If you love *The Perfectly Imperfect Woman*,
discover Milly Johnson's other books, available
in paperback and eBook now

The Yorkshire Pudding Club

Three friends fall pregnant at the same time. For **Helen**, it's a dream come true. For **Janey**, the timing couldn't be worse. **Elizabeth** doubts if she can care for a child. But soon the women find themselves empowered by unexpected pregnancy.

The Birds and the Bees

Romance writer and single mum **Stevie Honeywell** has only weeks to go until her wedding when her fiancé Matthew runs off with her glamorous new friend Jo. It feels like history repeating itself for Stevie, but this time she is determined to win back her man.

A Spring Affair

'Clear your house and clear your mind. Don't let life's clutter dictate to you. Throw it away and take back control!' When **Lou Winter** picks up a dog-eared magazine in the dentist's waiting room and spots an article about clearing clutter, she little realises how it will change her life …

A Summer Fling

When dynamic, power-dressing **Christie** blows in like a warm wind to take over at work, five very different women find themselves thrown together. But none of them could have predicted the fierce bond of friendship that her leadership would inspire …

Here Come the Girls

Ven, **Roz**, **Olive** and **Frankie** have been friends since school. They day-dreamed of glorious futures, full of riches, romance and fabulous jobs. Twenty-five years later, things are not as they imagined. But that doesn't mean they have given up.

An Autumn Crush

Four friends, two crushes and a secret … After a bruising divorce, **Juliet Miller** invests in a flat and advertises for a flatmate. Along comes self-employed copywriter **Hattie**, raw from her own relationship split, and the two women hit it off. Will they help each other to find new romance?

White Wedding

Bel is in the midst of planning her perfect wedding when disaster strikes. Can she hold it all together and, with the help of her friends and a mysterious man she meets unexpectedly, turn disaster into triumph?

A Winter Flame

Eve has never liked Christmas. So when her adored elderly aunt dies, the last thing she is expecting is to be left a theme park in her will. Can she overcome her dislike of Christmas, and can her difficult counterpart Jacques melt her frozen heart at last?

It's Raining Men

Best friends from work **May**, **Lara** and **Clare** are desperate for some time away. So they set off to a luxurious spa for ten glorious days. But when they arrive at their destination, it's not *quite* the place they thought it was …

The Teashop on the Corner

Spring Hill Square is a pretty sanctuary away from the bustle of everyday life. And at its centre is **Leni Merryman**'s Teashop on the Corner. Can friends **Carla**, **Molly** and **Will** find the comfort they are looking for there?

Afternoon Tea at the Sunflower Café

When **Connie** discovers that **Jimmy**, her husband of more than twenty years, is planning to leave her for his office junior, her world is turned upside down. Determined to salvage her pride, she resolves to get her own back.

Sunshine Over Wildflower Cottage

New beginnings, old secrets, and a place to call home – escape to Wildflower Cottage with **Viv**, **Geraldine** and **Stel** for love, laughter and friendship.

The Queen of Wishful Thinking

Lewis Harley has opened the antique shop he always dreamed of. When **Bonnie Brookland** walks into Lew's shop, she knows this is the place for her. But each has secrets in their past which are about to be uncovered. Can they find the happiness they both deserve?

Milly Johnson is a joke-writer, greetings card copywriter, newspaper columnist, after-dinner speaker, poet, winner of *Come Dine With Me*, *Sunday Times* Top Five author and winner of the RNA Romantic Comedy of the Year award both in 2014 and 2016.

She is obsessed by nice stationery, cruising on big ships and birds of prey. She is partial to a cheesecake or twelve but hates marzipan.

She was born and bred in Barnsley where she lives with her fiancé Pete, her teenage lads Tez and George, a spoilt trio of cats, Alan the rescue rabbit and now Bear the Eurasier pup. Her mam and dad live in t'next street.

The Perfectly Imperfect Woman is her fourteenth book.

Find out more at www.millyjohnson.co.uk or follow Milly on Twitter @millyjohnson

milly johnson

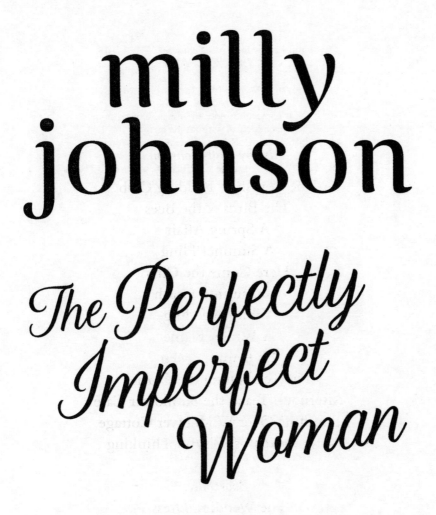

The Perfectly Imperfect Woman

**SIMON &
SCHUSTER**

London · New York · Sydney · Toronto · New Delhi

A CBS COMPANY

First published by Simon & Schuster UK Ltd 2018
A CBS COMPANY

3 5 7 9 10 8 6 4 2

Simon & Schuster UK Ltd
1st Floor
222 Gray's Inn Road
London WC1X 8HB

www.simonandschuster.co.uk
www.simonandschuster.com.au
www.simonandschuster.co.in

Simon & Schuster Australia, Sydney
Simon & Schuster India, New Delhi

A CIP catalogue record for this book
is available from the British Library

Hardback: 978-1-4711-6398-2
Trade Paperback: 978-1-4711-6176-6
eBook: 978-1-4711-6178-0
eAudio: 978-1-4711-6316-6

Typeset in Bembo by M Rules
Printed and bound by CPI Group (UK) Ltd, Croydon, CR0 4YY

This book is dedicated to Jill Craven, my wonderful friend who sadly died in April 2017. Jill was the best and most dedicated librarian in the world, a woman passionate about books and the best supporter of authors there could be. She was with me from the beginning, giving me time, showcasing me, forcing my books upon unwitting readers until they started buying them uncoerced. She was a fabulous and lovely woman and I miss her terribly.

Do something for her, even if you never knew her . . . if you don't know what to buy someone for Christmas, buy them a book. Buy an audio book for someone so they can listen to it when they're ironing, or driving in the car, or in the bath, or can no longer read a real book, or are too fragile to turn pages.

Keep reading, keep books –
and most of all – keep libraries alive!

Your flaws are perfect for the heart
that is meant to love you

ANON

Chapter 1

'CHEESECAKE? CHEESE. CAKE?'

If the situation hadn't been so dire, Marnie might have laughed at her mother coming across like an uppity Peter Kay.

'Yes, Mum, cheesecake.'

'You are not telling me that you're leaving your job to . . .' Judith Salt couldn't finish off the sentence because the words were too ludicrous. Her mouth gave an involuntary spasm as if she had just bitten down on a pastry filled with battery acid.

Marnie might as well have said 'I'm going to be a stripper' or 'I'm working in a brothel' instead of 'I'm making cheesecakes for a living', though illicitly peddling sugar and fats was right up there with those sinful occupations, in the world according to Judith Salt.

Cheesecake was where it all started for Marnie really. Nearly twenty-two years ago, when she had first encountered the word.

Puddings and desserts were not allowed in Salty Towers, as Marnie came to think of both her childhood residences.

At least not *proper* desserts: eclairs, cake with fudgy layers, a knickerbocker glory with a tower of whipped cream. Dessert was a banana, a baked apple, yogurt (low fat) and peaches that set her off gagging when her teeth made contact with their suede-like skins. Marnie's diet at home was micro-managed and that included school packed lunches: no Penguins or Mr Kipling cakes for her in her Tupperware box. She wasn't allowed to go to the birthday events of other children where there might be – *drum roll* – party food. If Marnie had been asked to give one word which summed up her childhood, she would have replied 'hungry'. Hungry for food, hungry for attention, hungry for love.

Then, in the summer of 1994 old Mrs McMaid with the pronounced limp and the guttural Scottish accent moved in next door and Judith Salt thought it might be a nice gesture if ten-year-old Marnie offered to run errands for her in the six-week holidays. Her eight-year-old younger sister Gabrielle didn't have the spare time, what with her singing, ballet, piano, flute, elocution and Spanish lessons. She had shown a natural propensity in all of these things, so Judith told anyone who cared to listen, therefore they were to be encouraged. Marnie had shown no such talents, which is why she escaped all the extra-curricular activities. She didn't mind; she'd seen Gabrielle dance in a show and decided she had all the lightness of a Yorkshire pudding made with cement and was grounded for a week by her mother for tittering in the performance. And Sarah Brightman certainly had nothing to worry about. So Marnie was sent off to do her Christian duty and be of service to Mrs McMaid, with a firm dictate that she was not to be given any food whilst she was there as she was on a strict diet for health reasons.

It was torture for young Marnie because Mrs McMaid made jam, and lots of it. And she told Marnie how wonderful it tasted slathered on her fresh-from-the-oven white bread and warm scones, with curls of creamy butter that she kept in a big jug of iced water in her fridge. And she let Marnie whisk up bowls of cake mix, which smelled better than the baked end product, and line tins with circles of pastry for fruit tarts. Marnie's stomach growled more that summer than it had in all her previous years put together.

'Och, it's a shame I canna give you any food, hen. What's the matter wi' you?' Mrs McMaid asked her one day, absently handing her a jam spoon to lick before hurriedly snatching it back.

'Nothing,' replied Marnie with a sigh loaded with disappointment. 'Mum just doesn't want me to get any fatter.'

'But you're no' fat,' Mrs McMaid exclaimed, and her grey shaggy eyebrows creased in consternation. 'In fact your mother and your sister could dae with fattening up a wee bit. It's nae good fir you walking roon wi' all your bones on show.'

And she passed the spoon back to Marnie whose hand almost shook with a seismic wave of joy as she reached out to take it and lift it to her lips. Her tongue snaked out in slow motion towards the sugary raspberry jam and when it made contact, her taste buds began to sing soprano. She closed her eyes and savoured the rush of sweetness and then she swallowed with a satisfying gulp.

Then the guilt washed over her like a tsunami.

Her mum would know. An all-seeing camera in the sky would report her sin back and she began to sob and Mrs McMaid enfolded her in a floral-scented cuddle and said over and over again, 'It's no' right. It's no' right at all.' Then she gave her another spoonful to help her feel better.

Contrary to her belief, her mother could not smell the licks of raspberry preserve on her and the relief that she was not indelibly permeated with it was palpable. That night she dreamt of swimming in a huge lake of jam, like an enormous ball pool filled with red berries instead of plastic spheres. She couldn't wait to run around to Mrs McMaid's the next morning in her cleaning clothes. She decided she was going to risk a mouthful of cake mix next.

But that day, instead of a sponge or scones or biscuits, she found that Mrs McMaid was making a cheesecake. The disappointment fell on Marnie like a hod full of bricks carried by a drunken builder.

'Cheese cake?' Marnie wrinkled up her nose. She envisaged a pile of melted smelly goo in the middle of a sponge and was a little bit sick in her mouth. 'That sounds disgusting.'

'Just you wait and see,' laughed Mrs McMaid, unwrapping a packet of Digestives. She put them in a plastic bag and gave them to Marnie to crush carefully into crumbs with the rolling pin whilst she melted a block of butter in a pan. Then she combined both ingredients until the crumbs were all soaked, then she pressed them flat in the bottom of a round tin with her potato masher before putting it in the fridge.

'That's the base. Now comes the topping,' said Mrs McMaid, taking a tub out of the fridge. 'This is crrream cheese. Mascarrrpone.' It had a wonderful exotic name, especially with all those rich, rolling, Scottish 'r's, far nicer than Edam, thought young Marnie. She beat at the strange white stuff with her wooden spoon, then whipped up some double cream until it stood in soft peaks when the mixer blades were lifted out. She put them both in her blue and white stripey bowl, and added some unholy white sugar which she stored in a jar with odd dried-up bendy brown sticks.

'That's vanilla,' said Mrs McMaid and held up the sugar jar for Marnie to sniff. The little girl felt her nasal receptors sigh with delight. 'All the way frae Madagascarrr'. It sounded somewhere dangerous and dark where spice wars might occur.

'And then there's this,' said the old lady, adding a pinch of something into the mix from an old square tin she brought down from her shelf. 'Ma secret ingrrredient, passed doon frae ma motherrr 'n' her motherrr's motherrr,' she added in a low voice full of drama. Then she whispered what that secret ingredient was and told Marnie never to tell anyone else. A mere nip of it would make her cheesecakes different to anyone else's, promised Mrs McMaid.

Then, with her large spatula, Mrs McMaid plopped the creamy mix onto the cooled crumbs and put it into the fridge for an hour before removing it from the tin and pouring over the raspberries and strawberries and bilberries that she had softened in a pan with a large spoonful of the vanilla sugar. Marnie was mesmerised as she watched the shiny glaze walk across the top and drizzle down the sides onto the plate. Oh my, the cheesecake looked wonderful, the best of all the cakes they had made in the summer.

They cleared up the kitchen, did a bit of dusting and then Mrs McMaid said:

'If you and I were to test oot the cheesecake, would you tell yer mammy?'

Marnie swore on the big bible that Mrs McMaid kept on her sideboard that she wouldn't. So, they set up two deckchairs in the corner of the garden where the pale pink roses smelt of honey, then Mrs McMaid poured out two glasses of her homemade lemonade and passed Marnie a funny fork where the left outer prong was thicker than the others, and a whole equilateral triangle of the very berry cheesecake served up on one of Mrs McMaid's lovely plates with blue-bells painted on it.

Nothing could have tasted better. Nothing in the whole wide world was finer than Marnie's first mouthful of that cheesecake. As they sat in the sun Mrs McMaid recounted all the flavours of them that she'd made in her time – and long before the fad came over from America, she said. Some with rum and raisins, others with chopped-up Mars bars in them, lemon and lime ones, salted toffee ones ... And the bases – ginger nuts, crumbled coconut macaroons, minty chocolate biscuits ... so many variations. Marnie wanted to make them all with Mrs McMaid. And the old lady laughed and said that they would – and more.

Mrs McMaid made cakes for fun and for profit. She made them to give to poor old souls who went to the same church as she did and needed a pick-me-up. And she made them for the woman from the big teashop in Ossett who pretended to her customers that she'd baked them herself.

'But that's lying and cheating,' said Marnie, one day when the tea-shop woman with the fat legs and high heels had collected her load.

Mrs McMaid jiggled her old battered purse.

'It is sort of, but I don't mind,' she replied. 'I might as well sell a few because I could never eat all the cakes I love to make.'

'I could,' said Marnie and Mrs McMaid laughed and then asked what they should do that day. Marnie could choose. Anything she liked.

'A rum and raisin cheesecake,' said Marnie. It sounded naughty, illegal and exotic.

'Rum and raisin it is,' agreed Mrs McMaid, who produced

from her pantry a jar of raisins which had been soaked in rum and were fat and sticky and smelt wickedly intoxicating.

That late August afternoon, they sat in the garden with a pitcher of Mrs McMaid's blood-orangeade and a slice of rum and raisin cheesecake. It was Saturday and Marnie would be back on school on Monday.

'But I can still come after tea and at weekends and half-term is only six weeks away,' said Marnie, wishing she never had to go back to school again but could stay here with Mrs McMaid making cakes – even if they were for Mrs Fatty-legs.

'Of course you can,' said Mrs McMaid. 'You're always welcome in ma wee hoos.' And Mrs McMaid suddenly put down her plate, lifted up Marnie's face with her small, thin hand and smiled at her.

'If I'd have hed a daughter, I'd've wanted her to be just like you, Miss Marnie.'

And Marnie didn't say it aloud but she wished she *had* been her daughter and not Judith Salt's. She knew then that she loved Mrs McMaid with her whole heart and knew that Mrs McMaid loved her back as much. Marnie felt as if the sun wasn't only shining outside that day, but inside her too, as if she'd swallowed it.

The next afternoon, Marnie went around to Mrs McMaid's with a cooked chicken leg that her mother had sent, and found the old lady at the bottom of the stairs, cold and lifeless with her body all twisted up. Marnie rang for the ambulance and waited with her old friend until it came and a minute before it pulled up outside, she took Mrs McMaid's secret ingredient tin from the shelf and put it into her bag. It hadn't felt wrong to do so then, and it never had since. Mrs McMaid would have wanted her to have it. She knew without any doubt she should be its rightful guardian now.

Marnie didn't make any more cheesecakes for years. Not until she had grown up and bought her own house and someone at work asked if she'd donate a cake for a fundraising event. She made a raspberry cheesecake with a sprinkle of the secret ingredient and she remembered that wonderful summer and dear Mrs McMaid and her kindness. Marnie's cheesecake went down a storm. No one had ever tasted anything like it. It had that indefinable . . . mmm, they said. And whatever it was, it was magic.

Chapter 2

Four months before the cheesecake conversation with her mother, Marnie walked into Café Caramba HQ in swanky central Leeds to find the new head of Merchandising in situ in his office. He was certainly a sight to warm up the frosty first working day of the year, her dilating pupils decided: tall, slim, dark hair with an unruly wave, brown-black eyes, sharp suit and a bleached-tooth smile worthy of a Colgate commercial.

If ever a man suited his name, it was Justin Fox, Marnie came to realise over the next fortnight. He was super good-looking with an arrogant swagger in his shoulders that said he was quite aware of his effect on the female workforce – and Glen from accounts. Marnie couldn't stop her heart giving an extra thump of pleasure whenever her eyes came to rest on him, but she had no intention of advertising the fact. It wasn't her fault, she kept telling herself, it was just her body reacting to 'the type' of man it had decided was a match for her. Jez, Robert, Harry, Aaron – all tall, dark, handsome snappy dressers. All tall, dark, handsome, complicated arseholes. And she didn't want another one walking into her heart and stamping all over it with his size twelve lawn aerator spiked shoes – thank you!

She suspected that she was pretty safe from Mr Fox though. She had never felt the warmth of his tobacco-brown eyes coming to rest on her back/bum/tights whenever she passed his desk or when they were in meetings together. No flirty banter bounced between them, no hunting for her attention occurred. She pigeon-holed him as the sort who would go for skinny, leggy, blondes, and she was none of those things. And that could only be good news.

Marnie knew that she functioned much better without a man in her life, corrupting her focus. Whenever she didn't have one of them trying to screw with her head, she could plough her energies into creating, forecasting, delivering. Work made her happier than any man ever had and she loved her job. She'd been at Café Caramba for six years now and worked her socks off for the company. When the last department head – Jerry 'Tosser' Thomson – left two years ago, there had been no one better to inherit the mantle than Marnie, even though HR had a bias towards men for the top jobs. No man wanted Beverage Marketing, though, because it was in a terrible state so the job slid easily to her. But Marnie Salt proved that she could turn a ship around in a force fourteen crosswind. Beverage Marketing was no longer a joke barge but a sleek cruise liner. There was even a waiting list in HR for people who wanted to join its crew and Marnie's reputation, as captain, couldn't have been higher. She was recognised throughout Café Caramba as naturally gifted at organising; an ideas person, an intuitive grafter with foresight who scoffed at comfort zones and a trailblazer for female employees of the company because there had been no other women top execs there – ever. Though Café Caramba, on paper, did most things that a progressive twenty-first-century workplace should be doing, the fat cats liked to see men in their boardroom, give or take the women in wipe-clean aprons pouring out coffees and distributing sandwiches. There wasn't so much a glass ceiling there as a two-foot-thick lead one covered with razor wire.

Three and a half weeks after Justin Fox joined the company, Marnie arrived at work expecting nothing but a normal day. She took the escalator and made a right through the first set of double doors, where the Product Development team sat under the leadership of 'Sweaty' Andrew Jubb, who could only achieve eye contact with women when their pupils were situated on their tits. High on the agenda was a morning executive huddle at one of the tall tables that the superboss Laurence Stewart-Smith had had implemented around the building. Standing meetings got to their point quicker and were over faster was his reasoning, and he was right. Laurence had transformed a number of failing companies into major success stories with streamlining initiatives like this. He was a business genius, adored by shareholders, oiled over by his minions who secretly thought though, beneath their fawning smiles, that as a human being, Laurence was an utter first-class knobhead. But Marnie knew that this morning, thanks to the fabulously shaped mug she'd sourced in the far east, Laurence was going to be a suitably impressed knobhead. They'd carry the company logo much better than the very ordinary ones they used at present. She had the sample in her bag and couldn't wait to present it to him – in front of an audience. She'd had too many of her best ideas pirated in the past, so now she made sure that they all bore a big fat Marnie Salt stamp on them.

As excited as she was about the morning get-together, still her thoughts drifted to Justin when she passed his office. She'd noticed that he didn't wear a wedding ring. But he had to have a partner, she reasoned. He was far too gorgeous to be on a shelf. And he was definitely straight because he flirted heavily with the canteen ladies who brought the refreshments into the boardroom meetings, sending them twittering off like a swarm of sparrows.

Straight on through Merchandising, she took another right into her department: Beverage Marketing, which had once been a merry band of six, but was now a small barrelful of four jolly apples with two rotting, maggoty additions. There was herself, of course; Arthur, a year away from retirement and solid as a rock; Bette, quietly efficient, who did her job and went home and Roisean, the office gopher who was bright and sweet and would end up running the company one day. Then there was Vicky, a twenty-nine-year-old busybody – and the thorn in her side, the stone in her shoe, the hair in her sandwich: Elena. A cocksure graduate eight years her junior who would have garrotted her own mother to get a rung further up the corporate ladder. She was head girl in the 'to get on in anything you have to be a cock' school of life. She'd presented well in her interview for the job and Marnie had since cursed herself for being sucked in by her superficial charm.

'Morning,' Marnie called to them all collectively and as usual received three cheerful echoes, one grumbly mumble and a blank. Within the minute, Roisean had put a coffee on her desk, just as she liked it.

'Thank you, love,' smiled Marnie.

Roisean coughed then gave her front teeth a discreet rub with her finger. It was code for *you've got lipstick on your incisors, boss*. Marnie swept her tongue over them and then test-smiled for Roisean who gave her the thumbs up. Little considerations like that made the day slide on a smoother track, Marnie always thought.

Elena and Vicky were gossiping. Again. And, if the look over the latter's shoulder was anything to go by, Marnie was the subject. Again. Marnie wasn't a hardline boss but Vicky pushed her buttons almost as much as Elena did. They faffed about every morning chatting and drinking coffee between signing in and starting work and now those faffs were getting too long to ignore.

Marnie, on the other hand, had logged on to her iMac and pulled up a report she needed for her meeting before she had even taken her coat off. She took a glug of coffee, pressed print and nothing happened. Her desk printer had been on the blink for a while and this time the usual bang on the side with the flat of her hand technique failed her.

'Elena. I've sent you a file. Could you run it off for me please?' Marnie asked her still-gossiping deputy. 'And Vicky, ring maintenance and get them up here as soon as, to look at my printer.' Her lips were curved upwards but she wasn't smiling as she added pointedly, 'If you have the time.'

'What's Roisean doing?' asked Elena, looking down her thin ski-slope of a nose at her boss.

'Yes they are urgent, thank you, Elena,' replied Marnie with a tone in her voice that sent the folie à deux begrudgingly back to their desks.

Marnie opened her diary and checked what was coming up next week. The yearly job reviews were pending. She would recommend that Roisean, Arthur and Bette be given pay rises and would have no qualms in telling Elena and Vicky that they needed to pull their socks up. Vicky was as slack as a prostitute's elastic. Elena was a much better worker when she wanted to be, but sullen and difficult to get on with. Neither of them felt part of the well-oiled machine the way Linda and Annie had, both happily on maternity leave.

Burke and Hare, as Marnie had privately renamed them, were more like people who would nobble the cogs given half the chance. She had an awful foreboding that Linda and Annie wouldn't come back either and she'd be stuck with the terrible twosome.

Five minutes later, Elena strutted across to Marnie's desk in her really tall stilettos. Marnie hadn't been the only one to notice that her clothes had become decidedly more figure-hugging, her heels higher and her lipstick had inched from orchid pink to slapper red since Justin Fox had joined the company. She held her hand out for the report but Elena put it down on her desk instead. Marnie tried not to let the growl inside rush out of her throat as she thanked her, albeit through gritted teeth.

'Pleasure,' replied Elena, sounding as if her duty had been about as pleasurable as cauterising the linings of her nostrils with a red-hot poker. She turned on her ridiculous heel far too fast to keep her balance, stumbled and did a comedy walk that said, *I am going to recover this and not fall flat on my face.* Then she fell flat on her face in a none too graceful way whilst her left shoe flew off her foot, did a perfect double pike back in the air and came to land on the back of her head. Arlene Phillips couldn't have choreographed it better.

'Oh dear,' said a male voice from behind Marnie. She turned to see Justin Fox striding into the department.

'My ankle, my fff ... bloody ankle,' Elena was crying. A big pink toe bearing chipped purple nail varnish was protruding from her now laddered black tights. Justin rushed forward like a gallant knight although he was hardly crushed in the queue to help.

'Here, lean on me. You came quite a cropper there. I'm surprised you didn't make a crater in the floor.'

Marnie had to turn around to compose herself. Schadenfreude was shameful, but just for once, she allowed herself to savour it.

As if Elena's embarrassment didn't have enough elements to it, her dark blue skirt had collected a million light-coloured fibres from the relatively new carpet and she appeared to have snapped the heel of the shoe that had managed to stay on her foot.

'Is this yours too?' asked Justin, picking up not only the escapee stiletto but a floppy gel Party Feet insert.

If Elena had gone any redder her head would have blown off her shoulders.

He examined the long pin-heel of the shoe, which looked decidedly tatty at close quarters. 'My goodness, no wonder you fell.'

'I think you ought to go straight to the medical room,' said Marnie, in her best concerned boss voice which she knew would feel like a hundred bees stinging Elena's ears. 'Look, your ankle is swelling up terribly.' And it was. Ballooning. It was almost a cankle. On its way to being a thankle.

'I'll take her.' Vicky stepped forward and Elena put her arm around her shoulder. She couldn't have hopped off faster if she'd tried.

'Are you all right?' Justin asked Marnie who was covering up her mouth and really really trying hard to look sympathetic. Had it been anyone else, it would have come naturally but not with Elena and it probably wouldn't have with Vicky either. But then, she was wicked, she'd heard that often enough to believe it might be true.

'I'm fine,' she coughed. 'Just worried about my colleague.'

'I brought these for you to cast your eye over before the meeting in . . .' he consulted his watch. A black-faced Rolex. As classy and striking as he was. '. . . ten minutes.'

'Thank you,' said Marnie, taking hold of the sheets of paper he was proffering, but he didn't let go of them. Then he leaned in to her and said in a whisper: 'Something tells me you rather enjoyed that little floorshow.'

Marnie gulped and gave a demure pat to her chest. 'I think you are very much mistaken, Mr Fox.' It wouldn't have convinced a grand jury.

'See you in . . . nine minutes and counting,' said Justin with a lazy grin and Marnie's heart gave a perfidious kick. *No, no, no.* She heard her brain protest. *Not again.*

Chapter 3

The day ended on a high. Elena and her fat ankle had gone home and, starved of her partner in crime, Vicky was quiet and actually did some work. Everyone in the executive meeting was impressed by the new shaped mug and Marnie received three billion brownie points. And she noticed Justin smiling at her as she talked through the pricings and argued why they should adapt this shape and ditch the old one. He had a flirtatious sparkle in his eyes and her own eyes kept being drawn to his, as if they were twin sparkly light-seeking moths. Her feet almost hovered above the ground as she walked back to her car that day, but the closer she got to home, the more that buoyant, airy feeling began to subside. The weekend loomed drawn-out and depressing in front of her as it had done for too long now. Marnie hated Saturdays and Sundays, for however much she tried to tell herself that she was married to her work and didn't need a man in her life, those two weekend days exposed that statement for the lie it was.

It was a particularly lonely phase as she was both boyfriend-less and best-friend-less and it followed the worst Christmas she'd had for years. She'd intended to spend it sharing a house with her boyfriend of twelve months, Aaron. Her on-off-on-off boyfriend of twelve months that is, who had finally decided in August that she was the one he wanted to spend the rest of his life with. So, she'd sold her furniture and her flat only for Aaron to tell her, on the day of completion, that he'd made a mistake and was still in love with his ex.

Her best friend Caitlin wasn't on hand to pick up the broken pieces as she was besotted by a high-flying city banker called Grigori and she spent all the time she could down in London with him. He was rich and handsome and successful and very posh and Caitlin had changed in the short time they'd been together. She'd become glossier and more groomed and – though Marnie hated to admit this – less fun, more staid and worst of all, distant. She'd denied having elocution lessons, though it was obvious from the slower, more measured way that Caitlin had started to talk and the strange shapes her mouth formed on certain words, that she had. And when Marnie rang her for a chat, Caitlin always seemed to be in the middle of something and said she'd call back. She didn't always. This, the same Caitlin who had had a real go at Marnie for not giving her friendship time when Aaron arrived on the scene.

Caitlin had been single for over two years when she met Grig-ORRR-i, as she'd started to pronounce it. No wonder she'd sucked him up like a dehydrated woman falling face down in an oasis. Marnie couldn't have been happier for her friend – then she'd met him, and she could have been very much happier for her because Grigori was a plank.

He might have been good-looking and clever and super-brainy and drive a Maserati but it was quite obvious that he didn't like Marnie from the off, because the disapproval came off him in waves. She had first met him in person at the night do of an old school-friend's wedding. Caitlin left Grigori and Marnie to 'get acquainted' whilst she nipped off to the loo. Marnie had opened conversation, but Grigori had turned away and wended his way out through the guests instead. Marnie was gobsmacked by his rudeness and she did wonder what Caitlin had told him to provoke that reaction. She had broached the subject once but Caitlin waved it away and said he'd been absolutely whacked with tiredness that night. Marnie hadn't bought it and what she hadn't told Caitlin was that later on, she'd encountered him on the stairs when he was arseholed and he'd been far more friendly. Feeling obliged to give him a second chance to make a first impression, she'd asked him if he was enjoying himself and he'd pulled her towards him and stuck his tongue down her throat before she pushed him firmly off. He'd fallen down two stairs and called her the c-word and though Marnie had tried to forget it and chalk it up to the drink, she never quite had. One thing was for sure – he had come between them and their once-strong vow that no man would ever do that was crushed to dust.

She'd got into the bad habit of drinking too much at weekends to numb that gnawing hunger within her for company, for affection. She recognised she was in trouble when she began to think that sleeping off a hangover was a better alternative than being conscious, and had tried to cut down over the last couple of weeks.

But on this particular Friday, maybe because she'd been so high earlier on from her successful mug presentation and a little male attention from the hottest property on the trading floor, her spirits nosedived and she felt extra sad and pathetic that night. So, unable to satisfy the cravings of her heart, her body tried to compensate by feeding her something else and put her hands in the way of a giant bag of sweet and salty popcorn and a bottle of Tesco's finest Shiraz.

There was nothing on the TV but programmes about house renovations and dream sheds, a crap gameshow and the big film, which was about a man who couldn't forget his first love – far too near the knuckle for her. At times, when she was plastered, she could see herself more clearly than ever and the revelations hurt and bewildered her. Through the clarity that alcohol supplied, she saw that she had been lonely for a long time, far longer than she'd wanted to admit to herself. Even when she'd been with Jez, Robert, Harry and Aaron she'd still been lonely. It took a particular skill to be lonely in a relationship, she had noted. Sometimes she had lain in bed next to a snoozing Aaron after sex and marvelled at how alone she felt. There had been only inches between their bodies but she had never felt as if she were truly part of a couple. Even when they'd been mid-bonk, there had been none of that 'two become one' or 'bodies melting into each other' bollocks. They'd been more like two hard pieces of wood bashing together than two balls of Play-Doh squashing into a single big ball of pliant softness.

None of the men she'd gone out with had made her feel secure, cherished, needed, not after the initial courtship period was over anyway and they had full access to the contents of her underwear. She often wondered if any man ever could. Maybe the men who still held doors open for you after you'd been together for over thirty years only existed in books – written by women fantasising about the same thing. Maybe that's why Midnight Moon romance stories were so popular, because they contained the sort of mythical beings who rubbed your shoulders without thinking that it constituted foreplay, whipped you up a hot chocolate on cold winter nights, made you laugh till your cheeks hurt or set all your nerves jingling like the bells of St Clements simply by placing a hand on your waist.

In books men energised women; in her experience they sapped your energy to below zero level. Give or take the thump to the ego, it was almost a relief when the relationship limped across the finish line, but then she was left with just herself for company. During the week she could work late, plough everything she had into the job but nothing seemed to fill the chasm of emptiness that weekends brought – not even Candy Crush. She couldn't continue as she was, she'd decided, and forced her brain to come up with a rescue plan, and so it did. For years, she'd toyed with the idea of writing a definitive cheesecake recipe book but had never got around to it. Maybe that was what she needed to get her teeth into and transform her weekends into a brighter brace of days.

So, with a notebook at her side, that night Marnie refilled her wine glass, switched on her laptop and typed 'cheesecake' into Google and before long she had been dragged into the deep quark web of baking. Within a few clicks, she'd happened upon an amazing American site which led her to the Sisters of Cheesecake club where fanatics all over the world sent in pictures of their mad creations and recipes or asked for advice. It was a defining moment when Marnie realised that it was nearly 2 a.m. on Saturday morning and she was more than half-pissed and involved in a three-way heated argument with a woman from Calgary and another from Memphis about the base to topping ratio. Sad didn't even come into it. Weren't women of Marnie's age supposed to have wild dirty cybersex, not rows about baking?

The across-the-pond sisterhood were beating Marnie

down, forcing her to accept that a thinner base was desirable. Then in stepped a fellow Brit, declaring that thick bases ruled, having Marnie's back all the way. The brave British duo were declared losers of the lowest order but it didn't matter because the connection they made with each other was a winner. And that is how the paths of Misses Lilian Dearman and Marnie Salt first crossed.

Normally Marnie didn't engage with people she didn't know personally on social media. She had no interest in learning about how some woman she didn't know in South Shields had got on at Weightwatchers that week, or viewing some circulated footage of kittens or people's dinners or sharing petitions and patronising inspirational messages. The internet was a nest of fraudulent vipers as far as she was concerned. If they weren't fleeing from Nigeria and needed her bank details to deposit their millions, they were screwed up dickheads on internet dating sites waiting to pounce.

Wine, therefore, had been a strong contributing factor to how she ended up having an in-depth email conversation with someone purporting to be a sixty-six-year-old insomniac, who found the Sisters of Cheesecake site particularly well stocked with 'sanctimonious know-it-all bastards' with whom she enjoyed a good verbal battle. Her sleeps, Lilian Dearman said, though tardy in coming were superbly restful after giving those stuck-up frustrated old crows a pasting. Thin bases indeed.

Marnie opened up another bottle of wine as they messaged back and forth. Somehow the conversation segued from recipes for cheesecakes to recipes of disaster – i.e. Marnie's life. Lubricated by fermented grapes, a dam burst inside her and out it all poured in a torrent. Everything. Starting with Aaron and then reaching back in time to things she hadn't even told Caitlin. And Marnie went past caring if the person she was typing to was a genuine elderly lady, a *Daily Mail* reporter or a serial killer called Darren.

Despite her intentions to clean up her act, Marnie awoke very late on Saturday afternoon with a major hangover, egg on her face and no recollection of getting to bed at all. The last thing she remembered was telling Lilian about reading *Wuthering Heights* at school and having a crush on her English teacher, Mr Trent. Dangerous territory. What a bloody idiot. How could she have blurted out so many secrets to a stranger? Stuff she had locked away in boxes in her head and yet their locks had sprung at the merest tickle and the contents had come spewing out perfectly preserved in brain-aspic.

Marnie was a panicking mess; what else she had said that she couldn't remember?

She switched on her laptop, after taking two ibuprofen and a Red Bull and tried to log on to the Sisters of Cheesecake site but found that, despite being hammered, she'd obviously had the foresight to delete her account before going to sleep, probably to stop herself reading what she'd written to this 'Lilian Dearman' in the private message box. How could she be so thick and rational at the same time? Whilst she was in cringe mode, she also checked that she hadn't sent an embarrassing email to Aaron but no – there was nothing recent in her sent box to her overwhelming relief. What was there in her inbox, though, was an invitation from Miss Dearman to have afternoon tea with her at a mutually convenient time in the near future. She'd suggested the Tea Lady tearoom in Skipperstone, a market town near to the village of Wychwell where she lived. So, Marnie had given Miss Dearman her email address then. And probably her mobile number, house address, bank details, national insurance number, all her PIN codes and passwords as well.

Marnie had a shower and an omelette and, when revived, looked up Wychwell on the internet, because she'd never heard of it and it was probably no wonder as it seemed to be in the middle of a big forest somewhere in the Yorkshire Dales. Photographs of it on 'images' were more complimentary: twee little cottages standing around a village green, an ancient stone church with a crooked spire and a beautiful manor house on a low hill. There were no pictures of Lilian Dearman, though there were plenty of other Dearmans: Montague Dearman, Ebenezer Dearman, Erasmus Dearman, and more. All with very highfalutin names, stiff poses and handlebar moustaches.

And as Marnie had bugger-all entries in her diary and she was inexplicably intrigued now, she emailed back that she would like to meet up. At least that way, they could both see that the other wasn't a serial killer called Darren or a tabloid journo.

Marnie slobbed around in her dressing gown for the rest of the day feeling weak and wobbly. She had planned to go out and buy her sister a birthday card but ordered one from the internet to be sent directly to her instead. They didn't do presents. They never had. Only at Christmas, which was an ordeal in itself because Gabrielle was allergic to soaps, perfumes, wool and animals, didn't eat chocolates, didn't drink, only read certain literary novels, didn't want anyone else to buy her clothes and flowers set her hay fever off. Marnie spent from August onwards trying to source something that showed she'd put a bit of effort in, whereas Gabrielle bought her an M&S talcum and hand cream gift set in a *meh* flower fragrance every year. Gabrielle was brazen about her lack of effort in present-choosing.

Marnie looked again at her diary and found she had filled in some entries, in a looping drunken scrawl, when she'd been off her face. Amongst others she had blocked in a four-hour lunch on Wednesday with Hugh Jackman and a trip to Lanzarote with Justin Fox on Thursday. Saddest of all, she had booked the following Saturday and Sunday for a catch-up, spa and shopping with Caitlin. She was pathetic with a capital 'P' and she'd ruined her diary with the stupid inclusions. She ordered a new one from Amazon and then took out the recycling, noting that she'd put away two full bottles of wine. Usually after two glasses she was comatose. No wonder she'd told a perfect stranger her entire life story and filled her diary with pitiful gobbledygook. Regrettably, she had more chance of having lunch with Hugh Jackman than she did of a whole weekend catch-up with Caitlin or that holiday in Lanzarote with Justin Fox.

Chapter 4

A big part of why Marnie felt unable to really chill out at home was because it wasn't her *home*. It was just a house filled with someone else's furniture, none of it fitting her concept of 'aesthetic'. She was renting 34A Redbrook Row in Doreton on the outskirts of Sheffield on a short-term lease and she hated the damned place. She had shut herself away for Christmas and cried herself stupid in this alien house, where every room was decorated in miserable greys which reflected her mood perfectly. Her mother had gone down to stay with Gabrielle in Leicester for the festive season so at least Marnie didn't have to hide behind a facade that all was well with her. A lone Christmas was, at least, better than putting herself through the strain of all that acting.

Since moving into the house in early December, she had felt increasingly restless and agitated, unfulfilled and frustrated. She did love her job at Café Caramba, but she had to try so much harder than her male counterparts to be taken seriously. Sometimes life felt like such an uphill slog and she had too many anxiety dreams about trying to catch up with a figure in front of her whilst she could only walk in

THE PERFECTLY IMPERFECT WOMAN 27

slow motion, or screaming and no sound coming out of her mouth. The only light relief in her present existence was meeting Lilian Dearman in the cheesecake forum every weekend. Someone who may or may not be a sweet old lady. Someone who had a wicked sense of humour, whoever she – or he – was.

Marnie had set up a new account with the Sisters of Cheesecake and she was so glad she had because it had been the best entertainment. Without fail, for the last three Friday and Saturday nights Lilian had been causing merry hell on the far-too-serious baking forum to Ealing comedy standard and Marnie hoped that this weekend would be no different. Lilian operated under multiple personas to cause maximum havoc: BigBase, Yorkpud, Creamtop, Lilette amongst others. Marnie powered up her laptop to find 'Lilette' single-handedly battling an army of cheesecake fanatics as always. Marnie grinned, suspecting that Lilian was being deliberately controversial.

'I have on occasion had a very successful result replacing butter with extra virgin olive oil,' Lilian had typed, causing a woman from Kings Lynn to resort to capital letters in her vituperative response. Marnie waded in. 'Or goose fat. Though more sugar should be added to the crumb.' She chuckled heartily at the wave of abuse that started scrolling up on the screen, turned to scratch an itch on her neck and caught sight of her cheerful reflection in the mirrored glass door. She realised then that she couldn't remember the last time she'd laughed properly before this.

'What a bunch of old farts,' wrote Lilian on the forum private messaging page. 'How are you, dear?'

'I'm good,' replied Marnie. 'How are you?'

'Could be better. Crumbling spine, alas,' came the answer.

'More crumbly than a Digestive base, in fact. I've become intolerant of sleeping tablets but I've found a good debate wears me out and helps me to have a decent sleep. Have the new mugs arrived? How's Mr Fox?'

Lilian knew everything about the new swanky mugs and her involuntary attraction to Justin. In fact she seemed to know everything about Marnie, thanks to that first communication, which Marnie tried not to think about.

'I shan't be online for a couple of weeks,' Lilian typed after half an hour's jolly chat. 'I have to go to hospital on Monday to hang upside down like a bat. Or at least that's what happened last time I went on traction.' She added a couple of smiley faces but Marnie didn't feel comfortable making a joke of it.

'Doesn't sound too great,' she fired back. 'Hope it goes well.'

'Lots of love,' Lilian replied quickly. 'I am now off to bed early for a change. Sweet dreams. Hope you have something to report about Mr Fox the next time we converse.'

Marnie doubted it, but she was wrong to. It would shortly go from zero to ninety miles per hour, commencing with a screaming orgasm.

*

The next week began on a particular low as Marnie broke her resolve not to look at Aaron's Facebook page and found that he was in Sorrento with his girlfriend looking very loved up. They were staying in the hotel that Marnie had found online the week before they split up. She'd wanted to book it for them but he'd said that he didn't fancy Sorrento. He'd meant, of course, that he didn't fancy Sorrento with *her*. The next picture featured a close-up of his girlfriend's hand showing off a big sparkly ring. Marnie forced herself to close the app and gave herself a stern word when she felt a prickle of tears behind her eyes.

She had a lunch meeting on Monday with the departmental heads though Justin Fox didn't attend as he was away in London until Thursday. She got lumbered with Sweaty Andrew who put her off her quiche with his sour odour and bored her to death with his flawed vision of million-calorie dessert coffees. The days after that dragged uncharacteristically, though there was a retirement party on Friday lunchtime in the pub local to Café Caramba for the old bloke who worked in the post room to look forward to. It spoke volumes when that was the highlight of the week.

Clifford Beech had been in the building since before it was Café Caramba, even before it was the HQ of the West Riding Building Society and was Fraser & Lunn Insurance, where he was taken on as a school-leaver to be a post room boy and, over his fifty-year stay, he worked his way up to post room man. He liked it there; he had no interest in fancy job titles and no ambitions further than working in the post room, though he had trained many other entry-level post room boys and girls – some of whom were now management. He was as much part and parcel of the building as were the cavernous cellars which sprawled under the city and the oversized cockerel weathervane that spun on the rooftop and if someone had cut Clifford Beech in half like a stick of rock, they would have found the words 'post room' written through the middle. Thank goodness no one had, though, and he was able to retire healthy and intact.

More or less the whole building popped into the Dirty Dog on the Friday lunchtime to buy Clifford a drink, or give him a present or an envelope with money in it collected by their department. Laurence the CEO had done the formal gift presentation in the atrium: a set of golf clubs and two all-expenses paid tickets to a course in Spain for a week. Clifford was delighted to tears, especially because Laurence had the reputation of being tighter than a worm's arsehole and he'd been expecting a carriage clock. Marnie let her staff have an early and extended lunch break so they could join him and say their goodbyes. She went to the pub herself after they'd returned and would go home straight from there because she'd booked half a day off to sort out her car. She took with her the envelope of money that Beverage Marketing had collected for the old lad and a bottle of rum that she'd bought for him herself.

As she turned the corner into the Headrow, who should she see about to go into the Dirty Dog but Justin Fox and her heart gave a stupid teenage leap. The odd thing was that the more she had tried to avoid him, the more their paths seemed to collide. *It's Fate with a capital F,* said some stupid hopeful voice inside her that still – despite her back catalogue of disastrous relationships with men – clung to the belief that one of them would walk straight out of the pages of a Midnight Moon romantic novel and into her heart. Could he be the one?

The timing was off. It was far too soon after the Aaron debacle. Plus she didn't want to be distracted. She was throwing everything she had at the massive company overhaul and didn't want to zone out at her desk with a head full of soft-focus images of Justin Fox holding her hand as they strolled through a sunny field of cowslips. She needed to keep her mind on a track of cappuccinos, lattes, flat whites and espressos. Unrealistic hope was her worst enemy at the moment.

But even as she was thinking that, she pulled into the dis-
used doorway of a recently closed clothes shop and checked
her face in the mirror of her compact. Her eyeliner was in
place, her foundation hadn't clumped around the sides of her
nose and there were no Alice Cooper runs of mascara. She
touched up her power-red lipstick and bared her teeth to make
sure it hadn't transferred, then blotted her lips with a tissue.
Just for good measure, she gave herself a spray of perfume, then
tipped her head upside down and flung it back to trap some
volume in her thick black hair. She lifted each leg behind her
and checked over her shoulder for ladders then took a deep
breath, jutted out her more-than-fair share of breasts, sucked
in her stomach – whilst all the time a counter-romantic voice
in her head was tutting disappointedly – and walked the
remaining fifteen steps to the front door of the pub.

It was empty apart from a bleary-eyed Clifford who was
grinning like Michael from *Ryan's Daughter*, a couple of strag-
glers who didn't want to go back to the office and Sweaty
Andrew who was chatting to the man who threw Ben Affleck
right into the back of the shade, Justin Fox. Marnie could
feel his eyes on her sashaying bum as she journeyed across to
Clifford to give him a kiss and a hug, rum and the envelope.
The table behind him was covered in boxes and a stack of
other envelopes . . . and a line of cocktails, pints and shorts.

'Lovely Marnie, help me out here,' slurred Clifford. 'I can't
drink all these. Take what you want. There's a slex on the
beach, there's a snippery whipple, pina colander and that, I do
believe, is a . . . oh, I can't remember.' He pointed to a small
glass full of muddied liquid: a lethal blend of Baileys, vodka,
Kahlua, amaretto and cream. It had more calories in it than
one of Elvis's special burgers. But it looked deceptively innocent against all the others and so Marnie lifted that one and

chinked it against Clifford's glass, just before he was stolen away by someone who had decided he really should have a cup of tea and a sandwich from the buffet before he threw up. Marnie sipped her drink, trying not to notice that Justin Fox was on his way over, holding a tall glass that appeared to have half a harvest festival balancing on its rim.

'So you're partial to a Screaming Orgasm then?' was his opening line.

'Pardon?' said Marnie. Blimey, he did move fast.

'The cocktail. It's a Screaming Orgas— oh you didn't . . . did you think . . . Oh . . .' He threw back his head and laughed and Marnie saw how beautiful and white and even his teeth were. *Shark-like*, her brain said, which she thought was a bit unkind of it. 'I thought you knew what it was called,' he went on. Marnie didn't buy his innocence. Nice try, though.

Her laughter joined his nevertheless. 'Nope, I didn't know. I thought you'd been reading my diary—' *Shit, too flirty.* '. . . Er, so what did you go for then?'

'A very tame Tequila Sunrise,' replied Justin, touching his glass against Marnie's. 'Nice to meet properly over a drink instead of stale sandwiches in the boardroom. Or women sprawled over your carpet.'

'Yes, it is,' Marnie answered, feeling her cheeks begin to heat up. She flapped at her face. 'Hot in here, isn't it?'

Justin grinned as if he knew that the room temperature had nothing to do with why Marnie was standing in front of him with cheeks the colour of a red velvet cake.

'So, tell me what you really think of Café Caramba's new marketing slogan: *"Flat white – it's buzzing"*?'

'I think it's. . . very Laurence,' said Marnie diplomatically.

'I think it's very crap,' said Justin. 'What the fuck does it even mean?'

Marnie pulled an 'I have no idea' face.

'And let's not even talk about *"Make every day a Macchiato day"*. Good grief. Is this really the man who turns companies around?'

Marnie throttled back on a hoot of laughter. She should be careful, though. What if Justin was a spy? Laurence was surrounded by yes-men and if she was honest, Justin had been nodding very approvingly in the aforesaid Flat White meeting, where Laurence rode over everyone's ideas and implemented his own.

'He has some good concepts,' she delivered cautiously.

'Absolutely. Really liked the one for espresso. *"Black. It's the new black"*. Have to give him that.'

Marnie's lip curled. That had been her brainchild. She'd asked Laurence in a one-to-one meeting in December what he'd thought about it. 'Not a lot,' he had replied with a condescending sniff. Then he'd only gone and nicked it for himself and the whole building was raving about it. Marnie tipped the tiny cocktail down her neck and reached for another. There was nothing like a couple of screaming orgasms for blotting out some blatant plagiarism.

The next half-hour flew as they talked about Laurence and his mad company directives and the jargon spouted in the meetings. *Blue-Sky Thinking, Game-Changer, We're on a Journey, Thought Shower* – Laurence brought them all into play. Sweaty Andrew had tried to impress with a *Let's Get our Ducks in a Row* once, which had Marnie pretend-blowing her nose to cover up the involuntary snort she made. If she'd caught anyone's eye in that meeting that'd had the smallest amused twinkle in it, she'd have exploded. Now she knew that Justin was of the same mindset, she had better never look at him again when Laurence went cheesy-corporate.

Then their conversation crept beyond work boundaries and into the territory of personal. *So, Marnie, do you live in the city or commute? Where do you come from originally? Are you single?* He barely gave her time to bat back any questions to him; it was all about her, which was refreshingly unusual. Marnie hadn't had any lunch and those liqueurs were quickly going to her head and she felt very warm inside and dangerously receptive to his flattery. All worries that Justin might be a plant had dissolved. She doubted a Laurence-spy would have used the line, 'You know, your eyes are the most amazing shade of green.'

'I suppose I'd better get back to the hell-hole,' he said eventually with a loaded sigh. 'Walk back together?'

'I've got the afternoon off,' said Marnie. 'I caught the train in this morning. My car's poorly.'

'Well, you can walk part of the way with me at least.'

'Okay,' she agreed.

They both said goodbye to a totally plastered Clifford – Justin with a firm handshake and Marnie with a squashy hug – and Justin held the door open for Marnie on the way out. Aaron would have let it swing in her face.

'I'm glad I'm not driv—' was as far as Marnie got in the sentence before Justin grabbed the top of her arm and steered her right rather than left.

'So let's walk around the block and sober up a bit,' he said, turning into the dead end of a lane that went behind the pub.

'Ok-ay,' replied Marnie, thinking that this was slightly odd but she went with it, presuming his intentions were innocent. Then he suddenly stopped, pushed her against the wall and kissed her full on the mouth. Caught unawares, it took Marnie a long second to press him backwards, politely but firmly.

'Forgive me. I've wanted to do that since I was in the first meeting with you,' Justin said, his voice a low sexy growl. 'You had a navy blue suit on and red "fuck-me" shoes.'

Marnie raised her eyebrows. He had remembered what she wore? He had been lusting after her for two months? *Gulp.*

'I trust your wife doesn't know you're in the habit of kissing other women in dark alleys,' she said, hoping that he'd say he wasn't attached because she would have slapped his face if he was.

He grinned. 'I can assure you, there's no one in here.' He patted his heart with his wedding-ring-less left hand. 'Now do I have your permission to kiss you?'

No, piss off with your soft velvety lips, said the protective angel on her shoulder, though her mouth issued no such protest. She couldn't entirely blame the alcohol, although it played its part, but Justin Fox's obvious desire for her blew all sense out of the window. He took her silence for concession. This time his kiss was tentative, tender, gentle and Marnie felt a complimentary hardness as he pressed against her.

Then he broke away and apologised. 'Forgive me for being an absolute oaf. I have forgotten how to behave. This is what tequila at lunchtime and a marriage breakdown does for you.'

Marnie's hands rose, palms flat on his chest, forming a definite barrier between them.

'So you *are* married?'

'In name only. Honestly. We're in the final stages of our divorce.' He rubbed his forehead with his fingertips. 'Look, have lunch with me next week because a back alley isn't the right place for this conversation, especially not when we're both swimming with alcohol. I'll explain then, if you'll let me. And I'll behave. I'll try to anyway.'

He's married, said that angel. *Steer well clear.*

Yeah, but let him explain, argued something else with a

too-convincing voice. One that couldn't believe its luck that this tall, dark handsome exec actually fancied *her*. Yep, she knew she was being too easily bought by him remembering what she was wearing in that meeting. She wasn't even really sure if she had been in her navy suit.

'Maybe,' she said demurely, and opened her bag to retrieve a couple of tissues, because if she looked anything like Justin did at that moment, she might have been mistaken for Pennywise the clown. Her lipstick was smeared all over the bottom half of his face.

'Please let's keep this between ourselves,' he said. 'My divorce is complicated as it is and Laurence doesn't like work-place relationships. He doesn't want anyone to have what he can't have himself, the ugly old bugger.'

Relationships. Is that where he saw this going? Blimey.

Marnie held up her compact mirror for Justin to wipe his face and he laughed.

'We look as if we've been at a Billy Smart convention.'

He had such a lovely smile, said something soppy inside her and she knew she was in trouble.

As they exited the lane and moved onto the bustling Leeds Headrow, Justin turned to Marnie.

'Well, hope your car doesn't prove to be too expensive, and have a lovely weekend,' he said.

'And you,' she replied, at a respectable physical distance now.

'Mine will be hideous,' he said with a sorrow-laden out-breath. 'I want to fast-forward to Wednesday and that lunch. I'll pick you up at twelve from outside the library.'

And with that he was gone and with delightfully trembly legs, Marnie walked down to the train station feeling more like a sighing Disney princess with every step.

*

Over the weekend, Marnie grew a grin so large it had its own brain. Her thoughts were completely overtaken by her up-close and personal encounter with Justin Fox and there was no room in her head for researching her cheesecake book, mulling over her dissipating relationship with her best friend, Aaron and Sorrento, or Lilian Dearman and her disintegrating spine. Her frontal lobe was showing one film only: *The Snog*, which would have worn out by Saturday lunchtime had it been an old-style videotape. It changed a touch with each loop. She added in Justin holding her face in big square hands (though in reality they were quite long and narrow), kissing her eyelids, telling her that he had fallen in love with her the first time he saw her. She deleted from her memory the part about his mouth looking as if it had sustained third-degree burns from her lipstick. She added in that he kissed her again passionately in the middle of the street as they parted, throwing caution to the wind.

She lounged in the bath like a beached mermaid with expensive treatments on her hair and face. She went to Meadowhall and bought new underwear and indelible lipstick. And on Monday and Tuesday, not even Vicky's miserable countenance could dampen her smile. Roisean even asked her if she'd had 'a bit of work' done because she looked different somehow. Must be the effect of the onset of spring, explained Marnie, imagining Justin springing from a wardrobe onto her spread-eagled body. Time seemed to take a tantalisingly long journey to noon on Wednesday.

Despite anticipating that something would arise to scupper plans, nothing did and the allotted hour eventually arrived.

Marnie left the office early so she could reapply her make-up in the loo. Justin's car pulled around the corner just as she reached the library and she hopped straight in. He gave her knee an affectionate squeeze as she fastened her seat belt.

'I wondered if you'd remember,' he said with a lazy, sexy grin.

'I wondered if you would forget,' she replied, trying to keep cool which was difficult as her nether regions were fizzing.

They drove to a quiet country pub where, over halibut and an arty-farty fan of vegetables, they'd gazed into each other's eyes and smiled a lot like shy teenagers. Justin confessed that he hadn't been looking for romance at all, didn't even want to start something else whilst he was in the mess of his divorce but Marnie had hit him in the heart like a thunderbolt. And Marnie told him that she hadn't been looking for romance either but he'd ignited something within her that she rather liked the feel of. They'd had a ridiculously passionate fumble in his car afterwards in which he admitted that he hadn't had sex in fourteen months and so she had better watch out. He demolished her new flimsy knickers and, as she had no spare pair, she said that she'd have to go without them for the rest of the day and he replied that he'd better hide his crotch behind his desk all afternoon then because the thought of it would keep his erection so big they could have flown the company flag from it.

A month later, the affair was established and passionate. And it was wonderful, amazing, blissful and all-consuming and ticked all the boxes except one – the big fat box that had the word 'perfect' on the side of it, because her heart remained troubled by their relationship. She wanted to declare that they were a couple from the rooftops but that was strictly prohibited. Okay, so Laurence might have frowned heavily on romances in the workplace, which is why they gave no hint of any connection between them in Café Caramba HQ, but out of work should have been a different matter. Yet it wasn't. Justin had only ever been to her house once. She'd cooked a meal which he ate nervously as if he expected his wife to appear from behind the curtains. His nerves, however, had not shown in the post-prandial bonk but they'd reappeared when the hands of the clock touched on 9 p.m. Marnie had barely got her breath back before he had leapt into the shower and dressed to go and not even his profuse apology that he had to rush off could smooth over the disappointment. They never went out to dinner or to the cinema or for a walk in the park in case they were seen. He gave her the best of reasons why they had to behave so, at least for the time being: because of his children. Justin still resided in the family home even though he and his wife lived separate lives now – and he knew that sounded like a line, but he really was telling the truth. His wife was a first-class bitch and yes, she'd agreed to a divorce but only on her terms. Terms he had to strictly adhere to because if not, he knew she would keep his three small children away from him. Or worse, poison them against him.

Suranna Fox, it seemed, had taken a leaf out of Gwyneth Paltrow's book and insisted on a conscious uncoupling, which – Justin said – was a psycho-bollocks way of her drawing out the agony. It was making him depressed and thank goodness Marnie understood and wasn't giving him a hard time like any other woman might have. Did she know how much of an angel she was for understanding such an impossible, sticky, horrible situation?

So how could Marnie give him any grief? She kept her misgivings to herself and gave Justin lots of care and attention and sex and the affair continued under a blanket of secrecy. But it didn't sit right with Marnie at all.

Chapter 5

It was Friday night and once again Marnie was looking forward to a lonely boring weekend, even though she had been in 'a relationship' for six weeks and should have been going out for a lovely romantic dinner tonight and then dragging her man up to bed for lots of sex. Instead, she was in her pyjamas with a meal for one ready to shove in the microwave and only a bottle of Pinot Grigio for company. It was Justin's daughter's fifth birthday and he was having to spend the whole weekend with his family and extended family, who were coming up from Derby to stay with them. Justin lived in a des-res detached on the other side of Sheffield. Marnie didn't know the exact address, but the area, Highton, was well-known as a new village full of prestigious multi-bedroomed, multi-bathroomed executive homes. Apparently, he and his wife were going to finally attempt to tell the children on Sunday that Mummy and Daddy were going their separate ways. He was terrified of losing the love of his three young children. His family values made Marnie like him even more. Or was it love? She didn't know. She didn't want it to be love yet because she had promised herself that she would definitely not fall for another man who had complications and more baggage than Elton John took on a year-long tour.

She had barely given Lilian Dearman a thought in the past few weeks and suddenly felt bad for that, especially as she'd been going into hospital the last time they'd been in contact. She logged onto the Sisters of Cheesecake site and found a multi-peopled heated dialogue going on. *Have you tried intro-ducing a swirl of marmite into the mascarpone for a singular taste?* was the header of the thread, composed by 'Cheeseman'. It had all the hallmarks of Lilian.

Marnie, grinning, private-messaged her.

'Marmite would only work if you added parmesan to the crumb base. Are you out of hospital now?'

'Hello, Marnie! Yes, hospital did the trick. Am well enough to come on here causing mischief. I have missed you. How are you and are we finally going to have that afternoon tea this weekend? Are you free tomorrow? Do say yes.'

And because Marnie needed not to think about her lover being in the bosom of his family surrounded by kids who would probably hate her when they eventually met her, she typed,

'Yes, am free tomorrow and I would love to. Yes, yes, yes.'

*

Lilian Dearman was nothing like Marnie had pictured her. She'd visualised a second tiny Mrs McMaid, but Lilian was tall and willowy with long, wavy silver-white hair which added a femininity to her otherwise androgynous frame and square-jawed long face. Her eyes were the most striking fea-ture: large, bright and green, sharp and intense. Already in situ at the café table, Lilian stood, leaning on her stick, when she spotted Marnie and smiled from ear to ear.

'I recognised you immediately,' she said, holding her arms out wide and as Marnie embraced her, she breathed in a familiar scent of lilies wonderfully reminiscent of times past.

Not a serial killer then, or a reporter. She was just as it said on the tin – an old lady with a spine problem, thought Marnie, taking a seat across the table. She noted the silver top of Lilian's stick in the form of a greyhound's head.

'That's beautiful,' she commented.

'Had it years,' said Lilian. 'I've got a collection of walkers but this is my favourite. Had it made after Dido died. Most loyal dog I ever had, bloody marvellous creature. Had to rely on damned sticks since I was a child, thanks to a lineage of bloody interbred bastards,' she explained, at volume, causing the eyebrows of a woman on the next table to zoom up her forehead. 'Let's order first before we start to talk,' she went on. 'Afternoon tea with cheesecake, I thought. What else?' And she winked.

Marnie nodded her agreement and Lilian waved over a waitress.

'So how long were you in hospital for, then?' asked Marnie.

'Bor-ing,' said Lilian. 'Let's not talk about health but of things far more exciting. Mr Fox for instance. Have there been any developments?'

'A few,' said Marnie, more sigh than words. 'We are now a couple.'

'Excellent.' Lilian clapped her hands together. 'There's nothing like a bit of love in the air. I hope he treats you better than the last bastard.'

Again the woman on the next table – mid-macaron – turned around to give Lilian a glance of disapproval.

'Do join us,' Lilian yelled over, with an expansive beckon. 'Your attentions seem to be more on our table than your own anyway.'

Marnie snorted in an effort not to laugh. She'd got it very wrong thinking Lilian would be a quiet little old lady like Mrs McMaid.

'Aaron, wasn't it?' said Lilian. 'And I have to say, Marnie, your friend sounds a horrible trollop. I say *friend* … She should not have put Grigori before a chum of nearly eighteen years,' and she huffed and Marnie's mouth dropped into a long O. Was there anything she hadn't told Lilian Dearman that night of the two bottles of Shiraz? And was there anything Lilian Dearman hadn't remembered about it? She felt her cheeks start to heat up with embarrassment.

'I think I must have bored you rigid with the story of my life, Lilian. I shouldn't—'

'If you're trying to say that you shouldn't have got absolutely buggered on booze and poured out your heart to me, then save your breath,' said Lilian firmly. 'I could tell by your increasingly bad spelling that whatever you were drinking was taking effect but that stupid cheesecake site brought us together for a reason, my dear, and I have absolutely no doubt fate played a hand in it.' Her voice softened and a smile spread across her lips. 'I sensed a troubled soul that night and I very much think that you needed to say what you did because you'd kept it trapped inside you for far too long. Not good for you at all – trust me, I know this. What a vile family you have, dear. No wonder you have so much difficulty negotiating life. They've imprinted a faulty map in you. Totally understandable why you keep losing your way. I have the same map imprinted on me too. We have more in common than you could know.'

The afternoon tea arrived cutting off further apologies from Marnie, and what a feast. Three tiers of sandwiches, pastries and miniature cakes with a smaller fourth tier at the top, bearing a selection of cute cheesecake squares.

'Tuck in, dear,' said Lilian, stuffing in an egg mayo triangle and making exaggerated sounds not unlike those uttered when Harry met Sally. Marnie was less impressed. She detected cheap mayo and margarine not butter, and not spread to the edges either which was a cardinal sin in her book.

'I do hope you'll come to Wychwell for the May Day Fair in a fortnight,' said Lilian. 'Not as popular as it used to be when I was a girl, but we do still honour the long-held tradition. We desperately need some new blood in the village. The last fresh young May Queen was ninety-two and died a week after she was crowned.'

Marnie half-choked on her ham and mustard. She shouldn't have laughed, she really hadn't meant to.

'Anyway, I want to know all about Mr Fox,' Lilian went on, reaching for a cheese and pickle. 'Do you have a photo of him that I can see?'

'Oh, I never thought to bring one,' lied Marnie. The truth was, she didn't have any. The first time she'd taken out her phone to snatch a selfie of them, Justin had covered his face as if he were an A-lister with no make-up on and she was the paparazzi. He wasn't photogenic, he'd excused. It doesn't matter, it's for my eyes only, Marnie had replied but he'd insisted no. He couldn't afford to take any chances of it getting into the wrong hands. He'd meant the hands of Suranna, his wife, of course. Marnie had been cross at his presumption that she'd plaster it all over Facebook if they had a row. What sort of person did he think she was? But she hadn't wanted to cause a fuss, so she relented.

So, no, she didn't have a photo of him. Neither could she ring him on his mobile, she had to wait until he rang her. Nor could they venture out in public like normal couples or stay the night in a hotel. Not yet anyway. Not until his uncoupling was completed. Marnie felt her jaw tightening with agitation. Best to change the subject, she thought, and steer clear of Justin-talk.

'I found Wychwell on the internet. It looks beautiful,' she said.

'Oh it is,' Lilian agreed with an energetic nod as she reached for a cheesecake square. 'It's tired though, so awfully tired. I've not given it my best. I resented it for so many ... good GRIEF what a disgusting taste.' Her features scrunched up and her tongue waggled in her mouth like a Maori doing a Haka.

Marnie followed suit, picking a square from the top plate to see what Lilian meant. Bland, rubbery, with a soggy, too-thin base. If there was one thing she was an expert on, it was cheesecake.

'My, that is a let-down,' she said. 'Gelatine overload and too much cream to cheese ratio. What do you think, Lilian?'

'I haven't a bloody clue,' returned Lilian. 'I couldn't make a cake if my life depended upon it. I only ever go on those silly forums to cause havoc. I'm a bored old lady who can't sleep and I ache everywhere. Playing devil's advocate is one of the few pleasures I have left.'

Marnie stared at her soundlessly, then she threw her head back and laughed. 'Really, oh my, Lilian, you are brilliant.'

Lilian smiled. 'I'm awfully sorry if you thought you'd found a fellow patissier but trust me, the world of baking is much safer with me outside it than within.'

'Oh, it doesn't matter,' said Marnie, thinking that it really didn't. She was having a lovely time with Lilian although she did look much older than her sixty-six years of age. But for all her bodily wear and tear, her mind seemed as sharp as a box of needles. Lilian halted a passing waitress in her tracks and demanded, with politeness, that the bill reflect the uneatable cheesecake offering. She had a beautiful voice, thought Marnie. Her speech was crowded with rounded vowels and that secret extra ingredient that distinguished her from people such as Gabrielle, who could never have achieved that intrinsic tone, not even with a million elocution lessons. The magic voice equivalent of the contents of Mrs McMaid's tin.

The waitress nodded. 'Mrs Abercrombie buys them in but the woman that makes them isn't very good.' Then her hand shot up to her mouth. 'Oh 'eck. I shouldn't have said that . . . I meant they're made in-house but the cheesecake woman isn't very good.'

The knowledge couldn't be undone though and that nugget of info stored itself in Marnie's memory for another time.

'Then you should tell Mrs Abercrombie to find someone else. Especially at the prices she charges,' snapped Lilian, not accepting the excuse. As the waitress scuttled off, Lilian whispered to Marnie, 'Tasted worse than something I'd make.'

'Surely not.'

'Believe me – that bad. Anyway, moving on, did you visit your sister for her birthday?'

Blimey, thought Marnie, *she has the memory of an elephant.* Did she really tell Lilian it was her sister's birthday as well? What else? It might be easier to make a list of everything she hadn't told her.

'No,' said Marnie. 'We don't do family birthdays really. Apart from sending a card . . .'

'Yours to them arrives on time, not so the other way around.' She answered Marnie's wide-eyed look seconds later. 'You didn't tell me that, I guessed.' She tipped the teapot over Marnie's cup and then her own, sharing the last of its contents.

'We are a dysfunctional family par excellence.' Marnie smiled sadly. 'We—'

'My dear girl,' Lilian butted in. 'Unless you have the Dearman name, you have no real concept of dysfunction. Although I do have to say that your sibling makes my younger sister appear a saint by comparison, and that's quite an achievement. Rachel ran off with our uncle who managed to kill them both in a glider.'

'Oh no, that's awful,' said Marnie.

'Rachel was a psychopath,' sniffed Lilian. 'Totally devoid of feeling. I didn't shed a tear over the thought of her being dead, though I shed gallons when she was alive. I remain convinced she murdered our nanny—' she broke off, waved her hand and shook her head. 'I can't talk about her. She's spoiling my mood. Let's talk about you; you said you didn't know why your mother ever had children.'

Marnie gulped. 'Did I?' Although she must have said it, because she'd always thought it and it wasn't the sort of thing Lilian could have made up. She'd often wondered what Judith Salt had been like before looking after a toddler whilst pregnancy took its toll; and before her husband left her the month before Gabrielle was born and moved to Thailand to be with a clutch of women he'd hooked up with on the internet and never even met.

'I didn't have a proper relationship with my parents either,' said Lilian. 'Maybe that's why fate put us together. Two kindred spirits.'

Marnie nodded. It said something about the state of her life that the person she had most in common with was an old lady whom she barely knew.

'I wanted so much to be told I'd been adopted when I was younger,' Lilian went on. 'But I had too much of the family resemblance to be denied . . .' Her voice momentarily trailed off before she launched down another conversational avenue. 'Did you ever find out who your real parents were, Marnie?'

'No.' Marnie licked a blob of Chantilly cream from her finger. 'My birth wasn't originally registered. The authorities were tipped off that a child was abandoned in an empty caravan – that was me. Irish travellers, they thought. I have no way of knowing . . . well, a slim chance because I suppose anything is possible these days.' She shrugged. 'I can't say that I'd try to find them even if I did know.' *I'm not sure I could set myself up for another disappointment*, she said to herself, but not aloud. She felt Lilian's chilly hand fall on top of hers and she saw how thin the skin was. She had the hands of a ninety-year-old.

'I knew even before my sister blurted it out when I was fourteen that I was adopted,' Marnie went on, seeing a GIF of Gabrielle in her head screaming at her:

I'm glad you're adopted, you bitch. I'm glad we're not real sisters.

Marnie remembered the top note of shock that hit her first. The relief came second and bloomed to euphoria because it explained everything.

'. . . I'd always known I wasn't the same as them. For a start, Mum and Gabrielle and my "father" are all blue-eyed blondes.' She flicked her long black hair over her shoulder and pointed at her cat-green eyes. 'I can't tell you how many times it's been said that I look Irish.'

Lilian studied her. 'Yes, I noticed that immediately,' she agreed. 'Your lovely sharp cheekbones and colouring. Unmistakably you have Irish blood in you.'

'And my sister can eat three potatoes more than a pig

and stay the same weight and I can put on a stone just from watching her do it.'

Lilian Dearman hooted with laughter.

'She was named after an angel, I was named after a deranged woman in a Hitchcock film. I think that says it all.'

'Ah, but a very beautiful woman,' said Lilian. 'One with spirit and beauty and guile.'

Marnie agreed that she had spirit and guile all right. Her mother had never suspected how much cheesecake and jam she had eaten that summer of her tenth year.

'We lived next door to a lovely old lady . . .'

'Mrs McMaid,' Lilian interjected.

'Oh, I've told you about her too.' *Quelle surprise.*

'Only a little. Carry on. I want to hear more.'

Marnie caught a waft of Lilian's perfume as she waved her hand encouragingly for her to continue. It was very like the one Mrs McMaid used to wear. She'd had a large ridged bottle on her dressing table with a tasselled squashy pump which dispensed the scent of midsummer whenever it was pressed.

'Well, she baked cakes on a continual loop for other people: the church, local bakeries and sometimes just to give away to poor souls who needed cheering up.' Marnie didn't realise how her features softened when talking about the old lady, but Lilian saw. 'I think, though it might sound melodramatic, that she was the first person to show me any real kindness. She let me lick cake mixture off the spoon which was highly illegal in our house and I nearly spontaneously combusted at the first taste of her home-made raspberry jam. But she died at the end of the summer and autumn seemed so much colder without her in it. The first thing the new people did when they moved in was to dig up all her lovely raspberry bushes.' Marnie sighed. 'And the price they charge for them in supermarkets nowadays.'

'So you like raspberries, do you?' asked Lilian, with a disproportionate interest in the answer.

'I love them,' smiled Marnie.

'We have lots of raspberries in Wychwell,' said Lilian, adding cryptically to the air. 'It's a sign.'

Sign of what? wondered Marnie, thinking that Lilian might be a little more batty than she'd initially given her credit for.

'Tell me more about your Mrs McMaid,' Lilian prompted. 'She sounds marvellous.'

'She was – totally and absolutely marvellous. She might only have been in my life for a few weeks but I've never forgotten her. If I close my eyes sometimes, I can drift back in time. I can be in her front room with the massive squashy sofa and the crocheted cushion covers . . .' *And the scent from the pink roses which she cut from the bushes in the garden and put in coloured glass vases around the room. I can be breathing in Mrs McMaid's heady floral perfume and watching her scraping the vanilla caviar out of the beans as she stands at her scrubbed kitchen table.* 'I think one day I'd like to have a cottage like Mrs McMaid's.' She wasn't sure she'd spoken that aloud until Lilian Dearman replied to it.

'I have a spare cottage if ever you wanted to stay. The previous occupant was a very special old lady. Jessie was our last May Queen. Died doing "Agadoo" in the local pub on her ninety-second birthday. It was quite the most ideal way for her to go.'

Marnie gave a soft chuckle. 'She sounds formidable.'

'Oh she was,' nodded Lilian. 'And a superb tenant. A perfect match for Little Raspberries.'

'Little Raspberries?' repeated Marnie.

'All the cottages in the village have names: Little Raspberries, The Nectarines, Peach Trees ... I renamed them myself when Father died. Lionel – the vicar – thought it might help me to put my stamp on the place. Oh, that reminds me ... do you read?'

'I love to read,' said Marnie, watching Lilian bend to retrieve something from her bag. 'I read a lot, anything and everything. At the moment I'm halfway through an account of the Great Train Robbery.'

'Oh, I adore crime books. The grittier the better. I especially love a good murder mystery. I think Hercule Poirot and I would have got along very well had we ever met. But I don't suppose he ever came up to the North of England. Shame.'

Marnie smiled tentatively, not sure if Lilian was joking or not. She reached over to accept the coffee-table book which the old lady was holding out towards her.

'Talking of crime, this is about Wychwell. Lionel did it as a labour of love and I only had five copies made. It's not for public consumption, you'll see why when you come to read it. Take it, then you'll be acclimatised to us when you come to visit.'

'Thank you,' said Marnie. 'I'll bring it back the next time we meet.'

'Oh no, keep it dear. It's a present. You'll realise what a foul lot the Dearmans were, despite the name. Nothing dear about them at all. Bunch of bastards. Lionel did it very well; pulled all the skeletons out of the cupboards, which is why I can't let people like Titus Sutton read it. Titus is a distant relative and has mentally rewritten history ...' Lilian leaned in as if Titus Sutton might be within hearing distance and tapped her temple. 'In his head the Dearmans belong to a noble lineage, friends with royalty, rich as Croesus and God's right-hand men. Not the case at all; they were cruel arse-lickers. Although Lionel didn't quite use that expression when describing them, being a man of the cloth. "Toadying" was the euphemism he plumped for.'

Marnie thought she might enjoy reading about the Dearmans. She needed to get her teeth into something this weekend to stop her thinking about what might be happening over at Justin's house and Buster Edwards and Ronnie Biggs weren't really doing it for her.

'My family have owned Wychwell for generations,' Lilian went on. 'Henry the eighth gave the manor to my ancestor Edward Dearman as a reward for his loyalty when he was looting all the monasteries. Frightful man, according to history. Two-faced bastard. Staunch Catholic but knew which side his bread was best buttered. It was he who cursed us all.'

'Cursed us all?' Marnie echoed as a question.

'Oh, you'll read all about it in the book. He had a witch drowned in the well outside her cottage in the woods, hence the name of the village. Some harmless bugger who happened to have a black cat and grew comfrey, probably. She's supposed to haunt the place. I've never seen her myself but some say they've seen orbs of light through the manor windows at night. Usually after a heavy session at the Wych Arms, no doubt.'

'How very sad,' replied Marnie. 'Is the well still there?'

'Somewhere, but we lost it,' Lilian said with regret. 'Her cottage was burned down and the well closed up to seal in the bad luck, which was unfortunate as it tapped into a spring and was the only clean water around. Probably why she was so healthy and the rest of the village was riddled with pox. It didn't get rid of the curse at all. Of course, it might have helped us if we'd fornicated outside the family occasionally.'

Macaron woman on the next table slammed her china cup down onto her saucer in a gesture of disgust. It had no effect on Lilian whatsoever.

'Do come for the May Fair, Marnie. Everyone dresses in medieval costumes, or as witches, apart from the Suttons who prefer their country tweeds. I can show you Little Raspberries. You never know, you might take a liking to it.'

'Thank you, I'll put it in my diary,' said Marnie, not committing herself to a promise because country fairs weren't really her scene and she had other plans for that May Day weekend. Lord knows why Lilian Dearman was so keen to show her an empty cottage. She could hardly live in it and commute to Leeds every day, if that was what she was thinking.

The waitress brought the amended bill and Lilian snatched it deftly up from the table.

'Let me get it,' insisted Marnie.

'Absolutely not. I invited you here, so the onus is on me,' replied Lilian, foraging in her bag and pulling out a purse which was battered and bright purple and fat with notes. 'You can get the next one.' She counted out the exact cost and then added a fifty-pence piece to the saucer.

'Okay, I will then,' Marnie said as Lilian struggled to her feet, stiff from sitting down for so long.

As they walked out, Lilian took Marnie's arm for balance.

'It's no fun at all getting past sixty when you have defective genes. I'm old before my time.'

Marnie didn't comment, though she remembered how sprightly Mrs McMaid had been in her eighties. Even after all these years, Mrs McMaid continued to pop into her thoughts on a regular basis.

As the duo walked into the street and then around the

corner, Marnie knew instantly that the huge vintage black Rolls Royce parked very badly must be Lilian's. It made every other car near it look like a Matchbox toy.

'We always have the best weather at the fair. It hasn't rained on our May Day celebrations for over a hundred years. The bloody weather hasn't cursed us at least,' Lilian said, opening the door to the Rolls and sliding her stick across the seat into the passenger side footwell.

'Oh my,' gasped Marnie as she took in the beautiful interior of the Roller. With its walnut dash and many dials, it looked more like the cockpit of a private jet.

'It was Daddy's car,' said Lilian. 'Hideous man. He hated it so he never drove it. That's why I can because I don't have any memories of him associated with it. I'm thinking of leaving it to my groundsman when I die. You'll like him. One of very few men on the planet who isn't a bastard.'

Marnie couldn't help the giggle that escaped from her lips. Poor Lilian must have suffered at male hands in her life. It wasn't really anything to laugh about but her delivery was just too funny.

Despite her frail frame, Lilian turned to Marnie and embraced her with a grip worthy of a WWE wrestler. As she did so, Marnie caught a whiff of face powder and talcum and the bottom notes of that lovely perfume and as a picture of Mrs McMaid puffed past her brain like the lightest of warm breezes, Marnie now knew for certain that they both wore the same fragrance. *How delightfully odd and wonderful*, she thought.

'Dear Marnie, you are exactly how I thought you'd be. What a joyous hour I've had,' Lilian said, with feeling. 'Do come and see me soon. May Day falls on a Sunday this year so we will be celebrating on the actual day rather than the nearest weekend to it. Always has stronger magic when we do that.'

Marnie smiled. She believed that there was a little magic circulating in the world. Like Mrs McMaid's special ingredient. And whatever magic had brought her and Justin together at Clifford's retirement do. Yes, there was still some around, for sure.

'I'll see,' she said, helping Lilian into the Roller. Then, she stood and waved as Lilian pulled out onto the road at a snail's pace, testing the impatience of a car driver who had slowed down to allow her to manoeuvre out. He beeped on his horn and Marnie saw a long arm being extended through the window of the Roller, one finger held aloft. Then Lilian sped off as if the drugs squad were after her, the sound of a chirpy double-pip on her horn trailing behind her like a tail.

Chapter 6

History of Wychwell by Lionel Temple
with contributions by Lilian Dearman.

Edward Sutton Dearman was a brutal, feared man in the county. When Henry VIII embarked on his project to dissolve the monasteries between 1536 and 1541, Edward saw his way to bring himself to the attention of the king at court and his toadying demeanour was attractive to the king's vanity. Edward, it was said, could smell a priest hidden in the walls of a house as sure as a dog could smell a rat. Ironic that he convinced his fellows that this gift was God-given and not witchcraft.

As a reward for his duties, Henry ejected the Lord of the Manor Sir Percival Shanke and his immediate family, executing them for their allegiance to the Catholic faith, and gave the house and lands to Dearman.

Dearman forcibly married Elizabeth Swannecke, the niece of Percival's wife, but after a succession of miscarriages, Dearman – who had made many enemies through his ruthless ambitions – decided there was black magic working against him.

In the woods resided a widow, Margaret Kytson. Some in the village, fearing the increasingly psychotic and paranoid Dearman might point the finger of blame at them, suggested that Margaret could be a witch stirring up evil. Indeed, Margaret grew medicinal herbs to trade for goods and was said to have a black cat. The villagers arrived mob-handed at Margaret Kytson's cottage and found no cat but a newborn baby. In a kangaroo court, she was found to be guilty of witchcraft against the Lord of the Manor and sentenced to be thrown, along with her cat, down her own well which tapped into a natural spring. When no cat was found, Dearman was led to believe the cat was changed into the child to disguise it and invoke sympathy. Upon death the cat would show its bones, he was told.

As Margaret and the crying child were lowered into the well, she cursed the villagers and said that no one who bore the Dearman name would ever know happiness. The well was immediately demolished and covered over to seal in the bad luck and Margaret's cottage was burnt to the ground.

Six months later, Elizabeth Dearman gave birth to a healthy son and Edward knew that he had done the right thing in executing the witch and the child. As he rode into the village with his newborn to show the villagers his heir, his horse bolted and threw them to the ground, killing them both instantly.

Fearing the wrath of Margaret, the village (called Aldwell originally) was renamed Wychwell, in an effort, maybe, to appease her spirit. The well still exists somewhere in the woods and though the exact location cannot be traced, it is thought to be somewhere to the south west of the village (see Chapter on Little Raspberries).

Elizabeth married Edward's younger brother John, and had five children by him: Henry, William, James, Nicholas and Anne. By adulthood only James and Anne were still alive. James had married Catherine Blount who was barren. Desperate for an heir, it is said that he impregnated his own sister and he and Catherine raised the issue as their own. Anne, who was unmarried, was declared mad when she had safely delivered twin boys and interred in Bedlam asylum.

Flipping heck, thought Marnie, reading the first pages of the book which Lilian had given her that afternoon. She was home by herself waiting for a delivery from Ping Pong's Chinese takeaway in Eccleshall Road. Justin had sent her a cheeky text saying that he wished he were snuggled up in bed with her instead of in the midst of people he couldn't stand and that his son had broken out in spots, which was probably the onset of chickenpox. She wasn't stupid, she knew he was laying the foundations of why the children wouldn't be getting to know about the divorce this weekend. She ached to be with Justin openly and completely and though he informed her of all the tiny steps he and his wife were taking to dissolve their marriage, she was starting to question whether they were just walking on the spot. But then again, she had never been in a relationship with anyone who had children before. She wondered if Gwyneth and Chris had taken this long.

There was an old adage that you could fool everyone else, but not yourself; but it was rubbish because Marnie was very good at doing exactly that. She had learned to rationalise away anything that threatened to bash her in the heart, that held up a pin to those little bubbles of tenuous delight that came her way so rarely. The skill was born from some internal self-preservational part that wanted to see her happy, but this frustrating situation with Justin had gone on for so long now that it was really contesting her powers of self-delusion. Her brain was starting to ask itself some awkward questions and despite all the expert assurances Justin gave her, she was finding it harder and harder to keep convincing herself that she wasn't being spun a very elaborate yarn.

Angrily, she picked up her mobile and replied to Justin's message in emphatic capitals:

I DONT THINK THIS IS WORKING. LET'S CALL IT A DAY.

Her finger hovered over the send arrow. She imagined him falling into a tailspin on receiving it. Then she imagined him replying with a cool, YEAH, WAS THINKING THE SAME. She flew into a panic and deleted the text. What on earth was she doing? He'd told her he knew that this wasn't a traditional courtship but she had to trust him. He was under a lot of pressure. She should give him the benefit of the doubt. She'd promised she would. Not all men were bastards.

The doorbell rang and just for a second, her heart gave an excited little kick that it might be Justin surprising her after all. But it wasn't. It was her chicken and mushroom Cantonese-style arriving from Ping Pong's.

Chapter 7

Two more weeks passed with Marnie still in limbo. She'd been right, of course. The children still didn't know that Justin and Suranna were separating because the little boy had been quite ill with chickenpox, which he kindly then passed on to his sister and you couldn't drop a bombshell of that magnitude into the laps of poorly children, could you?

On the Wednesday of that week, Marnie walked into the massive atrium of Café Caramba and immediately felt something strange in the air, something amiss, something not quite right. It was nothing she could put her finger on: the snooty receptionist ignored her as per usual, there was the regular buzz as people rushed past her on the escalator to go to one of the two floors above, either because they were late or keen; but it was present like a gas in the air, waiting for the moment to jump out of the cupboard dressed like a clown to scare her half to death. Or maybe it was the warm wind of change for the best, she thought hopefully. They couldn't carry on treading water for ever.

She got off the escalator and, as always, made a right through the first set of double doors where the Product Development team were having their usual morning huddle. She said a cheerful good morning to Sweaty Andrew, who replied a cheerful good morning to her boobs. Then she walked past Justin Fox's office, giving him only a cursory glance, which belied the thump in her heart. Oh, how she wanted to stop and flash her secret smile to him that said, 'Remember what my lips were doing to you yesterday afternoon on the back seat of my car?' All the more reason to keep her attention fixed forward. The affair had remained secret for almost two months and that was because they'd never let their guard slip. *Careless talk costs lives*, as they said in the war, adapted to her own version: stupid mistakes result in all sorts of crap.

Straight on through Merchandising, then a right into her own department. Her mood immediately sank to find that Elena was back at her desk after a week and a half off with 'women's complaints'. Starved of a counterpart with whom to gossip, Vicky had got on with her work and kept her head down.

'Nice to have you back, Elena,' Marnie lied sweetly.

'Good to be back.' Elena's reciprocating smile was as false as her natural pout.

In her bag, Marnie's phone bleeped. She pulled it out to see a reminder flash up for the Wychwell May Day fair on Sunday. Marnie winced guiltily. She wouldn't be there, despite giving Lilian the impression she might. The weather forecast was brilliant for the weekend and she had decided to take the bull by the horns and insist that Justin spend Saturday with her moseying around the villages of Derbyshire and then they stay in a hotel overnight so she could – at last – wake up with him the next morning, which happened to be her thirty-second birthday. She'd found a beautiful olde worlde hotel off the beaten track with a suite that had a huge

four-poster bed and a hot tub for two on a private patio. It
hadn't been cheap but it would be worth every penny.

The clock hands crawled around to eleven forty-five. As
soon as the big hand on her watch had touched the nine, she
picked up her bag, stood and smoothed down her skirt.

'Roisean, I'm taking a long lunch. I have a business meeting with Justin Fox.' They had decided that avoiding each
other entirely could cause as much suspicion as flirting. There
was nothing wrong with announcing a legitimate tête à tête
every so often.

'Lucky you,' said Roisean, clicking her tongue.

'You think?' said Marnie.

'He's certainly a looker,' said Roisean.

'I'll put in a good word for you,' Marnie winked at her.

'No, you're all right but I'll hold the fort. I'm not going
out anywhere.'

Marnie hated lying, especially to Roisean. She wanted to
be able to say to her that she was taking a long lunch with
Justin because he was her boyfriend. Or better still – her
fiancé. She'd even started doodling 'Marnie Fox' on her notepad at home (never at work of course) to see how it fitted. It
sounded like a name that kicked ass.

She was meeting Justin on the other side of Leeds, at a
pub called the Blue Boy which didn't look much from the
outside, but inside it was newly refurbished with large comfortable leather seats and sofas with lots of private alcoves.
She ordered two baguettes, a half and a pint of diet cola and
waited, nervously drumming her fingers on the table because
she was worried about telling him she'd booked the hotel. She
had the awful feeling that she'd been too reckless and would
lose her money because he wouldn't go. Then annoyance
began to replace any anxiety as half an hour passed and he

still hadn't arrived, leaving barely time to eat never mind have a snog in the car. But her tight pout instantly softened when she felt Justin lean over her from behind, enveloping her in a cloud of Joop and issuing a throatful of apologies that he hadn't been able to get away from Laurence. Then he went and spoiled it all.

'. . . Then Suranna called,' he said, shaking his head. 'I have no idea what's wrong with her at the moment. I'm jumping through every hoop she's putting in front of me and it still isn't enough.'

Marnie hated hearing the 'Suranna' word. It made her into a real person, one who was still joined to Justin in holy matrimony, even if he did call it 'unholy matrimony'. It was obvious that she was clinging on to him for grim death, using every excuse in the book to keep him consciously coupled to her. Didn't she realise how stupid she was making herself look? How desperate and deluded? Marnie had a vision of Suranna hanging on to Justin's leg every morning when he set off to work, with him dragging her down the path towards his company car.

She changed the subject quickly. 'I got you a prawn baguette. Hope that was okay.'

'Er . . . yes. Not really hungry though. Had a huge breakfast with the law firm lads.'

She bit down on what she had been about to say, *But you knew you were coming out to lunch with me*, because she didn't want to sound as whiney as his wife. She was getting sick of constantly having to hold her tongue, though.

'You okay? You look stressed,' he said.

Marnie took a deep breath and, given the cue, dived straight in.

'You know it's my birthday on Sunday.'

'Yeeees,' he said, drawing the word out so slowly that it made her wonder if he'd remembered. Then again, she'd told him in a very heated moment.

'Well . . .'

Her mouth stopped suddenly, like a Shetland pony faced with Beecher's Brook.

'What?'

It came out so fast it was almost one long word. 'I've booked us a night away in a hotel. Not too far away in Derbyshire. And in the room where Mary Queen of Scots stayed. It has a four-poster and . . .'

His face, creasing in awkward regret, told her everything she needed to know and had really known from even before she had made the reservation.

'I can't, Marnie.'

'Say it's work,' said Marnie with an unashamed tone of pleading in her voice.

'She'd know it wasn't.'

Marnie felt close to tears. Hot, annoyed, frustrated tears. 'But you went away golfing with Laurence a few weekends ago.'

'Yes, but that *was* work.'

'I feel like I'm having an affair with a married man.' The words burst out of her and she had to quickly gather the reins on the volume.

'Well, technically, you are.' Justin picked absently at a prawn.

'You know what I mean, skulking around, having to wait for you to ring me, meeting in secret, never being able to spend the night together.'

She had bought him a daft tie with foxes on it, but he had left it in her house because he couldn't take it home with him.

Suranna would ask where he got it from and she'd know he was lying if he said 'a rep' or that he had bought it for himself. *Suranna Suranna Suranna*. Marnie felt like the second wife in *Rebecca*.

'I know. It's hard for me too,' he said, stealing a look at his watch. 'Come on, let's have some "us" time.'

By which he meant a shag in the car. Her car. They'd only had sex once in his car and all traces of her had been removed immediately afterwards with squirts of Febreze and a sticky roller thing.

Marnie stood up to go with a resigned sigh. Maybe she could make him change his mind by 'doing his favourite' on her cloth rear seating.

Which she did. But he didn't.

There wasn't enough time then to do anything else that she might have benefitted from, not that she was bothered because she knew she would have had to fake anyway; her head was too full of disappointment to let lust come to the fore. She followed Justin back to the office and again felt that strange foreboding in the air as she walked through the revolving doors. It was thicker now, more pronounced, as if it was a fat spot, filled with infection, pushing up from below the surface of the skin, ready to make its vile appearance.

It was at precisely half-past three when the zit burst and the pus covered everyone on the trading floor. Marnie had been talking on the phone to Laurence when she heard the noise from departments away. Arthur and Bette looked up from their desks and then put their heads back down again. They wouldn't stop trying to balance a sheet if there was a sudden earthquake and the roof fell in.

Marnie tried to focus on her conversation but one ear

was now cocked to whatever was going on. A woman was shouting.

'WHERE IS SHE? WHERE IS THE SLAG?'

Vicky, Elena, Roisean, the whole of Beverage Marketing now, including the older ones were looking at each other raising their shoulders, mouthing 'what's that' at each other. Even Laurence, at the other end of the phone, was asking what on earth was going on and Marnie had to reply that she had no idea.

Then from around the corner appeared a short, Weeble-like woman wearing a blue swingy pinafore. Behind her, Dennis, the world's most ineffectual security guard, was wheezing as he tried to keep up. The woman was facial-scanning everyone as she passed them, matching them up to a photofit she held in her head.

'Madam, Mrs . . .' pleaded Dennis, grabbing hold of the Weeble's arm, but she shook him off forcefully and the effort swung her round slap bang in front of Marnie's desk. The little woman's eyes widened then narrowed. It seemed as if she'd found a match.

'You,' she levelled at Marnie with a non-too friendly stab of her finger.

'I'll ring you back, Laurence,' said Marnie, putting down the phone. The woman's rotundness did nothing to stop her from throwing herself across the desk to grab a handful of Marnie's hair so when Dennis pulled her back, Marnie was dragged over the desk with her. The woman had demonic strength and she wouldn't let go. Marnie instinctively groped around for something to use as a weapon, found a stapler and launched it but it flew way off target. The woman was going to scalp her in a moment if she didn't do something. She was aware of Arthur now, trying to dislodge the woman's fingers. Marnie made her right hand into a claw, lashed out in the direction of the woman's head, felt her nails rake against soft skin and heard a sharp yelp as she let go. Marnie staggered backwards, her head pulsing with pain, to see the fat little woman clutching her face before she recovered and lurched forwards again with a cry worthy of Braveheart. This time, though, Dennis and Arthur were able to secure her and Roisean dived defensively in front of her boss forming a cross-shaped barrier.

'You bitch, you bitch,' the woman kept repeating over and over again. A large audience had now gathered. It seemed as if the whole building had come to gawp at the floorshow.

'What the hell . . .' said Marnie, fighting back tears which the hair-pulling had brought involuntarily to her eyes, their flow not helped by her humiliation at being the target of this lunatic's attention.

'Hell? Hell? Yes I'm in hell because of you, you . . . bitch. Do you know who I am?' screamed the woman, spittle flying from her mouth. 'Because I know who you are. You're the slaggy tart who is fucking my husband.'

Chapter 8

There was a pin-drop silence to end all pin-drop silences, only broken by an eventual snigger that had Vicky's stamp all over it.

'What?' asked Marnie, hardly hearing the words above the sound of her heartbeat which had both transferred itself to her ears and acquired the speed of a bullet train.

'Oh, don't play the innocent you ... you ... bitch.'

'I knew it. Didn't I say?' Vicky's voice again, in a delighted, barely covered whisper.

Marnie noticed how tight that swinging frock looked around the woman's middle. She wasn't fat, she was pregnant. Heavily pregnant. Her brain started spinning in stark contrast to everything around her which had frozen into stock-still mannequin mode. Even Dennis looked like a waxwork of himself.

'But ...' Inside Marnie's head, some clear, no-nonsense part tried to take command of the situation and find some logic in this surrealism.

Suranna? Is this Suranna? Or a stray nutter who didn't like the look of her. The first option seemed more viable on quick reflection.

'Suranna?' Marnie asked.

'Don't you dare use my bloody name.' There were four jagged red stripes raising on her cheek.

'Is that a baby?' Marnie's finger stretched forward.

Suranna gave a bitter hoot of laughter. 'What do you think it is – blocked wind? I'm pregnant with my husband's child, you ... you ...'

More names ensued. A whole thesaurus-worth of insults. Many of the older ones in the department probably didn't realise there were so many words for a tart.

Marnie's brain switched into calculator mode. She heard Justin's voice in her head: *I haven't had sex in fourteen months*, but whatever was in Suranna Fox's belly had got there during the last nine.

'You're not with him any more,' said Marnie, blood hissing and pounding in her ears.

Suranna indicated her stomach. 'Er, I obviously am.'

'Someone fetch Justin,' Roisean said.

'You've split up,' said Marnie.

'No we haven't,' countered Suranna, pulling a face.

'Stupid bitch.' A voice to her right. Elena. Marnie turned her head and saw the Olympic gold medal of smirks gracing her mouth.

'Apparently Justin's not in the building,' someone else said.

Marnie was in shock. Nausea gripped her stomach with hard bony fingers and squeezed. 'I didn't know. I didn't know.'

'Course you didn't,' Suranna sneered, her teeth bared. Her cheek looked terrible, as if she'd been clawed by a tiger. Then suddenly she seemed to deflate between the two men holding her and started to cry.

'Come on, love,' said Arthur, pulling a chair over and pushing Suranna Fox down onto it. Someone else handed her a tissue so she could dab at the blood peeping from the scratches; someone else dropped to their knees at her side, took her hand and began talking softly to her. She was enclosed in a circle of warmth and sympathy whereas Marnie stood alone, banished to a hinterland of coldness and disgust.

Burned by her shame and with a compulsion to get out of the building before she was poisoned by the air in it, Marnie reached down to the side of her desk, grabbed her handbag, snatched the coat from the back of her chair and cut through the assembled crowd, conscious of the attention on her, aware of their sniggers and chatting and judgements firing into her back like Robin Hood's arrows. Eyes fixed forward, she was glad that her legs worked independently of her brain because she would have fallen to the floor like a marionette without a puppet master if she'd had to consciously move them.

She felt as if she couldn't breathe, as if Suranna Fox and her compassionate entourage had sucked all the oxygen out of the immediate area. Shame powered her stride. She stole a glance into Justin's office but it was empty, his chair pushed backwards against the wall as if he'd vacated it in a hurry. All sorts of horrible thoughts were crowding her brain, demanding further examination and answers and she was afraid to let them sharpen into focus. As she approached the door which led out onto the upper floor of the atrium, it swung back in her face too quickly for her to avoid it hitting her squarely on the cheekbone. The man on the other side started to apologise profusely but she raced past him, down the escalator, past the reception desk, through the door and out into the car park, tears stinging her eyes. For a second or two she couldn't remember where she had parked her car. Left, or was it right? *Think, Marnie, think. Right. It was right. It's there.* Her hands were shaking as they fumbled in her bag for her key. She unzapped the car, threw herself inside, fired up the engine and willed herself to calm down, uttering words of self-comfort because on top of everything else she didn't want to bloody crash. *You're okay, Marnie. You didn't know. It's not your fault. Keep calm. Breathe.*

She pulled down the visor above her head and looked at herself in the vanity mirror to find that her own cheek was swelling up thanks to clumsy door man. She nosed the car carefully out of the car park and felt a wash of blessed relief as it blended with the anonymity of the city traffic. As she waited for a red light to change, Marnie scrolled through the names on her Bluetooth car phone directory until she came to JF. She rang him, for the first time ever, and it went straight through to voicemail. She disconnected the call. Should she leave a message, she asked herself. The answer came flying back at her, *Yes of course she bloody should.*

Straight to voicemail again. 'It's me, Marnie. Can you please ring me back. I need to speak to you. It's urgent.' She tried to keep the emotion out of her voice but failed as a fat hiccupping sob broke out of her throat just before she quit the call. The lights changed, she pressed down on the accelerator and stalled. The BMW behind gave an impatient beep on his horn which set Marnie's nerves jangling. *Pull yourself together and ignore that swanky wanker,* she told herself sternly and set off as smoothly and calmly as she was able, homeward bound. Except it wasn't her home, it was a rented semi because she had sold her lovely flat last year so she could move in with another luggage-laden twat.

She rang Justin again to find that his line was engaged. Three minutes later his line was free but he didn't pick up. She suspected he wasn't going to ring her back after all. She parked the car securely in the garage, rather than leave it on the street as she usually did, just in case she woke up in the morning to find SLUT written all over it in red paint.

Once inside the house, she locked the door behind her, closed the vertical blinds at the front window until they were mere slits and finally felt her nerves begin to stand down. She made herself a coffee, aware that her hands were shaking and then slumped onto a chair at the kitchen table. Her brain felt as if it was a multiplex cinema. On screen one, IMAX, 3D with Dolby surround sound was Suranna Fox holding on to her hair with her limpet grip. On screen two, Vicky and Elena standing like two old fishwives, arms crossed over their bosoms, lapping the spectacle up. On screen three Justin, a pastiche of all his best convincing lines flowing out of his lying gob. He hadn't had sex in well over a year. Details of the painstakingly slow conscious uncoupling. How could she have been so stupid? Sorry, amend that – how could she have been so stupid *again*? Why didn't she ever learn? Why was she so bloody selective with what she believed? Why hadn't she seen that the only real reason why they screwed in her car, why he never stayed over, why they couldn't be seen in public together was because he was still very much married to a woman he was still sleeping with. Her mother was up there on screen four: *You have no one but yourself to blame, you stupid, unthinking, unfeeling girl.*

What the hell was she going to do? She couldn't go back to Café Caramba. Ever. She couldn't walk into the office, shrugging off the judgements and opinions of everyone around her and carry on as if nothing had happened. She wasn't Sharon in the canteen who had been caught having sex in the lift with a temp during a drunken office party (Laurence had outlawed them since) only to walk back into work the next day as if shagging in a moving box was a standard part of the job description. If anyone new joined the company, Shagger Sharon was always pointed out as an interesting feature: *Those are the toilets, that's the coffee machine, there's Shagger Sharon who was caught flattening the lift floor buttons.* Until today, Marnie had never appreciated how much of ballsy – or barmy – woman Sharon was. But Marnie's misdemeanours wouldn't be treated so casually. She would get all the blame, she knew. She was the scarlet woman, the seductress. All claims that she had no idea Justin's wife was pregnant would be greeted with disbelief and scorn. People like Elena and Vicky would fuel the fires of her fornication.

She didn't know she was crying until she felt a wet drop on her hand. Followed by more, much more. She began to think that the flow might never stop.

Chapter 9

Marnie didn't sleep. Those four cinema screens were all playing on a loop in her head and she contemplated getting up and going out to the supermarket to buy some Nytol, but decided that would be a worse ordeal than staying in with insomnia. Mr Sandman might have been keeping his distance but Mrs Agoraphobia had paid her a visit, it seemed. Every noise outside the window, every car that passed made her heart delay its beat and then kick hard. She'd hoped that Justin would arrive at her door with an explanation. Maybe Suranna wasn't pregnant and she'd just shoved a cushion up her dress – after all if she was deranged enough to storm into the office creating holy hell, then she was nuts enough to try that stunt. But what if she really was pregnant? And if Justin had lied about sleeping with her, what else had he said that wasn't the truth? She suspected the answer to that lay between 'most of it' and 'everything'. She'd not only been reeled in by him but she'd put the hook through her own lip.

She had more chance of Leonardo DiCaprio dressed all in black, shinning up her drainpipe with a box of Milk Tray than she had of falling unconscious. She tossed from side to side in bed with her mind torturing her until she was forced to get up and make herself a hot chocolate. She usually walked around the block, breathed in some night air, reset her body clock but that wasn't going to happen tonight. She added the last of the cheap brandy that she used for cooking to the mug and glugged it back in large throatfuls.

Eventually, due to sheer mental exhaustion, she dropped off on the sofa and was woken by a persistent knocking early the next morning. She flew straight into panic mode and was shaking as she peeped through the blind to see a man with a parcel. He caught her looking and waved and she felt obliged to go to the door. It wasn't for her though, but for Melissa next door at 34; she was 34A. Postmen and delivery drivers were always getting it wrong. It didn't help that her door didn't have a number on it and she'd told the landlord when she first moved in. He'd said he'd sort it but he never had and she didn't see why she should.

She caught sight of the clock in the kitchen as she went to put on the kettle. It was ten past nine and ordinarily she would have been at work an hour now. She could imagine the whole building gossiping about her. Vicky and Elena in particular, spreading their venom and she wondered if Justin was being discussed with the same malice. She should ring HR and say she was ill but when she picked up the phone and started dialling the number, she couldn't do it. She burst into tears and allowed herself to dissolve helplessly into them, battered down further by the stick of her mother's words telling her what a trouble-causer she was, a selfish little tart who couldn't keep her legs shut.

After half an hour of wallowing, she knew that she had to do something more constructive than use up a load of tissues. She couldn't just sit in the house for ever and pretend none of this had happened, she had to get herself out of this mess. It wasn't as if it was the first time she'd wished she had sunk into the earth and it had closed over her head. She could run courses on it: *How to land yourself in the shit and then find a way out of it until it happens again. Ten pounds, including light refreshment.* She took a pad and a pen out of the drawer and began to scribble down a plan of action. Justin was the first word that came to mind. She wrote down his name followed by a large question mark. What was the likelihood that she and he would run off into the sunset together? Given that he hadn't as much as sent her a text to see if she was okay, the answer was zero. However, the soft, deluded lobe in her brain began to fire 'what ifs' at her. *What if his wife damaged his phone and he hadn't got her messages? What if his wife had trapped him by saying that she would kill herself if he attempted to contact her? What if . . .*

Oh shut up. A weary sigh resonated from some pissed-off part of her that usually couldn't get a word in but was now claiming centre stage. A part that said things she didn't want to hear so she pressed it down until it couldn't speak. *Justin Fox is a gutless twat and if he'd been anything like a real man he would have been in touch. He hasn't, because he doesn't care. There is NO OTHER EXPLANATION so wake up and smell the bloody coffee, you daft cow.*

The truth hurt as surely as that door swinging back in her face had, more if she were honest with herself. Justin was not going to ride up to her front door on a white charger to declare her his one true love. She had just written the word 'wanker' next to Justin's name when she heard the sound of broken glass and shouting. Horribly familiar shouting.

'COME OUT, YOU SLAG, I KNOW YOU'RE IN THERE!'

It was Suranna Fox again; that angry, vicious squawk was unmistakable.

Marnie ran upstairs to peep through the blinds at the front bedroom window and saw Justin's wife smashing Melissa's car up with a mallet. Melissa's car with the personalised MS reg plate. She'd obviously traced the address but not quite got it right. She'd seen the very girly Beetle parked outside (red with black ladybird spots and eyelashes on the headlamps). the row of fairy ornaments in the flowery borders, the pink curtains and the dream-catchers at the windows – as opposed to the very plain numberless house next door.

'You didn't think I could find out where you lived, did you ...' Marnie watched as Suranna picked up one of the stone toadstools from Melissa's garden and lobbed it at her window, scoring a bullseye if the sound of more glass breaking was anything to go by.

Marnie looked at the little fat woman, face red with fury, stomping up and down Melissa's path and a wave of unexpected pity hit her from left field. She was going to be horrified when she realised she'd targeted a poor innocent hairdresser. There would be no points scored for her when the police arrived, as they would very soon, because nothing got past nosey Mrs Barlow in the house opposite, or the Neighbourhood Witch as she was better known.

Marnie went downstairs, picked up her mobile and sent a text message to Justin telling him that his wife was getting herself into all sorts of trouble in Redbrook Row and needed him. Then she deleted his number.

The police arrived in record time and took a very distressed Suranna Fox away. Marnie had no idea if Justin turned up or not because she stayed in the kitchen and set up her laptop on the table there. Suranna's arrival on the street had made her mind up for her: she couldn't remain here where the neighbours would know soon enough why there was a pregnant woman lobbing fairytale bric-a-brac at windows. She was five months into her tenancy and had only recently filled in the forms to continue the agreement. They'd been sealed up in an envelope ready to send, although she kept forgetting to buy stamps. Thank goodness for her shit memory.

Marnie emailed the estate agency and said that she had changed her mind and would be vacating the property as soon as possible. She hadn't a clue where she was going to go instead but she'd find somewhere, though that somewhere depended on where her new job would be because she wouldn't be working at Café Caramba any more.

She drove around to the walk-in doctor's surgery. She thought she might have had a struggle convincing the doctor she needed some time off work with stress because she was a rubbish liar, but she burst into tears as soon as she sat down. The doctor gave her a sick note for a month and prescribed some tablets to lift her mood and help her to sleep. Try some mindfulness too, suggested Dr Singh. Marnie promised that she would although her mind was already full and she wanted it emptying instead.

She emailed HR a succinct message to tell them that she had been signed off for a month and sent them a photo of the note, promising to post it as well. When she got back to Redbrook Row, she saw that a window fitter's van was parked up and a man was busy mending Melissa's front bay. She was a quiet young woman and Marnie felt so dreadfully guilty. She wouldn't have known what to say to her – how would that conversation go? *Hi, Melissa, sorry that my lover's pregnant wife turned up and smashed up your house and car instead of mine.* She slipped into the house thankful that Melissa wasn't outside.

Marnie cancelled the hotel in Derbyshire. She contemplated going there alone rather than wasting the money but sleeping in a four-poster by herself would have been sadder than sad. She lost the hundred-pounds deposit, but she'd just have to write it off against her own stupidity.

At six o'clock, after scraping away a microwave meal for one that she couldn't eat, her text alert rang and she leapt on it.

Are you in?

It was Caitlin. She couldn't deny she wanted to see Justin's name more on the screen but seeing her friend would be a very close second.

YES !!! x

Have your bday present. Ok to pop round? x

OF COURSE XXXXX

Marnie had planned not to leap on Caitlin as she walked in through the door but she couldn't help herself. She needed to hug someone so badly. She needed someone to hug her even more.

Chapter 10

The Caitlin of old would have brought wine with her, kicked off her shoes and curled up on the sofa. 'Okay, tell me everything, all details, leave nothing out,' that Caitlin would have insisted. She would have listened intently, made all the right noises (even if she thought Marnie had been an arse) and then leapt over to give her a hug. Only then would that Caitlin have kindly and softly offered her true opinion as she had done in the past: *Marnie, do you think that maybe you scared him off a little by falling too fast? Marnie, didn't you think that he might have been lying about driving an Aston Martin when he'd forgotten his wallet three dates on the trot?* But that Caitlin wasn't around any more. She'd got a little colder and more distant with every passing year. That Caitlin didn't bear much resemblance to this one who had rolled up in a Vivien Westwood suit with expertly microbladed eyebrows and an immobile forehead.

Caitlin perched on the edge of the sofa, hands on her lap as if she was at a job interview. She refused the offer of a coffee or a tea, said she was detoxing and was only drinking water at the moment. Obviously not tap water, only the bottled stuff with a French name, which Marnie didn't have so she'd do without. Besides, she couldn't stay long. She and Grigori were going out to dinner with her parents.

'So, go on then, tell me what's wrong,' said Caitlin, with more of a tired air than Marnie wanted to acknowledge. So Marnie told her. The lot. Everything. And then she waited – hoped – for Caitlin to be the Caitlin of old and make her feel better. The way that Marnie had made her feel better when Danny Bradford had bonked her cousin and Will Brown had told her he had gone off her because she was crap at sex. And when Grigori had said that, before he took her to meet his parents, she should work on changing how she laughed because it sounded a bit common. That wonderful, infectious bray of a laugh that Caitlin was known for had to go. And her clothes. And did her accent have to be quite so broad Yorkshire? Marnie had asked her if she was sure she really wanted to be with a man who was so hyper-critical. She said she did and slowly but surely, Grigori had turned her into Margaret Thatcher.

'So, let me get this straight,' said Caitlin in that strange slow way she talked now as if each word had to be vetted for accent and pitch before it emerged from her mouth. 'You didn't realise that he was still very much married, though he wouldn't go out in public with you or stay the night?'

'No. I know it sounds stupid—' Marnie began, but Caitlin cut her off.

'How old are you?'

'You know how old I am, Cait—'

'Yes, I know I know. You're thirty-one, days away from being thirty-two and isn't that just a little too old to be making this sort of mistake? It sounds to me as if you knew exactly what the situation was but chose to ignore it.' And she laughed, a new Caitlin laugh, a hard, breathy mini-*guffaw* that carried the words *how vey vey vulgar* as passengers.

'I believed him, Cait,' said Marnie, tears racing up to her eyes. 'He was so convincing. There's no love without trust. So I trusted him.'

'You've trusted them all,' said Caitlin, wearily. 'Don't you have any BS detector? Haven't you learned anything from being dumped on over and over again?'

'Do any of us?' Marnie returned, a little annoyed at Caitlin's judgement. 'Maybe we only see it for other people, Cait.' They'd always said to each other that it was the world's easiest thing to give advice but much harder to take it. In the past they'd accepted they weren't the wisest girls when it came to men. One of Caitlin's exes left his own engagement party to nip over for a bonk with her before racing back to it FFS. She hadn't had a clue that he was even seeing anyone else.

'But this is stupid,' Caitlin came back at her. 'You must have known. The signs were obvious. More than obvious. Even to someone in a coma. Don't lie to yourself and me. You *knew*.'

'He said he and his wife were consciously uncoupling. I might have been frustrated about the lack of speed of that process, but no – I didn't know.'

'Did you question him properly? No – you didn't, because you didn't want to face up to what you really knew. You never do. You don't learn. No wonder I—'

She pulled up her sentence short and shook her head, continued down another path. 'You've caused untold damage now, to yourself and others.'

Untold damage? Since when did Caitlin Tyler say *untold damage?* But Marnie was more concerned with what Caitlin had been about to say after the 'no wonder' line.

'No wonder I what?' she looped the conversation back to it. 'What were you going to say?'

Caitlin shrugged. Then she looked at her watch. Then she stood up from the sofa, carefully, like a model afraid that a paparazzo would shoot his camera up her skirt. 'Doesn't matter. I'm going to have to go . . .'

'No wonder I what?' Marnie was insistent. 'Just tell me.'

Caitlin sighed, then looked Marnie straight in the eye and quirked a perfect left brow, as far as the Botox would allow her to.

'Okay then, I was going to say . . . no wonder I didn't bring Grigori with me.'

What did that even mean, thought Marnie.

'Grigori? What's he got to do with any of this?'

Caitlin's hands fell onto her hips in a stance of meaning business.

'Marnie, you aren't interested in men unless they have some complication, some baggage. Think about it – every one of them,' Caitlin picked up her handbag, a very nice Lulu Guinness with a pair of red lips as a clasp, not unlike the lips on Caitlin's face, which were plumper than Marnie remembered them ever being before.

'And what the hell has that to do with Grig—' Then the icky penny dropped. 'Oh please, tell me that you're not suggesting I'd be after Grigori. Please don't tell me you keep us apart because you're afraid I'd try and steal him from under your nose.' Marnie let loose a shriek of disbelieving laughter, expecting Caitlin's to join it. Expecting Caitlin to tell her not to be so bloody daft.

'Yes, if you must know, that's exactly what I think.' Caitlin's expression remained stony.

'Really?' Marnie's jaw dropped so low, she could have fitted a football between her teeth.

'Yes, I'm afraid so. That's what I think.'

Marnie stared at the woman in front of her and knew that there was nothing of her old friend left in that Caitlin casing. She was an alien, a stranger. That her best buddy could think so badly of her flooded her body with a horrible cocktail of upset and anger which spilled over into words.

'I wouldn't touch that chinless wonder if he peeled his skin off and he was Ryan Reynolds underneath.'

'But you did, didn't you?' Caitlin threw back at her. 'He told me what you did on the staircase at Lucy's wedding.'

'What *I* did? You mean when he stuck his disgusting tongue in my mouth and I shoved him off and he fell down the stairs and called me a—'

'Oh, listen to yourself, Marnie,' spat Caitlin. 'He couldn't stick his tongue in your mouth from a distance, could he? He's not a fucking lizard,' – Marnie huffed loudly at that –'you'd have had to get up close and personal first. Don't you think I've thought it through?'

Marnie threw up her hands. 'You'd believe him over me? He was plastered, I was sober for a start and I would have never, *never* have done that to you. What a prick. He's had you changing the way you dress, how you speak, how you laugh and now you tell me he thinks he's so drop-dead gorgeous your best friend would come on to him?'

'And that is precisely why you are not invited to our wedding,' said Caitlin, taking her car keys out of her bag.

Marnie blinked in shock. She wasn't sure if she was most stunned by the fact that her so-called best friend – her oldest friend – was getting married and hadn't told her, or that she was marrying one of the biggest turnips on the planet. Or that Caitlin had believed her capable of such deception. They were all vying for top position. And all of them were winning.

'Happy fucking birthday. Don't bother buying me any-thing for mine. Let's end it there,' said Caitlin, dropping both the gift bag she brought in with her onto the sofa and her posh accent too. She sounded like the Caitlin of old for those few seconds before she speed-walked on her red-soled shoes towards the front door, slamming it hard behind her.

The bag fell off the sofa and the box inside slid out. It was an M&S toiletries gift set.

HISTORY OF WYCHWELL BY LIONEL TEMPLE
with contributions by Lilian Dearman.

There are presently twenty-four residences (including four derelict ones) in Wychwell plus an eight-bedroomed manor with its own boating lake, the Wych Arms pub, a post office-cum-general store, a village hall and a mobile library, which is a caravan in the church grounds. Also the church of St Jude the Apostle (patron saint of hope and lost causes). The Reverend Lionel Temple was born into the position as his father, Lionel senior, was also the resident reverend until his premature death aged only fifty-seven. Wychwell occupies 3,015 acres of land and woodland which surrounds the village on all sides.

The names of the cottages were chosen by the present Lady of the Manor, Miss Lilian Mathilda Dearman after the death of her father in 1988, as she felt many of the present names were too morose for such a pretty village and this process helped to put her unique stamp on Wychwell.

Every year on May Day weekend, the village honours the poor soul of Margaret Kytson and her unnamed child with a medieval fair. A May Queen is crowned. Sadly the fairs are poorly attended. Another tentacle of Margaret's curse, perchance?

Until the 1930s a 'Wychwell Pie' was made, each attempt aiming to be larger than the previous one, an idea borrowed from the famous Denby Dale Pie events in West Yorkshire. This tradition ended with the death of Lilian's grandfather Erasmus Fortescue Sutton Dearman and it proved too unpopular to revive.

Chapter 11

Marnie realised how ridiculous her situation was when she ran out of toilet rolls a couple of days later and didn't dare go out to the shop to get more. She felt as if a million watt light would pick her out and sirens would go off as soon as she stepped over the threshold and Melissa from next door would race out screaming abuse and try to attack her car with an axe by way of revenge. So, Marnie waited until it was dark before setting off for the supermarket in Doreton to buy some essential household basics: loo rolls, milk and bread. She had just passed the bottom of the wine aisle en route to the till when who should she see looking at bottle labels but Vicky. *Of all times, of all supermarkets.* This one was miles from where she lived, so why was she here? That old chestnut Sod's Law was obviously in operation. Marnie broke out in a cold sweat as she hurried to the self-service till and with shaky hands scanned the contents of her basket quickly, ready to abandon everything if she heard that stupid computer voice asking her to wait for an assistant. It didn't, but as she was bagging up her Warburton's loaf, she saw Vicky approach a manned till and realised that it wasn't her at all. In fact, hair style excepted, the woman looked nothing like her.

She knew she couldn't live like this, eaten up by worry and paranoia. She almost smashed into a van driving out of the car park and received a mouthful from the aggressive male driver. She drove into her garage, sped into the house, closed the door behind her, locked it and felt close to tears with the relief. There were so many beads of perspiration on her face, she could have made an eighteen-inch necklace out of them. Her phone went off in her bag – an email alert.

I do hope you are still coming tomorrow, Marnie. Here's my mobile number so you can let me know. 07970 . . . Lilian x

Her thirty-second birthday. She could either spend it holed up in this house wondering what Melissa at the other side of the wall was thinking, lamenting that she wouldn't be waking up beside her lover, hearing her mother's voice on a continual loop in her head that she was a trouble-causer, a tart, a disgrace. Or she could journey up to a small village in the Dales where only one person knew her, but that person was lovely and liked her.

She replied within the minute, to Lilian's mobile this time

Yes. I'll be there x

*

The sun was shining its little heart out the next morning. Marnie had managed a full six hours' sleep, a record since the Suranna Fox incident on Wednesday. She checked her phone, once again, for a birthday message from Justin and hated that she had. She might have deleted his number but she hadn't blocked it. There were no texts. And, for once, her brain wasn't drumming up excuses why that was. But what it had been doing, between the hours of six and seven, when she woke up for no reason and couldn't get back to sleep again, was dissecting her relationship with Caitlin. It had opened up lots of boxes in her head, full of information that she had stuffed away not wanting to acknowledge (oh, she was so good at that!). Caitlin could be great fun and witty but there was a cold side to her that Marnie had always been wary of. In short, Caitlin could be – and had been – a right cow sometimes.

As if her grey cells were on a major head de-clutter, it had dragged out lots of files containing memories that stung like wasps: how Caitlin hadn't wanted to be her friend at first and was a bit of a bitch at school, until Ali Scott-Marshall emigrated and Caitlin found herself at a loose end. How Caitlin resented Marnie having boyfriends when she was single but dropped her like a boiling brick when she found one of her own. Caitlin snogging the boy at a sixth-form college disco whom Marnie was nuts over, blaming it on strawberry-flavoured Mad Dog. Caitlin going to Julie Duckworth's party when she'd invited everyone in the class but Marnie (solidarity – not). Caitlin always managing to be last to the bar whenever they went out.

Then there was the matter of the Saturday job in the local shop that Caitlin had snatched from under her nose. Marnie had forgiven her all of these things because no one was perfect – oh boy, she knew that for a fact – but for Caitlin, her friend for so long, to believe the warped account of a man she'd known for less than a year over her own . . . well, there was no coming back from that. Their friendship was irrevocably dead. And it wasn't worth the funeral.

En route to Wychwell, Marnie remembered that Lilian had said something about dressing in medieval clothes. Not that it mattered because she didn't have any. If she wasn't allowed entry because she was in jeans and a T-shirt, then so be it. She had enough to worry about, never mind trying to find a last-minute fancy dress costume.

It was a lovely drive once she'd left the motorway. The road took her through the village of Skipperstone and she saw again the Tea Lady tearoom where she'd first met Lilian and a smile spread across her face before immediately shrinking back. How could her life have changed so much in the fortnight since then? She had gone from bouncing around like Tigger to feeling as if there were lead weights on her feet. She'd gone from being the first woman to run her own department in Café Caramba to a despised pariah. She'd gone from a relationship with a gorgeous, sexy, successful man to being estranged from a lying, cheating dickhead. Now she was rudderless, without direction, adrift, unloved and reduced to sneaking out of her house in the dead of night for bog rolls. It wasn't good.

And it was her birthday and she'd had no cards to open, apart from the one from Caitlin and Grigori that wasn't the usual 'best/special/great friend' card, but an arty one with abstract coloured blobs on it. 'Have a Very Happy Birthday love from Grigori and Caitlin x' she'd written inside. Even her bloody handwriting had changed. Plus, she'd not only added that twat's name, but put it first. Marnie hadn't displayed it on the mantelpiece where it would only have looked impossibly lonely and even more indicative of her Billy-no-mates status than none would have been, but binned it. It meant nothing. Caitlin had written 'love' whilst hating her for supposedly coming on to her boyfriend. Possibly her mother's and Gabrielle's were in the post, though it wouldn't have set a precedent if they had 'forgotten' to send one. They didn't believe in belated cards as they were, apparently, just another way for shops to money-grab, so if a card didn't arrive near enough on time, it wouldn't arrive at all.

She tried not to think of making love with Justin in a four-poster bed in wildest Derbyshire before a delicious breakfast and a slow drive back home, possibly via a country inn for a small vino and a light lunch, but concentrated on heading towards the privately owned realm that was Wychwell. She tried, but soft-focus images of the day she should have had kept poking through the net of her resolve and she had to keep bashing them back.

After Skipperstone, the scenery became quite beautiful: patchwork green fields, rich brown squares of ploughed land that reminded her of chocolate cake crumbs. Rivers tripping over stones ran alongside the road for a spell; in the distance the smoke-grey Pennines rested their heads against pillows of wispy clouds and a sheet of pale blue sky. Signs pointed to very Yorkshire-Dales-like sounding places such as Kettlehead, Mintbottom, Uttersthorpe. There were no signs for Wychwell, even though the satnav told her she was only three miles away now. The road started to weave left and right like a mad giant snake climbing up a hill before beginning a gentler curve over the top, one side flanked by high rocks wearing what looked to be hairnets, the other by forest.

Alerted by the satnav, she took a left turn down a two-way but very narrow lane darkened by the trees that arched above. *Wychwell, half a mile.* Marnie wondered if she was traversing the wood where the witch lay buried. No wonder they couldn't find the well; it was huge, dense. Then the trees began to thin and she saw in the near distance a church spire and buildings. With the window down, she could hear a pounding drumbeat and a tambourine-tinkle as she approached what looked like the remains of medieval village defensive walls. There was a large hand-painted sign reading 'CAR PARK FOR VISITORS' and an arrow pointing to an area with two vehicles in it and she pulled up in one of the many empty spaces. She walked towards a man sitting at a table where an equally rough sign advertised 'ENTRY TO THE FAIR'. He was wearing a long gold-blonde wig and a hessian tunic and was foraging in a sack at his side. Marnie waited for a polite amount of time and then coughed to alert him to her presence. His head snapped around and she wondered if the full beard and moustache that matched the hair were false too. He smiled and Marnie took a small involuntary step back in horror. His teeth were disgusting, brown and protruding and she bet that they smelt of cheese.

'Good morning. It's a pound entrance fee but you do get a glass of mead and entry into the raffle to win even more mead.'

His teeth appeared too big for his mouth. Poor soul, thought Marnie. His mother really should have had a brace slapped on those when he was a kid.

'Okay.' Marnie fumbled in her bag for her purse.

'Are you going in like that?' he pointed to her jeans and she noticed the cadence in his voice and an accent as he said *dat* rather than *that*. And, after taking a second look, she wasn't sure that he was wearing a wig and false facial hair after all.

'Well I . . . I don't have anything else.'

'You're welcome to dress up. We have some spare tunics here,' and he pulled one from the sack like a medieval Father Christmas. 'You'll feel more a part of it all if you do.' And he smiled and she tried not to look at his teeth, but they were dragging her eyes towards them as if they contained some strong magnets.

'Thank you.' Marnie paid over her money and took the hessian tunic from him.

'There's a five-pound deposit,' said Mr International Tooth Decay.

'Oh, okay,' Marnie got out her purse again. The man tore a raffle ticket number from a book of them, ripping a corner off the next one too.

'The tickets are too small for my big fingers,' he laughed nervously, and Marnie wondered if he was the simpleton that every village had. He looked a similar age to her – they would both have been the unpopular kids at school at the same time but for different reasons. He should really have had someone to watch out for him more, tell him about the importance of brushing his teeth. She felt a rush of sympathy for him.

'Thank you,' she said with a smile.

'Return it at the end of the day and I'll refund the money.'

'Okay, I will.' She set off walking in the direction of the music but he called her back.

'Excuse me, are you from around here?'

'Erm, no,' she replied. 'I'm a friend of Lilian Dearman's.'

'Oh, right. Ow.' His hand shot up to his mouth as if he'd bitten his lip. Hard to avoid with those gnashers – poor soul, she thought again.

Marnie crossed a bridge and entered the village of Wychwell and felt as if she'd gone back in time to a far more gentle era than the one that lay outside those tumbledown protective walls. In front of her, elevated above the rest of the village, was the Dearman manor house, which she recognised from images she'd looked up on the net. It was lovely, like a

jewel set perfectly on the mount of the hill. To the right was
the church with its tall, slightly warped spire and in front of it
stood a man with thick salt-and-pepper hair, also in sackcloth,
and a dog collar threaded into the black shirt underneath it.
Reverend Lionel Temple, she guessed. He was manning a
tombola stall.

'Can I interest you in a ticket?' he asked with some difficulty. His teeth were quite a mess too. He could have eaten
an apple through a barbed wire fence with them. 'A pound.
You could win some Marks and Spencer talcum powder or
a bottle of home-made wine, for instance. Every ticket wins
a prize.'

The gifts weren't very tempting. If she won the talcum,
she'd let them keep it.

'I'll take five pounds' worth,' said Marnie, thinking the zip
on her purse was getting some hammer today.

Luckily she didn't win the talc. She won five keyrings. She
took one and left the others on the prize table.

'Thank you,' said Lionel, or at least she presumed that's
what he said because it sounded like 'Boc-boo.' Then something like: 'All money goes to the church roof fund.'

Obviously, thought Marnie, wondering if there was any
church in Britain that didn't need roof repairs. 'Do you know
where I might find Lilian Dearman?' she asked.

'Yes, yes,' he pointed down the road. 'She's the bum baking
obbo noise onba big brum.'

'Pardon?'

'She's the one making all the noise on the big drum,' Lionel
repeated slowly and carefully.

Marnie thanked him, thinking that the fish didn't swim
very far in this gene pool, and walked towards the percus-
sion sounds. Cottages stood around a large village green,

all different, all pretty, if tired. That one could have done with a refresh of paint on its white facade, this one had peeling windows and the gable end needed some serious pointing. There were a few people milling about in peasant costumes and a stout man in the tweedy garb of a country gent holding court. At his side stood a tall, thin, figureless woman and Marnie wondered if these were the Suttons with their pretensions of grandeur and entitlement about whom Lilian had waxed lyrical. She spotted someone who she presumed was the May Queen: a young woman dressed in a floor-length white gown with a dark green cloak over her shoulders and pink flowers threaded into her long blonde hair. From a distance she looked like a shorter version of Gabrielle, which sent a shiver down her back. There was a red and white striped maypole in the middle of the grass; pastel-shaded ribbons hanging from its top were being nudged by the slight breeze and skipping around it with casual abandon was a young man in a step-in horse costume. Marnie did a quick full-circle scan for a giant Wicker Man and a fast-route exit.

'BARRNNEEEE.' The noise of the drum stopped as Lilian spotted her. She was dressed as a witch, complete with black hat. She waved and struggled to her feet with the aid of a stick. 'How boffy bo beeooo,' she went on, hobbling at her fastest pace towards her young friend, grinning monstrously. She threw her arms around Marnie, then stepped back and reached into her mouth to hook out a rotted-teeth fake cover. 'We're all wearing these and none of us can talk properly. Lionel bought them from eBay.'

Marnie snorted with laughter. 'They're too effective,' she said. 'I was beginning to wonder if toothbrushes were forbidden in these parts.'

'I'm delighted you came,' said Lilian, slipping her arm through Marnie's. 'Let us cut through the crowds and I'll show you around.'

She was either joking or delusional, thought Marnie, because apart from a scattering of people wandering about, there was hardly anyone there.

A tall, solid-built man was lumbering towards them, the human equivalent of a Shire horse. He doffed the floppy hat he was wearing as he neared them and Marnie wondered if he was in character or if that was standard practice. He looked like the sort of person who would be polite and reverential.

'Ah, Derek, come and meet my new friend,' said Lilian. 'Marnie, this is Derek Price, our churchwarden. Derek, this is Marnie. We met on the internet talking about cheesecakes.'

Derek smiled and it was an awful sight because he too was wearing the false cover over his teeth. Lilian chuckled. 'You look quite the part, Derek.'

'Everyone seems to be moaning about these teeth things, but I find mine surprisingly comfortable,' he said, grinning again and talking perfectly.

'Where's Una?' asked Lilian, looking around.

'Oh, she's having a lie down with a migraine,' replied Derek, with an accompanying sigh. 'I said I'd go and wake her up before the crowning. She doesn't take the sun too well. Or the heat. Or the cold. Or the rain.'

'No,' was all Lilian said to that with a polite, but strained, smile. 'Well, we'll see you in a little while then, Derek. You and Una.'

Marnie noticed the stave of lines that were carved into his forehead. They looked like a musical score.

'We'll be there, don't you worry.'

'Poor Derek,' said Lilian, when he was – just – out of ear-shot. 'His wife is a harridan. It's her that's put the slump in that man's shoulders and all those grooves in his forehead. He's such a gentle soul, too.'

Were there any equal pairings in the world, thought Marnie as they walked on. She could be forgiven for thinking there weren't, based on her own experiences.

'You see that house over there,' Lilian stretched her long arm out towards a very grand three-storey building with a pale yellow façade. 'That is the Lemon Villa where Titus Sutton and his wife Hilary live. The very very very distant cousins who believe that when I shuffle off this mortal coil, Wychwell will be theirs. They are my only living relatives, you see.'

Lilian said that in the same way that Marnie admitted Gabrielle was her family.

'I inherited Wychwell when I was thirty-eight and I didn't want it, I don't mind telling you that. I was more than happy to let Titus Sutton carry on running the estate.' She sighed then, and the sound seemed to come from a place deep inside her. 'I didn't fall in love with Wychwell until years after I owned it, Marnie. I didn't realise until it was too late how much it had been neglected. Half the properties are empty, most are in disrepair, four need completely rebuilding from the foundations up.'

Marnie noticed that there was no flaky paint on the Lemon Villa windows, no patches on the roof where tiles were missing.

'I'm not good with accounts and even if I were I doubt I could have found in the ledgers where it all went wrong. Titus is very . . .' she tapped her lip as she hunted around in her head for the right word, '. . . shrewd. It all looks perfectly above board, but I know it can't be.'

'You aren't still letting him handle your finances if you feel like that, are you?' asked Marnie.

'I have no choice. Someone has to do them and he's the only one who can understand his own bloody writing,' said Lilian. 'My father and Gladwyn Sutton pissed in the same pot, as they say. Old boys from the same school. Father couldn't be bothered with paperwork and he paid Gladwyn handsomely to deal with it all for him. Then when Gladwyn died, his son stepped seamlessly into his shoes. I, as a mere woman, had no say in the matter. I'd go as far as to say my father loved him, as much as a man without a heart could love anyone. Titus was the son he never had.'

The next two cottages were joined together, the second obviously empty, the first covered in just-budding honeysuckle.

'This is where my housekeeper lives.' It was really quite substantial yet looked tiny when compared with its huge yellow neighbour. The sign at the side of the door said that this was The Nectarines. 'Cilla Oldroyd,' Lilian went on. 'Her husband Griff used to be the estate groundsman but he retired early after a stroke. He's getting better, but slowly. Their daughter Zoe helps her mother and their son Johnny is the assistant to my present groundsman, Herv. Johnny is the festival fool today, prancing around in a horse costume. You'll have met Herv at the gate, the rather striking man who looks as if he's just walked off a Viking longboat.'

Marnie couldn't remember the man with the long blonde hair looking anything like a Viking. More like a young Hagrid that had fallen into a vat of peroxide and hard times. Then again her attention had been mostly fixed on those horrible teeth which she now gathered were (at least she hoped they were for his sake) false.

'Lovely family, the Oldroyds,' Lilian was saying. 'You'll

like them. And Herv. Oh my, you *will* like Herv. Our May Queen is quite besotted by him.'

'The woman in the green cape?'

'The very one,' answered Lilian. 'Ruby Sweetman. She's a teacher in Kettlebottom. She lives with her mother in Quince Cottage. Come, Marnie, I'll show you.'

They walked past a couple more cottages, obviously dere-lict from their half-absent roofs and glassless windows.

'I've never had a quince in my life,' Marnie admitted, look-ing at the cottage, the epitome of twee, complete with fishing gnomes by the door, a metal fairy wind-chime hanging from the porch roof and pink lacy curtains at the windows – very next-door-Melissa style. 'I've always wondered what they tasted like.'

'You'd think they'd be sweet, wouldn't you,' said Lilian and then wagged her finger, 'but not all fruits are, Marnie. Not all fruits are at all.'

Next to Quince Cottage was a shop with a rustic sign over the front door. Plum Corner Post Office. Even though it wasn't on a corner. Marnie was having twee overload. Even Snow White would have thrown up at all this schmaltz. Next to this – and on the real corner – was a pub: The Wych Arms, complete with thatched roof and magpie timbering.

'Nearly there,' said Lilian, guiding her down a short pot-holed lane serving a single building. 'I do so want you to like it. There. What do you think?'

It was a house, thought Marnie as they drew level to it. A small stone house with a dark pink door and bell-shaped pink flowers growing up the crumbly walls. The shabby window frames were also painted dark pink, though much of it had flaked off. The roof was intact but buckled in the middle, as if a giant had sat on it. Marnie couldn't understand why Lilian was so keen to show it to her.

'Come inside,' said Lilian, reaching into a pocket of her black dress for the keys. She opened the door and walked in, knocking her witch's hat off because the doorway wasn't full size. Marnie followed and a smell of unlived-in damp greeted her nostrils.

'Pongs a bit,' said Lilian. 'But then it has been empty for nearly a year.'

There was a sofa covered over with a plastic sheet and various pieces of dark wooden furniture dotted around the snug front room.

'I had it refurbished for Jessie only months before she died. Poor dear was delighted but barely had the chance to enjoy it. She'd never had a TV in her life before that. She developed quite a thing for Craig Revel-Horwood. Look at the kitchen, Marnie.'

The kitchen was long – twice the length and more of the front room and fitted with new oak units masterfully made to look as if they were as old as the cottage itself.

'Jessie was a wonderful cook,' said Lilian. 'She baked the most delicious fruit pies. All from the fruits that grew in and around Wychwell: bilberries, wild strawberries and raspberries, blackberries and apples, peaches and plums. Let me show you outside.'

Lilian unlocked the back door and they walked into the garden.

'Herv hasn't had time to keep on top of this as well but he has assured me he will make it a priority to sort it out for the next tenant.'

The grass was overgrown, as were the raspberry bushes and brambles that enclosed the garden but that didn't detract in any way from a loveliness that made Marnie catch her breath and she didn't really know why. The lawn sloped gently down towards a curling ribbon of stream and there was a bench situated near the bank so one could sit and watch ducks and geese glide past. There was a bridge – one person wide – across to the woodland on the other side, the probable site of Margaret Kytson's cottage, Marnie recalled from the book. All unspectacular ingredients of a scene, but together they formed something tranquil and beautiful.

'There is someone I could let this cottage to, but he's not the right fit so I've been thinking about giving him one of the others. You, however, are,' said Lilian, resting for a few moments on the bench. 'As soon as we began communicating via the Sisters of Cheesecake, I thought, *Marnie would be perfect for Little Raspberries.*'

Marnie smiled, but awkwardly. She wasn't quite sure what Lilian was saying.

'I know you can't remember much of the interchange you and I had that first night, but your typing didn't indicate you were that inebriated, give or take the odd spello,' said Lilian with a soft smile.

'Trust me, I was way beyond drun—' Marnie interrupted.

'Please, let me finish,' Lilian interrupted back. 'You were speaking from the clear, calm eye of some storm happening inside you. A deeply desperate and distressed place. Don't ask me why I know that Little Raspberries and you are a match because I have no rational explanation. I just do and I don't tend to ignore my intuition when it shouts. I felt the same when I heard about Jessie Plumpton needing a place and it was the right decision to let her have it.'

Standing facing her, Marnie was struck by how green Lilian's eyes were. Cat-green, like her own. They went very well with the witch costume. It all added to the bizarreness of the day.

It wasn't that Marnie wasn't tempted. It would be luxury

to sleep and not be afraid of being awoken by mad Suranna Fox turning up on her doorstep, or to live in a place where she had no chance of bumping into someone she knew from work. But she'd be bored out of her tree living here. She was a doer, not a relaxer. She couldn't sit in a garden for more than five minutes without having to get out a notepad and scribble down some ideas for how to put Café Caramba coffee in front of an even wider audience of consumers and drive it home to Laurence that he'd been wise to give her a chance at heading up a department.

Laurence.

The name yelled in her brain. *Oh lord.* What would he have had to say about what had gone on? Not only were two of his workforce involved in an illicit affair, but one of that workforce's wife had come in and gone all Bruce Lee in front of the whole trading floor. He would be beyond fuming. Could he sack her? Probably not for bonking a fellow executive but he'd find a way of winkling her out of the door. He'd take the man's side of course and use what had occurred as an excuse not to elevate women to the top positions. She'd done a huge disservice to the sisterhood.

Lilian stood up.

'If you ever want to get away from the rat race or need somewhere quiet to stay, then come and spend some time in Little Raspberries,' she said, again linking Marnie's arm for support.

'I will,' said Marnie. 'Promise.'

'All is not well behind that smile of yours, Marnie Salt,' said Lilian, without missing a step. 'You can't fool me.'

They walked back through the cottage and whilst Lilian locked the back door, Marnie poked her head into the spacious larder. Mrs McMaid used to have one that led off from her kitchen, stocked to the gills with wonderful things that she hadn't seen before – clumpy brown sugar and sticky green angelica, home-made butter with salt crystals in it and clotted cream with its rough, crusty top.

'There's someone else I'd like you to meet,' said Lilian, as they wended back to the centre of the festivities, though she had to take a breather outside the post office. She was old before her time, thought Marnie with a sad inner sigh. They headed towards a road that Marnie presumed wound its way up to the manor house. Kytson Hill, a pointy sign indicated. A pale-green cottage stood back from it. They had to bend under the low-hanging boughs of a large apple tree in the front garden to continue down the path. Before Lilian's hand touched on the handle of the door, it opened and an old lady emerged, wearing a long black dress and a cape, with her hair in twin white buns by her ears. She looked like a negative of Princess Leia's grandma.

Lilian greeted her warmly. 'Emelie, come and meet Marnie.'

'I was just on my way,' said Emelie, shutting the door behind her. She held her hand out towards Marnie. 'I've heard so much about you from Lilian.'

'All good, I hope,' Marnie smiled back at the sweet-faced Emelie.

'All very good,' said Emelie, nodding her head.

'How are you today, my dear?' asked Lilian, giving her friend a kiss on her cheek.

'I'm fine. More to the point, how are you?' asked Emelie. 'You look pale.' She reached up and touched Lilian's face gently in the manner of someone who was very fond of her.

'It's the black, sucks all the colour out of your skin,' said Lilian, waving away any inference that she could be less than

well. She took Emelie's arm. For all her age, the older lady
was steadier on her feet than her friend.

'Have many people arrived?' asked Emelie, a soft lilt to her
words, Marnie noticed, and the hint of a speech impairment
in the way she pronounced her 'r's.

'The usual piddling amount,' sniffed Lilian.

'Ah, that's a shame. But, so long as the May Queen is
crowned to protect us all, it doesn't matter how many people
witness it.' Emelie patted Lilian's hand and smiled at her. It
sounded to Marnie as if they all needed protecting from Titus
Sutton more than from a long-dead witch.

They went back down the hill to the green where a small
crowd, but a crowd nevertheless, was gathered now. Three
children were holding the ribbons attached to the maypole
and were running around it, weaving the strands into a
tangle, then running the opposite way to unravel them. A
woman was adjusting the flowers in the May Queen's hair,
personal-stylist-style.

'Lionel, come and meet my friend Marnie.' The vicar was
duly summoned over.

'Ah, this is your famous Marnie. We've met, sort of,' he
said, holding out his hand and Marnie's joined it in a firm
shake. 'But nice to meet you formally.' He had taken out the
tooth plate and his real teeth were even and displayed beautifully as he smiled.

'Looks like Ruby Sweetman is taking her role very seriously.' Emelie grinned mischievously.

'I wonder why,' said Lionel, with the tone of someone who
knew exactly why.

'Well, Herv is doing the crowning after all,' Lilian replied.

*Herv? The hairy bloke on entrance ticket duty? Well, he must look
better out of the sackcloth then*, thought Marnie. She couldn't

imagine that Ruby was at the end of a very long queue for his attentions.

She studied the May Queen whilst Lionel and Emelie and Lilian were talking amongst themselves. Ruby looked about the same age as herself, long golden hair, large blue eyes, perfect nose but the overall effect was let down by the mean line of her mouth. She set Marnie on edge; it wasn't for any reason she could put her finger on. Maybe she was predisposed to not favouring the blonde/blue-eyed combo.

Someone barged past knocking Marnie into Lionel who courteously steadied her. The man in tweed, the one with the flat cap, waistcoat and expensive boots – Titus Sutton. He clapped his hands to summon attention to himself.

'Ladies and Gentleman,' he addressed the small crowd. 'Thank you all for coming to this auspicious occasion where we crown our most beautiful May Queen and honour her.'

'Lionel, you should be doing this,' Lilian said to the vicar.

'Be complicit in a pagan ceremony, whatever would the bishop say?' replied Lionel.

'He need never know. Titus is bound to spoil it.'

'Magic, if you believe that old tripe' – Titus sniggered behind his hand as if he was in a play and telling the audience something he didn't want the rest of the cast to know – 'is at its strongest on May Day, so based on that we should all be in for a wonderful, happy, fruitful year. Protected from the wicked witch of the well.' He said the sentence with relish and drama and Lilian responded, none-too-quietly.

'Well, really! She wasn't wicked. If her spirit heard that, she'd be very cross.'

Titus heard but ignored her and carried on. 'So, it is with great delight that I ask that the May Queen be crowned. Who crowneth the queen?'

'I do. Herv Gunnarsen.'

Blond Hagrid appeared from behind them. Blimey, he's massive, thought Marnie. He'd taken those revolting teeth out and she could see what Lilian meant about him looking as if he'd just walked off a Viking longboat. His *real* leonine blond hair fell past shoulders wider than a double wardrobe. Yep, now she understood why the May Queen's heart was melting before their eyes, although hers didn't quicken in the slightest. It was learning at long last. Hip-bloody-hurrah!

Herv held a floral crown in his hand, yellow flowers twisted with ivy leaves. He lifted it above Ruby's head with his left hand and with his right he fumbled in his trouser pocket under the sackcloth. He brought out a piece of paper and began to read from it.

'Oh May Queen. Please protect your people from the old magic that exists in de village. May your goodness and beauty overcome anything dat threatens to harm us.' *There was that accent again.* Scandinavian, Marnie guessed. She wondered if he was putting it on to match his Eric the Red image.

'This year, may you show us where you are so we can lay you to rest and we can all finally be at peace with one another.'

Well, I don't think Sir Ian McKellan has got anything to worry about, Marnie sniggered inwardly. His acting was about on par with Gabrielle's.

The big blond man screwed up his script then and attempted to return it to his pocket, except he couldn't find the gap in the sackcloth. The woman who had been adjusting the queen's hair earlier bobbed forward and took it from him, otherwise they could have been there all day waiting for him to put it away. Now ready, at last, to perform the final part of the ritual, Herv lowered the crown onto the May Queen's head, which he had to do at an angle because her face was tilted up to his and if she'd been a cartoon, red love hearts would have been pumping out of her eyes.

A cheer erupted from the gathered throng and Ruby's head swivelled now so she was proffering her cheek. Hairy Herv bent and kissed it and Ruby's lips spread into a smile that threatened to engulf her whole head.

'Let the festivities begin,' said Titus Sutton and a band consisting of a drummer, a penny-whistle, a tambourine and someone on a triangle started up.

Lilian immediately hobbled over to him with rage powering her steps. 'Titus, that was unforgivable of you, mocking the ceremony. And to call poor Margaret wicked can only bring bad luck, as if we haven't had enough. The reason we have to do this ceremony is because she was unjustifiably executed. Vengeful magic of innocents is very powerful.'

'Dear lady, I apologise wholeheartedly,' said Titus, hands out at his sides and smiling as a crocodile might try and assure a salmon that he had no intentions of scoffing him. It was quite obvious to Marnie that he was a patronising git. And a liar because he didn't look sorry at all. Margaret's curse hadn't touched him, if his house was anything to go by. Or his wardrobe. He was clad in the very finest of country gentleman's attire, which must have cost a small fortune. He made Chris Eubank look like Charlie Chaplin.

'He is an odious man,' Emelie confided quietly to Marnie. 'Wychwell has been more than good to him and all he had to do was be reverent today, because it's important to Lilian. Griff Oldroyd has always made the speech before, but he has laryngitis at the moment. Lilian will be furi—' She snapped off the word as Lilian came back to them at speed.

'Well that doesn't bode well,' she said with huffing

impatience. 'Not well at all. Mocking poor Margaret. How could he? Wicked witch indeed.'

Lilian's eyes were shining with angry tears.

'It's done, Lilian, the queen is crowned,' said Lionel in a calm but firm voice, squeezing her hand as he spoke. 'It will be fine.'

'Let's have some mead,' suggested Emelie. 'You'll feel better after one of Lionel's magic potions.'

A young, slim girl with a blaze of long red hair arrived, with magnificent timing, at their side with a tray of drinks. She was dressed like a wench in a Hammer Horror film.

'Go on, Marnie, you have to toast the health of the May Queen,' Lilian urged, nodding towards the plastic beakers which contained bright gold-coloured liquid. 'Lionel makes it. He and David at the Wych Arms have competitions to see who can make the best mead—'

'But I always win,' Lionel broke in, taking beakers from the tray and passing them to the ladies. 'Thank you, Zoe,' he said to the wench-waitress. The skin at the corners of his eyes crinkled as he chuckled and Marnie thought that he must have been a very handsome man in his youth.

'They hold a lot of public tasting sessions, so you can see there are worse places to live,' Emelie smiled and Marnie had to agree with her. As quiet and villagey as it was, living somewhere like Wychwell would be far preferable to living in Redbrook Row at the moment.

As Lilian continued to savage Titus Sutton for cocking up the ceremony with her friends, Marnie indulged in a spot of people-watching, in particular the dynamics between the May Queen and the Viking, which would make a good Midnight Moon title, she mused. Except this story didn't look as if it would have the traditional happy ending. They were drinking mead now and talking together. Ruby was playing with her hair coquettishly and her body was swinging slightly as she stood in front of him, whilst he had his arms crossed protectively against his broad and impressive chest. Her body language said, 'I'm yours for the asking, in fact you don't even need to ask – just take me now.' His said, 'I'm being polite but still keeping my distance because I'm not interested.'

The mead was sweet and toxic. Marnie could feel the first sip going to her brain at warp speed and she thought she'd better not drink too much more of it if she was driving. She watched Titus Sutton knock back his cup in two gulps, in comparison to the tall, slender, dull-looking wife at his side, holding hers with her pinkie finger slightly stuck out, as if it were a cup of Earl Grey. Titus was talking to the May Queen's mother now and guffawing at something, but Hilary Sutton's smile was strained, as if she felt obliged to show approval.

The 'fool' in the half-horse costume was bouncing around the maypole, making people laugh. He looked as if he was having a whale of a time. Actually, he looked as if he was wrecked. Marnie imagined that it wouldn't take very many of those meads to get everyone else feeling the same. Main ingredients: honey and petrol.

'Marnie,' Lilian's voice cut through her reverie. 'Why don't you stay the night? I have a spare bedroom in the manor. Actually I have seven, but one is always made up. You can carouse into the night with us. Your car will be perfectly safe.'

Yeah, right, thought Marnie. The last thing she wanted to do was *carouse* into the night. Knowing her, she'd probably confess the sins of her life to the whole village and that would be another part of England that she'd have to avoid like the plague.

'Thank you, but I'd better be going soon,' she replied,

whilst looking at her watch. 'I've got some . . . er . . . files to look at before work tomorrow.'

'You have to stay for the food,' Emelie entreated with enthusiasm. 'We all go up to the manor and it's quite an occasion.'

As curious as Marnie was about seeing the manor, she had a long drive back home and work in the morn— . . . No, she didn't, actually. Really, there was nothing stopping her going up to the manor with them all, except for some inexplicable reason, she felt that she had to go. She'd kept her promise to visit and should leave now.

'Herv, come and meet my friend,' Lilian waved over at the blond man and he waved back, made his excuses to the May Queen and wended his way over to the three women and Lionel. Close up it was even easier to see why her royal highness was in full-on flirty hair-flicking mode. He was quite a dish if you were in the market for some eye candy, which Marnie most categorically wasn't. She'd always thought the long hair look on men was a bit girly or 'aged rock star' and hadn't seen anyone yet who could carry it off with perfect aplomb – until now. All that mane, a killer smile plus knicker-meltingly blue eyes – but not the same blue as the Salt family eyes. Herv's were much lighter; softer and yet more intense at the same time. And infinitely warmer: the difference between a Caribbean sea and a bloody cold Arctic one. Her knickers were not melting though. They had been coated with the strongest fire-retardant on the market and were totally impervious. He could have been Gerard Butler with a bouquet of red roses in one hand and bottle of warm massage oil in the other and still the permafrost would have remained intact.

'Herv, this is my friend Marnie. Marnie, this is Herv

Gunnarsen, my gardener and groundsman and maintenance man and ... what did we decide your job title was in the end, Herv?'

'I don't think that we ever did.'

'The word *Herv* should be added to the Oxford English Dictionary,' Emelie giggled girlishly. 'The definition should read *man who does everything*.'

Emelie was a sucker for his charms too, it seemed.

'Nice to meet you, Marnie,' said Herv, holding out his hand towards her. It engulfed hers in a warm, gentle shake. 'So where did you meet Lilian then?'

Lilian answered for her. 'We met online talking about cheesecakes. We have great fun and some rapier-sharp battles with truly hideous people. Idiots from all over the world.'

Marnie winced visibly. 'If that sounds tragic, it's because it is,' she said quietly to Herv.

He laughed and it was a deep rumbling sound, as if it came from the very core of him.

'I'd better get back,' Marnie said again. 'I've got a two-hour drive ahead of me. Should I leave my sack on the rack?'

'I need to return your deposit,' said Herv, hunting around himself again for his lost pocket.

'No, it's fine. Keep it in the collection box.'

'That's very kind of you,' said Lionel.

'Oh Marnie, it has been lovely to see you again. Please say you'll come back. I'd love you to see the manor,' said Lilian.

'I will, I promise,' said Marnie. 'I'll stay longer next time.'

Someone called Herv's name and he indicated that he'd heard them with a wave of his arm. 'Nice to meet you, Marnie. I hope I see you again, too.' His smile said that he meant that.

'Yes, bye,' she said. 'Nice to meet you.' She daren't look to her side where she could just see the May Queen dangling at the edge of her vision. Probably casting a hex on her.

'Ladies and gentlemen, to the manor,' shouted Titus, summoning everyone to follow him.

'That isn't his job either, that's mine,' said Lilian crossly as the crowd began walking towards Kytson Hill.

Marnie gave her a hug and it appeared that Lilian didn't want to let her go.

'Little Raspberries is there for you,' she said again. 'It doesn't like being empty. I think you could help solve that problem.'

'Go and eat and enjoy the rest of your day,' Marnie commanded. 'We will be in touch with each other again very soon.'

'Let me know when you reach home safely,' said Lilian.

'Will do,' replied Marnie. 'Lovely to meet you too, Emelie, Lionel.'

'Very much likewise,' said Emelie, her lovely face lit up by her smile and Lionel reached over to shake her by the hand again.

She took a few steps, turned, blew a kiss to Lilian and set off towards her car, wondering why she felt the need to get away so quickly because there was nothing waiting for her at home. She didn't even have a home.

Emelie had started to walk up with the others but Lilian and Lionel remained, watching Marnie until she was out of sight.

'Do you reckon it is her?' asked Lilian. 'I'm so sure of it.'

'Oh, I don't know, dear Lilian,' said Lionel, shaking his head slowly. 'But I don't think you should hope too much.'

'She looks so Irish, her colouring, her eyes, Lionel,' insisted Lilian. 'And the dates tie up exactly. There's a reason why she came into my life. I *know*, without any doubt, that's it's her.'

*

Marnie's drive home was smooth and unhindered and she barely saw any traffic on the roads, which was good news because she tackled most of the journey on automatic pilot as her brain was whirring. For a reason she couldn't fathom, her visit to Wychwell had stuck a huge wooden spoon in her life and stirred everything up. As if it weren't agitated enough already.

She had just short of a month before her doctor's note ran out – and what then? What was she going to do? She also had to decide about where she was going to live. She could go back to the estate agent and tell them she'd changed her mind about changing her mind, but she knew she wouldn't. She had never liked living in Redbrook Row and now she carried a big fat greasy memory of shagging Justin in it. A very married man. She felt sick at the thought.

The closer she got to Doreton, the bigger the knot of dread in her stomach grew. She expected to see Suranna throwing bricks at the right house this time, but there was no activity other than a kid racing up and down the pavement on a bike. Still, her skull prickled with anxiety as she zapped open her garage door and it was only when she was safely inside number 34A that her nerves began to settle.

She was a wreck. She texted Lilian to say that she was home and safe but she was neither. This wasn't her home and she didn't feel safe. She felt on edge and stressed and tense and terribly guilty about what had happened to Melissa's house and car. She felt mad with worry about what she was going to do about her job. How could she possibly go back there? She couldn't. So what the buggery bollocks was she going to do?

*

Somehow, in the wee small hours when Marnie was forced to finally shut down and recharge, her brain gave a great sigh, put its hands on its hips and set out to build something from the broken pieces of her life, then attempted to present it to her as a dream. It cobbled old memories of Mrs McMaid with new information about Jessie and her pie-making in Little Raspberries. It pulled in Wychwell and Lilian Dearman and their first meeting in Skipperstone in the Tea Lady tearoom then sat back and waited. It was as worthy a plan as Marnie brought to the corporate table in Laurence's boardroom.

Marnie woke up at just after seven a.m. with her head spinning. She sat at the kitchen table with a very strong coffee and raked over the ridiculous notion that was resolutely sitting in her little grey cells. She couldn't. How could she? It was stupid. Wasn't she supposed to be an intelligent woman, and here she was having the thoughts of a madwoman. But desperate thoughts came to desperate people.

She got dressed quickly. She had emergency shopping to do in Tesco.

Chapter 12

That afternoon Marnie sat at a corner table in the Tea Lady in Skipperstone trying not to believe that she was about to make the biggest tit of herself imaginable. Then again, how much worse could it get? She tried to concentrate on the menu in front of her because if she started thinking about what she was about to do, she would walk out.

A young waitress in a liveried black dress and white apron emerged from a door behind the till counter and waved to her. 'Mrs Abercrombie will see you now,' she said. Marnie stood up on shaking legs and picked up the large food container she had brought with her. She followed the waitress down a short corridor and knocked on the door at the end.

'Come in,' boomed a deep, smoky voice.

The waitress opened the door for Marnie then left her to it. Marnie walked into the small office balancing the plastic box with one hand, the other extended towards Fiona Abercrombie, a large buxom woman with short, cropped white hair and long dangly earrings.

'Mrs Abercrombie, Marnie Salt. Thank you for seeing me

at such short notice.' Marnie's own voice was a confident act belying a jelly interior.

'Do sit down.' Mrs Abercrombie indicated the chair at the other side of her desk.

Marnie sat and rested the box on her knee.

'Ten out of ten for balls,' said Mrs Abercrombie. 'You intrigued me.'

Marnie had rung her that morning with the opening line: 'Mrs Abercrombie. I have to say that as much as I love your tearoom in Skipperstone, your cheesecakes are appalling.' She'd expected the phone to be slammed down. It hadn't been.

'Are those samples?' Mrs Abercrombie pointed to the box.

'Yes.' Marnie peeled the lid from the large square container and lifted out the contents. Squares of cheesecake sat on foil. Marnie took her through the various flavours as every one was different.

'Lime and ginger, white chocolate and raspberry, trillionaire's shortbread, old English trifle, chocolate rum truffle, prosecco and strawberry, honeycomb and caramel.'

'Goodness. You are inventive,' said Mrs Abercrombie with a note of surprise in her words.

'I can also do a gin, tonic and lemon one, pina colada, dark chocolate and coconut ... well, any flavour you like. Even liquorice.' Marnie handed her a plastic spork from a packet which she'd also brought.

Mrs Abercrombie dived straight into the trifle cheesecake.

'The fruit didn't have a lot of time to sit in the sherry so the flavour will be lacking, but I usually soak it overnight,' Marnie explained, trying to read from Mrs Abercrombie's expression what she thought. Was that a slight nod of approval?

Mrs Abercrombie moved on to the trillionaire's shortbread now. There, a definite 'mmm' sound of appreciation.

'Discretion absolutely guaranteed,' said Marnie, which was obviously the wrong thing to say as Mrs Abercrombie shot her a look.

'Erm ... I mean that I have no idea what your present set-up is,' Marnie quickly amended, 'but, if you bought your cheesecakes from me, no one need think anything other than that they are made in the Tea Lady's own kitchens.'

Crisis averted. Mrs Abercrombie moved on to the next sample.

'Who else do you supply?' she asked, after swallowing a mouthful of the chocolate rum truffle.

'No one. I was taught by the best cheesecake maker in the world, who trained under Gaston Lenôtre in Paris,' Marnie lied. 'Family circumstances prevented me from pursuing my chosen career as a patisserie chef, but I have finally decided that I can no longer deny the reason I believe I was put on earth for. I have no interest in opening up a café or a shop, I don't want to deal with the general public, only business to business.'

Lies came so easily when you half-believed them yourself, thought Marnie. No wonder Justin was so seasoned at them.

'Interesting,' said Mrs Abercrombie, studying the taste. 'I detect something quite unusual. Too subtle to interfere, but a definite presence. What is it?'

Mrs McMaid's secret ingredient, that's what it was.

'Ah, a pinch of something Lenôtre passed down to my mentor, and she to me. I would be breaking a solemn vow if I revealed it.'

'Intriguing,' mused Mrs Abercrombie. 'They are excellent. What are your hygiene standards like?'

Marnie forced an affronted look. 'Exemplary,' she said. 'You could do operations on my kitchen table. I have the highest standards.'

'I would insist on a contract being drawn up, of absolute discretion. I would insist on a visit to your kitchens and the possibility of spot-checks. All cakes must be boxed at your end in my packaging which vans will collect and distribute. I have fifteen outlets. Have you time to sit down now and discuss full terms and conditions?'

'Yes,' Marnie said with a dry throat, so she coughed and repeated the word. 'Yes.'

Mrs Abercrombie pressed a buzzer down on an old-fashioned intercom system on her desk. A crackly voice answered, 'Yes, Mrs Abercrombie.'

'Janet, have two teas sent through, please.'

Mrs Abercrombie drove a ridiculously hard bargain, but the profits would give Marnie a living wage – just. Nothing like what she earned at Café Caramba, but enough so that she didn't have to survive on Cup-a-Soups and tins of tomatoes as she had for a spell in her first bedsit.

She sat in the car and took lots of calming deep breaths before setting off back home. Her mother's voice was shouting in her inner ear, even more furious than usual: 'What are you thinking, you stupid girl?' She wasn't thinking, was the honest answer. She was going with the flow, albeit a very strange flow.

That was step one. For step two, she picked up her phone and scrolled to 'recent contacts'. Lilian Dearman picked up immediately.

'Marnie, my dear girl. What a lovely surprise, how are you?'

'Lilian, did you mean what you said about Little Raspberries? Could I rent it from you? Could I—'

Marnie was cut off by an exhilarated Lilian.

'Of course, of course. I'll ask Herv to cut the lawn and we will have it ready for you. When are you thinking of coming?'

'Tomorrow, is that too soon?'

'It's not soon enough. I'm delighted. I'm absolutely delighted.'

As soon as Marnie got home, she set up a mail redirection
service and informed the estate agent of her new address
so they might forward anything that came for her until it
kicked in. There was no point in changing all her documen-
tation because she didn't know how long she was going to
be staying in Wychwell: a few weeks at most, she figured.
Then – who knows?

She'd sold nearly all of her furniture to move in with
Aaron, so she reckoned she could get most of what she
owned into her trusty Renault. She called in at the local
Quality Road bargain store because they always had a bank
of boxes for people to take and then she emptied her kitchen
cupboards into them. Books filled another two boxes, her
clothes went into her three suitcases and her laptop, printer
and stationery went in another. She filtered the items before
packing and put plenty of things into black bin liners for the
charity shop. For instance, she would never again wear the
suit she had on when Suranna Fox was trying to scalp her.
She would drop off some surplus bedding at the animal shelter. Amongst them the sheets that she and Justin had rolled
around on when he visited that one time. And the towel he'd
used when he came out of her shower – when he'd washed
off their sex-odour and her perfume to make himself neutral
for his wife.

By suppertime, her life was all packed up. She had a few
boxes that she couldn't fit in the car and rang her mother
to see if she could store them in her cavernous garage. Her
mother sighed and said that she supposed so. Everything

Marnie said to her seemed to exasperate her. Marnie said she'd call round in the morning.

For once, she had no trouble at all going to sleep that night. She couldn't remember the last time she'd slept so well or so deeply.

Chapter 13

The family home – Salty Towers II – was a substantial terraced town villa just outside Penistone. It had high ceilings, period features and large square rooms. Despite the chunky central heating radiators, Marnie's principal memory of the house was that it was always cold. Judith had never liked the house; she had preferred the one they had before in Wakefield. The one they'd had to move from. Because of Marnie, as she was so often reminded.

Marnie hadn't seen her mother since she'd dropped off her present before Christmas. She rang once a fortnight – never the other way around – and sometimes her mother picked up, sometimes the answering machine did. The conversations were always short and dutiful: was her mother all right, did she need anything? Her mother always replied that she was perfectly fine and if she wanted anything, she would ask. There was little more to the interchange than that. Marnie had long since learned that any attempt at telling her mother what was going on in her life was met with indifference, although she sometimes still tried, ever hopeful of a breakthrough.

Marnie carried her boxes into the garage, storing them neatly at the back, then went into the house. Her mother hadn't put the kettle on, she wouldn't have even thought to. Marnie thought she'd lost weight that she didn't have to lose; the skin at her neck looked more sunken in than usual and gave the impression that her head was being supported by tent poles. She was huddled in a thin cardigan, a step away from teeth-chattering.

'It's cold in here, Mum,' said Marnie.

'I'm not putting the central heating on in May,' said Judith. 'Besides, I'm not sure it would make any difference.'

'Well it would,' argued Marnie. 'You'd be warm for a start, you look frozen.'

Judith walked over to the mantelpiece and took a card from it which was propped up against a clock. 'I've never liked this house,' she said and Marnie knew what was coming next. 'I never wanted to leave the lovely one we had in Wakefield. Here.' She handed the card to Marnie. 'I didn't have a chance to post it.'

'Oh, thank you,' said Marnie thinking that all roads led to the lovely house in Wakefield, and the wonderful rose-tinted life they'd all led there until she ruined it. She could have started a conversation about Charles Manson and in three steps, her mother would have bent it around to the lovely house in Wakefield.

'So where are you going?' asked Judith.

'I'm staying in the Dales for a while.'

'The Dales? Whatever for? How are you going to get to Leeds every morning from the *Dales*.'

She imbued the word with all the disapproval that she might have saved for a sewerage leak.

Marnie braced herself for the onslaught that would surely

come. 'I'm not working in Leeds any more. I've got a new job, for now anyway.'

She really hoped her mother wouldn't ask what that new job was.

'Gabrielle has a new job too,' said Judith, nibbling a rough edge from one of her short, neat nails. 'It involves a lot of travelling to New York.'

'Oh, good for her,' said Marnie, fearing that it had come out sounding sarcastic.

'Business class too. She doesn't travel anywhere these days unless it's first class, she says.'

Marnie did her best not to react. Her job would sound extra shit at the side of Miss Bloody Perfect Gabrielle's international career. She would have to lie if asked. She couldn't tell her mother the truth.

'How long are you intending to leave that stuff here?' asked Judith.

'A few weeks. Is that all right?' Surely it would be, considering that her boxes and a chest freezer were the only things in the garage. Her mother didn't drive; she took taxis when she needed to go anywhere, or someone from her bridge club gave her a lift.

'I suppose so,' said Judith; her stock, weary phrase. 'What sort of job are you doing now, then?'

International envoy for Yorkshire, Marnie was tempted to say. *It involves lots of travelling to the space station – beat that, Gabrielle.*

Then Judith said under her breath, 'I don't suppose it'll be an upward move,' and Marnie felt the hairs on the back of her neck begin to rise.

'I've opened up a cheesecake factory,' she heard herself saying as her mouth broke loose from the straps tethering it to the sensible part of her brain.

There was an obvious silence after that, broken only by Judith Salt's jaw hitting the floor. Then her mother said:

'CHEESECAKE? CHEESE. CAKE?'

'Yes, Mum, cheesecake.'

'You are not telling me that you are leaving your job to—' The sentence was severed and Judith's face formed that mask of disappointment that Marnie had seen so many times and Gabrielle had seen just the once, when she had failed her Grade 8 flute for playing some bum notes.

'Yes, I'm telling you exactly that.' *I'm thirty-two, I'm not asking for your permission*, Marnie added to herself before continuing. 'Look, I know what you're thinking but I'm a big girl now and I—'

'HUH.' Judith's single hard note of acerbic laughter held a library's-worth of words.

Marnie sighed. She wouldn't get through to her mother. She never had and probably never would. She might not have needed her permission but, however much she tried not to, she really, really would have liked her approval. If this had been Gabrielle, she might have been praised for her derring-do and enterprise (despite embarking on a sinful relationship with sugar and fats), but this was Marnie and the old adage of blood being thicker than water always held true in the Salt family.

'Well, it's your own life, I suppose,' supposed Judith Salt yet again. 'Yours to make a hash of if that's what you want to do. As you say, you're a *very* big girl now.'

Marnie wanted to point out that the 'very' hadn't been there when she said it. But she knew that was another sly dig. A size fourteen wasn't big, but it was when you came from a family of willowy saplings. Her BMI wasn't pulsing out danger lights, she was healthy, could put her socks on without turning a dark shade of aubergine and went in and out in all the right places. She certainly looked healthier than her mother did at the moment: pale and brittle, more so than usual.

Her mother was talking under her breath now, quiet words that weren't meant to be overheard, apart from one that was: *disappointment.*

Tears rushed to Marnie's eyes. Despite all those years of hearing that word levelled at her, she had never quite hardened herself to it. It hit the bullseye of her heart every time. And though she had always swallowed it in the past, this time she couldn't.

'Yes, Mum, I know I am,' she said, struggling to keep the wobble out of her voice. 'You've always made that perfectly clear.'

'Can you blame me? After all the trouble you've caused.' Judith Salt flew back at her sharply, eyes narrowed and glittering with anger.

'All the trouble *I* . . .'

But Judith hadn't finished.

'I wonder about your sanity sometimes, Marnie. I really do.'

'What?' That was one she hadn't heard before and made her mouth curve with disbelief, a smile with no humour in it that further infuriated Judith.

'Yes, you would find it funny. Who throws away a career to go and make . . . buns?'

'I'm not exact—'

But Judith was on a rant now.

'You were awkward from the off. You wouldn't sleep, such high maintenance.' She shook her head disapprovingly. It took Marnie a few seconds to realise her mother was talking about her as a baby.

'You mean when you adopted me? When I was one?'

'You were manipulative even at that age.'

Marnie did laugh then. A high-pitched bark of incredulity.

'I was one year old, Mum.'

Marnie thought there was nothing new left to hear from her mother but she was wrong. The word cheesecake had taken the stopper off a bottle and it wouldn't go back in. Things that Judith Salt had been holding back for years started frothing up inside her.

'He would never have left me if it wasn't for you. I thought you'd glue us back together, but you didn't you drove us apart.'

'I drove . . . ? Glue? What do you mean?'

'They told me I couldn't have children. He agreed to adopt, to save us, but he couldn't take to you. He wanted his own child. He wanted a son. When he found out I was carrying another daughter, he left. Don't you see?'

Marnie swallowed. *Dad.* The father that wasn't really hers and that she couldn't even remember. The one who had to pay maintenance for her and had resented every penny of it.

'I see that he was a real catch.'

Judith screamed at her. '*She* was our little miracle. *She* would have kept us together. He would have loved her if you hadn't put him off having a daughter.'

Marnie got it now. Gabrielle. All hopes and dreams had been transferred to her sister. All the sins of the father heaped on the adopted daughter. The cuckoo in the nest.

'Is that what you really think, Mum?' *Mum.* The word didn't fit properly in her mouth. It never had.

'And I was right,' screamed Judith. 'You spoiled everything. You tried to alienate my family from me. We had the perfect school . . .'

Marnie felt the heat of discomfort flare in her stomach. 'I have to go.' She couldn't have that conversation. Not again.

'You destroyed us. Gabrielle would have gone to Oxford or Cambridge, her teachers said so ...'

'Goodbye, Mum. My mobile number is the same if you need anything.'

She opened the door and Judith's voice followed her out, at a pitch that Marnie had never heard before.

'I don't need anything from you. Don't ring me. And stay away from my daught—'

Marnie shut the door behind her, slicing off her mother's words. She didn't even realise she was crying until she felt the itch of tears on her cheek.

Marnie walked away from her mother's house. She had never thought of it as home; even when she was a little girl it had always felt as if there was a plastic layer over everything that stopped her being part of the Salt family. She might have had their name, but she'd never been one of them.

She was running away because she'd been a disappointment to herself. Possibly even more than she was to her mother. And that really was saying something.

She opened the birthday card in the car. It wasn't a daughter one with a gushy verse about how special she was, but a generic one with a drawing of a woman in a stylish hat and an impossible figure. Inside was blank except for one word, 'Mum', and a cross that followed it, so tiny it looked as if it had been written under duress.

Marnie threw the card on the passenger seat and drove on.

HISTORY OF WYCHWELL BY LIONEL TEMPLE
with contributions by Lilian Dearman.

There have been a few sightings of ghosts in the manor at Wychwell, none substantiated, except for one relatively new entity which has been spotted on a few occasions in the long upstairs gallery, as seen from outside. The ghost takes the shape of an orb of light which travels slowly from one side to the other. Due to the chemical compounds used to make the window glass, the orb appears in a pinkish-purple hue. As such, the 'ghost' has acquired the nickname 'The Pink Lady'.

Chapter 14

There was a small welcoming committee when Marnie reached Little Raspberries: Lilian and a buxom lady with a tight greying hair bun and the fresh round face of a dairy maid. Lilian was sitting on the low wall in the sunshine, the other woman was cleaning the outside of the window. Lilian's face was lit up with a broad smile and her arms were open wide to greet her. Marnie couldn't ever remember anyone else being that happy to see her.

'How wonderful you are here,' she said, throwing her arms around Marnie. 'Cilla, come and meet Marnie.'

Marnie recognised the name: Lilian's housekeeper. Cilla wiped her hands on her apron before bouncing over to shake Marnie's hand with the reverence of someone meeting the Duchess of Cambridge.

'Delighted to meet you, Marnie,' she said, and that delight showed in her big beaming smile.

'Cilla has polished Little Raspberries from top to bottom for you,' said Lilian. 'And Herv has cut the grass.'

'There was no need, really,' said Marnie.

'Well, it's done,' countered Lilian. 'And you're coming to

lunch with me up at the manor, I insist. Zoe – that's Cilla's daughter – makes a wonderful sandwich. Leave the unpacking for later.'

Marnie was peckish now, she had to admit. She'd intended to stop off at a café and have some breakfast but the altercation with her mother had wiped her appetite away. Instead she'd pulled in to a lay-by for ten minutes and sobbed her heart out. Then she'd cleaned her face with a wet wipe, freshened up her make-up and stuck on her stock 'fuck 'em' mask. It'd had a lot of use in the past few years.

'I'm parked there,' said Cilla, nodding towards the car across the lane. 'I'll run you both up.'

So Marnie bowed to the order and together they took the very short journey through Wychwell, up Kytson Hill past Emelie's cottage and along the rising winding road to the manor. Lilian chattered all the way, like an excited schoolgirl welcoming a French exchange student to whom she was desperate to show things. She more or less jumped out of the car to talk to the young man who was mowing the strip of lawn in front of the great house. Marnie recognised him as the fool at the fair. Cilla's son Johnny.

'You've worked like a medicine on her,' said Cilla, opening the car door for Marnie, because she had a dodgy child-lock, she explained. 'I haven't seen her that giddy for years.'

'I have no idea why,' said Marnie, with a soft smile. 'But I'm glad if I have that effect on her.' And she was. It wasn't every day she went from zero to hero in two hours and if she were honest, her ego needed it.

'And so am I,' said Cilla, gently touching her arm and studying Marnie's face. 'For all her being the lady of the manor, she's not had the happiest of lives. Are you related?'

'Lord no,' chuckled Marnie. 'Not at all.'

'You're not even some distant cousin?'

'Not as far as I know.'

'Come on you two, stop gossiping,' called Lilian.

'You'll see why I asked soon enough,' said Cilla as she followed Marnie inside.

The hallway was vast and oak panelled, a room from a bygone age. Marnie looked around for a suit of armour standing to attention and found two on sentry duty at the bottom of the wide staircase.

'Wow,' she said.

'The east wing is new, the original burned down in a fire two hundred years ago. Attributed to Margaret Kytson of course, as is everything else that goes wrong here,' explained Lilian.

No sooner had she finished speaking than a block of plaster fell off the ceiling and landed at Marnie's feet. She jumped back a step in shock.

'The house likes you,' laughed Lilian. 'It's making itself known to you. Say hello back, Marnie.'

'Hello . . . manor house,' said Marnie, feeling daft.

'Come on. Let me show you something.'

Lilian started walking up the staircase which registered her footsteps with satisfying creaks. Portraits hung on the wall, men in powdered wigs and military uniforms, women with ruffs and puffed crinolines.

'Meet the family,' said Lilian. 'My father's portrait is worth a lot of money but I refuse to have the old bastard hanging on my wall, so I replaced it with this – Rose Dearman, my great grandmother. My great grandfather brought her over from Ireland. It was thought she was a gypsy and he had her privately educated as a lady to pass muster.' And Lilian, with a grand hand gesture, presented the portrait to Marnie. A woman in a long green dress with cat-green eyes and black hair piled high on her head. In her hand she held the most delicate shamrock, barely discernible. Her cheekbones were high and sharp, a faint smile of mischief dancing on her dark pink lips. At her feet looking up adoringly at her was a silver greyhound. Marnie did a double-take. The resemblance to herself couldn't be denied, but surely Lilian didn't think this was any more than coincidence?

'Beautiful isn't she?' said Lilian. 'None of us ever had her looks, alas.'

'You have her green eyes, Lilian,' said Marnie.

'I'm the only one who did. Another reason for father to call me an anomaly. I wouldn't have minded inheriting more of her qualities but the bloody awful Dearman genes dominated. Faulty stock and pig-ugly.'

It was true that all the other subjects on the wall wouldn't have won any beauty contests, even given the kind hand of the artists who must have had a nightmare trying to prettify the hideously fat ancestral couple with their big noses and thin lips.

They walked together along a galleried landing, the outer wall made up almost entirely of windows.

'This is where people say they see the ghost,' explained Lilian. 'An orb of light travelling along here in the dead of night.'

'Any idea who that ghost is?' asked Marnie. She didn't believe in them, but that didn't prohibit her from enjoying a good story.

'Could be anyone, although she is known as the Pink Lady,' sniffed Lilian. 'Although it's only in the last thirty years or so that she's made an appearance. Could be Father, though he's more likely to be a poltergeist throwing things about and making his presence known. Mother would have been a wailing woman. And I can't see Rachel returning here. She hated the bloody house. If she was haunting anywhere, it would be a casino in Monte Carlo. I reckon it must be Margaret Kytson. It's the only answer.' And she winked.

Chuckling at that, Marnie followed Lilian around the upstairs, saw the priest hole where Percival Shanke had unsuccessfully hidden his confessor. Marnie, alone, went up the steps to the tower which afforded the most fantastic view of Wychwell and the thick wood that almost completely surrounded it. It was all very grand but awfully tired. The carpets were bare, there were spider cracks in the windows, rotted frames. It must have been freezing in winter in some of the rooms and it would have cost a fortune to light up all the fireplaces to counteract the chills.

'I've brewed the tea,' Cilla's voice shouted up towards them.

'Oh, come on, Marnie. We've been summoned,' said Lilian, walking down the staircase holding on to the beautifully carved bannister. 'I'll show you the rest of the house after we've eaten.'

They walked through an old library where the smell of lavender polish hung heavily in the air, then into a snug with heavy black velvet drapes and mahogany panelling to all the walls. They passed through into a long dining room with a table that must have seated thirty people, Marnie guessed. Doors there led into a bright conservatory, a sharp contrast for the eyes after all that darkness.

'This is my favourite part of the house,' said Lilian, leading Marnie over to the round table placed near the window and set for two. 'You can probably see why.'

The view from the window was that of a small lake. The garden it graced wasn't a typical manor layout with symmetry and order, but was wild and beautiful. She could see a small square building in the distance and what looked like a short jetty.

'That's the boathouse,' said Lilian. 'I used to take a boat out on the lake and just drift off to sleep in it. I always felt safe in the middle of the water' – she sighed as if visited by a happy memory – 'away from my bastard father and my psychopathic sister. Come and eat.'

The table was not laid with a couple of simple sandwiches, as Marnie had expected, but a buffet lunch fit for the King of Tonga. To coin a phrase relevant to the moment, Lilian's housekeeper really had pushed the boat out.

'My mother was barred from taking a boat out after trying to capsize it and drown my father,' said Lilian with a nonchalance that suggested this was nothing out of the ordinary.

'I didn't notice a portrait of her on the wall, or did I miss it?' asked Marnie, choosing a cucumber sandwich and marvelling, at first bite, how Zoe Oldroyd had managed to make such a simple concept so delicious.

'There is no portrait,' said Lilian. 'Mother was transparent. Even for the weakest watercolours. No substance to her at all. Her happiest years here were when she was locked up in the tower.'

'Good lord.'

'She was having an affair with her psychiatrist. We always believed the banging and thrashing noises were her having electro-convulsive treatment.' Lilian laughed. 'Which I suppose she was. It's all in the book. I told Lionel to spare us no blushes. It's not for public consumption anyway, thank God.'

'I haven't got that far,' said Marnie, trying not to spit crumbs. 'I'm at puritan times.'

'Ah yes, James Sutton Dearman. Made Bacchus look

like a vestal virgin. Used to organise county orgies. The Lemon Villa was his personal whorehouse. Secretly, behind closed doors of course. Outwardly his tongue was so far up Cromwell's arse he could taste his toothpaste. My family have always been so very good at obsequiousness.'

It was such a beautiful tranquil setting in the sunlit room looking out at the lake that Marnie temporarily forgot her life was in such a mess. She and Lilian munched on the tiny sandwich triangles and pastries without saying anything and the silence was as warm and comfortable as the buttered crumpets.

Conversation started up again when Cilla, beaming with pride, brought in a pink nest of meringue, filled with cream and fat raspberries.

'I'll get too used to this,' said Marnie. 'I'll be up here every day for this treatment.'

'Oh do, you'd be very welcome,' urged Lilian.

'I'd be as fat as a house.'

A very big girl. Her mother's voice came from nowhere, booming in her ear, and as if Lilian had heard it too she asked about her.

'What was your mother's opinion about you moving to the back of beyond?'

'Funny, I was just thinking about her. Not much actually. She thinks I'm a fool, although there's nothing new there.'

'Well you aren't,' said Lilian firmly. 'You're a big girl and entitled to live your life as you see fit.' Her face assumed a quizzical look at Marnie's ensuing smile. Marnie wondered if she was psychic.

'I've packed in my job in Leeds and from Monday morning I'm going to be making cheesecakes three times a week for the Tea Lady in Skipperstone. I'm the jewel in the crown of my mother's disappointment,' announced Marnie, as Lilian crunched her knife into the meringue.

'How wonderful,' said Lilian, ignoring the latter part of the sentence. 'How enterprising and smart of you. I bet your sister wouldn't have spotted such an opportunity and dived straight into it like you did.' She delivered a crumbly triangle of dessert to the plate that Marnie was holding up.

'What should I do about rent, Lilian?'

'Oh, don't talk such nonsense.'

'I don't expect to live here for free.'

'I won't hear of such talk. La la la. You're my guest. No one pays rent in Little Raspberries. It's the law. Cream?'

A conversation for another time, Marnie decided, not wanting to throw Lilian's kind hospitality back in her face. 'Why not.'

'I gather that the delicious Mr Fox is no more,' said Lilian, tilting the cream jug over Marnie's meringue.

'He was married, Lilian. Very married,' said Marnie, wondering why it was so easy to talk to Lilian, why she could give so much away – even sober now – and not feel judged. 'His wife stormed into my office and she was pregnant with their fourth child. She attacked me in front of the people I work with. I felt so ashamed, I had to get away fast. Then she drove to my house the next day and smashed up my neighbour's car and her front windows thinking they were mine. My mother always said that I was the sort of person who attracted trouble like a magnet. I think she was right abou—'

There was a cough from behind them and Marnie's head shot round.

'Sorry, I didn't want to interrupt you.' A young woman was standing in the open doorway holding a coffee pot. The girl with the red hair who was the mead-distributing wench on the day of the fair. Zoe, Cilla's daughter.

'Just leave it here, dear, and we'll pour it ourselves,' said Lilian. 'Please close the door on your way out, Zoe.'

Zoe rushed in, said a very quick hello to Marnie, and rushed out again.

'She's a lovely girl,' said Lilian dropping her head close to Marnie's to add, 'but hasn't the finesse of her mother. Anyway, you were saying . . .'

'I couldn't go back in to work, not after what happened. And I didn't want to stay in that house.'

'Understandable,' said Lilian, nodding. 'You never did settle there, did you? And what did Mr Fox have to say – the bastard?'

'He didn't ring, he wouldn't answer my calls either. I can't believe I was such an idiot.' She poured the coffee into the fine china cups that bore the Dearman coat of arms and their family motto: *Aurum Potestas Est*. She recognised it from the book that Lilian had given her about the village.

'I had a torrid affair in my twenties,' said Lilian. 'George Purcell and I were the talk of the vale. George was married, too. We were going to run away together but when it came to it . . . chicken-livered—' Lilian huffed, unable to find a word strong enough to describe her lover's perfidy. 'Oh, Marnie, talk is a very cheap currency for sex. The heart does get more discerning for the breaking, my dear, but it did take me a long time to get over George Purcell.' Lilian's smile spread upwards, touching her lovely green eyes and made her look so much younger than her years.

'I'm not sure my heart has learned any lessons,' said Marnie. 'I fall from one disastrous relationship straight into the other. But,' and she clapped her hands together, 'no more.'

Outside the *zuzz* of a petrol strimmer starting up punctured the summer stillness and Herv Gunnarsen came into view from stage left. His hair was loosened, falling past his shoulders. He looked like some sort of gardening lion.

'Ah, now there is a man,' said Lilian, with a sage note in her voice. 'I think most of the women in Wychwell wish they were thirty years younger. Although youth obviously does not guarantee his affection.'

She meant Ruby Sweetman, of course.

'Yes, he's quite a looker,' replied Marnie. In fact, Herv Gunnarsen was too bloody handsome for his own good, even if he was far from her usual slim, suited, dark-haired, executive, dickhead type. Not every handsome man was a git, she knew, but – without exception so far – the ones who made her own pupils dilate seemed to be. She certainly wasn't going to hop from a Justin frying pan into a Herv fire.

Herv had stopped the strimmer to rotate his shoulder. A very muscular shoulder, it had to be said. Marnie wondered if he was aware he had an audience and was doing his best Diet Coke-break-man impression.

'He's our newest addition,' said Lilian. 'We need more of them. Half of the properties in this village are empty. He's from Norway.'

Ah, she was right then with her Scandinavia guess. 'Did you find him on a cheesecake site too?' asked Marnie, her own eyes twinkling now.

'Actually, yes,' replied Lilian.

'No way.'

'Of course I didn't, you silly girl. He was a teacher. On an exchange visit at the school where Ruby Sweetman works. A very unhappy teacher, to boot. Herv's heart wasn't in it at all. Channelled into a career that was a bad fit for him, anyone could see that. He's an outdoor boy, a fixer, a doer. Ruby brought him to the Wych Arms, I met him, we talked, I needed a groundsman. You can guess the rest.'

Marnie could imagine that meeting. Within five minutes of conversation starting up, Lilian would have winkled his life story out of him.

'He's a good man, Marnie. You could do much worse.'

Marnie turned her head around to Lilian to see if she was she joking and when she found her expression serious, she let loose a bark of laughter.

'Lilian. As if I want to go down that road again.'

'Oh, of course you will, you must,' said Lilian with unveiled impatience. 'Love is the reason God gave us hearts.'

'And to pump blood around our bodies to keep us alive.'

'A secondary function,' Lilian pooh-poohed Marnie's sensible notion. 'Herv is one of those rare souls whose contents are as wonderful as the package they come in. As are you.'

Marnie gave another hard chuckle which infuriated Lilian. 'Don't you dare scoff at me, young lady. In some things I'm not as batty as I'm painted. I know a proper match when I see one. You'd be good for each other. He's a gentle man and patient, kind, he'd court you, put you on a pedestal. And you'd have terrific sex.'

'Lilian!'

'Darling girl, of course you would. It's the best thing ever when there is parity in a relationship. Not that you'd know with your past choices. You're too content with crumbs from the table. As was Herv with that tramp of a wife of his. She left him for his best friend, can you believe? Smashed his heart. Then came crawling back. Luckily, by then, he didn't want her and that broke hers.'

'Yes, well, Cupid is a bit of an arse, Lilian. He fires his golden arrows into some and his lead ones into others for the hell of it. Given a choice I think we'd all fall for the good ones, the nice guys, but life isn't like that.'

'I know, and unrequited love is the cruellest of things,' Lilian paused then to pop a raspberry into her mouth before continuing. 'Ruby Sweetman would marry Herv tomorrow, yet he has no feelings for her. But he took an instant shine to you. Asked me all sorts of questions about you after the crowning of the May Queen.'

Marnie didn't tell Lilian that her first impression of Herv was that he was the village numpty, but she held her hand up to stop Lilian saying more.

'I don't want to know. I'm taking a break from men for a very long time.'

She would have to be careful though if what Lilian said was true because she didn't want to lead anyone on. She knew how being on the begging, ever-hopeful end of a relationship felt only too well. She had a PhD in the subject. She would avoid Lilian's gardener like the plague until any misguided affections withered and died on his vine. 'I'm sure your Herv is wonderful, Lilian, but I'm not interested.'

Lilian thought about that for a second and then conceded. 'You're right of course. You need time to recalibrate your gauges. They're very off track. Now, eat your meringue,' she commanded. 'No more talk of unhappiness or of love one cannot have. This, as they say, is the first day of the rest of your life.'

'Precisely.' *Dear, well-meaning Lilian*, thought Marnie. How could she really know the nature of love, having spent her whole sixty-six years in this quaint Wychwell prison? How could she really know anything of life?

Chapter 15

It didn't take Marnie long to unpack the car and move into Little Raspberries. By teatime her new kitchen cupboards were full of her baking equipment, her clothes were hanging in the wardrobe and her sheets were on the bed. The bedroom was at the back of the cottage and two deep bay windows afforded a view of the newly clipped lawn and the stream. It would be nice to be able to pull back the curtains in the mornings and not worry about seeing Suranna Fox standing on the street with a chainsaw.

She made herself a coffee and settled down with her new book: *Country Manors Part One – Buyers and Cellars*, which was nothing like as innocent as it sounded. 'Makes *Fifty Shades of Grey* look like one shade of beige', was its tagline. The author, Penelope Black, wrote about the comings – literally – and goings of a small English village, complete with a devastatingly handsome lord of the manor and what he liked to get up to in his specially adapted cellar with the local women, whose stupid husbands were blissfully unaware of what was going on under their noses. It was riveting stuff and the series had taken the world by storm.

She felt truly relaxed until someone knocked on the front door and she almost shot out of her skin and she knew she wasn't out of the stress and anxiety woods yet. She opened it up to find Lionel Temple there, dog collar in place at his throat, bottle of wine in his hand.

'Hello, Lion . . . Mr Lion . . . I mean Mr Temple,' she stuttered, not quite sure what best to call him.

He chuckled. 'You can call me Lionel, Mr Lion if you prefer. I don't want to disturb you, but—'

'Come in, do, please,' said Marnie.

Lionel stepped over the threshold and wiped his feet on the doormat.

'My, it feels lived in already. And smells like it too.' He took a long sniff upwards.

'I've not long since put a pot of coffee through, would you like one?' asked Marnie.

'I would, thank you. That's no ordinary coffee smell.' He followed her into the kitchen where Marnie took a mug from the cupboard and filled it from her trusty old machine.

'It's caramel coffee. Is that okay?'

'Sounds wonderful.' He handed her the bottle. It had a rustic label on it, the writing calligraphic. 'Last season's bilberry,' he explained. 'It trounced David's rhubarb and ginger in the Christmas taste session.'

Marnie laughed. 'Thank you. I can open it if you'd rather.'

Lionel declined the offer. 'No, that's for you. A *welcome to your new home* present.'

'That's very kind,' said Marnie, putting it on the kitchen table. 'Please take a seat. How do you take it?'

'With the merest touch of milk to cloud it and no sugar, thank you.'

When she turned from the fridge, it was to find Lionel flicking through her *Country Manors* book.

'So this is what everyone's talking about. I did want to peep inside and take a look but they don't have it in the village library.'

'I thought it was about country life,' Marnie blurted. It was an obvious lie and Lionel grinned, not taken in at all.

'I've sat many an hour at this table talking to Jessie,' said Lionel wistfully. 'Eating fruit pie. She was a wonderful gossip.' He laughed and Marnie thought it sounded like the laugh equivalent of church bells. Deep and resonant and joyful. 'She is sadly missed.'

'Well, I'm a cheesecake specialist, if that's any consolation,' Marnie replied, having a sudden vision of taking tea and cake with the vicar every week. Not something she would ever have imagined doing before.

'Yes, Lilian told me so. Though ...' he held up his hand to reinforce the disclaimer, 'she wasn't gossiping about you. Fascinating story of how you came into contact with each other.'

'Yes, it's very odd,' replied Marnie. She wondered if the vicar was here to suss her out, work out what her intentions were. He was understandably protective of Lilian, and she had no qualms about allaying any fears he might have.

'I did get the feeling that Lilian thinks we might be related, but we're not of course.'

'Oh, you've seen the scarlet gypsy woman on the wall then,' Lionel said. 'In the very kindest way I shall tell you that Lilian sometimes sees what she wants to see.'

Time to put the cards on the table, thought Marnie.

'If, by any chance, you're afraid that I'm here to take advantage of Lilian, Mr Temple, can I just say that I'm not. This is a bolthole for me for a short time. I shall be paying rent and—'

'Please, please, dear lady,' Lionel interrupted and refused to let Marnie continue. 'I am not here to vet you. I really am here to welcome you, with no hidden agenda. For however much Lilian's memory is dissipating, her judgement of people remains sharp and steadfast.'

Then they definitely weren't related, because Marnie's judgement – at least of men she fancied – was more than crap.

'Thank you, Lionel. I know you must all care for Lilian and her welfare very much.'

'Well, some more than others,' replied Lionel. 'She hasn't had the easiest of lives, despite being born into such privilege. But then it's people that enrich us, not money, of course. *Aurum Potestas Est;* the Dearman family motto sums it up for them all – immediate and extended family – *gold is power.* Except for dear Lilian. If only the line could have continued under her.'

'Lilian gave me a copy of the book you wrote,' said Marnie with a wry smile. 'It doesn't pull any punches.'

'As Lilian requested. I do pride myself on its accuracy, although I did have to check all the facts thoroughly. Lilian has a tendency to rewrite history when she dictates her memories.' He gave her a wry smile of his own, before he drained his cup and then got to his feet. 'I won't take up any more of your time. I just wanted to say welcome. I don't know if you are a believer or not, but Sunday service is at eleven a.m. There's no pressure to attend, but I do like to play to an audience. An actor always gives a better performance when every seat is full.'

'Thank you,' replied Marnie. She wouldn't be attending. Christianity hadn't done her any favours in the past. 'And thank you for the wine, *Mr Lion.* I shall put it to good use.'

At the door, Lionel Temple turned and then turned back,

as if he had been about to say something but thought better of it. Then he decided to say it after all.

'Marnie, be careful in Wychwell. It's full of old families who are averse to change and anything new, unless you happen to be Herv Gunnarsen of course. He's even got all the men fluttering their eyelashes.'

Marnie grinned. 'I will.'

'Not everything is as sweet as it might at first seem,' he warned her then wished her goodnight. And as Marnie closed the door, she thought that she remembered Lilian saying something very similar only two days before.

Chapter 16

Marnie slept soundly in the back bedroom of Little Raspberries and strangely what nudged her awake was the silence. Her ear was attuned to the sounds of Redbrook Row: the traffic, the opening and closing of garage doors, gates squeaking open and then shutting again, Mrs Barlow's dog yapping as they set off for their walk at eight precisely every morning. She opened her eyes to a strange room flooded with warm light as the morning sunshine pushed through the pink curtains and, keeping her head on the pillow, asked herself what the bloody hell she was doing here.

This time last week she was head of Beverage Marketing, a suit, loved up, with her eye on world domination. She'd had a game plan: she *would* get on the board and who knows, might even be sitting in Laurence's chair when he moved on to turn another sinking-ship company around. Now she was in the middle of nowhere, having flown here on a whim, living in a house owned by an old lady she barely knew and was about to embark upon a 'career' making secret cheesecakes for a wage that might keep her in pints of Guinness, but her Lulu Guinness days were definitely gone. This was all beyond madness.

Her mobile, charging on the bedside cabinet, showed that she'd received a voicemail. A message had been left by Fiona Abercrombie. They were coming to inspect her kitchen that afternoon at one o'clock. Could she please confirm that was all right?

Cilla Oldroyd had scrubbed the kitchen clean for Marnie but she still gave it an extra once-over before the formal inspection. Mrs Abercrombie would need sunglasses because the gleam from the worksurfaces was so bright.

She arrived at precisely one, carrying a serious clipboard and wearing white gloves, which she proceeded to run along, under, on top of and inside the cupboards, surfaces and appliances in Jessie's ex-pie factory. She scribbled things down, looked serious a lot, studied whilst chewing the top of her pen and then declared that Marnie's kitchen was Abercrombie-friendly and had more than passed muster.

Over a relaxed coffee, she went over her requirements. Marnie was to supply twelve foot-square cheesecakes of three different flavours every Monday, Wednesday and Friday, unless otherwise directed. These would be collected by a refrigerated van at eight o'clock on those days. The office would dictate what flavours they required four days in advance. Payment would be made by BACS. The first van would arrive on Monday morning, unless Marnie could manage Friday. From the extensive flavour list that Marnie had supplied, first-off they would require, four apple crumbles, four cream teas and four rum truffles. Marnie said she could get a Friday order ready, no problem.

Did Marnie have a business name for her records alone, Mrs Abercrombie asked. Something nice and anonymous, i.e. not 'the Secret Cheesecake Maker'.

'McMaid's?' suggested Marnie; it just came to her. That would do, said Mrs Abercrombie.

Mrs Abercrombie offloaded a stack of flat-pack boxes bearing the mendacious words 'Tea Lady Instore Bakery' and then she zoomed off in her Audi TT.

Marnie had told her that a large separate fridge for Tea Lady usage only was on order. It wasn't, but it would be by the end of the day. She also needed to buy a lot of ingredients and cake tins. The day was taken up with shopping for those. It kept her mind away from what happened exactly a week ago: Suranna Fox storming the building, her life falling down a well – and one that felt as deep as any Margaret Kytson was thrown into.

But thanks to Mrs McMaid and Lilian Dearman, she hadn't quite reached the bottom. Yet. She had a ledge to rest on, to recoup and rebuild. She had no idea how permanent the ledge was, but it was holding for now.

The fridge was delivered the next morning. She'd had to pay forty pounds more for it to happen, but that was okay. It was either that or wait until Monday and she needed the kitchen to be fully operational as soon as possible.

She had hoped to relax in the garden and read a couple of chapters of *Country Manors* down by the stream, but the heavens opened that afternoon and so she read at the kitchen table instead whilst eating a baked potato. The lord of the manor – Manfred Masters – (who it was suspected had warlock's blood in him) had just seduced the gamekeeper's wife, Eunice, who had shown herself to be – in plain parlance – a right goer, despite making all that jam for the local WI. Manfred could have charmed the knickers off anyone, but the author had still managed to make him sound like a decent bloke. It was fairly obvious that Eunice was merely using him, though.

Marnie couldn't wait until Manfred, who was falling in love with her, found out.

Just as Marnie was reaching a very juicy part, there was a knock on the door. She was surprised to find the May Queen herself on the doorstep, clutching a bunch of flowers.

'I'm not disturbing you, am I?' asked Ruby.

'No, not at all,' fibbed Marnie.

'I brought you these. Moving-in present.'

'Thank you very much. That's so sweet.'

It became obvious after an awkward silence that Ruby was angling to come in and Marnie was too polite to say, 'cheers then' and shut the door in her face. So she invited her inside.

'Can I get you a coffee or a tea?' She remembered Lionel's gift. 'Or a glass of wine, maybe?'

'Thank you, a glass would be lovely. Mr Temple's is it?'

'That's right.'

Marnie noticed how preened Ruby was, as if she was dressed for business rather than pleasure. She'd done a Body Language and Presentation course at Café Caramba and it had been rather insightful.

There was a prickle in the air as they waded through conversational niceties. Marnie played the game, until Ruby revealed her real reason for being there. She also made sure that she sipped the industrial-strength wine very slowly herself, but refilled Ruby's glass in the hope that it would oil her tongue and they could get to the nitty-gritty.

Information was duly traded: Ruby's family had always lived in Wychwell. Her father and mother were divorced and he'd moved back to Skipperstone. Ruby was a twenty-nine-year-old primary school teacher and was a member of Skipperstone's am-dram society. She liked to sew, knit and read but not trashy stuff like the *Country Manors* thing that everyone was talking about. Her mother – Kay – worked part-time both in Plum Corner post office and in a mini supermarket in Mintbottom.

Marnie was more than careful with the information she gave out and forgave herself the odd untruth. Had she enjoyed the May Day festivities? – yes (true). How had she met Lilian? – on a baking site on the internet (true). What brought her to Wychwell? – she was in between jobs and taking some time out from the rat race (half-true). The line of Ruby's questioning then become very telling: was Marnie single – yes (true). How long was she planning on staying – not that long (true). When was the last time she'd had a boyfriend – too long ago to remember (lie). Was there anyone she had her eye on? Marnie wanted to answer, 'Herv Gunnarsen,' and watch Ruby spontaneously combust, but she answered 'absolutely not' instead. If Ruby Sweetman wasn't here to warn her off Lilian's rugged Viking gardener, Marnie would have not only eaten someone's hat, but the head inside it as well.

Ruby was knocking back the wine under the impression that Marnie was drawing level with her. If Marnie had had so much as a full glass of the stuff, there would have been a repeat of what had happened with Lilian on the confessional night she couldn't remember. She wouldn't have bet that her secrets would have been as safe with Miss Sweetman as they were with Lilian.

Eventually the H-word reared its mane-like head.

'Have you met Lilian's groundsman yet – Herv?' Ruby asked. A discernible sigh was tagged onto the end of his name, Marnie noticed.

'The bloke with the hair and the beard?' Marnie played dumb. 'I just said hello at the May Day event. Lilian introduced us.'

'He's gorgeous isn't he?' Ruby let Marnie fill up her glass again and then Marnie pretended to top up her own.

'I can't say that I really noticed,' sniffed Marnie. 'I go more for the dark, slim, short-haired-type myself.'

'I heard him asking about you up at the manor house,' said Ruby with a smile stapled to those thin lips of hers.

'Oh? Can't think why. Maybe he's just nosey.'

'Expressing an interest, possibly?' Ruby began to run her hand around the rim of her glass until it made a really annoying sound.

'It's not reciprocated, in case you're asking,' Marnie mirrored the fake smile. 'I'm not interested in men.'

'Oh, you're gay?' Ruby's relief was obvious.

'No, not gay, just not interested. Especially not in a handsome man who would probably be more in love with himself than he ever would with me.'

Marnie didn't mean to say that. She suspected Ruby Sweetman was the sort of person who would store such a slip of the tongue for later use. She tried to rectify the situation immediately.

'I mean . . . not every man as good looking as him will be an arse . . .' She was aware she could be making things worse. 'I'm sure he's great but . . . I wouldn't be his type anyway, even if I wanted a man, which I don't . . .' She was digging herself a hole and she'd need a sixty-foot ladder to get out of it if she didn't shut up. 'Are you and him . . . an item? I thought you looked . . . er . . . nice together at the May Day event.'

'Really?' Ruby looked delighted by that.

'Yes, when he was putting the crown on your head. He looked at you quite . . . quite . . . er . . . tenderly.'

'We're *very* good friends,' said Ruby with emphasis, smile not stapled on now; rather it was adhering to her lips with the glue of joy. 'He's my best friend, in fact. We're keeping it platonic, though. For now. He moved here after his marriage broke down. His bitch of a wife left him for his best friend so he needs time to heal before he starts another relationship. Early days.'

'Yes, you could understand him wanting some cooling-down time after that sort of betrayal,' nodded Marnie. 'How long has he lived here then?'

'Three years, six months.'

Marnie snorted and tried to convert it into a sneeze. *My, he was a slow healer. Or not.* Her third-last boyfriend had used the same line, that he liked her but he didn't feel ready to get back on the relationship horse. But sex was permitted. Strangely enough, not only did he get back on another horse but he ended up marrying the horse and getting it pregnant within two months. They'd had twin foals by that Christmas.

'I'm sure it's only a matter of time before he's ready to love again,' said Marnie diplomatically, thinking that Herv Gunnarsen was keeping Ruby at arm's length for good reason because if he gave her the nod, she'd have shinned naked up his drainpipe before his neck had straightened up. She bet anything that Ruby had already chosen her wedding dress.

'It'll be nice to have someone in the village who is the same age as me,' said Ruby. 'Apart from Herv there's no one else, they're all old farts.'

'What about Zoe Oldroyd?' asked Marnie.

'She's only eighteen. I have nothing in common with a cleaner over ten years younger than me.' Ruby's words had a definite slur to them now. Her nicey-nicey mask was slipping. '. . . Although I do feel a bit sorry for her having to work up at the manor when she wants to go to university and do languages. She got really good A-level grades, but she can't.'

'Why not?'

'Probably because she has to take over from her mum when she retires. They'll lose their house if not. They've worked for the manor for generations. It's *tradition*.' Ruby gave the word a scathing tone. 'Stupid people. Little people. Lilian Dearman pays them a pittance and they'd all line up to wipe her backside if they could. Lionel and Derek hang on her every word, that silly Emelie won't hear a word against her, it's like living in medieval times. I hate it here.'

'Why don't you leave then if you dislike it so much?'

Ruby didn't answer but really she didn't have to – because Herv Gunnarsen lived here, that's why. And she was waiting for him to make his move.

'I think I need your toilet,' Ruby said, standing up and then falling straight down again. 'Whoops.'

'Upstairs to your left,' said Marnie, hoping that Ruby would decide to go home now. She'd obviously done what she set out to and it was less to do with being part of the welcoming committee and more to do with warning Marnie off. She might as well have lifted her booty like a cat on Sunday and sprayed Herv Gunnarsen as he crowned her. Well, Ruby had no worries on any score. Let her crack on.

To Marnie's relief, when Ruby came downstairs her first words were, 'I'd better go. I've got an early start in the morning. We're taking the children to the Viking museum in York.'

'That sounds like fun,' lied Marnie. She wondered if Ruby would be imagining Herv in the costumes, running at her intent on ravaging her.

Ruby picked up her bag. 'Thank you for your company. We should do it again soon. Do you like the theatre and acting?'

If Ruby was angling for her to join the am-drams, she had

another think coming. But Marnie wasn't an idiot. She was all too aware of the adage 'keep your friends close and your enemies closer' and knew which one Ruby thought she was more likely to be.

'I occasionally go and watch a play, but I wouldn't want to be in one myself.'

Nor did she want to be sitting watching *Coronation Street* in Little Raspberries comparing cross-stitching projects. She had secret work to do in here for the Tea Lady which involved a few very early mornings per week and no one snooping around her space. Especially not someone who gave off such hostile vibes.

'Alas, I work unsociable hours. I'm a . . . freelance . . . copywriter in high . . . er demand,' Marnie added. That would get her safely out of any future invitations, she hoped. She opened the door and forced out a yawn. 'Thank you so much for the flowers, Ruby. It was very kind of you to make me feel so welcome.'

'A pleasure,' said Ruby. 'Lovely to meet you properly. Lilian was gushing about you so much, we were all quite intrigued.'

I'll bet you were, thought Marnie. 'Enjoy the Vikings.'

She shut the door and fought the urge to slide down it. This was what she hadn't factored into the equation – typical village life with nosey people wanting to pry into her business, bringing a jar of jam (or rather flowers) and demanding part of her soul in exchange. She poured out the last of Lionel's bilberry wine, closed the curtains and locked the door. Then she picked up her book and slid back into her story of an untypical village life where no one was curious why Manfred Masters' manor rocked with ear-splitting sounds of intercoital ecstasy, especially when the moon was full.

Chapter 17

On Friday morning, Marnie started work at 3 a.m. in plenty of time to make the Tea Lady's cheesecakes. She was surprisingly nervous, ridiculously so. *Why are you worrying? You have my special ingredient to help you.* It was as if Mrs McMaid's voice had drifted into her head like smoke. Her eye glanced up at the square tin on the shelf, the one she had taken on the day she found the lovely old lady had died. She'd filled it back up many times over the years and what was inside never failed to work its magic, adding that little something that everyone tasted but no one was quite sure what it was.

She got to work: stewing the apples, crushing the biscuits for the base, whipping the cream to a soft peak, melting the chocolate slowly so it was smooth and glossy and not grainy and stiff. A sprinkle from the secret ingredient tin went into the mix before the cream and the cheese met. By seven o'clock, all the cheesecakes were in the new tall fridge in their boxes ready for the van to collect, which it did, exactly on time. It was a black van with blacked-out windows and no signwriting. The driver wore black sunglasses to add to the air of mystery. Marnie waved goodbye to her first consignment

of cakes then collapsed at the kitchen table with a strong
coffee that didn't have a chance of keeping her from sleep.
She was woken up two hours later by a loud knock on the
door. She opened it to find Herv Gunnarsen there, looking
taller and wider than the door frame.

'Good morning.' He was holding a letter. 'I met the postman at the end of the road.'

'Oh, thank you,' smiled Marnie, taking it from him.

'You've been cooking,' he said.

'What gave it away?' said Marnie, sounding more sarcastic
than she meant to.

'You have sugar on your face. And the apron of course.'
He grinned and Marnie wiped where he pointed to. There
was loads of it. She must have been resting on a sugar pillow
on the table.

'Thanks,' said Marnie, for want of something better to say.
'And thanks for the post.'

He wasn't making any attempt to move from the doorstep, she noted. Well, she wasn't going to invite him in for
a cuppa and a cosy chat after what Lilian had told her. That
would have been blatantly encouraging him, leading him
on. Better to err on the side of rudeness than politeness, then
he knew where he stood with her. 'Was there something . . .
you wanted?'

'Lilian would like to know if you'd lunch with her. She
sent me to ask you.'

'Oh, right, er . . . yes, yes. That would be lovely. What time?'

'Twelve. Can I tell her that would be okay?'

'Yes. I'll be there,' said Marnie, catching sight of a figure
walking past the end of the lane – the woman who had been
adjusting Ruby's hair at the May Day fair. Her mother, Kay,
presumably. Bloody marvellous.

'Good.'

'Thank you . . . Herv.' God, his eyes were ridiculously blue and they were trained very intently on her.

'Oh and *Velkommen til landsbyen,* as we say in Norway. Welcome to the village.'

He really did have a nice smile. She felt something inside her chest respond to the curve of his lips and wanted to slap it.

'Oh, cheers.'

'A pleasure.'

'Bye then.'

She shut the door on him, literally and figuratively. No, she was not going to give any man an inch for him to take a mile for a very long time – possibly ever. Not even a paragon of virtue such as Herv Gunnarsen. Lilian was right though, because if the way he had been looking at her was any indication, he had definitely taken a shine to her. His pupils had been so dilated that she could have climbed in them and cadged a lift up to the manor. Whilst she stayed away from men, her life was uncomplicated and stable. Let them in and chaos ensued. Message received and understood. Finally.

She went upstairs to wash the 'sugar pillow' properly off her face, wondering why Lilian had sent Herv down to ask her in person and hadn't just phoned herself. The minx.

Marnie called in at the shop on her way to the manor for a bottle of wine, because she didn't want to turn up empty-handed. A large woman with ankles so fat they looked as if the skin was melting over her shoes was talking in a low voice with another woman standing behind the counter – her second viewing of Kay Sweetman that day. Their conversation snapped off as soon as Marnie entered so it wasn't difficult to guess what the subject matter had been, especially as the last words she heard were '... feet under the table'.

Marnie browsed around the small wine section whilst the air crackled with a silence so pregnant, it was calling out for gas and air. Ankle woman had finished shopping but she wasn't going anywhere, probably because she couldn't wait for Marnie to leave so they could carry on with their theories of why she was staying in Wychwell, and what Herv Gunnarsen was doing on her doorstep this morning.

Marnie lingered for far longer than she needed to out of mischief, forcing the two women to strike up a staged conversation to fill the silence.

'Are you feeling all right now, Una? Derek said you had another one of your migraines at the weekend,' asked Kay.

'Yes. All that drum banging didn't help. And he can't do anything without making a noise. He's like a carthorse. When he dusts it registers on the Richter scale.'

Ah. Una Price. The woman who put the mass of frown lines on lumbering Derek's face. So that's who ankle woman was.

Marnie eventually approached the till, feeling Una's eyes sliding up and down her.

'That'll be eight pounds ninety-nine,' said Kay with a shop smile that looked more like a grimace. It wasn't hard to see who Ruby had inherited her string-thin, sneery lips from. Marnie slowly took the purse out of her bag, giving the questions time to rev up. She could feel them pushing at the starting gates in the women's throats. When none were forthcoming, she turned to Una, looked her straight in the eye, smiled and said,

'Phase Eight and Zara.'

'I beg your pardon?' Una appeared puzzled.

'You were staring. I presumed you were curious where

my clothes came from: Phase Eight top and my jeans are from Zara.'

'I wasn't . . .'

'Was it my hair? Leeds then – Russell Eaton. Or my shoes – Office. Or was it my make-up? Clinique foundation. It's very good. This one is Vanilla.'

Una was flustered then, her cheeks started loading with pink.

Kay fumbled in the till for the change and dropped a pound coin on the floor.

Marnie stared silently at Una who clearly wasn't used to face to face confrontation, preferring to operate behind people's backs. Say what you like about Café Caramba, but they didn't half send you on some really useful psychological tactic courses. It was amazing what havoc an intense gaze could cause. Equivalent of a laser gun when used properly.

Kay rose up from behind the counter and put the money into Marnie's waiting hand.

'Thank you,' Marnie said, smile fixed on with superglue. She walked out of the shop with a swagger in her step and knew that she'd given the two women enough to chatter about for the rest of the day probably. *You didn't get that in a town corner shop*, Marnie giggled to herself.

A man was watering the cheerful hanging baskets that hung at either side of the pub door. As soon as he spotted Marnie, he climbed down from the ladder and walked towards her, holding out a meaty paw.

'Hello, we haven't met,' he said. 'I'm David Parselow and you must be Marnie.'

He looked more like a butcher than a publican, thought Marnie, with his stout physique and fuzzy red sideburns.

'I am. Nice to meet you, David.'

'I heard that the vicar has been trying to bribe you with his bilberries,' he grinned.

'Oh the wine, you mean,' said Marnie, after a moment's confusion.

'Don't let yourself get acclimatised to his rot. I'll leave you a bottle of my rhubarb and ginger on your doorstep later so you can try some proper stuff,' he said.

'Thank you,' said Marnie. 'That's very kind.'

He looked with disdain at the bottle in her hand, 'I tell you, you'll never drink that shop-bought stuff again.'

'I shall look forward to being converted,' Marnie replied.

As she walked past the green, she mused how strange it was that she liked some people on sight and usually got that sort of judgement right. It was when she fancied people that she got it so wrong.

Johnny Oldroyd was cutting the grass on the green with a drive-on petrol mower. He was wearing headphones and his mouth was moving as if singing to a track. He looked at total peace working in the sunshine as if he was content that Wychwell was the extent of his world and he wasn't bothered about anything beyond those collapsed village walls.

She passed Emelie coming out of her sweet little cottage with a parcel as she walked up the hill towards the manor. Emelie was delighted she'd come to stay, she said, because Lilian was over the moon. Made a change to have a positive effect on someone, thought Marnie. More intoxicating than Lionel's bilberry wine. When she reached the manor, Herv was on his knees at the side of the porch, weeding. He even looked tall in that position.

'Hello again,' she said, wondering if Kay Sweetman had a pair of binoculars trained on her ready to report back to her daughter.

'Hello.' He took an exaggerated look at his watch. 'You're late.'

'I've been socialising with my fellow villagers,' Marnie replied, not stopping to chat. 'Enjoy the sunshine.'

'Marnie.' He called her name and when she turned, she found him standing. His body language suggested that he wanted to tell her something in confidence.

'I am not sure that Lilian is so well. She was fine first thing this morning but since . . . She's having one of her spells.'

'Oh,' said Marnie, wondering what 'one of her spells' consisted of. 'Is she sick? Should I call in and say hello or . . . go back home?'

'No, she wants to see you, she was most specific.' Marnie noticed that his accent was thick when his voice was quiet. 'Bodily she's okay, but she's confused again. She has called me Griff three times this morning and she has never done that before. Please let me know what you think of her.'

'Okay,' Marnie nodded, doubt in her voice because she hardly knew Lilian really. Would she notice things out of the ordinary more than he or Cilla or anyone else who saw her more often might? 'I'll report back.'

She rang the bell and Cilla answered the door, her features etched with worry. Nevertheless, she smiled at Marnie and told her to go straight through to the conservatory where Lilian was waiting for her.

Lilian struggled to her feet with the aid of her beautiful greyhound stick as soon as her visitor entered.

'Dear Marnie, how lovely of you to come. How are you settling in?' Then she leaned in to whisper, 'Have you started making your secret things yet?' and she tapped the side of her nose.

'The first batch this morning. If I'd known I was coming

for lunch, I would have made an extra one.' *She sounds on the ball to me*, thought Marnie.

'What a shame,' said Lilian, 'next time. Come and sit down. Sheila has made us another wonderful lunch.'

'I brought you some wine; it's just from Plum Corner but I didn't want to come empty-handed,' said Marnie, thinking, *who is Sheila?*

'Thank you, Marnie. That's kind of you but you really didn't have to. We will have it later at the party.'

Cilla walked into the room with a plate of warm pastries, still wearing that worried look on her face. Then Marnie remembered from reading the Wychwell book that Sheila had been Cilla's mother, her previous housekeeper. Cilla looked at Marnie as she gave her head a little shake that said, *she's not right.*

'This all looks lovely, Cilla,' said Marnie, emphasis on the name.

'Sheila, dear. Cilla will still be at school,' Lilian corrected her, patting the chair at the side of her. 'Come and sit down and let's eat. How did you sleep in Little Raspberries?'

Marnie poured out some tea from the large silver pot.

'Very well,' she said. 'Like the proverbial log.'

'It was always my favourite of all the cottages,' said Lilian, clapping her hands. 'I knew you'd like it.'

'I do. It's very cosy,' said Marnie, but concern for Lilian was nagging at her too now.

'Isn't it a lovely day, Marnie. I feel very content today.'

Lilian started chewing delicately on a pastry whilst staring wistfully out of the window, not at the garden and the lake, but at somewhere far beyond them. Marnie studied her and thought her profile rather beautiful.

'I'm so glad I found you,' Lilian said at last and turned

slowly to Marnie. 'It is my greatest joy that you came back into my life.' She reached over for Marnie's hand and squeezed it hard, desperately affectionate.

Marnie smiled and wondered if she should ask what she meant. She didn't want to upset Lilian. She looked happy in her confusion. She tried gently.

'What do you mean, my dear friend? I haven't been away. Are you mixing me up with someone else?'

'From Ireland,' Lilian said, as if it were Marnie who had forgotten. 'I knew it was you. I told Lionel. Have you met Lionel yet?'

'Yes, I have,' said Marnie.

'He never married,' said Lilian with a laboured sigh. 'What a waste. Some lady missed out on a wonderful husband there.'

Cilla walked into the room to check that everything was all right and if Lilian wanted anything else.

'No, I think we are fine, Cilla,' said Lilian and Cilla's face relaxed into a smile. Lilian was 'back in the room'.

'They worry about me,' said Lilian to Marnie when the housekeeper had gone. 'And they also worry that when I pop my clogs they won't be safe. But they will. Safer than ever.'

Lilian seemed fine after that, episode over, as sharp as if she'd spent all night in the knife drawer, as Mrs McMaid used to say. After a jolly lunch, she took Marnie into the very large formal drawing room to show her the treasures that were exhibited in the glass cabinets there. Marnie wasn't a great lover of pottery but she did think Lilian's collection rather impressive. They were all very different but what they had in common were lines of gold criss-crossing over them.

'They were broken and then mended Japanese-style,' Lilian explained. 'There's a name for it that escapes me. I've collected them for years. Wonderful, aren't they?'

'They are indeed,' agreed Marnie. It was entirely believable that Lilian would rescue broken things.

When Marnie came to leave Cilla rushed out to speak to her.

'You've brought magic with you,' she said. 'I haven't seen her laugh like she has today in a long time.'

The next few weeks passed in a blur. Marnie settled into her routine of cheesecake making three days per week. Mrs Abercrombie increased her order by a third and seemed very impressed by the arrangement. Marnie had a rather cursory email from Café Caramba asking when she intended to return to work. Fortified by a glass of David Parselow's rhubarb and ginger wine, she replied in a similar tone that she wouldn't be back and also she wouldn't be working her notice. She was shaking when she pressed send. She had jumped off a cliff and had to pray that the landing was softer than it looked. But what else could she do? She couldn't go back so the only way was forward.

She had swapped power suits, high status and traffic-heavy journeys into the city for slow-paced, anonymous baking in a sleepy Dales village. She didn't know how long this present arrangement would last because Marnie was a doer and she *knew* she would get very bored very quickly here in Wychwell. She enjoyed thinking up and implementing new ideas, improving the status quo, seeing results, feeling that surge of adrenaline rushing through her veins. Even so, she was enjoying the sunshine and sitting on the bench down by Blackett Stream reading books and newspapers. Film rights to the first three *Country Manors* books had been bought by Hollywood, according to the *Skipperstone Trumpet*. Marnie had been equally fascinated by the story behind the novels.

The first two books had been out on shelves and the third half-finished before its touch-paper found the match. Then – *boom* – shops couldn't buy the books in fast enough, with the result that the author Penelope Black had just climbed onto the ladder of Britain's richest people – and she hadn't entered on the bottom rung either. Or he. The identity of the author was a secret which only added to the coffers as people bought into the mystery. Marnie wondered if she should write a book now that she had all this spare time. She'd tried once but given up by page three and decided that she was destined to be a buyer and a reader rather than a seller and a writer.

Exactly a month to the day after Marnie had moved to Wychwell, Laurence sent her a personal letter, surprisingly. Not surprisingly it wasn't very complimentary. If she'd lived at Hogwarts, it would have been a *howler*. Her unprofessionalism in quitting her position without the proper notice period had been recorded officially, he said, by which she read that she'd get a shit reference. She'd been too conditioned to expect the worst when it came to people.

It became a regular event that Lilian came to her for lunch on Tuesdays and they talked for hours about anything and everything. Marnie loved to hear the stories about the Dearmans, for there seemed to be no end to their iniquity. Gambling, whores, murder, sexually transmitted diseases, bestiality, madness . . . the Dearmans made the Borgias look like the Osmonds. Marnie set a table down by the stream and they ate cheese and pickle and egg mayo sandwiches and the 'cheesecake of the week'. Marnie read *Country Manors* aloud to Lilian as they drank a glass of David's or Lionel's wine – as bottles appeared on her doorstep as if they had been delivered by an alcoholic fairy.

Sometimes, Marnie made Lilian laugh lots by exorcising the ghosts of her doomed relationships with her witty narrative. Except for the Justin Fox episode, because she couldn't forget the sight of pregnant Suranna Fox reduced to doing what she'd felt she had to, and there was nothing funny in that. And sometimes, when it felt safe to do so, they touched on those things that sat deep under the seabed in Marnie's heart, things that never failed to cause her pain when they were exposed to the salt of the water. Sometimes Lilian cried with her, for her.

On Saturdays Marnie would lunch with Lilian at the manor. Often they took a walk around the gardens which had been artfully created to appear wild.

'Griff Oldroyd was a master gardener,' Lilian told her one day as they watched Herv dredging the lake, 'but Herv is something even more special. The Picasso of horticulture. Teaching's loss is our gain. Thank God that bloody woman of his broke his heart and he fled her and found us.'

He was a nice man, Marnie had to agree. Always polite, kind; always with a smile playing on his lips. But he was a man all the same, and was therefore to be avoided. Her heart was not at home to callers, even if they were as perfectly perfect as Herv Gunnarsen.

Chapter 18

Marnie had been living in Wychwell just over six weeks when she first saw the ghost of the Pink Lady. The days had been especially warm and a thunderstorm was badly needed to puncture the heat. On the evening before the rain came, the air was so thick, it was almost unbreathable and despite having the windows open, she couldn't sleep. She tossed and turned until two o'clock then got out of bed to walk around the green to tire herself and reset her bedtime routine. Everything was so silent when she ventured out into the night. The whole of Wychwell was asleep, with their windows open at full stretch.

Marnie sat on the ornate memorial bench dedicated to Jessie Plumpton and marvelled at how different this place was to any she had ever been to. She had settled into village life far easier than she would have thought possible. She loved the fact that Plum Corner sold such a motley array of goods, though she much preferred to visit it on the days when the owner Roger Mumford was running it and not when Kay Sweetman was serving. She loved that the vicar was like an omnipresent being and Marnie bumped into him lots and he was always up for pleasant chat. She loved the gentle elderly people living there: Dr Court and his wife who were a sweet old cat-loving couple, and Cyril and Alice Rootwood who walked around the green three times a day with their tiny ancient Yorkshire Terrier, Richard. And Lilian and Emelie, of course. She often saw Emelie sitting out in the garden watching the birds gather around all the treats she laid out for them.

Ruby Sweetman hadn't visited since with her 'keep your enemies closer' fake friend routine and Marnie was glad about that. She hadn't spoken directly to Titus at all. He had passed her a couple of times in his E-Type Jag and she'd waved him on once when her car had had right of way, but he hadn't given her the slightest acknowledgement as would have been polite. She'd bumped into his wife Hilary the previous week and they'd said hello. Hilary had asked how she was settling in and Marnie replied, *very well thank you*. The interchange had been no more than that but Marnie got a surprisingly warm vibe from her. And she'd been taken aback by her voice. She would have expected Hilary to have a mousey squeak, not one so resonant and beautiful. She could have read the news with that voice.

There was a massive full moon hanging in the sky like a giant shiny bauble. Marnie was staring hard at it, trying to imagine a face in it, when she felt a presence behind her.

'Penny for your thoughts.'

Marnie whirled around to find Herv. 'You scared the living daylights out of me.'

'Or should that be nightlights. Mind if I join you?'

'Not at all,' she said. 'It's a free country.'

'Couldn't sleep?' he asked, taking his place at the side of her. A respectful distance between them, she noted.

'No. I thought a walk might help.'

'Me too. Even though we are sitting.'

His accent was subtle but ridiculously attractive. Marnie felt her heartbeat increase both in speed and volume in the quiet. Bloody pheromones. They were slave to no one.

'Lilian's garden is looking really lovely at the moment,' said Marnie eventually, feeling that the silence should be broken.

'I do my best,' Herv said, with a little laugh. 'But Lilian, she is full of strange ideas and plant combinations in her effort to stamp out the past. Apart from the lake, the garden is totally different to how it was when I first came. She has changed everything her family had there, every shrub and flower. This year I have to put lilies everywhere. The big ones, the bright ones, the smelly ones.' And he pinched his nose.

'Stargazers?' asked Marnie, with a smile.

'She wants them everywhere,' said Herv, nodding 'I tell her, "Lilian, you shouldn't try to change the past, it can't be done and especially not with big smelly flowers", but she doesn't listen. She is stubborn like a mule.' And he growled in amused frustration.

'She's been very good to me, mule or no mule,' said Marnie.

'Where did you live before you came here?'

'South Yorkshire,' she answered, being slightly evasive. She didn't want anyone snooping into her background.

'What did you do? Did you have a job?'

'I was head of Beverage Marketing in a firm that produces coffee.'

'You were?'

'I was.'

He whistled, genuinely impressed. 'What made you have such a life change?'

My lover's pregnant wife tried to kill me in front of the whole building and I couldn't stand the shame of going into the office again, she said inwardly and wondered what his reaction would be if she voiced it. That would stop his pupils dilating when he saw her.

'I wasn't happy. Sometimes you just need to get away.'

'I recognise that feeling,' said Herv. 'When my marriage broke down, I had to get out of Norway. I wanted nothing familiar.'

'You were married?' She asked out of politeness, though she knew this already.

'Yes, for two years only. I was happy. I thought Tine was too but she was . . . was happier with my friend.'

'Ah,' said Marnie, with a grimace. Happened to men too, of course; she knew that women could be twats as well.

'Then she wasn't happier with my friend and wanted me back. I couldn't. The trust had gone. It was very hard for me. Maybe it was meant to be, because I came here and I feel absolutely in the right place. How could you not love this view?'

They both looked at the moon hanging above the manor. And then their eyes were distracted. A strange blush-coloured light was journeying slowly from left to right along the gallery.

'Can you see that?' Herv asked.

'I most certainly can,' replied Marnie with a gulp. 'The Pink Lady?'

Herv was fascinated. 'I have never seen it before. Wow, it's amazing. I wouldn't have believed.'

The pink light faded to nothing yet they carried on watching, waiting for it to make a reappearance, but it didn't.

'Do you like ghost stories, Marnie? Ghost films?'

Marnie's warning flag shot up the pole. She suspected immediately where this could be going.

'I can take them or leave them,' she said, wrinkling up her nose.

'There's a cinema in Skipperstone . . .'

'Anyway, I'd better get to bed, I think my walk has done the trick. Goodnight, Herv,' said Marnie quickly and stood to go.

'Oh, goodnight. Do you want me to walk you back?'

'No,' she said firmly. Too harshly. 'Thank you,' she added in a softer tone.

She was annoyed with herself then. He was only going to ask her to go to the bloody cinema with him, not propose marriage. *God, she was ridiculous.* But she knew what would happen and had to stop it from starting. They'd go out, he'd be kind, her starving heart would open up, fed by the morsels of his attentions. She'd fall hard and deep despite feeling that something wasn't quite right because it never was, but she'd press the override switch and plough on, falling ever deeper and harder. Then the complication would start to show itself, because there always was one. Probably in this case that his heart was still full of his ex-wife, and then her world would come crashing down on top of her and she'd be capsized into a sea of heartbreak. Either that, or Ruby Sweetman would throw herself off a cliff and she'd be blamed for it all.

No. No. No. No. No.

HISTORY OF WYCHWELL BY LIONEL TEMPLE
Contributions by Lilian Dearman.

In 1844 Sir Rodney Dearman, a friend and drinking partner of Branwell Brontë, driven insane by syphilis, forced
the parish priest to conduct a marriage ceremony in his
church between himself and his prize stallion. Luckily Sir
Rodney died before the marriage could be consummated.
Though as Rodney was still married to Cordelia, mother
of his five children, his actions could be, at best, described
as bigamous.

Chapter 19

It was Marnie's turn to go up to Lilian's for lunch the next day. She hadn't slept very well at all, but it was less to do with the heat and more to do with Herv Gunnarsen about to ask her if she wanted to go to the pictures. Although, thinking about it in bed, maybe she'd been a bit ahead of herself; what if he'd merely wanted to tell her that there was a horror film showing, and wasn't proposing he take her to see it? In which case, she'd made a proper tit of herself. Anyway, whether she'd got it right or wrong, she'd probably scared him off for good with her Linford Christie sprint away from him. She was, therefore, quite relieved that he waved at her from across the slope of lawn when she approached the front door of the manor as if there was nothing untoward between them. She hadn't murdered his ego, after all; she wouldn't have wanted to do that. And, if he *had* been about to ask her out, she'd saved him from her blunt refusal by cutting him off at the pass, giving them both the opportunity to keep things platonic and safe and uncomplicated. It was for the best, really it was.

Cilla was in the hallway filling up a vase with roses when she walked in.

'Morning, Marnie,' she smiled, full of beans.

Marnie knew that when Cilla was happy, all was good with Lilian.

'She's waiting for you in the conservatory.'

'Thank you, Cilla,' she replied.

But something wasn't quite right, she could feel it as soon as she had stepped over the threshold. It was as if the manor had its own moods and they coloured the ambience. Marnie had grown to love the old house and its quirkiness. She loved the old gentleman's smoking room that was now a snug where Lilian liked to listen to music, and the breakfast room with its floor-to-ceiling windows that made the most of the morning sunshine. She loved the tower and the library full of beautiful leather-bound volumes and hundreds of Lilian's paperbacks and the magnificent drawing room full of Lilian's precious broken-mended treasures. The manor's personality was always very much in evidence, as if it were made up of layers of all its best times. It never felt cold or hostile and despite its size, Marnie knew why Lilian was happy to reside in it alone. But the manor was less like a house and more like a living thing with emotions (and yes, Marnie knew that was bonkers). Today, the manor felt worried. There was something threatening, an electric portent. Just as the skies outside were warning of thunder.

'Marnie, dear, Marnie, come on in,' yelled Lilian, sitting at the table by the conservatory window. 'What an odd day, don't you think? There's quite a storm brewing and the view is spectacular when that happens. It's better from the tower, of course. I always used to go up there when there was a thunderstorm. At least when Mother wasn't fornicating with her doctor. The heavy air has given me quite a headache. I've had two of those little tablets shaped like bullets and it hasn't made a scrap of difference. Now you are here, I bet it disappears in an instant. So, what have you been up to since, when did I see you last. Christmas?'

'Tuesday,' said Marnie, not sure if Lilian was joking or not.

'Was it only Tuesday? It feels like much longer. Let's have some lunch and then I think we'll go boating on the lake before it freezes over. It once froze enough for us to skate on and we invited the children who were in the village to come and slide with us. One of the few happy memories I have of my childhood. Now, tell me what flavours you're going to do next week for the place we cannot mention.' She placed a shushing finger against her lips and Marnie sat and began to tell her about the next cheesecake order, but she noticed that Lilian was finding it hard to concentrate and kept asking her to repeat what she'd just said.

She couldn't eat anything either. Not even Cilla's cheese pastries which were her absolute favourite. She kept pressing at her temple with her knuckle and despite saying she was all right, she obviously wasn't.

'Lilian, shall I go and get you some more tablets?' Marnie asked.

'Titus shouldn't have mocked Margaret Kytson. I knew no good would come of it. It's disturbed her spirit. She will be walking amongst us again and who can blame her.'

Marnie didn't mention that she'd seen the Pink Lady in the gallery last night, but she felt something unpleasant trip down her spine.

'Don't tell Father that we're taking a boat out,' Lilian looked over her shoulder. 'He's not in a good mood at all.'

Marnie was worried now, plus she thought that Lilian's colour had changed since she arrived. She looked so dreadfully pale. Lilian needed a doctor; no, an ambulance, her intuition said. She got up from the seat to ask Cilla to ring for one, on the quiet because she knew that Lilian would protest.

'I'll go and get you those tablets,' she said, but before she took a step, Lilian made a grab for her hand.

'I'm so glad I found you, Marnie.' And then tears began to pour down Lilian's face as if a pump was behind them. Marnie wrapped her arms around the old lady, who held on to her with the force of one afraid of falling.

Cilla arrived with dessert and the smile she had been previously wearing dropped like a stone. Calmly, so as not to frighten Lilian, Marnie mouthed at her to get an ambulance and Cilla turned on her heel, the creaks on the floorboards telling of her haste.

'Would you like to lie down, Lilian? Do you think that might help your headache?' suggested Marnie, her voice low and gentle.

'I wish I'd taken care of Wychwell more,' said Lilian, sniffing hard. 'There's so much to do.'

'I think Wychwell is perfect as it is,' said Marnie, as Lilian increased her grip. 'This damned headache,' she said, knocking her temple hard with her knuckles. Marnie could feel tears soaking through her shirt.

'Cilla's gone to find something to help you get rid of it,' said Marnie, holding her, trying not to let her worry show.

'Marnie, don't leave me.'

'I'm not going anywhere. Shhh.'

'Don't let them take me there again.' Lilian sounded frightened.

'Where, darling?'

'*There.*'

'No one is taking you anywhere, I promise.'

Lilian's crying was that of someone in the grip of true

panic. This really was something Marnie hadn't seen in her before. Then she started to mutter gibberish, none of it making sense, words but not words. And all the while Marnie tried to soothe her, talk away whatever was troubling her and when Lilian's crying stopped, Marnie thought she'd managed to finally calm her. Her breath against Marnie's neck began easing. Then there was no breath at all.

Marnie would always remember the last sigh of air against her skin, the moment when Lilian left them. Sense told her it was a mere exhalation; her heart told her it was Lilian's spirit whispering away from her body. Marnie went into automatic pilot. She screamed for Herv, for Cilla. She put Lilian on the floor, tilted back her head, attempted to breathe her own life into her. Then everything became a speeded-up blur: Herv and Cilla and the paramedics pouring into the room. Herv's arms peeling her gently away, holding her and Cilla as the medics went into action. But Lilian had gone, her eyes said she wouldn't be brought back because she had moved on to somewhere else and the door had closed behind her. Marnie remembered the paramedics looking at each other, agreeing to stop, checking their watches, saying that the time was twelve forty-one. She remembered Lionel racing over the front lawn in the pouring rain just as Lilian was being placed in the ambulance. She remembered him taking off his glasses to wipe the tears streaming from his eyes.

Chapter 20

A post mortem revealed Lilian had died from a massive bleed on her brain. She couldn't have been revived.

The village seemed to divide into two camps: those whose heads took the lead and were more concerned with what would happen to the manor now that the last of the Dearmans had gone, and those who were led by their hearts and blundered through the week, business as normal because they didn't know what else to do. Cilla and Zoe turned up to work every morning as usual, as did Herv. They all wanted the manor to look perfect for Lilian's wake, their last duty to her. Kay and Una were in gossip heaven in Plum Corner. David at the Wych Arms shut up the pub for two days as a sign of respect. As for Marnie, she locked herself away in Little Raspberries, dragging her sadness around with her like Jacob Marley's chain. She fulfilled the Tea Lady's orders, but her heart wasn't in it. For her, it was like losing Mrs McMaid for a second time and not only the woman herself, but everything she was to her: an anchor, a confidante, a friend. Like Mrs McMaid, she had barely got to know Lilian Dearman but at the same time felt as if she had known her for ever. She cried a lot.

She needed to go to the supermarket in Skipperstone the following Tuesday and as she stepped out of her cottage, it was as if a cloud had descended upon the whole of Wychwell, as if something integral was gone. She didn't want to see anyone or talk to anyone. Just as it was for Herv, Cilla, Emelie and Lionel and all people who loved Lilian, the period between her passing and the funeral was a bubble of time in which they existed alone, working out their grief.

On the day of the funeral, Marnie made her cheesecake order then went to bed as usual, but couldn't sleep. She got up, showered then put on her best black suit for the funeral and though she knew she looked smart in it, the mirror threw back a disappointing reflection. She was tired and it showed; and though make-up could give her cheeks colour they didn't possess, it couldn't cover the puffiness under her eyes. It didn't matter, she wasn't attending a fashion show; but she wanted to appear at her best to say goodbye to someone she truly loved, a woman so close she almost felt part of her. They would bury a piece of Marnie too when they buried Lilian today. Once again she felt like a balloon torn from someone's warm safe hands and sent adrift to be buffeted by cold uncertain winds.

The church bell was ringing a solemn single note, its peal sad and sombre, summoning the people of Wychwell and those beyond too – people of the Dales, old families who had tenuous connections to the Dearmans and the village. Outside the church, Marnie saw Herv looking strange but handsome in a black suit, black tie, his mane of hair tied behind him. He gave her a small wave just before Ruby stole his attention. She hugged him, put her arms around his waist and her head against his chest, claiming comfort for a level of sadness Marnie wondered if she really felt. *What an opportunity to seek sympathy,* she thought and immediately rebuked herself for being mean. Her mother was right, she was no sweet and sensitive Gabrielle – Miss bloody Perfect Perfection herself. She was her anti-Christ equivalent: Miss Imperfectly Imperfect. The family misfit with her black hair and green eyes – Little Miss Trouble who grew up to be Miss Gullible, Miss Stupid, Miss Alone.

Lilian had understood because she'd been the same. And now she was gone. Unwanted tears forced themselves out of Marnie's eyes and she flicked them away with her fingertips, hoping that no one had seen them, unlike Ruby Sweetman who was dabbing her eyes with a lace handkerchief and all the fragility of a Jane Austen heroine. She'd probably have a fainting fit mid-ceremony from the vapours.

'Are you all right, Marnie?' a soft voice at her shoulder asked. She turned to find Derek Price the churchwarden there.

'I'm okay,' the words came out on a croak.

'You should sit in the front row in the church,' he said close to her ear. 'You meant a lot to Lilian. More than most people here.'

Marnie could imagine what his wife Una would say if she was so presumptuous to sit in the front row. It might have mattered to some where they were positioned, but not to Marnie.

'Or you can sit with Una and me if you'd prefer,' he smiled.

'Thank you, that's very kind,' she said.

'Derek.' Una's shrill voice summoned him to return to her immediately. Derek gave Marnie's shoulder a squeeze and he walked back to his wife, no doubt to be told off for consorting with the enemy. Although the only thing she'd really done to have that label bestowed upon her – as far as Marnie knew – was to have been spotted with her friend's daughter's love interest standing on her doorstep.

Lionel appeared at the church doors, dressed formally for the ceremony in cassock, surplice and stole. He invited everyone inside where Lilian's coffin had lain overnight, as she'd wanted. The church was filled with flowers of all colours. Stargazer lilies scented the whole building. They'd all been cut from her garden, Marnie knew. Herv had done this for her.

Titus Sutton had bagged himself the best seat in the house, obviously. His tall, thin, dour wife Hilary sat rigidly beside him. A heavy-set man in a business-like pinstripe suit with large facial features, whom Marnie didn't recognise, sat at the front on the right-hand side. Herv, Marnie thought, might have sat with Cilla, Johnny and Zoe had Ruby not curled her arm around his like a hungry boa constrictor and pressured him to sit beside her and her mother. Griff was playing the organ and beautifully so. She saw Lionel beckon her to the front but she waved that she was fine a few rows back, behind the villagers. Emelie moved seats to join her.

They sang before any words were spoken – Lilian's favourite hymn: 'Praise to the Lord, the Almighty'. Lionel's voice rang out as clear and pure a sound as one of his church bells, his faith affirmed in the lyrics. There was a silence after the song had ended, one soaked in drama and emotion. Then Lionel began to speak.

'We are gathered here to celebrate the life of our dear, dear Lilian,' and his voice crumbled like an Oreo base with too little butter in it. There was an uncomfortable lapse whilst he struggled to regain his composure and when he did, he apologised, but throughout the whole sermon it became evident his strength was a big dog on a weak leash. It was clear his affection for Lilian ran deeper even than Marnie had thought.

Marnie's tissue was in shreds now. Emelie handed her

another and when Marnie turned to her to mouth *thank you*, she found the old lady's bright blue eyes cloudy with tears ready to fall down her powdered cheeks.

'When Lilian asked me to sit down and discuss what should happen when this day came, I really didn't really want to,' said Lionel, after a fortifying breath. 'The thought of saying goodbye to her wasn't something I wanted even to contemplate, but she was most adamant that it would be played out to her script. She even ordered the sunshine.' A slight ripple of laughter from the assembled mourners. 'Lilian Dearman was the last of a noble line. And she was the greatest of that line. I think you all know the word she reserved for her antecedents.'

'Bastards,' mumbled someone and a flurry of loud *shhh*s ensued.

'Lilian only gave of herself what she wanted others to have. Those who have known her longest, have not necessarily known her the best.' Whether intentional or not, the vicar's eyes drifted to Titus on the front row. 'Lilian Dearman entered this world on January the first 1950, by caesarean section. She was a Dearman and as such was not destined to arrive without drama and ceremony.' A trickle of affectionate laughter at that. 'She was born into a life of privilege and yet it was the simple things that made Lilian tick, those that money cannot buy, which marked her as very different from the rest of her family. When she refused to take part in the Pickering Hunt because foxes deserved better, her father locked her in the tower of the manor for a week for that insubordination, but she never did go hunting.

'Her father labelled her: *imperfection personified*. To that I say *glorious imperfection* –' He shook his fist, his voice now strong as the gesture. 'Lilian Dearman was the most perfectly imperfect woman I ever met. Generous, stupidly so, sweet, kind, principled ... loving. Loving to the ex-racing greyhounds she adopted, loving to people, even loving to things: plants, her home, her books, her collection of mended treasures which she displayed so reverently and she was a faithful and loyal friend—' he hiccupped, stalled, recalibrated, 'and we shall all miss her in our different ways.

'For instance, Cilla, her beloved housekeeper, will miss her insistence that on very hot days, she should abandon the cleaning and go and sit in the garden with Griff. I quote, "Life is too short to be changing beds when the sun makes a rare appearance in this bloody country".' In the front row, Cilla was nodding as if she was a toy full of fresh batteries. 'Emelie will miss their deep and rewarding relationship, David will miss her over-zealous testing of his home-brewed beers, wines and spirits and I will miss the girl whom I've known all my life.' Lionel's voice cracked and he had to pull his handkerchief out of his pocket, taking a few moments both to blow his nose and to compose himself. Then he left the pulpit and approached the coffin, placing his hand gently on the top. 'I invite you all, for a moment, to think of a precious memory of this ... this lady who has been so wonderfully kind to all of us. Our lady of the manor. Lilian.' He dropped his head, and everyone followed his lead and did the same.

Marnie thought of meeting Lilian for the first time in Skipperstone and how the old lady's face had lit up on seeing her. She thought of Lilian flipping the bird out of the window of her Rolls Royce before she zoomed away. She thought of sitting in Lilian's conservatory and hearing stories of her family and thinking – at the essence of it all – how similarly the track of their lives had run. And how it had taken hardly any time at all to fall in love with Lilian Dearman.

They sang the Lord's Prayer, Derek, David and Lionel supplying a perfect bass descant they must have been used to. The echo from the last note hung like smoke in the air.

'Please, friends, people of Wychwell and beyond. Would you follow Lilian into the churchyard where we will say our final goodbyes,' said Lionel.

The pall-bearers appeared and lifted Lilian's coffin onto their shoulders. Griff began to play the jaunty 'Bring Me Sunshine' and people started to sing along with it as they stood up. Lionel followed the coffin out of his church, Titus making sure he was immediately behind him, heading up the temporal procession.

'Lilian's favourite song. She loved Morecambe and Wise,' said Emelie with a smiling sigh and Marnie thought that it was fitting. Lilian Dearman was the sort of person who would bring the sunshine along with her if it wasn't there.

Herv smiled and nodded at her as he passed; Ruby gave her the evil eye. Marnie didn't care, she was looking at the coffin and thinking how surreal it was that her friend lay lifeless within it.

Emelie and Marnie were among the last out. 'Can I hold onto you, dear?' the old lady asked.

'Of course,' said Marnie, crooking her arm and walking slowly in tune with Emelie's pace.

'She didn't want to go in the family crypt underneath the church,' said Emelie. 'She wanted to be outside with the flowers.'

'I can't say I blame her,' said Marnie. 'From what she's told me about them.'

'Dear Lilian,' said Emelie, dabbing at her eyes with her handkerchief. 'I shall miss her so much. She was the best of people. The very very best.'

The sky was blue and cloudless today: the sun had

returned after a week of cloud and drizzle as if it had hon-
oured a diary date to shine down on them all as Lilian's
body was lowered into the ground in a large plot near an
ancient cherry tree. It had flowered late and when the breeze
stirred, the blossom billowed in the air and fell upon the
mourners like confetti.

'Look, it's like the wedding she never had,' said Titus too
loudly. Marnie noticed Lionel casting him a very unchris-
tian look.

With a voice strengthened now by duty, Lionel began the
final goodbye.

'We entrust our beloved Lilian Mathilda Dearman to your
mercy, in the name of Jesus our Lord, who died and is alive
and reigns with you, now and for ever, Amen.'

'Amen,' echoed the crowd.

'Ladies and gentlemen of Wychwell only, if you would
please make your way now up to the manor house for private refreshment and the other business in hand,' Lionel
then announced.

'What's the other business in hand?' Marnie asked, as the
crowd began to disperse.

'The reading of the will. It's Dearman tradition that it
immediately follows the funeral. That was one thing at least
that Lilian hasn't kicked against,' replied Emelie, opening up
her handbag and taking something out.

'Well, I'll walk you up if you like and then disappear.'

'You will not,' said Emelie firmly. 'You are now part of
Wychwell, Marnie. And Lilian thought more of you than
she did of those racing off to see how much richer they will
soon be. I'll catch you up. I just want a few moments to say
my own goodbye to Lilian. Wait for me by the gate, would
you? I won't be long.'

'Of course.' She noticed then that Emelie had a handful of small white flowers. Edelweiss. She knew what they were because she'd been in the school production of *The Sound of Music*. She'd been a grumpy nun. Gabrielle had been Julie Andrews. Her overriding memory of the play was the audience trying not to giggle at her rendition of 'The Lonely Goatherd'. She heard that one of her parents had likened it to the sound of someone being goosed by a giant amorous porcupine.

Standing by the gate, Marnie watched Emelie drop the flowers gently onto the coffin, all the while talking as if Lilian were lying there able to hear her. Then Emelie crossed herself slowly, blew a kiss into the grave, then turned and walked towards her.

Chapter 21

Up at the manor house, there was a buffet on the dining table that would have defeated Henry VIII, and trays full of champagne, or sparkling wine – Marnie's palate wasn't discerning enough to tell. She walked in, glad that Emelie was holding her arm because she might have chickened out otherwise, especially as she heard Kay say to Una, 'What's she doing here?'

'Ignore her, Marnie,' said Emelie. 'Lilian was never fond of the Sweetmans. She called them the Sourmans.' She let loose a childish giggle and it made Marnie chuckle too.

Lionel was heading towards them with two flutes of fizz which he handed to them.

'You did very well, Lionel,' said Emelie. 'It can't have been easy for you.'

'It was the hardest service I've ever led,' replied Lionel. He looked tired, thought Marnie. The whites of his eyes were pink, the usually conker-shiny irises a dull mud colour today.

'It's the end of an era,' said Roger the postmaster, joining them. 'Wonderful service, Lionel. Wonderful. Lilian would have been sad she missed it.'

'She didn't,' said Emelie. 'She was there. We could all feel her.'

'I haven't seen you for a while, Emelie. Someone said they'd seen you posting a parcel in Skipperstone. I hope you aren't being unfaithful to me,' said Roger with a grin.

'Who would say such a thing?' said Emelie, suddenly serious. 'Village people can be such gossips.'

When Roger moved away, Emelie confided in Marnie. 'I did post a parcel in Skipperstone. I didn't want him asking who I was sending things to in London. He can be very nosey.'

A sudden burst of Titus's laughter filled the room, interrupting everyone's conversation.

'All hail the new lord of the manor,' Marnie overheard David say behind her. 'Someone's happy at least. He'll have moved in here by twilight. You mark my words.'

It was obvious to everyone that Titus was counting down the minutes to accepting his title.

Marnie caught sight of Herv at the other side of the room. He looked like a Norse god who had decided to take a job in a bank. He was standing with Ruby who was nibbling delicately on a sandwich enjoying the temporary illusion of being in a couple with him, though it appeared as if he wished he were elsewhere. She watched him scan the room, felt his eyes lock with hers. He waved, he smiled then he made, Marnie presumed, his apologies to Ruby and headed across the room to her. Ruby's expression turned murderous and Marnie thought, *why is it that at every stage of my life I have made so many enemies?* Herv was two steps away from her when Titus cut straight in front of him.

'Herv,' he bellowed so most of the room could hear him. 'I hope you're going to be staying around, at least. I need a good gardener.'

It was as if a bucket of water had been tipped over Marnie's head. She hadn't considered the full extent of what Lilian's death would mean. There would be changes, lots of them. She wouldn't be able to stay in Little Raspberries rent-free for a start. And Lilian herself had said that Titus didn't want strangers in the village. There had been no written rental agreement; he could throw her out tonight if he chose to, unless she decided to sit tight as a squatter.

Marnie slid from the room and into the conservatory where she stood by the window and gazed out at the tranquil lake. She heard again Lilian's account of the day when her father fell into the water trying to scare away a heron and her mother pressed his head under the water with an oar hoping to drown him. There were so many more stories of Lilian's to tell, Marnie hadn't known her long enough at all. And now, all the ones that weren't in her memory or Lionel's book were gone for ever. She was gripped by a sudden sense of it all being so unfair. She had loved and been loved by only two people in her whole life, two old ladies full of fun and joy and kindness. And she had lost them both.

'Marnie, how are you doing?'

She felt Herv's hand on her shoulder, large and warm before he lifted it away abruptly, as if fearing she would shrug it off. She wouldn't have.

'Well . . .' she smiled sadly.

'Of course, stupid question.' He cleared his throat. 'I've been thinking about you but I didn't know . . . if I should . . . leave you alone.'

She really had scared him off that night of the Pink Lady sighting. She'd felt rotten about that since it happened and had the overwhelming urge to tell him that it wasn't the idea of going to the cinema with *him* that had set her off running

like Usain Bolt with a firework up his backside, but *anyone*.
A nice man like him would be better staying away from
such a fuck-up as herself. But here was neither the time nor
the place.

'Thank you, that's very sweet of you but I'm a big girl . . .'

A very big girl now. Her mother's voice came from nowhere.
She ignored it and carried on.

'. . . Anyway, how are *you*, Herv?'

'I don't know,' he replied. There was no sparkle in his blue,
blue eyes today. 'I feel numb, I think. As if something very
significant has gone from my life.'

His shoulders were slumped, weighted with sadness. She
felt the need to reach out to him, comfort him, do something
to convey that they were together in this, but she overcame it.

'I don't want to work for Titus,' Herv went on. 'I think I
shall . . . probably leave soon.'

She wasn't prepared for the effect his words had on her, as
if something had kicked her insides – hard – causing a real
physical pain.

'You can't leave,' she said hurriedly, before collecting
herself, taking a breath. Herv had become as much part of
Wychwell as Lilian's lake and Little Raspberries. He belonged
to it now. 'I mean, that would be a real shame, Herv. You're
happy here. Lilian thought so much about you.'

'And you,' said Herv. 'She loved you. She worried about
you. She asked me to keep an eye on you if anything happened to her.'

Now, say it now, prodded a voice in her head.

'Herv, I'm so sorry about running off from you that night.
It was so rude of me.'

He smiled. 'Don't worry about it. Lilian told me—'

But he didn't get the chance to finish his sentence because

Titus's booming voice cut off his words. 'Come on, everyone, now, into the great lounge. Time for the reading of the will.'

With a gentle hand on her back, Herv marshalled Marnie back into the dining room where they followed the others into the drawing room, newly relabelled by Titus. No doubt he would have new tags for all the rooms by end of play: the conservatory would become the orangery, the dining room would become the grand dining room, the snug would revert to being known as the gentleman's smoking room again. Hilary would probably be banished out of his sight to the ladies' sewing room (i.e. tower) – if she was lucky.

The room had been set with all manner of motley chairs collected from around the house. There weren't two vacant ones together so Marnie ushered Herv forwards to the one Ruby had saved for him and was obviously desperate for him to occupy, if her manic waving was anything to go by, whilst she herself insisted on taking the one in the back corner, next to the cabinet containing Lilian's favourite broken/mended ceramics. She couldn't see a lot of what was going on at the front of the room because her chair seemed to be lower than everybody else's plus she was positioned behind the very large Derek.

The man in the pinstripe suit was standing in front of the beautiful desk by the window. He called loudly for order and all twittering instantly stopped.

'Good afternoon, ladies and gentlemen. For those who haven't seen me before, my name is Falstaff Wemyss of Wemyss, Whitby and Sons, solicitors at law. For those who have seen me before, you will know that it has always been a matter of tradition that the reading of the Dearman will takes place on the day of the funeral. Usually a formality, give or take personal disbursements to the staff.' He unfolded the arms of a pair of gold-rimmed half-moon glasses, put them on to read and, after a throat-clearing cough, got straight down to business.

'The last will and testament of Lilian Mathilda Dearman. To my loyal housekeeper and her family Cilla Oldroyd, I leave the sum of twenty thousand pounds. To my gardener Herv Gunnarsen, I leave the sum of five thousand pounds. To my friend Lionel Alistair Temple I leave the sum . . .' Mr Wemyss broke off, sighed, took off his glasses and gave the arm a quick chew before continuing. 'To my friend Lionel Alistair Temple, I leave the sum of twenty thousand pounds. David Parselow – five thousand pounds, Emelie Tibbs, two thousand pounds, the Maud Haworth home for cats – three thousand pounds, Miss Marnie Salt fifty thousand pounds . . . blah blah.'

The gasp that arose then seemed to suck all the air out of the room. Then chatter, raised voices, mumbles of surprise, shock, anger. Marnie felt heads turn to each other, then further round to seek her out and she wished her chair was even lower. If she had been nearer to the window, she might have jumped out of it. Titus Sutton was on his feet, glaring at her with the full force of his big bulging eyeballs.

'Please sit down, everyone,' said Mr Wemyss, wearily. 'It doesn't really matter what this will says because there isn't any money so I'm afraid no one is getting a penny.'

Titus, having just sat back down, sprang up again. 'What? What are you talking about, Wemyss?' He could barely be heard against the rising babble.

'It's quite simple, I'm afraid. Miss Dearman didn't have any cash.'

'Don't be stupid,' yelled Titus. 'She owned a bloody village.'

'Yes, she did,' replied Mr Wemyss, matching Titus for

volume. 'But she spent her whole personal savings on the upkeep of the said village because the village pot is almost dry. And the said village has been left in its entirety to a person or persons who wish to remain anonymous.'

Even Mr Wemyss was having trouble being heard above the chatter in the room now. 'And that person, in accordance with the wishes of Miss Dearman, has requested that Miss Marnie Salt should manage the estate for them in return for a nominal stipend.'

The level of noise in the room went off the scale. Titus was throwing up his hands in all directions, so much so that he looked as if he were breakdancing.

'WILL YOU PLEASE SIT DOWN AND BE QUIET,' roared Mr Wemyss. 'And that includes you, Mr Sutton.' Like water thrown on a fire, the volume dropped, first to a hiss, then eventual silence.

'Thank you,' said Mr Wemyss. 'Now, as I said, Miss Dearman died virtually penniless. The estate, from what I believe, has been entirely funded by Miss Dearman from her own personal fortune: wages, maintenance et cetera. It will fall to the aforesaid Miss Marnie Salt, as estate manager, to reconstitute the fortunes of Wychwell and restore it to its former self-financing glory. Or as Lilian put it so masterfully in her instructions – *unbugger it up*.'

'I absolutely reject this,' Titus protested loudly.

'I'm afraid you have absolutely no choice in the matter and must legally hand over all records,' said Mr Wemyss, in a voice as calm as Titus's was enraged. 'To withhold them will incur criminal charges,' he added with a warning note.

'Who is the new owner? I insist you stand up,' said Titus, leaping out of his seat yet again to face the villagers and scan the expressions of every one of them for clues.

'As I said, Mr Sutton, the new owner wishes to remain anonymous,' Mr Wemyss repeated, sounding bored now by Titus's big man act.

'How did they know they've inherited it if *this* is the reading of the will?' asked Una Price in a huffy voice.

'I think it's quite obvious that Miss Dearman told them before she died,' replied Mr Wemyss, looking at her over the rim of his glasses as if she were a fly he'd quite like to swat.

Titus was still livid. 'It's outrageous. I shall be seeking legal advice.'

'I *am* the legal advice,' growled Mr Wemyss. 'There are no loopholes, Mr Sutton, so don't be wasting *your* money, for a change.'

'What did you mean by *your money for a change*? What are you insinuating?'

Mr Wemyss, refusing to get into a slanging match, especially with a man he was delighted to see in a delicious state of hubris, lifted up his brown battered briefcase, said a parting 'Good day to you all,' strolled down the aisle in the middle of the chairs but turned right to reach over to Marnie in order to hand her his business card before he walked out through the door.

'Miss Salt, please ring my office at your earliest convenience for a meeting.'

If Marnie had come to Wychwell to escape bad feeling, judging by the sea of eyes trained hard on her now, she couldn't have made a worse move if she'd tried.

Chapter 22

There was no oxygen in the room. Marnie needed to get out. She could feel her head grow light. She saw Kay Sweetman's mean mouth twisting, heard Titus shouting over that he wanted 'a word with you, lady', then Lionel telling him to calm down. Una's jaw was moving ten to the dozen as she stood with her arms crossed indignantly over her bosom and though Marnie couldn't hear what words she was dispensing, she would have bet none of them were congratulatory. Marnie pushed her chair back and half-sprinted from the room. How could everyone hate her for something she'd had thrust on her? How was any of this her fault? She hadn't inherited the damned village, but whoever had had made her the scapegoat. She wanted quiet and a comfortable spot in the background and this . . . this . . . *git* had dragged her into an ice-cold lime-light. Why her? She didn't want any complications; she just wanted to make cheesecakes three times a week in peace and read books about sexy lords of the manor and what they got up to in their cellars. Actually, she wasn't sure she wanted to do that any more. Even the word 'manor' at the moment was enough to make her throw up.

She was at the front door when she heard Herv's voice behind her, calling her name. Seems he was taking Lilian's request to 'keep an eye on her' seriously.

'Are you all right?' he asked.

The stupid question to end all stupid questions. 'Not really, seeing as you ask,' she snapped and felt bad for that. Again.

'Come on, I'll walk you home.'

Her legs were shaking. She didn't realise how much until her feet touched the gravel path and she stumbled, righting herself just in time. She willed herself not to faint on Herv Gunnarsen or fall flat on her face Elena-style in front of him. Then again, how much worse could today get?

'Slow down, I can't keep up,' said Herv. She slowed, even though she wanted to get into Little Raspberries as soon as possible. She couldn't think of anything to say to him as they walked side by side, until he asked the question that must have been on everyone's lips.

'Marnie, are you the new owner?'

Marnie halted abruptly and twisted to face him. 'No, I am not. Is that what they think? That I've inherited the manor and conjured up this ... charade for ... whatever reason. I don't know what that could be.'

'Hey, it doesn't matter if you are. It was Lilian's to leave to whoever—'

'It's not me, Herv. I didn't know about any of this. I don't even know what it means.' Marnie started walking again and Herv jogged at her side.

'You have no idea who it is?'

'No idea at all. I presumed it would be Titus who inherited the manor. Like everyone else did. Including Titus.' She rolled her eyes. 'Who would do this to me?' Second in line to inheriting must be Lionel, she reasoned. But he would be perfectly capable of managing the estate himself and wouldn't need someone else to do it for him.

'Someone who values you, obviously,' said Herv.

'Is it though, Herv? I've worked in business and I know that people hire someone to do all the dirty work so they can keep their hands clean. Then they get rid of them.' An idea came to her that – stupidly – she hadn't considered yet. 'I won't do it. I'll tell Mr Wemyss, I refuse to do it. No one can make me. Then I won't have to worry about people throwing bricks at my window.'

They were steps away from Little Raspberries.

'Do you want me to come inside with you for a little while?' Herv asked.

'Absolutely not,' replied Marnie, scrabbling in her bag for her keys. 'Thank you but I want to be by myself.' She spoke to him in a tone he didn't deserve. She dropped the key and Herv reached down for it. He was as calm as she was all over the place. He'd be a rock in a crisis, she knew. Everything Lilian said he would be and more.

'Here let me.' He opened the door for her and she knew he was concerned that she was a jittery mess of shock and confusion. But she couldn't cope with kindness. Not today. She wouldn't know how to handle it.

'I'm sorry. Thanks for the offer, but I really need to be alone,' she said.

'It's okay,' he said, his voice gentle, understanding.

She shut the door hard on him as if he represented the whole traitorous world and she wondered how she would keep the scream spiralling up within from breaking out and shattering all the glass within a five-mile radius.

'What next?' she shouted skyward. 'What else have you got in store for me?'

Her phone chose that moment to vibrate in her handbag. She took it out to find a message from a number she recognised immediately.

> **Just in case you've erased my number it's Justin. Can we talk. Please.**

She didn't reply to the message, but her brain did anything but ignore it. It obsessed on why he had contacted her, what he wanted from her, what must have been going through his mind. She told herself that she didn't care about what he might be feeling, but she was lying and she knew it. She didn't trust herself to reply to it. Not at the moment. She wished she could get a ticket to another planet, away from Justin effing Fox, Titus Sutton, wills, manors ... everything.

She poured herself a glass of water, forced herself to take a breath, then flipped open her laptop. Then she took Mr Wemyss's business card out of her handbag and wrote him an email.

```
Dear Mr Wemyss
    Re: managing the Dearman estate.
    Thank you but I think the new anonymous owner
has made a mistake. I will not be accepting the
position. Please tell them to find someone else.
    Yours very sincerely
    Marnie Salt
```

She had no compunction about pressing the send button. There was no waver of indecision present in her index finger. Problem solved. The owner would soon know that she had no intention of being the public whipping boy and the rest might soon realise that the title of village upstart had been thrust on her and that she had not sought it.

Why was this all turning into such a mess?

She locked the door, uncorked a bottle of Lionel's strawberry wine and poured herself a large glass. But before she took her first sip, she made sure her laptop was out of reach because the last thing she wanted to do was get blasted and start up a conversation with anyone else on a cheesecake site.

Chapter 23

Marnie awoke with a brass band playing in her head. Ironically she'd just had the one glass of wine the previous night to avoid a hangover and instead found that a stress headache par excellence had taken up residence in her skull leaving no room for thought; which would have been good if the thump hadn't been so relentless and painful. She had some ibuprofen, pressed a cold cloth against her forehead and tried to sleep some more. She ignored the insistent vibration coming from her mobile phone until it began to annoy her too much. She expected to see Justin's number flash up but the missed calls and four voicemails were all from a landline that she didn't recognise. She pressed to hear the first message, expecting to hear either an automated one about PPI or news of a consumer survey, and got ready to hit the roof.

Message 1: (woman's voice) Gerry, it says to leave a message. Should I leave one or ring back or try again later. (man's voice in the background) Ring her back later.

Message 2: (woman's voice after very long pause) I should leave a message, Gerry. Oh hello. Is this recording? This is . . . (cut off)

Message 3: (woman's voice in style of robot from *Doctor Who*) This is Jean Smith and this is a message for Gabri— . . . no for Marnie, daughter of Judith Salt. Can you ring me back please?

Message 4: (woman's voice) Oh hello. I left a message. It's Jean Smith and I live next door to your mum Judith Salt. I got your number from her address book. I forgot to leave my number it's . . . (cut off)

Marnie sat up and rang the number stored in her 'recent calls'. A man answered almost immediately, reciting the house number clearly and precisely as people of a certain generation do. She presumed this was 'Gerry'.

'Oh hello, this is Marnie Salt. I think it must have been your wife who left me a message' *(or twelve)* 'on my voicemail asking me to get in touch.'

'Ah yes. Marnie. I'll just pass over . . . er, pass you over to Jean.'

Marnie waited patiently for Gerry to convey to Jean who was on the phone, then slightly more impatiently when Jean seemed to take forever to pick up the receiver and start speaking.

'Hello, Marnie, I hope you don't mind that I rang you,' Jean said at last. 'I didn't think it was right, you see. I wasn't sure that you knew. I had a feeling that she hadn't told you.'

What was the bloody woman on about, thought Marnie, who was really not in the mood for any of this encrypted bollocks. 'I'm not with you, Mrs Smith. What do you mean?'

'Oh, you don't know, do you? Gerry, she doesn't know. I knew it. I'm sorry to have to tell you on the phone, Marnie but it's your mother. She died last Wednesday.'

*

Life was an unfeeling bastard, to coin Lilian's favourite word, thought Marnie. It had no sense of occasion, no duty of care. It didn't consider that two deaths in one week might be a bit much for anyone. Especially when they were the deaths of two such significant women in her life, albeit for very different reasons. One had done her best to trample her underfoot, the other to reconstitute the broken pieces. One she had known all her life, one she had known for just a small part of it, yet it was upon the news of Lilian's death that her heart had cracked more. Marnie received the news that her mother had died with a strange objectiveness that worried her greatly. She should have been thrown into chaos as other daughters would have been, surely? What sort of person did that make her, that she had cried harder over a woman she barely knew? She didn't want to be that person. She wanted to be upset and hurt and be like everyone else.

Marnie rang her sister and whilst she waited for her to pick up, her anger started to grow and that was good because at least she was feeling something.

'Hello.'

'Gabrielle, it's Marnie.'

Silence.

'Gabrielle?'

'Oh.'

That small word was loaded with the weight of many more.

'I've had a call from the woman who lives next door to Mum.' Silence at the other end. 'Gabrielle, are you still there?'

'Yes, I'm here. I presume you've heard, then.'

'About my mother dying, yes, funnily enough I have. When were you going to tell me? Don't you think I had a right to know that my mother had died?'

More silence before Gabrielle answered. 'Look, where are you living? Mum said you'd moved.'

'I'm in the Dales.' *Was this really happening?* 'I'll drive down now. It'll take me two hours.'

'I can't meet you today. I've got a business engagement I can't miss. I'll meet you tomorrow at the house. I'll text you the time.'

And there the conversation ended. And Marnie was left in no doubt why she had no template for a normal relationship with anyone.

By the early afternoon, she had packed a suitcase, driven away from Wychwell and booked herself into a Premier Inn five miles from Penistone. A place where the receptionist smiled at her as she handed over the key to the room and the waitress was nice to her in the restaurant. They didn't know her as a village pariah or the black sheep of the family. She needed that anonymity today as much as she needed oxygen.

Marnie cried in the room, not because her mother had died but because she was the sort of daughter who hadn't cried when she'd heard that her mother had died. They were tears of confusion and self-loathing.

She had a long drawn out dinner to kill time, watched a film, had a bath. The next morning she had a long drawn out breakfast and read a Sunday paper at the table, though she absorbed little of its content. Gabrielle had texted her to say she would be there at the family home at twelve. Marnie got there to find Gabrielle's Porsche in the drive – top of the range, obviously, complete with personalised number plate. Things her mother would have taken as proof that Gabrielle was a good and successful daughter.

The front door was unlocked; Marnie walked straight in

to find her sister putting crockery into boxes. The room was almost stripped bare. Gabrielle had the grace to look startled as if she were a burglar disturbed by the house owner.

Other sisters might have run to each other seeking comfort, but there wasn't only a lot of water under the bridge between the Salt sisters, there were a few islands, an oil rig and a heavily armed Checkpoint Charlie border complete with armed guards as well.

'I was going to tell you,' were Gabrielle's first words. 'Mum left instructions with me what to do if she died. I had to respect them.'

Marnie matched her for cold, barely concealed hostility. 'Well the lady next door thought I had a right to know sooner than you obviously did. And being the elder child, I would tend to agree with her.' She waited for Gabrielle to give her the 'you weren't her child' speech and didn't know what she would do if that happened. She'd heard it too many times to tolerate it again. This time might very possibly result in a thump.

'Nosey old cow. It wasn't any of her business,' snapped Gabrielle, putting a Himalayan salt lamp into a black plastic bag. It was still boxed and sealed with a round sticker. Marnie's Christmas present to her mother. 'Mum had her own way of doing things and she shouldn't have interfered.'

'I could at least have helped you pack things up,' said Marnie.

'I can manage.'

Marnie knew why she hadn't asked. Gabrielle would have made a beeline up to their mother's bedroom for the jewellery. She needn't have worried, Marnie didn't want any of it.

'What happened to her?' asked Marnie.

'She had a heart attack on Wednesday. Massive, apparently. She wouldn't have suffered. Nosey Jean next door found her.

She had a key. She knocked to see if Mum wanted some vegetables from their allotment and when she didn't answer the door, she let herself in.'

'I see.'

'She rang me because she had my number in case of emergencies. I said I'd ring you.'

'But you didn't.'

Gabrielle let go of a long annoyed breath before answering that. 'I was going to ring you the day before the funeral.'

'Which is when?'

'Tuesday. So I would have rung you tomorrow to inform you of the arrangements.' Now she was packing a stack of saucers and putting them in a box. It was all so laughably matter of fact. As if they were talking about going to see a play.

'And would you have? Had Mrs Smith not told me?'

Now Gabrielle stopped what she was doing and scowled at Marnie.

'Of course I would have. What do you take me for?'

Best not answered, thought Marnie. She looked around the kitchen. The oven, the washing machine and the fridge weren't there any more, she noticed.

'It's all gone to charity, as she requested, in case you're wondering,' said Gabrielle, following the track of her eyes. 'Oh, and I've put a red box in the garage next to the others you left. It's got some stuff of yours in it.'

'What sort of stuff?'

'I don't know. Just stuff. Photos, school books. The door's open. The house is going up for sale this week so you'd better move them sooner rather than later.'

'You're not hanging about, are you?' Marnie gave a mirthless laugh.

'Is there any point in doing that?'

'I'll take them with me now.'

'The service is at the crematorium at eleven. The car is leaving from Benson's funeral parlour on Summer Street at quarter to. There will be refreshments there after the service. I've arranged everything as she wished. She didn't want flowers apart from a customary display on her coffin and I've ordered that. I'll send you a cheque for your due when the house has been sold after I've paid off the funeral costs and whatever else is owed.'

What could she say? She was as excluded in her mother's death as she had been in her life. 'I'll go and get my boxes,' said Marnie, defeated.

'Don't spoil it, Marnie. For once, please don't spoil things for her,' Gabrielle appealed to her, just before the door closed. Marnie didn't answer.

*

Marnie rang Mrs Abercrombie and told her that her Monday delivery wasn't going to happen because her mother had died. Mrs Abercrombie said she was very sorry to hear that and would the Wednesday delivery be there as normal. If so, could she add four pina colada cheesecakes to the order. Marnie said of course. She understood there was little sentiment in business.

Marnie stayed at the Premier Inn for a second night and booked in for a third. She went to Meadowhall and bought a black outfit because she hadn't brought one with her. She trailed around the shops rolling the thought around in her head that she was buying a dress for her mother's funeral and was both fascinated and perturbed by her detachment.

A therapist might have put it down to shock, she hoped. Or that it was a natural consequence of how she had been treated.

She had never felt loved by Judith and yet she'd been brought up in a house where the love for her sister had been so thick in the air it had choked her like smoke sometimes. She'd known that from an early age. She couldn't even remember a time before it. Judith had fed her, clothed her, covered all her material needs. She had gone to parents' evenings, made sure she did her homework and brushed her teeth, but it all felt as if she were going through the motions rather than actually caring. Marnie had been naughty sometimes, just to claim notice, attention – negative was better than nothing. She'd poured her love onto toys but teddy bears didn't cuddle back, dolls didn't reciprocate kisses. She'd got used to love being one-way traffic.

She awoke very early the next morning with her pillow wet from the tears that leaked from her eyes as she dreamt. Her mother, features softened with affection, was holding out her arms for Marnie to run to. But she was older and her accent tinged with a Scots burr.

'Ma wee Marnie. I've always loved you. I never knew how to show it, but I did. I really did.'

Dreams could lie so cruelly sometimes.

Chapter 24

For the second time that week, Marnie stood in front of the mirror checking her reflection, dressed in black. But on the first occasion she hadn't considered wearing a white suit and kicking against convention. A white suit and long black hair, a two-fingered statement against all those blondes in black suits that she would encounter today. A white bullet-proof vest might have been a good idea too. Her mother's funeral congregation would be full of poison-leakers hissing behind Marnie's back like the nest of vipers they were. *What poor Judith had to put up with. Thank goodness she had St Gabrielle the Immaculate Contagion in her corner.* Today of all days, Marnie had to keep her dignity intact, her head held high, her trap well and truly shut. They would be waiting en masse for the black sheep of the Salt family to ruin her mother's interment and she would not give them the satisfaction.

Marnie had dressed carefully: mid-calf plain dress, long jacket – also plain. Shoes: demure heel, hair pinned up in an artful but not too showy bun, no hat. Make up, subtle. No bright red lips that a wayward daughter might choose to hint at subversion, but rose pink. Never had it been so important to strike the right balance between respectful and classy.

She arrived at the funeral parlour at ten-thirty. Gabrielle was already there, along with a man Marnie didn't recognise. Her sister's usual type: older and no Prince Charming, smart clothes, moneyed, if the penis-extension convertible in the car park was anything to go by. He introduced himself as Duncan, Gabrielle's fiancé, which came as a surprise but Marnie didn't bother to ask how long they'd been affianced. His handshake was limply polite, indicating that he already knew her by reputation.

Judith's coffin was in position in the back of the hearse with a modest cross of white flowers on it, as befitted someone who went to church every Sunday and paraded herself as the good Christian, charitable woman she was. 'Her organs might not have been worth donating but people would have benefitted from her quality clothes and white goods.' She'd have enjoyed the congregation talking about her like that in absentia.

Gabrielle made sure she herself occupied the middle back seat in the limousine. Marnie wondered if that was to keep her away from Duncan; her sister needn't have worried on that score.

Marnie felt her nervous levels ratchet up when the car reached the crematorium. There were a lot of people clustered outside the doors. She spotted Uncle Barry – her mother's brother – and his wife, Auntie Diana, in the midst of them and she felt her jaw tighten with tension. Towards the end of the 1990s, Judith hadn't spoken to them for two full years. Marnie's fault again, obviously. Marnie had hoped she would never see either of them again. On the lists of people for whom she was *persona non grata*, she was in indisputable first place on theirs.

Marnie kept her head up and her eyes resting on no one as she followed the coffin down the central aisle of the crematorium chapel. A CD was playing classical music as people filed to their seats. It would have been chosen to impress rather than it being meaningful. Something like 'Bring Me Sunshine'.

The young smooth-faced vicar gave a resumé of Judith's life. He filled everyone in on where she was born and went to school and how she liked to knit squares for blankets to be shipped out to Africa even as a child. He said that she had an older brother called Barry; he didn't mention that he was a twat. He said that Judith was very much in love with her husband Tony and that marriage was blessed with a daughter and an adopted daughter but sadly it was not to last. He didn't say that Tony ran off to shag half of Thailand and that he'd never laid eyes on his real child. They sang 'The Lord Is My Shepherd' and Gabrielle folded, turning to Duncan for comfort as she dabbed at her eye with a delicate handkerchief so she wouldn't smudge her eyeliner. Marnie's composure slipped on the second verse and she didn't know if it was because she was genuinely emotional or because it was a sad hymn with beautiful words which were renowned for making people cry.

When the vicar asked them all to sit and think of their fondest memory of Judith Salt, Marnie tried her best to conjure up a time when she had felt like the true daughter of a mother. In thirty-two years there had to be something. She raked desperately through her memory banks and came up with nothing but that perpetual feeling of being on the cold outside of a family she should have been part of, of her Christmas presents being a much smaller pile next to Gabrielle's. Of being told that no she couldn't have a birthday party like her sister because no one would come. She had no recollection of being cuddled when she fell, of her mother's joy when she had achieved something: her gold survival badge in swimming, a certificate for the perfect mark in a French exam, first place in a teenage cake-baking competition. Not one.

When the curtains closed and 'Eine Kleine Nachtmusik' started up, Gabrielle began to wail. Marnie wanted to wail, she wanted to feel so much emotion that she out-wailed her sister. But if she had, she would have been accused of attention-seeking, so she could only sit and murmur a message in silence. *Rest in peace, Judith. I wish you could have loved me. I wanted you to so much.*

Chapter 25

She should have gone home after the service, she really should. She should have listened to her intuition and as soon as the limo dropped her back at the funeral parlour, she should have taken her car keys out of her bag and driven straight to Little Raspberries. But she didn't. Instead she bowed to convention and joined the others in the funeral home function room to partake of finger food and small talk, because she wanted to prove to those people who had expected her not to do her duty by her mother – 'adoptive mother' as the vicar had so made the distinction – that they were going to be disappointed.

There was a generous buffet with accompanying tea and coffee. No booze, because Judith didn't drink, apart from sips of communion wine that is.

Her mother's neighbours Jean and Gerry Smith were there and said hello to Marnie and how sorry they were for her loss. They were nice people, friendly and she was grateful to them for rescuing her from feeling like a spare prick at a wedding. Jean said that she hoped she hadn't caused any trouble in ringing her and Marnie assured her that she had done the right thing. The vicar came over to shake her hand and deliver the stock phrase that he too was sorry for her loss. He also, on the quiet, apologised for having said that she was adopted and that it was a directive he should have overridden. Marnie was appreciative of that disclosure and said that it was fine. She understood.

A lady from the church came over to introduce herself and said that she hadn't realised Judith had a second daughter, which was telling but not unexpected. She said that Judith's washing machine had been given a lovely new home. The recipient – her neighbour – had been very thankful. The conversation wasn't exactly thrilling but Marnie was glad of it and chatted about the banal with her until their tea cups were drained. Up to that point, all had been well. Marnie stuck to mingling with strangers with whom she could chit-chat superficially. She'd stay until people started to leave, she decided, and not give anyone cause to comment that she had been the first to go.

She tried to ignore her Aunt Diana who, with her scowl and stabby pointing in her direction, was making her best attempts to make sure Marnie knew she was the subject of a character assassination. Marnie knew that her aunt would have enjoyed nothing better than for Judith's renegade 'daughter' to create a scene, thus fulfilling Diana's prediction that she *would* create a scene. All the more reason for Marnie not to bite and behave impeccably. Aunt Diana was the world's biggest snob and had never forgiven Marnie for puncturing the illusion of her perfect world. Even after all those years, the fires of her hatred were still burning, and the feeling was mutual. Aunt Diana had been cruel to her. Cruel and unfair. In her attempt to preserve her ego, she had tried to destroy Marnie's.

The vicar began to make his goodbyes. Marnie took that as a cue to prepare to say hers. She started to walk towards Gabrielle and swanky Duncan but who should cut in front of her but her Aunt Diana and her big black feathery fascinator that sat on her head like a dead crow.

'Wait long enough and a bad penny will turn up,' Diana snarled. Having been denied a reaction earlier, she'd decided to hit Marnie directly with her cattle prod of confrontation. From the blast of her flammable breath, it was obvious Aunt Diana had been swigging from the silver hip flask of vodka she had always kept in her handbag. Marnie had known about her secret drinking since she was a child. Everyone knew about Diana's secret drinking because the more she drank, the more her accent turned into Princess Anne's. As worst-kept secrets go, it was right up there with Liberace's being gay.

'Excuse me,' said Marnie, politely side-stepping her. But Aunt Diana wasn't having that. She caught Marnie's arm in a death grip and halted her step.

'You were the worst thing that ever happened to the family. You were never part of it,' she said through clenched teeth.

The hairs on the back of Marnie's neck began to stand to attention. She really did need to get out of here.

'She wouldn't have had a heart attack if it hadn't been for you.' Diana's voice was rising. 'The strain you put her under all your life. It killed her. You killed her, you little bitch.'

'Let go of my arm now,' said Marnie, enunciating each word clearly so there could be no misunderstanding.

'You think you are something, don't you?' Diana growled, like an evil entity from a Stephen King film.

'I won't tell you again, get off my arm, Diana.' Marnie said, hanging onto her cool by the fingertips.

'Oh, you're threatening me now are you?' said Diana, loudly so that everyone could hear.

'What's going on here?' Uncle Barry strode over as if he were The Rock. Close up, Marnie could see that the years hadn't been kind to him. Or rather he hadn't been kind to himself, because the ridiculous comb-over of too-brown hair put twenty years on him rather than the intended effect of taking them off. He'd never been a looker but she didn't think he had that far to drop.

Despite the fact that his wife had her claw stuck into Marnie, it was to his niece that he addressed the question. 'What are you up to?'

'This little scrubber is pretending she's better than us all now,' scoffed Diana.

'What?' snapped Marnie in disbelief.

Diana laughed. 'She's baking buns for a living and she thinks she's Raymond Blanc.' She pronounced it as 'blank' but it still punched Marnie's pride right in the motherboard.

She levered Diana's hand off and Diana yelped dramatically. 'Did you see that? She stuck her nails into me.'

Then Gabrielle appeared, with Duncan and his hand-made shoes.

'What's going on?' she said, a tremor of panic evident in her voice.

'Diana's pissed, Barry's turned into He-Man and I'm going home,' said Marnie. 'You know where I am if you need anything.'

Gabrielle's face started to crease into tearless distress. 'I knew you'd spoil it. I've been waiting for you to start all day.'

'For the record, they started on me, Gabrielle,' said Marnie, adding under her breath, *'Where's Jeremy Kyle and his lie-detector when you need him.'*

'Don't let her upset you, love,' said Uncle Barry, pulling Gabrielle into his shoulder. His head twisted nastily towards Marnie. 'Go on, get out. You've done what you always do, ruin it. I see the years haven't changed things. Once a liar, always a liar.'

Liar.

If any word could have sprung the lock on Marnie's self-control, it was that one. She could have taken the sneers, the asides, the withering looks. But not that word. Not now when she was a grown-up who could fight back. This time she wasn't going to be sent away to the naughty step to think on her actions.

'Liar?' she threw the word back at her uncle.

'She's trying to cause another family rift, as if one wasn't enough,' Diana announced to the room. 'I didn't speak to poor Judith for years because of this one.' She pointed to Marnie as if she were exhibit A and years of repressed anger and injustice started to fizz up inside Marnie as if she were a shaken-up bottle of warm cola. It wouldn't be settled. There was only one way for it to go and that was out.

'You didn't speak to poor Judith for years because of *this one*!' Marnie yelled back at her aunt but her finger was extended towards Barry. 'Yes, this piece of shit that you accused me of trying to seduce.' She took a leaf out of her aunt's book and addressed the slack-jawed audience. 'Yes, ladies and gentle-men, this paragon of virtue, this fine specimen of manhood standing before you – my Uncle Barry – who said to his fourteen-year old niece "It's fine, it's not as if we're related, is it?" and "It's not as if you're a virgin".'

Marnie turned on her aunt then, who strangely wasn't so vocal any more. 'And you know exactly what you saw, however much your booze-addled brain tried to convince you otherwise. And so you know why I kneed him in his scrawny bollocks. Because he's a letch, a perv, a sex-pest, a dirty, filthy paed—'

'Get out,' screamed Gabrielle, tearing herself away from Uncle Barry whose head was growing so red it was in danger of melting his comb-over. 'No man could ever resist you, could they, that's what you think, isn't it? You're the disgusting one. You ruined my life because you couldn't keep your knickers on.'

'You spoilt, evil, little . . .' As Marnie stepped forward with her fists clenched in hard knots, the whole of the Salt family, including the despicable in-laws, closed around her sister in a defensive wall. The moment crystallised, and Marnie felt the tenuous thread between herself and that loathsome cluster break. She had never been one of them, would never be one of them. Why had it ever been on her list of aspirations?

'I think it would be better if you left,' said Duncan, his voice level but hostile.

'So do I,' said Marnie. The walk to the door was a matter of twelve steps but it felt like twelve hundred.

'I never, *never* want to see or hear from you again,' bawled Gabrielle as Marnie opened the door.

'Fucking ditto,' Marnie threw back over her shoulder.

'And I'm not sending you any of Mum's money. She told me not to give you any anyway,' screeched the woman who had been her sister.

'Stick the money up your arse, Gabrielle. Or buy yourself a personality. Either way, I don't bloody care.'

The fresh air felt like the first breath of oxygen after emerging from a sealed box. Her whole body was shaking with rage, with upset, with emotions she couldn't untangle.

She stalled the car in her eagerness to set off and knew

she wasn't fit to drive. Her plastered Aunt Diana would be safer on the road. The young vicar knocked on her window and scared the bejesus out of her. He asked if she was all right and though she said she was, it was an obvious fib. He invited her to follow him to the vicarage and have a cup of tea and a chat and his kindness brought tears to her eyes that her mother's death hadn't. She declined and said that she wanted to go home but she appreciated his concern, and she really did. She would probably have crashed if he hadn't taken those few minutes to help calm her and make her realise that the whole world wasn't on her back.

She pulled in at the first café she came to on the A1 and ordered a coffee and sat down in a booth sipping it and thinking, pulling apart what had just happened but as usual, where her family were concerned, it didn't make much sense. Her aunt had always looked down on them all. She wanted to the be the one the Joneses kept up to. She lived a life of show and illusion: a brand-new Range Rover on the drive – bought on HP; dressing room full of Jacques Vert whilst her visa bill was in quintuple figures. Double-fronted detached house with ornamental pond – crippling second mortgage. Golf and Rotary club membership, hob-nobbing with councillors – the fur coat and no knickers brigade. They went on a yearly cruise on a cheap inside cabin yet bragged to all and sundry that they'd booked a suite and had dined at the Captain's table. They'd polished out the stains on the veneer of their marriage by editing the manuscript of their life. Fourteen-year-old Marnie Salt – no blood relation – had come on to her uncle and the subsequent rejection of her advances had induced her to knee him in his knackers. Even the fact that Diana had witnessed her husband's hand slipping down the front of his niece's shirt, a second before she turned into the

Karate Kid, hadn't made any difference. If anything, it made matters worse, because Marnie had to be quashed completely for the truth to go away. Obliterated.

It hadn't been the first time his hands had wandered, either. Marnie had managed to jump away from him before, but he'd caught her off-guard that day as she was concentrating hard, sitting at the table doing her maths homework, trying to catch up with all the work she'd missed. *Come on, love. It's not as if you're a virgin, is it?* And though there had been two years of non-communication between her mother and Barry, Judith had said to her once – after they had finally been reconciled – 'I *know* my brother, Marnie. And he would *not* have been capable of such a disgusting act.' Lying to herself was always more preferable than believing uncomfortable truths.

Lilian's voice came to her as she looked at the bill for the coffee, 'Your family are shits of the highest order, Marnie.' And Marnie laughed and a tear escaped from her eye at the same time. Still, there was a bright side to today, she never had to see Uncle Barry or Aunt Diana again. Or Gabrielle. She knew she wouldn't be invited to the wedding, and what a relief that was. She couldn't wait to tell Lil—

Just for a second there, she imagined going back to the manor, sitting in Lilian's lovely conservatory with the view of the lake and telling her old friend about what had happened today. She wouldn't be able to demonstrate to her the smacked-arse expression on her Aunt Diana's face when she'd hit her with both barrels from the home truths gun. They would never again put the world to rights over a slice of cheesecake and a glass of Lionel's raspberry wine. She knew as the days passed she would feel the loss of Lilian far more than she ever would her mother. Lilian, who had made her feel as if she really were the person she'd always wanted to be. Lilian who had given her a home that she had settled into as surely as if it had been a nest custom-built around her. Lilian who had decided, along with the new owner of her beloved Wychwell that she – Marnie Salt – was the person who should manage the estate, rescue it, *unbugger it up,* and love it as she had done.

She'd do it.

If she was going to be disliked, it might as well be for a good and worthy reason. She would pat Wychwell back into shape for Lilian, whatever it took to do it. She went to her car, took out Mr Wemyss's business card and rang him to tell him as much.

Chapter 26

Unknown to Marnie, the previous night there had been a meeting in the Lemon Villa. The whole village had been summoned – except for Marnie, but then it looked as if she wasn't at home anyway. Her car hadn't been there since Saturday but sadly, it appeared to Kay Sweetman that she hadn't done a moonlight flit because she could still see her things in Little Raspberries when she peered through the window.

Titus, who had called the gathering, obviously took charge. Everyone sat around the table in his dining room; Hilary and Pammy Parselow bustled around distributing refreshments to everyone before it started. For those who had not been in the Lemon Villa before, it was quite eye-opening how opulent the interior was. *Homes and Gardens* magazine perfect. There were no damp patches on the walls or draughty windows for Titus and Hilary Sutton.

Titus knocked on the table with his teaspoon to stop all the twittering.

'I thought we should have a formal meeting in the light of . . . recent events.' He chose his words carefully. 'I can see absolutely no reason why the new owner of Wychwell has decided to stay anonymous. Can we all swear that none of us around this table is Lilian's chosen heir?'

'I think that is unfair to ask,' said Lionel, immediately bringing suspicion to his door. 'They have no obligation to declare themselves. Whoever he or she is has done so for a reason.'

'What possible reason can there be?' asked Kay Sweetman.

'There is only one reason and that is because they don't want to. We are therefore forced to accept that. Besides, they have delegated the running of the estate to Miss Salt,' replied Lionel. 'It is her we will have to deal with respecting any village matters.'

'I think it is her,' said Ruby. 'Then if she does something unpopular, she can just fend off any blame on "the new owner".' She drew two emphatic quote marks in the air.

There was a nodding of heads at that and low grumbles of agreement.

'But who is to say that it is someone who lives in Wychwell?' asked Herv. 'Maybe Lilian decided to leave it to someone outside the village.'

'Who? Margaret Kytson?' scoffed Titus, causing Kay to humour him with a chortle.

'Maybe Margaret had a descendant we don't know about,' put in Hilary. 'Lilian was always so keen to make amends for what had happened to her at the hands of her ancestors.'

'Go and fill up the teapots, Hilary,' said Titus dismissively. 'What a ridiculous imagination you have.'

Hilary coloured and Lionel, angered by Titus's put-down of his wife was driven to defend her.

'I don't think it's ridiculous at all. Lilian was fascinated by family trees. She and I worked on her own for years. She may have discovered something that hasn't yet come to full light.'

'Or maybe someone is about to sell our houses from under our feet,' snapped Una.

'They can't sell any houses,' countered David, who didn't say much but when he did, he always spoke considered sense and fact. 'The manor cannot be sold, only inherited. The houses cannot be sold, only rented out by the estate.'

'How come you know so much about it, all of a sudden, David Parselow?' asked Titus with narrowed eyes.

'I thought everyone knew that. It's not rocket science, is it?' David answered. 'Admit it, we've had it far too good for far too long. We pay stupidly cheap rents and between us all we have creamed off the estate and yet here we all are, in a "state of shock"' – he wiggled his fingers in the air as Ruby had done – 'that Lilian has been subsidising us all out of her own money for years.'

'But we didn't know that, David,' said Roger.

'Oh come on, Roger, how much is the rent on the shop and your flat above it?'

Roger pursed his mouth, gravely affronted. 'I don't think that's anyone's business but—'

'Okay, I'll tell you what I pay on the pub. I pay twenty pounds a month. And I've always paid that. My father paid even less. And that covers all my heating, my water, my rates, any maintenance. And because I hardly have any customers, I also get a business stipend from the estate – a loyalty payment, as she called it. I hold my hands up' – and he did, physically – 'I didn't question it. I didn't go to Lilian and say that she should put my rent up and stop paying me a bonus. I took it because it was offered and I believed that the estate was so rich it could afford to do that.'

'I don't think that Marnie pays anything on Little Raspberries,' sniffed Una. 'From what I gather . . .'

'I don't think she's the only one who doesn't pay rent though, is she?' asked Lionel, his voice rising, his eyes sweeping across everyone in the room. Kay Sweetman lowered her head immediately. 'For a start, half the cottages in Wychwell are standing empty and have done for years since their residents died and so they're bringing in no revenue whatsoever.'

'No one who stays in Little Raspberries has ever paid rent,' put in Alice Rootwood, who lived in Orange House and had always thought that they'd had it too good to believe.

'Precisely,' Lionel went on. 'It's a charity cottage, given to whoever needed it: Jessie Plumpton and before her my great uncle Jack. And I happen to know that it sits very heavily with Marnie that she lives there rent-free, but it was Lilian's cottage to let it to Marnie on whatever grounds she chose. And that was their private business, not ours.'

'How do you know all this, with respect, Mr Temple?' asked Ruby, her veneer of politeness stretched thin over a depth of annoyance. 'She's only been in the village for two minutes and suddenly she's the flavour of the month.'

Emelie made a nervous cough. 'I think you are being unfair, Ruby,' she said. 'Lilian knew her very well and they were incredibly fond of each other.'

'It's very easy to be fond of someone when you know they own a manor and are ill,' Ruby threw back. 'Don't you thi—'

'Marnie isn't like that at all,' Herv cut her off, his voice hard. 'Don't make out that their trust in and respect for each other was fake when it wasn't.'

Ruby, doubly wounded by Herv turning on her and defending her arch rival, shrivelled into herself.

'Titus, you did the books for the estate. How was it that you didn't know that Lilian was in so much financial trouble?' asked Emelie, finding her voice now. And her courage.

Titus, annoyed beyond belief that this question could have come from Emelie Tibbs, a woman his father detested and for good reason, managed to overcome his impulse to scream back at her that she shouldn't be here in this meeting, in this village. She shouldn't even be sharing the same air as the rest of them considering what she was, what she came from. He switched on his best patronising smile instead. 'My dear Emelie, what are you inferring?'

'I'm not inferring anything,' she came back at him, mirroring that fake smile. 'I'm merely asking why you didn't see what trouble she was in. Or maybe you did?'

Titus's facade slipped. 'Lilian only let me see what she wanted me to see. I had absolutely no idea of any of this. My family have advised the Dearmans for generations. We are kinfolk. Do you think I would have let this happen if I'd known?'

'Yes, I do,' said Emelie defiantly.

Titus's face coloured. Anticipating a war, Lionel stood up and held out his hands, a gesture of peace.

'Look, let's keep the heat out of this. We have had the meeting as agreed and we are no further forward. We do not know who the new lord or lady of Wychwell is. All we do know is that we are in a mess and Lilian Dearman made plans before she died with this person to place Miss Salt in charge of the estate. We can do nothing other than give her our support and let her get on with trying to rescue the situation. Lilian trusted her and we should do the same.'

'Who is this Miss Salt anyway?' asked old Dr Court. They were the oldest living couple in Wychwell and the possible changes were very worrying to them. 'I mean where has she come from?'

Titus had his suspicions but he wanted to keep that to

himself for now. Until he knew for certain. Until he had checked out a few things.

'Lilian met Marnie on the internet,' said Cilla, merely answering the question and not expecting the uproar that followed.

Johnny Oldroyd didn't say a word though because he'd met his girlfriend through the internet and she was brilliant. Titus, however, took that as being the best possible indicator that Marnie was a crook.

'Lilian wasn't a fool, Titus,' said Lionel, keeping tight rein on his temper. 'She was an insightful judge of character.'

'Aye, great judge of character if she's run off,' huffed Una.

'Marnie will be back, I have no doubt about that. Lilian didn't put her faith in people lightly,' said Lionel, adding to himself *with one most blatant exception* and flicking his eyes towards the odious Titus.

Herv stepped in again. 'What you all may be not taking into consideration is that Marnie and Lilian loved each other. Lilian died in Marnie's arms. I was there, it was terrible for her. She tried to bring Lilian back and failed.'

'How convenient,' tittered Kay Sweetman.

'Please tell me you aren't insinuating that Marnie killed Lilian,' said David.

'Well, if the cap fits.'

'How dare you,' bawled Lionel, with a growl in his voice that none of them had ever heard before. He was joined by others who thought to imply murder was too much and Kay, who'd been expecting a hail of 'hear hears' not jeer jeers found herself shamed into silence.

'If I can continue,' boomed Herv. 'For Marnie to have this trauma and then to discover that she has been landed with a burden of responsibility she was not expecting which would bring with it all this hostility ... well, maybe she needed some time away to sort out her head, as you might say.'

'Well said, Herv,' said Derek, which earned him a thump on his leg from his wife.

'What if she puts our rent up to a thousand pounds a week?' asked Una.

'She can't,' replied Roger. 'Surely? Can she? Titus?'

Titus cleared his throat. 'Well, theoretically, yes she can.'

'There are laws to stop that,' said Ruby.

'Because of the original charter, set up in 1538, Wychwell is not subject to general English law with regards to properties et cetera,' explained Lionel. 'If Miss Salt is in charge, then – with the permission of the owner – she can do as she pleases.'

'And if we all refuse to pay?' said Kay with a defiant twist to her lip.

David Parselow, who wasn't a fan of the Sweetmans, was only too happy to answer her.

'Then we'll all be out on our arses, won't we?'

Chapter 27

Marnie was just lifting the last box out of her car when Lionel Temple arrived at her side.

'Here, let me take that from you. It looks heavy.'

It was the red box full of things which Gabrielle had decided were Marnie's. She hadn't a clue what was in it.

'Thank you,' said Marnie, nudging open the cottage door for him. 'Put it anywhere for now.'

He carried it inside and placed it on the kitchen table. When he turned around, he had a wide, beaming smile on his face.

'You came back,' he said. 'I knew you would.'

'Yep,' said Marnie. 'I did.'

'Tea or coffee, I'm not fussy. Plenty of milk and two sugars, please if you're offering.'

'I'm offering.' Marnie put on the kettle and thought how lovely it was to be back in the cottage. It felt glad to see her again, crazy as it sounded. Warm and welcoming.

'You look very smart,' said Lionel, when Marnie brought two mugs of tea into the lounge. She hadn't had a chance yet to change out of her black suit.

'I've been to a funeral,' said Marnie.

'Not anyone close, I hope.'

'My mother's,' replied Marnie, thinking that at this point a normal person would show some emotion: their voice would crack, their lip would tremble.

'Oh, my dear girl, I'm so sorry,' Lionel sighed heavily. 'I presumed you'd taken some time out for yourself, not that you'd had to endure another death so soon after Lilian's. Are you all right? Can I help you in any way?'

'We didn't get on,' said Marnie, sitting in the large squashy armchair and dragging the small coffee table over so it could serve them both. 'She always regretted adopting me. That's not my imagination, by the way. She told me so plenty of times.'

Lionel shook his head as if stumped for words.

'I know it's a ridiculous thing to say, Lionel, but I was much closer to Lilian than I was to my mother. She unknotted years of shit for me.' Then her hand shot to her mouth and she apologised for swearing.

'Don't,' replied Lionel softly. 'I've always believed men of God should exist in the real world of swearing, shouting, drinking and not in some lofty plain above it. If swearing offended me, I could never have had Lilian Dearman as one of my closest friends.' He laughed, that deep, church-bell-like sound again, and it made Marnie smile.

'I expect I've been the talk of the town in my absence,' she said.

'Of course you were. We even had a meeting about you.' Lionel held his hand up then in an effort to allay her fears. 'Or at least about the situation. Some people will not take too kindly to change. But you had quite a few champions around the table too.'

'Oh?' asked Marnie, genuinely surprised by the 'quite a few'.

'Emelie Tibbs. She got right under Titus's skin. David, at the Wych Arms, myself of course. We've all had it too easy for too long.' He took a long sip of tea. 'And Herv, Lilian's gardener. He was very vocal in your corner.'

'Oh,' said Marnie, trying not to look as chuffed as she felt hearing that he had stuck up for her. She hadn't alienated him then by her abrupt behaviour after the will-reading. She was glad about that. The man must have the patience of a saint and the hide of an old rhino.

'Herv Gunnarsen is a good man,' said Lionel. 'You and he are proof that new blood is what Wychwell needs. Titus is a purist. He doesn't want anyone to live here who wasn't born here or married someone from here and the result is that half the properties are empty. I'm so angry at myself that I didn't see what was going on. Marnie, I think you will have quite a task on your hands and I came to tell you that if there is any-thing – *anything* – I can do to assist you, you only need ask.' He drained his mug in a single gulp and stood. 'Anyway, I shan't keep you.'

'Thank you, Lionel, that means a lot,' said Marnie. 'I don't suppose you know who the new owner is?'

'Your guess is as good as mine, Marnie.'

At the door she confessed to him. 'I didn't run off because of my mother's death. I left because I didn't want to do what had been asked of me. I even emailed Mr Wemyss and told him that I wouldn't do it.'

'But you came back?' smiled Lionel.

'I felt I had to. For Lilian.'

Lionel nodded sagely. 'She had faith in you for the right reasons then, didn't she?'

*

Marnie went to bed early because she needed to be up at the crack of dawn to make the cheesecakes for Mrs Abercrombie. As soon as the van had left with the cargo, she changed into something not covered in splashes of cream to meet with Mr Wemyss, who was operating from his Leeds office, and not the Richmond one, for the foreseeable future. She hoped that she didn't bump into anyone from Café Caramba in the city centre. Chances are she wouldn't, surely? If she did, she'd walk quickly on and not engage.

She was getting into her car when she saw Herv's truck pass the end of the lane. Then she heard the brakes screech. Then she saw him reverse at breakneck speed towards her.

'Marnie, you're here,' he called through the window so enthusiastically that she was convinced he would then bounce out of the vehicle to hug her, but he didn't. And she found herself a little disappointed about that.

'Yes, I'm here. I'm just going into Leeds to meet Lilian's solicitor.'

'I knew you would come back.'

His grin lit up his eyes. His grin lit up his whole face. His grin lit up the whole village.

'Lionel said that you'd stood up for me in the meeting you had. Thanks for that.'

Herv shrugged his very big shoulders. 'It's okay.'

How could he look that happy to see her? Could she really make anyone's eyes shine like that? Especially as she had a real habit of being abrupt with him.

'Well, I'd better get on.'

'See you around, Marnie,' said Herv. 'If you need me for anything, please ask. I'm working up at the manor until some-one tells me to stop. I think we are all carrying on as normal because we don't know what else to do. Maybe there is no place for me in the new owner's Wychwell.'

'I'm sure there will be.' said Marnie. 'In fact, if they've put me in charge of managing the affairs of the village, I'll make damned sure of it.'

'Thank you.' His grin became lopsided, flirty, and so damned sexy. 'Ah, so, you do think something nice of me then.'

'Of course,' she said. 'You're a good gardener.' She made it sound as if her reasons were from a purely business perspective. But they weren't.

Mr Wemyss was delighted to see Marnie. He had a dark green pinstripe suit on today and Marnie imagined that he had a pinstripe suit in every colour in his wardrobe. When they shook hands, his large one enveloped hers. He led her through into a huge wood-panelled room that looked very much like a solicitor's-office version of the gentleman's smoking room in the manor. He sat behind his desk in a gigantic leather chair and invited Marnie to take a seat at the other side. Then he buzzed on an intercom for a tray of tea to be brought through.

'I'm sorry that I told you I didn't want to have anything to do with the estate,' Marnie said, as he fiddled around with papers on his desk.

'Knee-jerk reaction. Totally understandable. Didn't believe a word of it,' Mr Wemyss replied.

The tea arrived. The lady who brought it served it up and after she left, Mr Wemyss got straight down to business.

'The present owner and Lilian decided that you would be the best manager ...'

'Who is it?' Marnie assumed she would be told now.

'I'm not at liberty to disclose that,' replied Mr Wemyss, much to her disappointment. 'They have, however, made a list of recommendations for you to implement.' Mr Wemyss handed over a large brown envelope. 'There is also a set of the manor keys in there. Your salary will be paid from the monies remaining in the estate account, as will the staff directly employed by the estate, namely the housekeeper, gardener and assistants. The coffers are very depleted but there is enough left for approximately six months. By which time I do hope that monies will be coming into the accounts rather than leaving them. That is certainly the hope of the present owner.'

No pressure then, thought Marnie.

'Re your salary,' continued Mr Wemyss, 'I wouldn't get your hopes up of buying a Ferrari with it.' And he looked at her pointedly over his half-moon glasses. 'Having had a cursory look at the accounts which Mr Sutton has – under threat of legal action – turned over to us, I can only wish you well.' He raised his eyebrows. 'The parts of the records which are legible – and I must say, there are few – make little sense. I'll have them couriered to the manor tomor-row morning.'

'I can save you some money and take them with me now,' Marnie suggested.

'Unless you've driven here in a flatbed lorry, having them couriered might be the wisest option,' Mr Wemyss replied.

'How is this going to work if I don't know who the owner is? How am I supposed to contact them? And where do I start?' asked Marnie.

'Email me any plans that you have in mind and I will act as broker between yourself and the new owner. He – for sake of ease let's say *he* rather than all that he or she nonsense – will directly communicate only with me. I shall forward his responses to you. The new owner has suggested you operate from the manor house. He thinks it will give you more leverage. Open the envelope. That should give you your starting point,' Mr Wemyss urged.

Marnie did as he requested and scanned the first of the new owner's instructions.

'Bloody hell,' was all she could think of to say.

The new owner was certainly going straight in armed and dangerous. Nice of him to hide in his shelter whilst sending her across a minefield in flip-flops.

It was lunchtime when Marnie left the building and office workers everywhere were pouring out into the city centre to shop and eat. Marnie could have walked back to her car the way she came – the long route past all the shops – or the short one past Café Caramba. Her feet were aching in her heels and she was tired from getting up at an unearthly hour to make the cheesecake order. She just wanted to get back home as quickly as possible. Plus she was strangely curious to know what it would feel like to be outside her old HQ again, to see the building but know it wasn't part of her life any more. She wouldn't bump into Laurence as he never strolled around the city, and was as likely to crash into Vicky or Elena either way, so she might as well choose the short route. She'd ignore them totally if their paths collided. She hadn't quite worked out what she would do if she bumped into Justin though.

She still hadn't replied to his text, but she hadn't deleted it either. She knew she shouldn't have opened it up as many times as she had done to try to second-guess what he wanted from her. She wouldn't respond, but still, she wondered.

She didn't see Vicky or Elena. She recognised someone

who worked in accounts but not well enough to say hello to, even in passing. Then she heard her name being called from across the street and froze. When she turned to the source, it was to find Roisean bounding towards her, grinning like a maniac.

'Marnie!' She threw herself at her old boss. 'It's so good to see you. Are you coming back?'

'No, I'm afraid not,' smiled Marnie, touched by Roisean's affection.

'Have you time for a quick coffee?' asked Roisean. 'Please. I've missed you.'

How could she refuse.

'I'm due back in ten minutes, but sod them,' said Roisean. 'I've got loads to tell you. Let me see if I can squash it all in in the time it takes us to drink a flat white.'

There was a small café along from the Dirty Dog: the Aloha. It had the tackiest décor in the world: plastic palm trees everywhere and a massive mural of a beach on the back wall. It wasn't a place likely to be frequented by any of Marnie's trendy nemeses.

'It's a bit shit but the coffee's good. And cheap,' said Roisean, queueing up at the counter. She insisted on paying. She'd explain why in a moment, she said and winked, sending Marnie off to grab a table.

'You look thinner,' said Roisean, when she brought the drinks over. She lifted the lid off a plastic pineapple on the table and spooned out some sugar into her coffee. 'I hope that's not from any stress.'

Marnie didn't want to bring the mood down by saying that she'd been to two funerals in the same week. 'I've cut out bread and potatoes,' she fibbed.

'I'd sooner die,' Roisean declared. 'Where are you living? I sort of tricked HR into giving me your address and I swung past but the house was empty. I emailed you too but I'm presuming you haven't logged onto the Caramba mainframe.'

'No. To be honest, I thought there would only be horrible emails.'

'Well maybe you should have,' Roisean scolded her gently. 'Everyone was really worried about you. I think quite a few people emailed you with nice messages.'

Marnie doubted that and gave a little huff of disbelief.

'I mean it. Obviously not Vicky and Elena, as you can imagine. But Arthur and Bette. Even Dennis the security bloke came up to see if we'd heard anything from you.'

'That was sweet of him,' said Marnie.

'I'm not going to wait for you to ask me what happened after you'd gone, you must be dying to know,' said Roisean.

'I am and I'm not,' replied Marnie. 'The whole thing gave me nightmares.' She looked Roisean square in the face then because she wanted her to hear this and believe her. 'Justin told me he and his wife were divorcing. I would never have gone into a relationship with him if I'd known he was lying about that. In fact, I'm not even sure anything he told me was the truth.'

'I knew that,' said Roisean. 'I think your reaction when his wife came storming in made that obvious. Either that or you should have left the job to go into acting. I felt gutted for you. Really sad. You looked heartbroken.'

Roisean believed her. Without any doubt. Boy it felt good that someone did.

Marnie had to ask. 'Is he . . . Justin still working there?'

Roisean huffed. 'Not only is he still working there but he's become bosom buddies with Laurence. He's so far up his backside, you can only see his feet these days.'

Marnie chuckled.

'He brazened it out, like Shagger Sharon did. He didn't come back into the office that afternoon, but the next day he turned up acting perfectly normally, as if nothing had happened.'

Marnie wasn't surprised. Justin had clearly been a master at compartmentalising.

Roisean went on with glee sparkling in her voice: 'Elena was given the job of acting head of department but, not to put too fine a point on things, she made a total balls of it. She has no people skills at all, as you know, and got everyone's backs up, she hadn't a clue what she was doing. Arthur had a blazing row with her one day. He called her quite a few choice names – we all sat there gobsmacked. We didn't know he had it in him.'

'Arthur?' Quiet, calm Arthur?

'Yep. She sent Laurence some wrong figures and then blamed Arthur for it. He didn't take it lying down, I can tell you. And he was obviously storing a lot of things that he thought he'd get out at the same time. Including what an absolute bitch she was to you and that maybe she realised now what a good boss you were. He gave her a right mouthful. And then he walked out.'

'Oh no . . .'

'He actually turned into Spiderman at one point, he said – and I kid you not – *with great power comes great responsibility*. You could have heard a pin drop.'

'But he's so close to retiring.' Marnie was very concerned.

'Ah, don't worry yourself. There'd have been a coup if he'd really gone. HR persuaded him to stay because Bette went down to tell them he was being bullied and she'd stand up in court and testify to it if it came to it. And so would

I, for that matter. Even Vicky ditched Elena and transferred to Communications.'

'Really?' Marnie hadn't expected any of this fallout. She'd imagined that she wouldn't be missed at all and the department would function better than ever.

'Yup. Then after Laurence made Elena cry in a meeting, she handed in her notice. She took her holiday entitlement and left straightaway. They talked Linda into coming back early to run the department and she starts on Monday. And guess who is the deputy?' She didn't give Marnie a single second to answer. 'Me. I've got a lovely pay rise and Linda rang me and told me on the quiet that she's not planning on staying long because she's pregnant again, so she's going to make sure that I'm ready to take over when she leaves. I can't believe it.'

'I can,' said Marnie. 'You were always far too competent to have a junior role.'

'I've only got this chance because they were desperate to keep some consistency.'

'It doesn't matter how you got it, the fact is you have and now you show them what you can do.' Marnie was delighted for her.

'What about you then, Marnie?'

Oh, where to start, laughed Marnie to herself. *Keep it simple.*

'I'm living in a small village in the Dales and I'm managing an estate.'

'Oh wow. That sounds grand.' Roisean looked genuinely impressed.

'It's certainly a challenge.' *That was one way of putting it.*

'I gather you and Justin are finished?' Roisean asked, giving her watch a quick glance.

'I never saw him again after that day. He just ran off and

hid like the rat he was. Not even a text from him.' She didn't mention the recent one that she'd ignored.

'Bastard,' said Roisean and sounded exactly like Lilian for that split second, which made Marnie smile.

'I tell you, Marnie, no man has given me a bigger thrill than when HR asked me if I would consider taking on that deputy's job.'

'One will, one day. But make sure that he's worth your affections. Don't sell yourself short.'

'I have an inbuilt detector for that sort of stuff,' said Roisean. 'I always thought Justin Fox was a slimy git. Can I have your mobile number?'

Roisean would end up as CEO of Café Caramba one day, Marnie was sure of it.

When Marnie got back to Little Raspberries, she found a printed A4 sheet on the doormat. An invitation to join the locals at an informal home-made wine tasting battle that night at seven. David Parselow had hand-written a note on the bottom.

> Please come. We need someone who isn't biased and can't be corrupted and if I win, I'll give you three bottles ;)

She was tempted. Not because of the wine but because she wanted to meet any awkwardness head on. She didn't want people to be wary of her and worried that she was going to turn into some power-crazed bitch. She even made it as far as across the road at ten past seven, then turned back. However kind the invite, she knew that tongues would start wagging when she walked in and she couldn't smile and be merry amongst them knowing what she was going to have to tell them in the next few days. She needed to be focused and detached because she was wielding a lot of power. And as Arthur so brilliantly put it, *with great power comes great responsibility*. She had to get it right, both for Lilian and Wychwell. Plus, she needed a clear head – and David and Lionel's wines were not conducive to having one of those.

The envelope that Mr Wemyss had given her contained details of her wage for causing carnage, which was actually more like pocket money. A pittance. It wouldn't buy her weekly requirement of butter for the cheesecake bases. Whoever the new owner was, he was taking the Michael and relying on her undertaking her duties primarily through a sense of loyalty to Lilian's memory rather than for the cash.

As she lay in bed that night, she replayed the conversation she'd had with Roisean. She'd been really touched that not everyone automatically presumed she'd been a heartless home-wrecker. And Arthur's opinion meant more to her than Laurence's if she was honest. She made up her mind to send a hamper of biscuits and chocolates to arrive on Monday to christen the new regime in the department, and to say thanks for their loyalty. She also made a mental note to look through the red box of things that she'd brought from her mother's garage. If she hadn't been so shattered she would have sated her curiosity and got up and done it there and then, but she was degrees away from sleep and her head was beautifully nestled on her pillows. She wasn't going anywhere now; it could wait.

She heard some drunken revellers coming out of the Wych Arms as her eyes shuttered down and she hoped that they'd still be as merry this time next week. Some definitely wouldn't feel like singing.

Chapter 28

Marnie woke up one minute before her alarm went off at nine a.m. She'd slept for ten solid hours. She used to survive on six when she worked at Café Caramba. She had a shower and some toast and then, with the brown envelope of doom in her bag, she set off up to the manor. She pushed open the heavy oak door and walked into the hallway. Lilian's essence was so obviously absent, the air trapped within the walls felt sad – and she knew it sounded ridiculous and she would never say it to anyone, but it was as if the house was grieving for her.

'Hello, house,' she said. 'Marnie here. Remember me.'

'Yes, I do,' replied the house.

Then Herv appeared from behind the staircase.

'You . . . silly bugger! You scared me stupid,' said Marnie, patting her chest.

'Lilian used to talk to the house too. And sometimes it would creak and she'd say, "Herv, listen, it's talking back to me"'. His eyes were smiling as much as his lips were at the memory. The thought came into Marnie's head, *His wife must have been a proper pillock.* She pushed it away and slid into work mode.

'I'm expecting a delivery.'

'It's already here,' he replied. 'I saw the delivery van pass my house so I came up early. I have put all the boxes in the dining room. I thought you might like to spread out over the table.'

'Great idea,' she said, ignoring the innuendo that he wasn't aware he'd made. And the naughty picture that flashed up in her brain.

'Would you like a coffee? Cilla and Zoe aren't in today. I told them that you might need some space and quiet to work. I know Cilla is very worried that she is going to lose her job and her house so if that's in the plans then maybe it would be better to tell the family sooner rather than later.'

'Why would that be in the plans?' said Marnie. It certainly wasn't in the new owner's initial plans and if it were, she would have fought it. Lilian thought very highly of the Oldroyd family. She wouldn't have wanted them to feel insecure.

'No one knows what is in the plans, that's the problem,' said Herv. 'Me too. What's the saying? *Last in, first out.*'

'That would be me then, not you,' Marnie pointed out.

'I'll make you a coffee,' said Herv.

'You don't have to. I'm not your boss, Herv,' said Marnie.

'I'm making you a coffee because I want to, not because I have to. I'm having one, I presume you'd like one too?' He phrased it as a question and stood waiting for an answer.

'Then yes, thank you.'

'Okay.' He turned in the direction of the kitchen and she cringed because she had somehow turned into the sort of screw-up who read three volumes of subtext in a simple line about putting on the kettle.

*

Marnie opened up the first file her hand touched on to get a flavour of what she was tackling. It would all have made more sense if it had been written in hieroglyphics because at least then the pictures might have given her a clue as to what was going on. She had a feeling that Gladwyn Sutton's writing was deliberately cryptic and, when she picked up a later ledger, found that he'd taught his son well.

Herv brought a coffee in for her, registering the expression of bafflement on her face.

'I can't make head nor tail of any of it,' she said.

'Can I look?' he asked.

'Help yourself.'

He bent over her shoulder and she caught the scent of him: something foresty and fresh and Nordic, something that his natural scents combined beautifully with, something that her senses approved of.

'What language is it?' he asked.

'Gobbledygook,' replied Marnie. 'This is going to be a nightmare.'

'You need to find the key to break the code.'

'I don't think Alan Turing could break this,' sighed Marnie.

'Can I help?' said Herv. 'I used to be a teacher.'

'What did you teach, Herv, espionage?'

Herv chuckled. 'Maths, History and Classics so I have a good head for these things. It likes to contemplate problems and solve them.' His arm whispered past her left ear as his finger touched the paper. 'See, this is an s though it looks like an f. And this is an e, though it appears to be an i, but the i is taller, like a lower case l.'

Marnie was half-listening, half-marvelling how large his hand was, how neat and square his nails were, how dark blond hairs started at the wrist and travelled up his arm.

'It's like one of those magic eye pictures. Once your brain is trained to recognise the patterns, it begins to see them more easily,' Herv went on.

'Well, if Titus can read this, I'm damned sure I can work it all out eventually.'

'Of course you can. Or you could ask him to give you the key to his coding.'

'Yeah, right.'

'I would be glad to help you.' The sentence faded before he reached the end of it because he supposed she'd refuse, but she surprised him. He didn't know it was a test on herself to see if she could accept a kindness from a man without presuming he had a hidden agenda. Herv, she thought, didn't deserve that insult again.

'Do you have time?'

'Of course.'

She pulled a chair out from under the table. 'Take a seat, my friend. Two heads are definitely going to be better than one on this.'

There was nothing in the rule book to say she had to do it all by herself.

Marnie stretched and her back gave a series of satisfying cracks. She'd been stuck in the same position for ages. It was past lunchtime and her stomach gave a rumble as if to remind her of that.

They'd managed to decipher the enigmatic handwriting to the extent that they were almost both bilingual – or quintilingual in the case of Herv because he was fluent in English, Swedish, Norwegian, German and Sutton now. Marnie could cover the basics in French, but she wouldn't have claimed to be proficient in it. It had been a sore point in her family that she achieved an A★ in her GCSE when Gabrielle, despite the extra private lessons, only got a B. Marnie was sent up to her room for gloating. She gave an involuntary chuckle when the memory came to her and Herv asked what she'd found so funny.

'I was thinking about something that happened half my life ago,' she said. And told him.

'You were sent up to your room for that?' he said, his tone disbelieving.

'I was too old for the naughty step by then,' smiled Marnie. 'I sat on it so much, my bum-print was ingrained in the wood.'

'You were a bad girl?' He looked at her through narrowed eyes.

'I tried not to be,' said Marnie. 'Trouble found me rather than the other way round.'

'I don't believe it of you,' Herv replied.

If he only knew, thought Marnie. 'Do you have naughty steps in Norway? Then again, I bet you were always a good boy, weren't you?'

'Of course,' Herv grinned. 'Plus we lived in a one-storey house – no steps.'

Marnie laughed. She couldn't imagine Herv giving his family the same sort of hassle she'd given hers.

'Do you only have the one sister?' Herv asked.

'Yep. And you? Any siblings?'

'Just me.'

'Lucky you,' said Marnie, a thought said aloud.

'You don't get on with each other?' he asked.

'Not at all,' replied Marnie. 'I doubt we will ever see or hear from each other again.'

Herv took a sharp intake of breath. 'That must be difficult for your parents.'

'Mum died, Dad was never on the scene. I say "dad" but I'm adopted.'

'I was adopted too,' said Herv.

'No way.'

'Yes, I was adopted when I was two.'

Marnie's curiosity was piqued.

'And how was it? When did you find out?'

'I was young, maybe six,' Herv answered. 'They didn't make a big deal about it. I saw a pregnant woman and I must have asked an awkward question. Mum said that she didn't grow me in her stomach, she grew me in her heart. It made me feel more special if anything. I was happy, I was loved.'

'Didn't you ever try and trace your real parents?'

'No. Mum and Dad were my real parents, as far as I was concerned,' said Herv. 'Did you?'

'I was found in an abandoned caravan,' replied Marnie. 'The only thing I know is that some Irish travellers had lived in it and that they were the ones who probably tipped the authorities off that I was there. Not really much to go on. I've always figured that I was surplus to their requirements.'

'Possibly,' Herv mused, 'but who knows why people give up their children. I think maybe often it is something they do because they have to rather than choose to.'

She shouldn't have started this conversation. It was taking her mind where it didn't want to go.

'Sometimes it is best to let the past settle and not try to rake it up again,' Herv continued. 'Plant flowers in it instead and let something good grow from it. That's why I didn't want to trace my birth parents. My life was a good garden.'

It was a nice way to think of things, a beautiful way. If you grew up in top-quality soil and not rocks and dry sand, of course.

'I bet your parents are proud of you,' said Marnie. Herv would be a perfect son, she would bet anything on that. The antithesis to her – the imperfect daughter.

'I hope so. Pappa died when I was eighteen. He was a teacher. I followed him into the profession because I wanted to make him proud, through some kind of misguided grief. It was okay but it wasn't me. Mamma died just after my marriage ended, it was a very sad time. She knew I wasn't happy in Norway, she told me to stop living for other people and so I came here and was introduced to Lilian and within the half hour I had changed my whole life.'

'You came over as an exchange teacher or something like that, didn't you?'

'That's right. I worked for a little while at the same school as Ruby Sweetman.'

'She likes you.'

'I know,' said Herv, with an awkward frown. 'But I . . . I don't . . .' He struggled to put his feelings into words and she knew that he was trying not to be discourteous.

'I understand,' she nodded.

'We . . . er . . . went out once for dinner. I wanted to say thank you. I didn't realise . . . what she felt . . . I was stupid. I didn't see it.'

Well, Herv, you must be either really thick or the world's biggest innocent, that voice inside Marnie said. She imagined that Ruby must have thought all her Christmases had come at once when Herv asked her out for that meal. She felt momentarily sorry for her.

'It was an odd one for me,' said Herv, brow creased as he recalled what had happened. 'I'm usually the one who loves too much. It was strange that . . . for once it was the other way round.'

I'm usually the one who loves too much. Could he see inside her head or was this one of those 'sensitive man' lines designed to loosen her knicker elastic? If she'd been a fly sitting happily on a web, she'd be detecting a subtle vibration now warning her to flit off because a spider was on its way. Or maybe, just maybe, she was doing that spider a disservice and he was simply happy for the company and didn't want to eat her and spit her out. Maybe that spider was actually one of the good guys with his kind, blue eyes and scent of pine forests.

'Coffee?' she said. She needed a break, food, some serious fresh air and a cold shower. Not necessarily in that order.

They had lunch at the table: Herv made a mountain of cheese and onion toasties and they must have been great brain food, because Marnie started making major headway on the deciphering of the accounts. But she half wished she hadn't because the news wasn't good. She found that the estate owned a farm between Wychwell and Mintbottom, leased to a Josiah Helliwell and no rents had been collected on it for over thirty years. Not only that but she discovered that an estate loyalty bonus of two thousand pounds had been paid annually to Mr Helliwell. Marnie couldn't remember reading anything about a farm in the book of Wychwell that Lionel and Lilian had co-written. She wondered, in that case, if they'd even known about it.

'It looks as if the estate has been paying this farm and the pub and the post office an annual amount to compensate them for having such little business. Who in their right mind does that?' said Marnie, scratching her head. 'Well that's going to stop right now and I'm going to instruct Mr Wemyss to collect all that back rent.'

It was bad enough that the most anyone paid to lease a house in Wychwell was twenty pounds a month, and that was the Wych Arms, but for the estate to be paying businesses for merely existing was ridiculous. And it got worse: Titus Sutton, she found, was given a 'family stipend' of ten thousand pounds a year and he paid absolutely no rent at all. And, if that wasn't enough fiddling, he was also paid handsomely for doing the accounts. It didn't need a financial expert to see that the Suttons had been ripping the Dearmans off for at least two generations. The estate had paid for all Titus's house furniture too – top-notch stuff – and the E-Type Jag he drove. Herv also found records of loyalty bonuses being given to two businesses that didn't even exist. No wonder Wychwell was on its knees. Marnie was furious.

She caught accidental sight of her watch and saw it was after seven o'clock. Herv had been hard at work recording the floor areas of the cottages so she could work out fair rents. His dark blond brows were lowered in concentration and Marnie had to call his name twice before he heard her.

'I didn't realise it was so late,' she said. 'We should stop before we go blind.'

'I was really into it. I can't believe what I'm reading,' said Herv, a yawn claiming his voice. He stretched and Marnie tried not to look at the chest muscles pushing against his moss-green T-shirt.

'Thank you for your help, Herv.' She could have carried on for much longer, but she needed an early night because she had a cheesecake order to make first thing in the morning. And she needed to call on Derek Price and get that job out of the way – although, on second thoughts, maybe she would leave that until she felt braver.

'Same time tomorrow?' Herv asked.

'I have something to do in the morning. What about after lunch? One-ish?'

'Aw, you don't like my toasted sandwiches,' Herv said, feigning upset, curling his bottom lip into a little-boy-hurt shape.

'They were wonderful, but I can't be here first thing.'

'Okay,' said Herv. 'I'll meet you at one.'

Herv lived in The Bilberries, a cottage just around the corner from Emelie Tibbs. She was looking out of the window when they passed and waved at them to stop. Seconds later she appeared at the door with a brown paper bag.

'Marnie, I went into the woods today and there are lots of wild strawberries. I thought you might like these for your cheesecakes. They are ripe and ready to be picked.'

The strawberries were tiny but very sweet. Marnie thought immediately of suggesting a new flavour to Mrs Abercrombie. The word 'wild' instantly made it something more desirable than bog-standard strawberry.

'Thank you, Emelie,' said Marnie. 'I might go and harvest a few myself at the weekend.'

It might have been the fading light of the day, but Emelie looked frail.

'Emelie, if you ever want to come up to the manor and walk around the gardens like you used to do with Lilian, please do,' Marnie invited.

Emelie clapped her hands together and beamed. 'I would like that so very much. And if you want me to show you where I found the strawberries, I'd be happy to.'

'That would be brilliant, thank you.'

Emelie went back inside then and Herv and Marnie

reached the bottom of the hill where Herv would go left and Marnie would cross the green to Little Raspberries.

'Well, cheers, Herv,' said Marnie. 'I don't think I could have made half the headway if you hadn't been there today.'

'Well, I can think of a way you can thank me,' said Herv, his eyes twinkling. 'I'm very partial to cheesecake.'

'Okay, I'll make you one.' She was surprised to find that she'd hoped he would have asked for more. 'Goodnight.'

'Goodnight, Marnie. See you tomorrow.'

It was only when she was halfway across the green that she began to wonder how Emelie knew about the cheesecakes.

Chapter 29

The next morning, Marnie made an extra cheesecake to the ones on her order – a wild strawberry one – to share with Herv that afternoon. When the van arrived to take them away, Marnie noticed Kay Sweetman hovering at the end of the lane. No doubt the regular van trips three times every week were tickling local curiosity. If asked, she'd say that she made pies, just like Jessie did, for a bakery. If asked by someone like Kay, she'd tell her to mind her own sodding business.

Marnie slept for three solid hours, then, showered and with cheesecake in her bag and a note to push through Derek Price's letterbox, she set off up to the manor. By a stroke of luck, before she could post it, she saw the man himself walking towards the church and she called to him.

He loped towards her, big friendly smile wide in greeting.

'Good morning, Marnie. And how are you today?'

'I'm good, Derek, but I wondered if I could have a word with you at some point in private. Up at the manor.'

'Well I'm a bit busy until this afternoon, but I should be free by four if that's any good. I'm not sure about Una though. She's—'

'No,' Marnie interrupted him. 'Just you. It won't take long but best done formally I think.'

'Sounds ominous,' said Derek, raising his brace of woolly eyebrows.

'Not at all, please don't worry,' said Marnie, quick to reassure him. At least, it wasn't ominous for him.

Cilla was dusting the staircase when Marnie walked into the manor. She said hello but her usually smiley face had an anxious cast. Marnie remembered then what Herv had told her.

'Look, Cilla, can I put you at your ease about something. Your job is totally secure, Zoe and Johnny's jobs are totally secure, and your home is totally secure. The manor is always going to need good staff.'

Marnie hadn't anticipated that Cilla would burst into tears. She had, it seems, been out of her head with worry. Marnie led her into the kitchen and made her sit down whilst she put on the kettle.

'Griff was worried that the new owner would slap a great big rent on us or turf us out. He feels so guilty that he can't work any more,' Cilla half-hiccupped, half-sobbed.

'The house is part of your wage though, Cilla. You wouldn't be expected to pay rent.'

'But when I retire, that'll all change, won't it? I was forty-two when I had Zoe . . .'

Marnie did the maths. Then she remembered something that Ruby Sweetman had told her about Zoe wanting to go off to university and she wondered if the girl felt obliged to stay working for the manor so she could keep a roof over the family heads.

'Cilla, I shall make the strongest case possible that you can stay in your cottage for life. Lilian would have wanted to look after you. No doubt Johnny and Zoe will be ready to flee the nest one day but don't worry that when you retire, you'll be out on your backside. That cottage must be cramped with four of you in it. I bet it'll be a relief when they find a place of their own.'

'It's cosy, I'll give you that,' said Cilla, with an attempt at a laugh. 'I think Johnny will stay around here, he's as happy as a pig in muck trailing around after Herv, but I know Zoe wants to go to university.' Marnie noticed Zoe appear in the doorway and then do a double-back out of the way when she saw that her mum wasn't alone.

'You should let her go then, Cilla,' said Marnie.

'It's the money though, isn't it,' said Cilla, blowing her nose on a disintegrated tissue that she'd taken from her apron pocket.

'Somehow most of them manage,' replied Marnie, pulling a new packet of them out of her bag and handing it to Cilla.

'Thank you, Marnie. We'd have been all right for money, you know, if we hadn't been silly with it. A few years ago, we invested in one of those sure-fire schemes. We shouldn't lose, he said, no one had before. But we had to accept that it was a gamble and there was a tiny chance we might. Anyway, we were unlucky and we lost everything we put in.' Cilla shrugged. 'It wasn't his fault, it was ours because that's what you get for gambling. He was so sorry, though, he felt so bad . . .'

'Who was this?' asked Marnie.

'Titus,' Cilla replied.

Marnie was livid when she walked into the dining room. She slammed the box with the cheesecake in it down on the middle of the table and made a deep growl of frustration. Herv was already there, poring over a ledger.

'My goodness, what's happened?' he asked.

'All roads lead to Titus sodding Sutton in this village,' said Marnie. 'I am going to have a great deal of satisfaction in cutting off his financial oxygen.'

'Can I buy a ticket to watch?' Herv grinned.

Marnie only answered with another growl.

'I'll go and get a knife and plates,' said Herv, rubbing his hands together. He returned with them minutes later along with two cups of coffee. Marnie had just about calmed down by then.

'I started at nine,' he said. 'You won't believe what else I found.'

'Oh, I would,' said Marnie.

'Titus has been also charging his golf membership to the estate.'

'Why am I not surprised?' Marnie threw her hands up in the air. 'I thought Lilian was supposed to be a good judge of character, so why didn't she see what he was doing under her nose?' It didn't make sense to Marnie.

Herv cut himself an enormous piece of cheesecake. 'My, this looks so good. What I think is she had no interest in money at all. In the days of her father there was plenty of it, so all the little swindles could be well hidden. But Titus is really greedy and hasn't stolen a tiny amount which wouldn't be noticed, he's bled the bank dry. He started looking after the accounts thirty-one years ago. Up to then, I found the Helliwells had been paying rent on the farm. I think they still are and Titus has been syphoning it off for himself.'

Every page of those ledgers brought sighs of despair of varying degrees. Titus had been like a kid in a sweet shop, it seems. Stealing the odd thing from the penny tray, then on finding he could get away with that easily, nicking the whole tray. Then upping his game until he was raiding the shelves in full view of the shopkeeper who appeared to be blind to it all. Had he inherited the manor as he thought, he might not have been able to sell it but he would have stripped it completely and sold all the portraits, even the panelling from the walls. Goodness knows what he would have tried to charge everyone in rents to finance his lavish lifestyle. He obviously didn't give Hilary any of his money because the last time Marnie spotted her, she'd recognised her beige stripey raincoat as the one on the Asda George TV advert.

Herv left at three-thirty with the rest of the cheesecake which he claimed 'for services rendered'. He was going out that evening with one of the teachers he'd befriended when he first came over to England, he said. He didn't say what sex that teacher was and Marnie hadn't asked but wished she had because, for a reason she was reticent to admit to, she would have liked him to have confirmed it was a male one.

The meeting with Derek cut out the teacher-gender second-guessing for a while at least. She was nervous about what she had to say to him, nervous about what carnage it might trigger. He arrived exactly on time. Cilla showed him through to the dining room. The smile was firmly back on her face after the talk she'd had with Marnie hours before.

'Take a seat, Derek,' Marnie said.

He sat awkwardly as if he had no right to be there. He was visibly tense, but not half as much as she was. *It'll be okay*, said a voice inside her. As if he'd take up the offer. He'd refuse and it would all go quietly away because he wouldn't dare let anyone know about it. She didn't know how to begin the conversation, so dived straight in and hoped for the best.

'Er, Derek. The new owner has asked me to ask you –'

Oh God '– if you would like to move into the old grave-diggers cottage. The rent would constitute part of your wage as churchwarden.' There, it was done.

Derek rolled the suggestion around in his mind, as if it were a toffee in his mouth and he were trying to determine the flavour. 'The old gravedigger's house. No one's lived in there since Diggory Hoyle died.' Could there have been a more convenient name for a gravedigger than Diggory Hoyle, Marnie thought. Doug Hoyle, maybe?

'That's right.'

She hadn't seen inside it herself but apparently it was quite habitable. For a single occupant.

Derek's eyeballs looked as if they were vibrating inside their sockets. It was a pretty clear indicator of the activity going on behind them. Then he said no more than the one word:

'Oh.' But that word was loaded with obvious meaning. It was the sort of 'oh' that a child might say when told that Santa had just landed on his roof.

'Yep,' said Marnie, waiting for more, which eventually came.

'Only one person can live in that house.'

'Yes.'

'I'd move out of the cottage I share with Una and go into there, that's what the owner wants me to do?'

'Well, he – or she – wants to know if that's what *you* would like to do.'

This was getting more awful by the second, thought Marnie with an inward groan. She was handing him an axe to smash up his marriage, that really couldn't be right.

'Me and Una would split up if I did that.'

Marnie gulped. She couldn't think of what to say to that. Then she saw Derek's mouth change from a tight moue of contemplation to a tentative twitch of a smile then on to a cavernous open mouth of delight.

'I'd love that. I'd bloody love that. When? When can I have the keys?'

Oh shit, thought Marnie.

HISTORY OF WYCHWELL BY LIONEL TEMPLE
Contributions by Lilian Dearman.

Emelie (Taubert) Tibbs came to live in Wychwell on 6th August 1941 with her parents Katerin and William and her elder brother Fred. They took up residence in Clementine Cottage (then Woodfield). Fred emigrated to New Zealand after the war and, following the deaths of her parents, Emelie moved into Little Apples on Kytson Hill. She was a modern languages teacher for many years at Troughton Grammar school and cites writing poetry, gardening and bird-watching as her hobbies.

Chapter 30

It appeared, from what Derek gabbled excitedly in the aftermath of the offer, that he'd wanted to leave Una for years but she was in charge of all the money. At least the little money they had, seeing as they'd lost a lot of their savings investing in a get-rich scheme. 'The bloke' had said that they'd been really unlucky, because no one had ever done so before. It didn't need a genius to work out who 'the bloke' was. Derek was under the impression that he alone had been caught out. Marnie didn't enlighten him. She'd keep her powder dry about that one for the time being.

Marnie had made a list of all the payments which came out automatically from the manor's accounts and scythed the dubious ones immediately. The so-called loyalty bonuses and Titus's ridiculous wage and his extras were top of her list. She didn't stop the stipend that Griff had been getting paid since his stroke; it was a piddly amount but taking it away would impact on the Oldroyd budget. There was more money in the estate account than she'd anticipated, but it wouldn't last the year. Marnie couldn't wait for the Suttons to find that the usual monthly standing orders hadn't gone in to their bank. *Bring it on*, she thought.

As she was cutting across the green on the way home, she heard an unholy commotion happening near the church. She saw Derek with a suitcase and a spring in his step walking away from his wife, who was yelling at him from her doorstep.

'You'll be sorry, Derek Price. You ungrateful, boring, useless shit.'

She could have called him any name under the sun and Marnie bet that it wouldn't have wiped that grin from his face. Of course, Una would hold her responsible and come gunning for her before too long. Great.

There was a bottle of Lionel's apple wine on her own doorstep when she reached Little Raspberries. She smiled, picked it up, walked into the cottage, locked the door, kicked off her shoes and headed to the kitchen for a glass. She was tired and ready for an early night. The forecast was good for the following day and she thought she'd take Emelie up on her offer to go strawberry picking in the woods. She intended to soak them in Pernod and black pepper then crush them and swirl them into the body of a cheesecake mix. She'd send a sample up on Monday with the driver and knew that Mrs Abercrombie would love it.

She opened the back door to let in some fresh air, poured herself a glass of Lionel's wine and picked up her new book: *Country Manors Part Two – The Wrong Side of the Blanket*. She needed something to dive into and lose herself. Manfred Masters had gambled and lost the manor to the arrogant Sir Titan Sonnett on a single game of poker, though it was obvious he cheated. So Manfred was going to take his revenge by seducing Titan's wife Lara. By page fourteen, it was looking rather as if Lara wouldn't take much persuading to exchange bodily fluids with Manfred. Whoever Penelope Black was, she certainly knew how to increase the heartbeat with a few well-placed verbs and definitely had a handle on village life. And there were some interesting euphemisms and innuendos as well. (*If you were my woman, Lara, I'd have pleasure licking you into shape.*) Marnie needed a cigarette after Chapter Four.

She'd had good intentions of having a rummage in the red box which she'd brought from her mother's garage, but she couldn't put the book down. Plus she needed a cheer-up and she knew she wouldn't find anything spirit-lifting in a box of memories attached to her family. Better to spend the evening in the company of fictional people who couldn't hurt her.

*

She woke up the next morning with sunshine streaming through the curtains bathing the room in a blush pink light. It was going to be the perfect day for a walk in the wood, she thought, if Emelie was up for it. She had a coffee and read another couple of chapters of her book and wondered if the author knew this area. It was too much to believe that the so-called fictional village of Wellsbury and its cast of characters had nothing to do with Wychwell and its inhabitants.

She bumped into Derek as he was coming out of the shop. He had a grin on him so big, it had its own moon. Marnie was almost embarrassed to ask him how he was, but felt obliged to.

'I've just had the best night's sleep I've ever had. No one snoring like a pig at the side of me, no one nudging me with their elbow telling me to go and get them a cup of tea,' he beamed and Marnie had to check that his feet were on the ground, because he looked taller, as if he were hovering above it.

'And ... how is Una?' She winced as she said her name.

'Don't bloody care,' came the reply. 'I feel like I've been let out of a windowless prison. Will you let the new owner know that they've done me the best favour in the world please, Marnie?' He grabbed her hand and began shaking it vigorously. 'I'm not sure I would ever have been brave enough to leave her if I hadn't been given this chance.' And off he strolled with his newspaper under one arm and a box of cornflakes under the other.

Marnie crossed the green and headed towards Little Apples. Outside Peach Trees, Dr and Mrs Court were standing with a young woman Marnie didn't recognise. As she neared, she saw that Mrs Court was holding a baby, patting its back with a gentle rhythm. Mrs Court was grinning even more than Derek had been.

'Morning,' Marnie said to them. It would have been impolite not to ask about the baby, but Mrs Court beat her to it anyway.

'This is our first great-grandchild,' she said, pride warming her voice. 'And she's called Sophia after me.'

'She's beautiful,' said Marnie.

'Would you like to hold her?'

'I'm not ... sure ...'

But Mrs Court was already putting the baby in Marnie's arms. 'There's nothing like the scent of a newborn is there?'

Marnie breathed her in as her hand touched the butter soft skin on her head and the downy fair hair.

'Is she good?' she dredged up a standard question.

'So far,' said the young woman. 'Drinks like a horse. I can't produce fast enough for her.'

The baby's legs were tucked up, resting on Marnie's chest. Her hand a perfect small-scale curled around Marnie's index finger, but it was the tiny nails that drew Marnie's eyes the most. There were fine lines at the tips as if they'd been French manicured by a master miniaturist.

'Hard to imagine that this time last week she was inside your tummy, isn't it Jasmine?' Mrs Court was saying.

'You could hardly tell I was pregnant, I was lucky,' Jasmine smoothed her hand over her almost flat stomach. 'I was four months in before I even had a clue she was on her way.'

Her mother screaming at her. 'How could you not know?'

'She's beautiful,' Marnie said, speaking to drown that voice in her head.

'Isn't she?' said Dr Court.

'Two pushes and a shove and she was out too,' said Jasmine. 'I didn't even have time for gas and air.'

Gabrielle sobbing. 'I'm glad it hurt. I'm glad you needed stitches. They should have sewed it up completely then you couldn't ruin anyone else's life, you bitch.'

The baby smelt of talcum, milk and something else that Marnie couldn't define. Something that drifted up her nostril and found the place in her brain that recognised it and remembered.

Marnie felt the baby's mouth gently butt against her shoulder. She placed her cheek next to her head, soaking up the warmth, the scent, the fragility, the life. It was sweet and unbearable and too much.

'I think she might be hungry,' Marnie said.

'I've just fed the little madam,' Jasmine said with a tut of joyful exasperation. 'Come on, you.' She picked Sophia from Marnie's shoulder. The baby was wearing a white Babygro, soft as newly fallen snow. Her small fist was now in her mouth and her dark blue eyes were fixed on Marnie from over her mother's shoulder as she stepped into the cottage. The sight grew suddenly painful.

'Congratulations, she's lovely,' Marnie smiled and walked quickly away from the Court family before they wondered why her eyes were wet with tears.

Her head swung around to Herv's cottage as she was about to pass it, looking for signs of life. Looking for a woman wearing his shirt opening the bedroom curtains, but they were closed. She wondered if he was still sleeping or still out. Her damned heart was incorrigible. She didn't need Herv Gunnarsen wafting his Norwegian pheromones her way and making her second-guess what might or might not be going on in his life.

Little Apples was one of the prettiest cottages in Wychwell, if one of the smallest, with very thick stone walls and a roof that had been put on in pre-spirit level days. The windows were tiny, but there were a lot of them. She knocked on Emelie's green door and heard a 'come in' from the other side of it. Tentatively she opened it a sliver but stayed on the doorstep. 'It's me, Marnie,' she called.

'I said, come in,' ordered Emelie cheerfully.

Marnie walked in, after wiping her feet on the doormat. A damp smell met her nose first before the scent of freesias, clustered in a pot on the telephone table by the door. Emelie was pulling a sheet of paper out of an old-fashioned typewriter which sat on a table at one end of her lounge. She balled the paper in her hands.

'The words won't come to me at all,' she said, shaking her head.

She had her lovely hair plaited over the top of her head

today and was wearing a white blouse gathered at the neck and a long heavily flowered skirt. She looked as if she had climbed down from an alp.

'I wondered if you were up for showing me where those strawberries were,' said Marnie. 'But if you're busy . . .'

'No, I'm not busy. I can't think straight today – ' she tapped the side of her head ' – I'm getting old.' Then she laughed as she launched the paper snowball at a mesh bin full of others, but it missed. Emelie bent to pick it up and stalled halfway with stiffness.

'I'll get it for you,' said Marnie.

'Thank you,' replied Emelie. 'Today my head and my body are united in defeating me. I'll go and get my boots. A walk and a stretch will do me good.' She pointed towards Marnie's trainers. 'Your shoes will get ruined in the mud. You can borrow a pair of my wellingtons if you're a size three or smaller.'

'Four and a half,' said Marnie. 'It doesn't matter, they're old ones.'

Marnie picked up the paper ball and noticed a clutch of words on it as she transferred it to the bin: *illicit, forbidden, love.*

'You like writing then?' she asked.

'Poetry mainly,' nodded Emelie, slipping her foot into an ankle boot. 'But I've been working on something else for a while now. It's a secret,' and she winked.

'Sounds intriguing.'

'All will be revealed one day.'

Marnie noticed on her bookshelf there were the three *Country Manors* sitting alongside a collection of important-looking hardbacks. She wondered how many more shelves in Wychwell held copies of that trilogy.

'Do you have anything to collect the strawberries in?' asked Emelie.

'I've got a carrier bag in my pocket,' replied Marnie.

'Take a basket,' said Emelie, pointing into her kitchen where there were three woven wicker shoppers of differing sizes hanging from nails in the beams. 'It's nicer to collect fruit in baskets, it doesn't get spoilt as much.'

'Thank you again' said Marnie, reaching up and unhooking the smallest. She put it over her arm and felt instantly like a country girl.

'Aren't you going to lock your door?' asked Marnie, when she and Emelie walked outside.

'What for? Hardly anyone locks their doors in Wychwell. It's one of the advantages of living behind the times,' chuckled the old lady.

The lip of the woods was just behind Little Apples and Marnie knew why Emelie had her sturdy boots on. There was a lot of mud.

'The rain comes down the hill and settles here,' explained Emelie as Marnie tried to negotiate the sludge, hopping between islands of more solid ground. 'It's got worse the last couple of years. Climate change I expect, that's what everyone seems to blame for everything these days.'

The woods were very pretty, Marnie found. They reminded her of the forest in her favourite childhood book, *The Enchanted Wood*, where the trees were darker than they should be and whispered 'Wisha-wisha-wisha' to each other. Gabrielle had scribbled all over her book but Marnie had been disciplined for the defacing. Then after she'd dobbed her sister in, she'd been put on the naughty step for telling tales – she could never win.

'In April the woods are like a carpet of violet with the bluebells,' said Emelie, stepping over the tree roots as sure-footed as a goat. 'And in autumn it is like walking in gold.'

Everything was eerily still in the woods. Marnie felt as if she were being watched.

'There are owls in here at night,' said Emelie. 'And I've seen a deer. A beautiful fellow with fine antlers.'

'Do the woods belong to the estate as well?' asked Marnie.

'Oh yes.' Emelie sighed. 'You know, I hope the new owner doesn't want to cut down trees to make Wychwell bigger.'

'Surely not,' said Marnie. 'It's big enough.'

'I'm glad to hear you say that. Some people think that you're the new owner, Marnie, and all this talk of a manager is a smokescreen.' Emelie's eyes narrowed suspiciously.

'That's boll— . . . rubbish,' Marnie threw back.

'Your ears must have been burning considerably last night. I went for my dinner with Lionel in the Wych Arms. The air was quite thick with the mention of your name.' She had an impish light dancing in her eyes. 'And I did hear about Derek leaving Una.'

'Oh Lord.' Marnie swallowed.

'I wouldn't worry,' said Emelie, halting to take a breath. 'At least not about that. Una managed to insult Kay by asking her if Ruby would be willing to clean for her.'

'Did she really?'

'Una hasn't lifted a finger for years; now that Derek won't be doing the cooking and cleaning for her she is terrified she might have to learn how to dust.'

'Is there anything wrong with her?' asked Marnie.

'Yes, she has terminal idle-itis,' chuckled Emelie. 'I warn you to watch out for her playing a sick card if you are thinking of increasing her rent. Her nerves, her migraines, her bad feet, her bad back. It's not healthy for a woman only in her late forties to be so lazy. Kay was most affronted that her precious schoolteacher daughter should be asked to clean for her.'

'I wish I'd been a fly on the wall,' laughed Marnie, as they started walking again.

'There was also a lot of interest in the vans that come to your house in the mornings,' Emelie added. 'I thought I should warn you.'

Which prompted Marnie to ask, 'Emelie, how did you know I made cheesecakes?'

Emelie's hand shot to her mouth. 'Marnie, I could have cut out my tongue, when I asked you if you wanted the strawberries for your baking in front of Herv. Lilian told me one day about the Tea Lady, but she swore me to secrecy. I can only apologise, it won't happen again. I certainly acted very dumb yesterday in the Wych Arms and didn't say a word. I hope that I haven't spoiled anything for you.'

'No, not at all. It went completely over Herv's head,' Marnie replied, hoping Lilian hadn't gossiped to anyone else. She was surprised. She didn't think Lilian would have sold on her secret.

There was a motherlode of wild strawberries in the wood, especially by the side of the beck that ran into the larger Blackett Stream.

'Some people say that the *Blackett* stream is named after Margaret Kytson's black cat, did you know?' Emelie informed Marnie as she picked her way across to a long-fallen tree and sat down on it to rest.

'I read about it in Lionel and Lilian's book,' she replied.

'Ah yes, the book.' Emelie smiled mysteriously. 'But it is sadly unfinished because there are so many secrets which have not yet come to the surface. And of course, the chapter we are all waiting for can only be written when poor Margaret is found.' They both took a moment to contemplate the vastness of the wood. 'Until she is laid to rest, Wychwell cannot move forward. That is what Lilian always believed: that it is anchored to the past with chains of poor Margaret's blood and Wychwell's guilt.'

'Has no one got any idea where the well is?' asked Marnie.

'Sadly not. And the wood is, as you can see, enormous. Lilian so wanted to give Margaret and her child a proper burial before she d—' She cut off her words then, and fell pensive, as if she were chasing something around in her head that refused to be caught. 'Now wait, Lilian did once say that she had an idea about where the well might be. She saw something when she was doing some research into the book and was looking at the accounts ledgers over at Titus's house. She said he wasn't very keen on letting her but he could hardly refuse. But she didn't write it down and then it was lost. She could never remember what it was.'

'I'm surprised she could read those ledgers. His handwriting is deliberately obscure.'

'Well, she must have been able to read some of it because I recall her saying that it was so obvious, she couldn't think how she'd missed it. She went through the ledgers again but couldn't find it the second time.' She lifted her shoulders and dropped them. 'I suppose if it were as obvious as she said, someone else would have noticed it too.' She smiled at that. 'And this was dear Lilian after all.'

As they talked and picked more strawberries, Marnie discovered that the lilt in Emelie's speech and the strange pronunciation of some of her words were down to the fact that she had been born in Austria and had never quite lost the accent.

'We had a large house in Salzburg,' Emelie told her. 'My father wouldn't bow down to the Nazis and he was arrested and ... "pressured". He was returned to us, fully complicit – or so they thought. We escaped, like the von Trapp family but without the music. My father was a scientist with code-breaking skills which were useful to the British so we were brought to England and changed our name from Taubert to make us fit in better. The government hid us in this village; obviously they must have paid Jago – Lilian's father – well for the inconvenience because it was clear that he hated us. It was very hard for people to differentiate between Austrians and Germans then. If you spoke German, you were automatically a Nazi to some people, who were hostile to us as a result. The Suttons in particular. Titus's father was a monster. No wonder his son grew up to be such a liar and a cheat.' Marnie noticed Emelie's expression of deep disgust. She thought she knew what that meant.

'Did you invest money with him too?'

Emelie gave a little trill of laughter. 'Not I,' and she shook her head slowly from side to side. My father always taught me that if something looks as though it is too good to be true, then it most likely is. Titus tried to take my money of course. It is foolproof, he said. Only high-risk investments would have paid off what he was promising, I told him and I was right. I know how to play the stock markets, my father was a very rich man in Austria but of course we lost everything when we came over here.' And she sighed heavily. 'I have never been back to Austria. I was too afraid of what I would find. Our house was taken from us, everything we owned. I never saw my dogs again.'

Emelie wiped her eye with a tissue that she pulled from her cuff and Marnie thought she must have worried about them so much. That's why Marnie chose not to have pets. Any attachments she made didn't tend to last very long.

'I have always seen through Titus,' Emelie went on, pushing her tissue back up her sleeve, 'but he has charm and finesse, or at least he had when he was younger. Now he is growing into the body he deserves, a swollen gout-ridden slug. I want to climb one of the apple trees in my garden and sprinkle salt on him when he passes. Ugh.'

Marnie started giggling at the mental image of Titus shrivelling under a salt-shower, which set Emelie off too and they laughed until their stomachs hurt. They ventured further into the woods to pick more strawberries but the mud defeated them. It was okay though, Marnie had enough by then. She didn't want to steal too many from the forest and waste them.

'What are you doing for the rest of the day?' asked Emelie as they left the shade of the woods for the sunshine.

'I shall take my book and sit in the garden,' said Marnie. 'I'm at a really good bit.'

'What are you reading?' Emelie studied her. 'Let me think. I can see you as a Daphne du Maurier girl. *My Cousin Rachel*, maybe? Lilian always liked that one. She will have told you all about her sister Rachel of course.'

'Oh boy, did she,' nodded Marnie, 'but I'm going to have to disappoint you. I'm reading *Country Manors*, the second one. I know it's trash, I know it's slightly porny, but I'm absolutely loving it.'

'Many people who didn't read before are reading those stories,' Emelie replied. 'It is like a blood transfusion into the book world. It can only be a good thing.' She pushed at her old, creaky gate. 'Marnie, don't forget where I live. Come and see me again soon. The door is always open and the kettle is always on.'

'I will,' said Marnie, looking up at the apple tree that stood in Emelie's front garden and imagined her hanging from the top bough with a bag of Saxa in her hand.

Herv's bedroom curtains were open when she passed. *Come on, chop-chop, get home. Nothing to see here,* said a bolstering voice in her head. She walked across the green and heard someone shouting at her, a male voice that she didn't recognise. Not her name but 'Hey, you there', as if he was telling her off for trespassing on his land. She wasn't surprised to turn and find the owner of that voice was Titus, walking towards her with a quick step. She prepared herself for battle.

'We haven't been properly introduced,' he said, holding out a large hand with short stubby fingers. 'Titus Sutton. Heard about you, obviously. Hope you're settling in.'

The last time Marnie had seen him, he'd been purple-faced with rage at the will-reading. He must know by now what she had found in those ledgers. Or maybe he thought she hadn't broken his coded handwriting yet. He didn't look like a man expressly worried as he stood before her with his oily smile. She didn't buy this super-matey routine, but she was intrigued by it. She'd bring him down soon enough, when she was ready. She shook his hand. 'Marnie Salt, pleased to meet you at last too.'

'Been meaning to say hello and reset, start off on the right foot,' he said. 'Shame Hilary isn't with me. She goes off to stay with her sister once a month. She's not been well for years. Hilary's a southerner. Alas,' and he guffawed, there was no other word for it. 'Anyway, very glad to have bumped into you. Must dash.' He made a pretence of walking off only to turn on his heel after a couple of steps. 'Meant to ask. Update of parish records, Lionel needs your date of birth. I'm just on my way to see him actually, I could tell him for you, if you like.'

'May the first, nineteen eighty-four.'

She saw a nerve in his cheek jerk.

'May Day, eh? And George Orwell's finest work. That's quite a statement birthdate, if I may say so.'

'I hadn't really thought about it,' said Marnie, which wasn't true.

'Splendid,' and with that, Titus set off in the direction of the church.

As she walked the remainder of the way home, she began to wonder if Lionel genuinely had asked for her birth date. It was an approximate one anyway, seeing as no one knew exactly when she had been born because her birth had never been registered by a parent. But Titus didn't need to know that detail. Parish records or not.

Titus didn't go to Lionel's, instead he thundered into the shop where Kay Sweetman was reading the latest *Women by Women* magazine behind the counter.

'You all right, Titus?' she greeted him, wondering why he was huffing like an old steam train.

'No, I am not,' he replied. 'Packet of my usual. I need something to calm my nerves.'

Kay opened the cabinet behind her and got out a packet of Titus's favoured brand of cigarettes. 'What's up?'

'That bloody woman,' he chuntered.

'Oh, her,' sniffed Kay. She knew exactly which bloody woman Titus meant. 'She's wrecked Una's marriage, have you heard?'

Titus hadn't, so Kay took great delight in filling him in with all the details.

'I wish she'd bugger off back to where she came from,' she remarked.

'I don't think there's much chance of that.' Titus gave a
bark of humourless laughter. 'There is no mysterious owner
of the estate. It's her, playing stupid games. I'd put my life
savings on it. I knew there was something else to this story.'

Kay was all ears. 'Oh, what makes you think that then?'

So Titus told her.

Marnie took her book out into the garden along with a can of
ice-cold cherry cola and an egg mayo sandwich. She'd found
a little wooden table hidden in an overgrown rose bush which
she'd washed down and positioned in front of the bench. The
stream looked thirsty; the banks were dry and crumbly and
she thought they'd welcome some rain. She looked ahead
at the wood and wondered if Margaret Kytson's grave was
within her sights. The wood surrounded Wychwell on all
four sides and unless they dug the lot of it over, they weren't
going to find it by design. Sometimes, when she was down
at the bottom of the garden, Marnie thought she detected
movement out of the corner of her eye but it was just a trick
the sunlight played when it found an opening through the
leaves and dived through them. She decided she wouldn't
have minded if it had been the witch, peeping behind a trunk
watching her.

The second book in the *Country Manors* series was much
better than the first. The characters were more rounded and
the action pacier, and it was very racy. There was a woman
featured called Kate Sowerby whom Marnie wanted to
punch. She reminded her of Kay Sweetman in the shop. They
even had the same thin-lipped mouth set in a perma-sneer.

The heat began to make Marnie drowsy. She read until
her eyelids felt too heavy to keep open and gave in to the
tiredness. It was so peaceful here. She hadn't imagined

she could ever feel such a level of calm, especially with all that she had going on: making enemies of everyone in Wychwell as she prepared to put up their rents, slash their bonuses, split up their marriages. She didn't want to raise Emelie's rent but she might have to, just a little so as not to mark her out as a special case and bring the wrath of the villagers down on her too. Then all thoughts of rents and Emelie and witches were washed away by tides of sleep creeping up on her, dragging her down into their warm waters of oblivion.

She had no idea how long she'd been asleep when she was suddenly awoken by the chill of a shadow falling across her. She was jerked from the depths of unconsciousness so quickly that she almost got the bends.

Kay Sweetman was bearing down on her, arms akimbo, measly mouth a downward arc like a croquet hoop.

'Can I please ask you what's going on between you and Herv Gunnarsen?' There was nothing polite about Kay's demand, despite the please.

'I beg your pardon? And what are you doing here?' It hadn't got past Marnie that Kay would have had to walk through her house to reach her.

'I knocked and when no one answered I came in,' said Kay, as if this was a perfectly reasonable explanation. 'So?'

'What on earth has it got to do with you?' asked Marnie, beyond affronted. How bloody dare she?

Kay's head pushed forwards and one hand left her hip to start waggling a finger at Marnie.

'I'll tell you what it's got to do with me, shall I? My daughter's very upset, that's what it's got to do with me.'

Does trouble have me permanently on the end of a fishing rod, thought Marnie.

'She's had to go to the doctors for some tablets to stop her crying, because of you,' Kay went on.

'Because of me?' squealed Marnie. What the actual ...? She really was getting absolutely sick and tired of never being able to escape from hassle. If she lived on a cartoon desert island with only a palm tree for company, they'd end up falling out with each other.

'Yes, because of you. Well, I'll tell you this for nothing, lady. I won't have my daughter depressed. You stay away from Herv and stop coming between them.' Kay's finger was exercising so much it was gaining muscle.

That was it, Marnie decided. No more Mr Nice Guy. She was an adult now. And self-employed. She didn't have to shut up and take any crap from anyone. She didn't have to bite her tongue for fear of getting sacked. She didn't have to stand the blame for fear of the naughty step or slapped legs. All the good that the strawberry-picking and slug-laughing and sunshine-sleep had done her today had been dashed away with a single wipe from Kay bloody Sweetman.

'Shall I tell you something, Mrs Sweetman,' Marnie got up slowly from the bench, her voice controlled, hinting at contrition. Kay Sweetman was a tall woman so Marnie still had to look up at her when she was fully on her feet. She smiled, giving no hint of the tirade to come. 'If I want to talk to Herv Gunnarsen, then I will. If I want to snog Herv Gunnarsen till his lips fall off, then I will, subject to his compliance of course. And if I want to move Herv Gunnarsen into my house and have naked orgies with him and invite half of Skipperstone along to watch, then I will.' Her voice was now at full volume. 'How dare you walk into my home and lay down your laws, and if your twenty-nine-year-old daughter's nose is put out of joint because the man she fancies doesn't fancy her back then tough tits. Tell her to grow up and move on. Now get out of my house before I grab you by your scrawny neck and throw you out.'

Marnie registered the expression of horror on Kay Sweetman's face. She'd taken the threat as a real one that would very likely be implemented – and she was right to. Marnie knew that she could look convincingly murderous because her mother had once told her that she was genuinely frightened of what she could be capable of, which had led her to the conclusion that her true parentage must be right at the business end of the dodgy scale.

Kay Sweetman began to scuttle back to the house, with Marnie in close pursuit behind her to make sure she went. It was as they walked through the kitchen that Marnie realised Kay would have seen the stack of flat-pack Tea Lady Bakery boxes in the corner. It didn't help her mood.

When Kay was finally out of the house, Marnie called after her in a calm voice that belied her inner turbulence, 'Thank you for coming. Don't do it again.'

'Not hard to work out why Herv Gunnarsen is sucking up to you and it's nothing to do with fancying you,' Kay threw back at her.

'Goodbye, Mrs Sweetman.'

Marnie shut the door, none too softly. She had no idea what Kay meant, nor was she going to ask her, but still the words wouldn't quite be as easily dismissed as the woman herself had been.

Chapter 31

Kay's invasion of Little Raspberries totally ruined Marnie's weekend. She had a dream that night riddled with vivid images of Titus and Kay hiding in her house, watching everything she did and then reporting it all back to her mother. Marnie woke up stressed and cross very early the next morning and decided that she might as well channel that black energy into compiling the first major report for Mr Wemyss to pass on to the new owner of Wychwell.

Based on what rental properties were going for in the Dales, she'd worked out what the Wychwell locals would now be paying if they hadn't been so heavily subsidised. But as much as she would have liked to have slapped the standard market prices on people like Kay Sweetman, she knew that Lilian wouldn't have wanted her to do that. The new rental system she'd come up with reflected the estate's loyalty to them without being a walkover.

Considering the price would include all their utilities and maintenance, they really couldn't complain. Marnie wondered, though, if the present residents did know that any maintenance work on their homes was part of their estate's pledge to them, apart from the Suttons of course, who had taken full advantage of that perk. Judging by the state of some of the brickwork and windows, she thought they might not.

Marnie also suggested that the four derelict cottages be restored and rented out too. On the records they weren't named after fruits like the others, but had their pre-Lilian names: Ironhall, Tin Cottage. Winter House, Summermoor. She asked that the villagers be given first option to rent any of the habitable cottages at the 'special rate'. Johnny and Zoe Oldroyd and Ruby in particular, because it might do her good to put a little distance between herself and a mother who still treated her as if she were six. All remaining empty cottages would be offered to people further afield and used for holiday lets, at full price. More people in the village should increase the footfall into the shop and the pub and help their businesses so they wouldn't need the estate funds propping them up as they had been doing.

She typed all this up and emailed it to Mr Wemyss so that he could forward it to the new owner. After her altercation with Kay, she was ready to let it ripple out towards the villagers that she wasn't to be messed with.

Rumbles of thunder began in the early afternoon. The sky started to blacken by the second, the clouds grew pregnant with rain. They were in for some serious showers, but Marnie needed to go out for brown sugar. She could have got away with white, but she was a perfectionist and brown sugar was far superior in a toffee apple crumble topping, giving it a chewiness that a white version wouldn't. It had just started to spit when she set off for the supermarket, heavy warm drops that the grass and the stream would welcome with open arms, she imagined.

There was a Tea Lady in Troughton, a small town with a big Tesco five miles away. Marnie thought she might kill two birds with one stone, see how her fare was going down and do her shopping straight after. She parked up in the supermarket car park and though the rain hadn't reached Troughton yet, she couldn't remember ever seeing the sky so dark during a midsummer day.

She had to wait ten minutes for a table to come free in the Tea Lady, but it gave her observation time. She watched the expressions of people partaking of afternoon tea and trying her squares of cheesecakes. No one was exactly jumping on their chairs declaring them the best they've ever tasted but there seemed to be a general air of 'yum' in the café.

When she was eventually seated, Marnie chose the cheesecake of the day – cherry and chocolate – and a pot of tea. And when she asked the waitress for the bill she asked if she could buy a cheesecake to take home because it was so delicious.

'Isn't it just,' replied the waitress. 'My favourite is the caramel and apple one, but it's not on this week. We've got a new cook in and she's fantastic. But we don't do a takeaway cake service, I'm afraid.'

'You should think about it,' said Marnie. 'I'd have taken a whole one off your hands.'

'I'll tell the boss,' said the waitress, smiling at the tip the nice customer had pressed into her hand.

So they were going down well, thought Marnie as she headed back to Tesco. Rumbles of thunder immediately followed crackles of lightning. She ran in and bought her sugar as the announcement came over the tannoy that the store would be closing in ten minutes. The rain was bouncing off the floor when she went back to the car and though her head and shoulders were dry, her jeans were soaked from the knee down. It was now falling so fast, before she switched on the wipers, it looked as if she was in the mid-cycle of a car wash.

The traffic was doing a slow-moving conga through Troughton. It halted completely outside the railway station, even though the traffic lights ahead were green. They changed back to red and then back to green and she was still in the same position and so Marnie presumed some poor sod had broken down. Other poor sods were waiting at a taxi rank to her left. There wasn't a shelter, a couple had umbrellas or hoods up, but the woman holding an overnight bag off the ground and standing last in the queue had neither and she looked drenched.

Then Marnie realised who it was – Hilary Sutton. She had that thin stripey beige raincoat on which had been dyed dark brown with rain and her shoulder-length grey hair was hanging over her face in soaked rats' tails. Even if she was a Sutton, Marnie couldn't have left her like that. She pressed down the window and called out. 'Mrs Sutton, want a lift?'

Hilary looked over, squinting in an effort to see who was calling her.

'It's me, Marnie. From Wychwell. Want a lift?'

Marnie was surprised that she accepted. She had thought that Hilary might have refused with a haughty, 'No thank you.' But she opened the door and said, 'I'm very wet. Do you have something I can put over your seat?'

'It doesn't matter, it's only rain, it'll dry,' said Marnie. 'Get in.'

So Hilary did, after quickly whipping off her coat and putting it in the footwell. 'Thank you,' she said. 'I've been stood there for ever. I'm dripping all over your car.'

'Don't worry about it,' said Marnie. 'It can't be helped.'

'I never usually have a problem getting a taxi there.'

'Been anywhere nice?' No sooner had Marnie asked the question that she remembered Titus saying his wife had been away at her poorly sister's.

'London,' replied Hilary. 'I go and see my sister one week-end every month. She's not very well.'

'Sorry to hear that,' said Marnie. Ahead the traffic had started to move, albeit at a snail's pace.

'I like to go there. I like sitting on the train and reading.'

'Me too,' said Marnie.

Hilary opened up her handbag to get out a tissue and started dabbing her face with it. Marnie saw that she had a copy of the first *Country Manors* in there. She wouldn't have thought Titus's wife would have been the sort.

'You too,' said Marnie.

'Sorry?'

'*Country Manors*. You're reading it too.'

Hilary looked slightly caught out, as she were ashamed of being seen with such a controversial tome. 'Someone on the train gave it to me to try. Have you read it?'

'I'm half-way through the second one.' The car was picking up pace now, thank goodness. 'I prefer it to the first but stay with it. The second one is a cracker, but you need to have read *Buyers and Cellars* for it to all make sense.'

'I will. Thank you.'

'She's certainly done very well out of it, hasn't she? The author?'

'Has she? I don't know.'

'They say she's earned ten million this year.'

'Doesn't make you happy though, does it?'

'I think I'd be considerably happier with ten million in the bank. Wonder why she doesn't reveal who she is.'

'I worked in public relations in London before I married Titus and came to live up here,' said Hilary. 'I can tell you exactly why: because all that intrigue is very marketable.'

Hilary didn't look like someone who had worked in public relations. She looked like someone who had never worked and did some needlepoint every so often when the job of counting her money became a tad too boring.

'I thought as much,' said Marnie, driving slowly through some deep pools of water at the side of the road. 'Quite a change for you then, leaving a PR job in London to come up to Wychwell.'

Hilary didn't answer for a while. When she did speak, she said something Marnie hadn't expected at all.

'I hate Wychwell.'

'Really?' She was even more shocked that Hilary had disclosed it to her.

'When I married Titus, the deal was that we'd live there whilst his father was ill and then we'd move down south. I'm a city girl. I can't be doing with all this green.'

The contemptuous way in which she said it, made Marnie chuckle and she immediately apologised for that.

'I'm sorry for laughing. I'm just surprised.'

'I like noise and shops and . . . life. If I didn't have an injection of London in my veins every month, I think I'd lose the will to live.'

'I like London, but I wouldn't want to stay there all the time,' said Marnie. 'I'm a town girl. Or at least I thought I was, but I'm enjoying village life give or take . . . er . . .' Hilary ended the sentence for her.

'Busybodies. And there's more politics in Wychwell than there is in the whole of the houses of parliament. And there's no children in Wychwell, simply a load of empty houses and a few people who think they're better than anyone else on the planet. Let me tell you, I was glad when I heard that you'd got the job of dragging it kicking and screaming into this century. I had a little giggle to myself when we were all in Lilian's will-reading meeting. I thought *good on you*, whoever the new owner is. I did hope it was you.'

Marnie was touched as well as taken aback. 'It's not me, but thank you for that, Hilary. You're one of very few supporters of change, though. I can't imagine my proposals will go down well.' She obviously hadn't checked the Sutton bank account yet.

'The shop and the pub haven't got any customers. There will be even more houses empty when the old ones die. Wychwell will be a ghost village in fifty years if something drastic doesn't happen. I might hate living there but I wouldn't want to see that.'

'I have plans,' said Marnie, aware that Hilary might be fishing for information for her husband, but somehow she didn't think so.

'Good. You do what you have to,' said Hilary.

'I will.'

'I liked Lilian,' said Hilary. 'I didn't have much to do with her because I think she was wary of me, because I'm married to Titus. I always thought that was a shame because I admired her. I think we could have been good friends if I hadn't had the Sutton name.'

They were just passing Scarpgarth Nursery school, which prompted Marnie to ask,

'Do you have any children, Hilary?'

'Couldn't,' she replied. 'Titus wasn't bothered anyway. He has a child. He doesn't think I know, but I do. I always have. He's never laid claim to her and I have no idea how he can do that.'

Marnie did.

A silence fell for a long minute then Hilary suddenly swivelled in her seat towards Marnie.

'I'm afraid I've lied to you. I haven't been to see my sister, I've been having an affair. There's a coffee shop around the corner here. You don't fancy stopping do you? I'll pay.'

Hilary's hands were shaking when she picked up her cup.

'I'm sorry, I don't know why I blurted that out,' she said. 'I haven't had anyone to talk to and I'm going slightly mad, I think. Probably the menopause. I hardly know you and there I am telling you my most guarded secret.' Her grey eyes were brimming with building tears. 'You could tell Titus and spoil my plans. I must be ill.'

Marnie reached across the table and squeezed her arm. She felt freezing to the touch.

'I give you my word, what happens in the Red Café, stays in the Red Café.'

Hilary smiled tentatively.

'I don't go down south to see my sister. Jennifer died two years ago but I didn't tell Titus. I just carried on going down there every month. I've known Julian and his wife for many years, as friends. Then dear Louise died, weeks before my sister did. Jennifer and I were very close, twins, identical. Julian and I helped each other through our grief. I don't think either of us thought our friendship would change into what it has.'

Marnie tried to think of something valuable to say. 'Wow' was all that came out.

'Titus and I haven't lived as man and wife for a long time. I'm merely someone who washes his clothes and pours him a brandy in the evenings after he's eaten the meal I've cooked.

I think I got used to living in the rut. I might always have been there as his unpaid servant had Julian and I not . . . found each other. I am making plans to leave Titus but I need to stay around for a tad longer. I want Titus never to forget the day, you see. I want him to realise exactly how much he has underrated me. But I shall be going very soon.'

'Wow,' said Marnie again.

'Julian told me of his true feelings last month. I didn't think my heart could hold so much joy. He's the most wonderful man.'

'Blimey,' said Marnie as a variation on wow.

'Tell me, I don't look the type.'

'You don't. I'm in shock.'

'I don't know why I told you. I don't trust very easily.'

'I promise I won't breathe a word,' said Marnie, notching a little cross on her heart with her finger.

'Julian has two children, both daughters, one pregnant. Beautiful girls. I shall be a sort of grandmother at Christmas.' Though the natural set of her expression was a sad, slightly haughty one, when she smiled it lent a softness and warmth to her whole face. As if a light had been turned on inside her.

'There will be children in my life at last. Not my own, but it doesn't matter. I shall love them as much as I would if they'd been mine.'

Her eyes looked glazed with a slick of happiness. Marnie wondered if Judith had had the same delight in her eyes when she found out she had been approved for adoption. Before she realised she'd taken in the spawn of Satan.

A waitress passed and Hilary gave her a ten-pound note and told her to keep the change.

*

Outside the rain was subsiding now and the sun was trying
to put in the odd appearance, when the clouds scuttling past
allowed it to do so. Hilary insisted that Marnie drop her
at Blackett Bridge and allow her to walk up to the Lemon
Villa so that no one would see them together and start
tittle-tattling.

'Thank you for listening to me, Marnie,' said Hilary as
the car pulled to a halt. 'And good luck with what you have
to do.'

'I'll need it,' said Marnie. 'Some people are really not going
to like me slashing all the monies they've been claiming from
the estate. They've all got to stop, I'm afraid.'

She waited for Hilary's expression to change but it
didn't.

'We don't claim anything from the estate ourselves. Titus
draws – *drew* – a wage for doing the accounts. He didn't need
to do much though: record things, chase rents when he had
to and arrange for maintenance when needed,' said Hilary. 'If
only Lilian had told him how bad things were, he might have
been able to help because he is very astute when it comes to
financial matters.'

He certainly is that all right, thought Marnie.

'He says that Lilian kept so much hidden from him, blundered on, made terrible decisions. Is he right? Is that what
you've found?'

So, Hilary really didn't know the truth of the matter.
Marnie decided to leave her in blissful ignorance. For now,
at least.

'I'm still trying to get to the bottom of it all, but yes, it
does appear that Lilian's decision-making wasn't that good.'
Lilian's decision to keep Titus in the job, anyway.

'Thank you for the lift.'

'Good luck yourself,' said Marnie. 'I hope it all works out for you, I really do.'

'You know, for years I believed that how Titus rated me was a fair assessment, until I learned from Julian that someone who doesn't know your value can't possibly tell you what you're worth.'

And with that, Hilary Sutton got out of the car, put on her soggy raincoat and set off in the direction of the Lemon Villa.

Later, Marnie was in the process of making herself a hot chocolate before bed when she remembered the red box. She took it out of the under-stairs cupboard and put it on the kitchen table but she suspected she'd be throwing all the contents away because it looked to be full of junk. There was a hideous pot vase she'd made at school. It must have been shoved away in a cupboard because it had certainly not been out on display, gracing a shelf. A flood of memories came rushing back to her: sitting at the potter's wheel creating it, giggling with Caitlin next to her, whose pot looked more like a giant erection. She had tried not to think about Caitlin because it hurt but they'd had some great laughs together and made so many plans that had come to nothing, as teenagers do: share a house, travel the world, have a double wedding.

There were a few old school books, a bracelet of her mother's which was hideous and plastic and probably why Gabrielle had decided she could have it. A small teddy bear – a souvenir from a school trip to Chester Zoo; a programme from a play Marnie was in and a clear plastic document folder. Marnie tipped the contents onto the table to find letters from the adoption agency, cards with Marnie's NHS and national insurance numbers on them and an old passport with a clipped corner. She opened it to see her eighteen-year-old self looking back at her, short cropped punk hairstyle, large bright eyes and lips set in a 'fuck you all' sneer. She wanted to climb into the photo and tell that girl she was all right, she was okay, she would survive. But to stay away from any man whose name began with a letter of the alphabet.

There was an envelope in the pile, handwritten to Miss Marnie Salt at her mother's address. The top had been slit open precisely with a knife, but the letter was still inside. Marnie took the two folded sheets of light blue paper out. The sender's name and address was written at the top, in neat handwriting.

Laura Hogg
'Evergreens
Sunningdale Avenue
Reading
Berkshire

It was dated 4 May 2002. Puzzled, Marnie read on.

Dear Miss Salt, or may I call you Marnie,
I hope you won't mind me writing to you, but I felt I had to ...

the letter began. She scanned it quickly to find out what it was about. Phrases leapt out at her from the page.

... I know what you must have gone through ... You must NOT think that any of it was your fault ... four years before ... I'm so sorry ... they should have prosecuted, then it wouldn't have happened to you too ... My parents never knew it was him ...

Marnie slumped to the chair and started the letter again, reading every word now. Reading every word of a woman who had once been a girl, like herself.

... I kept my son ... It has taken me a long time to trace you, using up quite a few favours – some possibly illegal, but as soon as I heard about you, I felt I had to find you. If I do not hear from you then I will presume you wish to be left alone, but please feel free to contact me and talk – any time you wish, I would be more than happy to be there for you.

By the time she had turned the page she had to wipe the tears forming thickly in her eyes. Tears of sadness for the girls they had been, tears of relief that she was not alone. And after the last word had been read, tears of anger that her mother had kept this letter from her when it could have made all the difference. Why had she kept it? Had she wanted to give Marnie some belated relief after her death? No, that didn't make sense because finding it now could only show how much Judith Salt had drawn out the pain for years when she could have stopped it. Or had she merely forgotten about its existence?

Marnie growled and that growl turned into a scream and with that scream, her arm lashed out sending her mug and all the things from the box scattering to the floor.

Marnie sank her head onto her arms and cried for her thirteen-year-old self who'd been so starved of love that when it came calling, she hadn't been able to resist.

Chapter 32

Marnie hadn't been able to sleep properly and eventually gave up the ghost and rose extra early to make the cheesecakes but her head was far from the task in hand. The contents of the letter she'd found in the box had been swirling around in her head, throwing it into turmoil. She wanted to dig up her mother and ask her why she hadn't told her about what Laura Hogg had gone through. She wondered if Laura Hogg's mother had called her a tart and slapped her face in anger and humiliation and walked around the house like a player in a Greek tragedy, back of her hand pressed against her forehead as she proclaimed, 'oh the shame'.

As Marnie waited for the van to arrive to pick up the cheesecakes, she took out a pad and a pen and began to write a letter to Laura Hogg but she didn't know how to start it.

A picture landed large and vivid in her head. A stiff-faced nurse, bringing her a warm cloth to ease the pressure in her breasts.

'It'll dry up eventually,' she said, her voice kippered and unsympathetic. She'd been right, of course. The milk had cried out of her breasts in the beginning, and unneeded had pined away in the end.

Marnie forced her focus onto the blank sheet of paper in front of her.

Dear Miss Hogg,

I must apologise for not writing but I never received your letter. I found it in my deceased mother's possession ...

No, she couldn't say that. She screwed it up into a ball and started again.

Dear Miss Hogg,

Thank you for writing to me all those years ago ...

But what if Miss Hogg was now married with children and had put this episode behind her? To get a letter might stir everything up again, as it had done for her. Maybe she should leave well alone. What was it that Herv had said once: *Sometimes it is best to let the past settle.*

She looked up the address on the internet and found that the Hoggs had lived there until 2005, but there was no trace of them after that. She felt bitter that Judith had robbed her of the opportunity to respond. As if she hadn't taken enough from her.

She started to write the letter she would have sent anyway. It didn't matter now that it had crossings out all over it.

I'm so sorry to hear what you went through ... I so appreciate you taking the time ... I wish I could have read this years ago ... I don't know why it was never given to me ... I don't know if it was misplaced kindness ... But it wasn't, she knew, because her mother kept bringing it up, and always with loathing prevalent in her

voice, long after the date of the letter, long after she must have
known about Laura Hogg and what had happened to her.

I'm glad it all worked out for you ... I didn't keep my baby ...

Tears slipped down her cheeks as she finished it, wished
Laura well. And her baby. The baby she'd been allowed to
keep. Then she sealed it in an envelope. Then she went over
to the sink, lit the corner of it with her chef's torch and held
it until the flames kissed her fingers. She'd always sent her
letters to Santa that way because someone had told her that
the smoke carried the words straight to his heart. She sluiced
the ashes down the drain and as the last of them disappeared,
so did the portal to those years. She had to close it up, nail it
shut, cement over it again or she would disappear down it and
drown in bitterness and anger.

She looked up at the clock to find it was nearly nine.
The van had never been that late before. She pulled up Mrs
Abercrombie's direct number on her phone and rang it.

'Fiona Abercrombie,' it was answered immediately, in her
usual clipped, business-like tone.

'Hi, Mrs Abercrombie, it's Marnie Salt here. Your van
driver hasn't turned up.'

'No, and he won't be doing so either,' said Mrs Abercrombie.

'Pardon?'

'I told you that if anyone got wind that we were being supplied by an outside caterer, the deal would be off immediately,
with no come-backs.' She sounded furious.

'No one could possibly have known,' replied Marnie.

'Then you should have been in here yesterday when two
women were shouting their mouths off *very* publicly and *very*
loudly about the cheesecakes not being made on the premises

but in a very scruffy little kitchen and they were going to tip off the trades descriptions office, environmental health and anyone else who'd listen.'

Then Marnie knew. It had to be Kay Sweetman. She was the only possible person who could have seen the boxes when she had stomped through Little Raspberries on Saturday.

'Did one happen to be very fat with short dark hair and the other a tall blonde?'

'Oh, know them do you? I rest my case. I shan't be ordering from you any more, Miss Salt, and I have to say I am very disappointed in you.'

'Mrs Abercrombie . . .'

'What?'

'Go to hell,' said Marnie and ended the call.

Five minutes later, Marnie was at the vicarage.

Lionel opened the door to find her holding a box. 'Good morning, Marnie, how are—'

'Lionel, would you like an apple crumble cheesecake?' said Marnie, interrupting him.

'I would absolutely love one,' he said, both surprised and delighted.

'There you go.' Marnie shoved the box in his hand, turned and walked back to the car where other boxes of cheesecakes were awaiting delivery. By the time Lionel had shouted a rather confused thank you, Marnie had her foot on the accelerator. She drove to the pub and gave David and his wife a cheesecake in the same manner, thrusting it hard into their hands. Then she went over to Dr Court's house and gave them one, then to Derek in the gravedigger's house, then to the Rootwoods. Then to the shop. Roger was behind the post office counter, Kay Sweetman was circulating stock.

'Hi, Roger,' said Marnie. 'I've made some cheesecakes. I thought you might like one.'

'Oh, I never say no to a piece of cheesecake,' said Roger, rubbing his hands together. 'Thanks very much.'

'I'll pop it here for you,' said Marnie, before marching back to the car for another. One that was covered in a gooey, sticky fruit sauce.

'I've got one for you as well, Kay,' said Marnie, fixed grin like a ventriloquist's dummy in place. 'It's a cherry one, look.' She approached Kay, opened the box, grabbed the back of Kay's head and pushed her face down into the dark red topping.

'If you want to fight with your gloves off, love, then I'm more than ready for you.'

It took Kay's brain seconds to register what had just happened and by the time she screamed, Marnie was already on her way to Una Price's house.

Herv was pointing the gable end of The Bilberries when Marnie strode up his lane carrying a box, wearing cheesecake blobs and runny dark cherry topping all over her white shirt.

'Hi, Herv, would you like a free cheesecake,' she said like a robot giving out special offers.

'Of course,' said Herv.

'Good, enjoy. With my compliments.' She held out the box out towards him, same deranged grin fixed on her mouth with superglue, but her eyes told a very different story. They were glassy with hurt and anger.

Herv took the box with one hand and caught hold of her arm with the other.

'What's the matter?' he said.

'Nothing,' snapped Marnie. 'Herv, let me go. I've got things to do.'

But he didn't let go, he did the opposite and tightened his grip, pulling her over his threshold.

'Sit down,' he said, 'I'll get you a towel.'

'If I stop moving I'll go mad,' she said, resisting him.

'You will stop moving and you will sit and you will go mad if you have to,' he said, with calm authority.

Marnie sat on the edge of his sofa. It suited the cottage but not him as it was very flowery and feminine. But it was soft and squashy and she could imagine that after a hard day's work, it would welcome Herv's big tired body like a hug.

He emerged from his kitchen and handed her a blue towel and she burst into tears and then buried her head in the towel, ashamed that she was making a fool of herself in front of him.

'I'll make you a coffee and then you can tell me what is wrong,' he said. 'Don't move from there.'

Marnie heard the kettle begin to boil and cupboards opening in his kitchen. The tinkle of a spoon. She wiped her face and dragged her finger underneath her eyes to remove any tear-melted mascara. There was lots of it, indicating she probably had panda-eyes, not that she cared. Herv returned with two mugs, handing one to her, before taking a seat in the armchair.

'Okay, let's start at the beginning,' he said. 'Why are you in this state and covered in cheesecake?'

'Because I've just shoved Kay Sweetman's head in one.'

'I see,' said Herv.

'And Una Price's. In a different one. Not the same one, in case you were wondering.'

'O-kay.' He paused for a moment, waiting for elaboration and when none was forthcoming he spoke again. 'Are you going to tell me why or do I have to guess?'

'I've been making cheesecakes for a firm that didn't want

anyone to know that they weren't made in-house by them. Kay found out and blabbed. I was warned that if that happened, my contract would be made null and void immediately.'

'Ah, the mystery black vans,' said Herv, now enlightened. 'They were picking up secret cheesecake orders.'

'I now have no job,' said Marnie and another tear slid down her cheek and she swatted it away, annoyed that it made her look weak and vulnerable. 'She didn't have to do that. She only did it because . . .' She stopped. *Because she thinks I'm after you* sounded like the stuff of playgrounds.

He pressed, 'Because?'

'Because she's a cow,' said Marnie. 'And Una Price. And we all know why she joined in.'

Herv chuckled. 'Drink your coffee,' he ordered.

She sipped at it and tried to think back to the last time a man had made her a cuppa. She couldn't remember. She wasn't sure if one ever had. She'd never been with anyone who woke her up with tea in the morning or whipped up a hot chocolate before bed. It was little considerations like those she yearned for the most. She bet Herv Gunnarsen was the sort of person who would make them. He took a drink from his own mug and grimaced.

'I forgot the sugar.'

He went to get some. He looked too big for the tiny kitchen. As if he were Alice in Wonderland who had just taken a potion. His head was only inches from the ceiling, and she'd noticed that he'd had to duck down through the front door too. Kindness emanated from him in waves and she knew why Ruby was mad for him because he was the perfect package: handsome, good company, considerate, hard-working with big strong arms that would close around you to give comfort. *Bet he's fantastic in bed,* said that annoying voice inside her, which she sent back to the corner post haste. Even though she had to agree.

'That's better,' he said, sitting back down. 'It's only half a teaspoon. I'm trying to cut it out completely but I have too much of a sweet tooth.' He opened his mouth and pointed to a canine. 'It's this one,' and he smiled and Marnie did too because it was hard not to catch one of Herv's smiles.

'I can guess why Kay did it,' he said.

'Can you?'

'She thinks I like you,' said Herv.

Marnie gave a little shrug. 'I don't know about that.'

'She's right, of course, I do,' he said.

'How can you not?' joked Marnie.

'You're a crazy mixed-up chick, but I like that too.'

She lifted her head and found his impossibly blue eyes and felt the crack of thin ice underneath her. She knew, if she let herself, she would fall very hard and very fast for this kind Norwegian man whom Lilian adored. That would mean a lot of pain when it all went tits-up. As it would, because it always did.

'Well you shouldn't like me,' said Marnie quickly, turning her attention back to the mug. 'I'm bad news. I should live on an island really because I have the extraordinary gift of getting on people's noses.'

'Up,' he said.

'Pardon?'

'You get *up* someone's nose. You get *on* their nerves. Or you get their goat. I think you should come to me once a week for English lessons.'

He was grinning, she could feel it, even though she was looking down at her coffee, because his grin warmed the room like a central heating radiator on full blast. He lifted the mug from her by the rim and put it down on the table and she felt the air between them shimmer like a heat haze.

'I do like you, Marnie. I can't help it.'

His hand came out to cradle her cheek, his fingers tender and warm on her skin.

'Don't, Herv,' she said, but she didn't move away, instead she closed her eyes and savoured his touch. Both of his hands were holding her face now, lightly as if she were one of Lilian's precious ceramics and when his lips gently grazed hers she felt a combustible mix of sunshine and hope and panic rush through her and it was all too familiar and a portent of disaster.

She pulled away.

'I'm sorry, Herv, I shouldn't have done that. I can't . . .' She stood up. 'Thank you for being so lovely, but I—' oh what could she say to explain why she shouldn't be here and why he should stop fancying her immediately and save them both the future heartache. She shagged a married man, that would do it. After what his wife had done to him, that would be as precise a hit as the knee had been in her uncle's crown jewels. But she didn't want him to despise her, as he surely would then – only to keep his distance, and to stay behind the platonic fence. Her heart would lap up this good guy like a starving cat would attack a bowl of cream if she let it. Herv Gunnarsen could make her the most vulnerable she'd ever been; then all sorts of things would come out of the woodwork and he'd hate her for what she was, what she'd done. '. . . I don't think about you in that way. I've had a shit couple of days and I shouldn't have given you the wrong signals, I'm sorry.'

'It's fine,' said Herv. 'I understand. Forget it and drink your coffee.'

'No, I should go,' she said. 'Thank you, but I should go.'

And she bolted out of his cottage hearing her body, soul and all her internal organs wildly protest. She was stupid, an idiot, a total fuck-up.

When she got back to Little Raspberries, she shut the door behind her and locked it. There was an incinerator in the garden and she filled it with the remaining boxes of cheese-cake. There were houses she hadn't called at: Emelie and the Oldroyds, to name two, but she couldn't face them. She set fire to Mrs Abercrombie's last order and stood staring into the flames, hypnotised for a while, thinking about Herv Gunnarsen's lips on hers and how he was probably the sort of bloke who would have kissed her for hours without it having to lead to more.

As the fire died to smoke, her phone tinkled the arrival of a text message.

Marnie, it's Justin. Can we talk?

As if she hadn't had enough today. She might have ignored him again if the morning hadn't gone in the way it had, but she found herself stabbing in a reply with a very angry finger.

What do you want

The answer came back immediately.

I need to talk to you. Please. Will you meet me?

When

That voice in her head screamed at her, *What do you mean, 'when'? Don't you dare.*

> **Friday? 2pm? The Peacock. That's near where you live isn't it?**

He didn't know she'd moved. She enlightened him.

> **Ive moved**

She didn't find him worthy of punctuation.

> **The Blue Boy?**

The Blue Boy, the last 'date' they'd had. When she'd done everything she could on the back seat to make him change his mind about spending her birthday with her. And failed.

> **Yes**

Thank you x said the text. She didn't reply to that.

Chapter 33

Marnie had an email from Mr Wemyss that afternoon to inform her that her recommendations had been approved by the new owner of Wychwell, apart from the rental cost she had agreed for Little Raspberries because no one ever paid for living there, it was an unwritten law; but she was to go ahead and implement her other suggestions. Marnie couldn't wait. She wrote letters to all the householders informing them of the new arrangements. In the case of Una and Kay, she put their rents up by an extra five pounds per month, not enough to have them seeking out the work-house, but enough to make a point. They would still be paying a quarter of what they would anywhere else plus all their heating and lighting and rates were thrown in. Titus's letter was especially long as she itemised everything that she had found he had been claiming for and demanded he pay it back.

She hand-delivered them as soon as she'd printed them out. Then sat back and wondered how long it would take for Mr Shit to meet Mrs Fan.

Nothing happened before bed, although Marnie was so keyed up for some reaction that she once again couldn't sleep and so decided to take herself off for a walk around the green to tire herself out.

There was just a fingernail snip of moon that night, bright against a velvety black starless sky. She sat on the bench after she'd done three laps and marvelled at how quiet everything was. The only sound was Dr Court's ginger tom stepping through the front-door cat flap. She liked it, though. She loved how the quiet of Wychwell seeped into her soul and she wouldn't have wanted to go back to a busy street in a busy town, or worse, a city like Hilary Sutton craved. Hilary hadn't adjusted to life here, but she had, too easily. Give or take the couple of village busybodies, as she and Hilary had touched on yesterday in the Red Café. She blurted out a giggle as she thought of Una Price opening up her door, standing there with her great saggy bosom propped up by her flabby arms, hint of triumph on her lips.

'What do you want?'

'I came to pass something on to you, Una.'

'What?'

'This.'

Marnie had picked up the cheesecake (thank goodness for the thick base she favoured) and slapped it straight onto Una's face like a clown's pie. It was a beautiful moment. Una had had a delayed reaction but a satisfying one. She'd screamed that she was blind. She had stumbled out of the house, slipped on some strawberry topping and landed flat on her bum on the road. She'd have an almighty bruise there by dawn and no Derek on hand to rub arnica into it for her, but Marnie didn't care. Or rather, she wasn't allowing herself to care.

Lilian would have hooted. They would have sat in her

conservatory and laughed until the tears rolled down their cheeks. Marnie looked across at the manor; it was such a beautiful house. Lilian had been so happy there in the last years of her life and it was a good thing, at least, that she'd died there and not in some impersonal hospital bed.

Then she saw it again. That pink light. But in the thick darkness she could also see a figure, she was sure of it. That was no ephemeral orb.

Marnie had the keys to the manor with her, on the same ring as her house key. She threw herself off the bench and across the green, past the end of Herv's lane, up Kytson Hill, fast as her legs would take her. Past Emelie's house, up the manor drive, key in her hand ready. She plunged it into the lock, barged through the door, flicked on the light and bounded up the stairs.

'Hello,' she called. 'Who's there?'

There was no orb of light, no spectral figure in the gallery. But deep in the belly of the house somewhere, she was sure she heard a door close. And ghosts, she knew, had no need of doors.

Marnie wasn't quite brave enough to hunt around the house then. Not because she was afraid to encounter a ghost, but a human. Was it the new owner or a burglar? Had he stayed in the house all night? When she went to the manor the next morning, she checked all the doors and windows and found them bolted from the inside, so whoever it was could only have got in through the front door. It had to the new owner, surely? Cilla and Herv had keys, but what would they be doing skulking around up there at stupid o'clock?

She was in the dining room scouring through the ledgers when Cilla and Zoe came in. Cilla greeted her cheerily. In the letter Marnie had given them, she'd offered Johnny and Zoe a cottage each if they wanted one, the rent to be included in their wage deal. Or if they didn't want to carry on working for the estate, she had offered them a much-subsidised one. In the case of Zoe, Marnie had proposed – and this had been endorsed by the new mystery owner – to help her with any costs she might incur if she went to university. She was sure by the following year there would be some money in the pot for that.

Cilla had confirmed, as asked, in writing that Johnny would very much like to move into one of the cottages and the promise to help Zoe was more than kind. And she requested that the new owner be thanked for confirming that The Nectarines would be theirs for the duration of their lives. Having it in writing meant a lot to Cilla and her nerves could climb down from high alert now. She was as chirpy as a spring sparrow though Zoe, Marnie noticed, was a little quieter than usual.

When Cilla brought Marnie a coffee, she closed the door behind her as if to impart a great secret.

'I thought I'd let you know that Titus has called a meeting for everyone tonight in the Lemon Villa at seven o'clock.'

'Oh really? That's interesting.' Not entirely unexpected though.

'I think you should be there too,' said Cilla. 'You are part of this village as well. The new owner's decisions affect you as much as us, I should imagine.'

'Thanks for the tip-off,' replied Marnie. 'Just out of interest, you didn't come up to the manor last night did you? About midnight?'

'Whatever for?' laughed Cilla. 'Nope, not me. Or anyone in my house. We were all tucked up in bed for ten latest. Why?'

'I was out walking and I saw the Pink Lady, so I ran up to catch her.'

Cilla shuddered. 'You're a braver person than me, then.'

Marnie had a sudden thought. 'There aren't any exits in the cellars, are there?'

'Not that I know of. And I know this place inside out,' said Cilla.

The cellars were the only place Marnie hadn't checked. She thought she'd take a look after she'd finished her coffee.

On the way out of the door, Cilla turned back.

'I heard what happened to Una and Kay yesterday. They've had it coming for a long time. Good on you, that's what Griff told me to tell you.'

Marnie carried on looking through the ledgers. What Emelie had said about Lilian seeing something in the pages that made her realise where the well might be had been niggling her. If it was here, Marnie was determined to find it.

When she eventually lifted her head to rotate the stiffness from it, she saw Herv in the garden through the window and her body began to respond to the sight. She'd thought of that fleeting kiss more times than she should have and wondered what would have happened had she not run off like a racehorse spooked by a gun. She knew she should go and clear the air because she didn't want things to be uncomfortable between them. She walked through into the conservatory and out of the doors, aware of her heartbeat increasing the closer she got to him.

'Morning, Herv,' she called. *Please don't hate me for being the rudest woman on the planet to you. Please don't ignore me.* He didn't. He turned and smiled and she wondered what the hell she was doing not letting him have free access to her heart. And all areas.

'Good morning. How are you today? Calmer, I hope?'

'Yes, much calmer,' said Marnie, although she didn't feel very calm next to him. She felt as if she'd been plugged into the mains. Her eyes dropped to his hands on the garden fork and she recalled how tenderly they'd cradled her face.

'Garden's looking lovely,' she said, scouring her mind for something, anything to say to him to show that she was okay with him, and wanted the same in return.

'Thank you. I do my best.'

'Is that edelweiss?' She pointed to the small white flowers covering a large patch of the garden. Lilian's tall lilies, standing in them, appeared to be growing in snow. It was an odd combination – but then, that was typical Lilian.

'Yes it is. Mountain flowers in a garden, not my idea,' and he clicked his tongue mock-disapprovingly. 'They need a different soil but Lilian insisted so I persevered.'

'You've done really well.' *God that sounds so patronising.*

'Thank you.'

The air between them was thick with unsaid words.

'Herv, about yesterday . . .'

'Don't worry, it's okay.'

'I don't want there to be any awkwardness between us.'

'There isn't, I promise.'

'Really?'

He gave a small nod. 'Of course, I understand.'

He didn't understand at all. He might have thought he did, but how could he?

'I like you,' Marnie said with a tentative smile. 'I would hate to think I gave you any wrong . . . any signals that . . .'

Herv tilted his head to one side and studied her intently.

'I can wait,' he said, his eyes twinkling.

'No one can wait that long,' replied Marnie, unsure if he was joking.

God he's sexy, said that ridiculous voice in her head. *Are you out of your tiny mind?*

'I don't suppose you fancy a trip down into the cellar with me?' she asked. 'Have you got a big torch?'

Well if that doesn't sound like innuendo, nothing does, the voice scoffed.

'Sure,' Herv answered her. 'What are we looking for?'

'A pink lady,' she replied.

The cellar, or rather cellars because there were eight of them, was accessed from the old boot room next to the scullery. Lilian had shown her underneath the house once, but it wasn't a very exciting place. It might have been when her grandfather was alive with his collection of valuable wines that her father either sold or drank. Now there were just empty racks and alcoves and lots of old furniture that was surplus to requirements covered in dust sheets.

The cellars were cavernous and chilly but there was nothing of interest down there. No secret doors – or trapdoors, for that matter, though she supposed that whoever she heard the previous night could have easily hidden themselves here until the coast was clear.

'It definitely wasn't an orb,' explained Marnie, 'it was a person, I swear it, a figure holding a torch or a light.'

'I have no answers,' said Herv, examining an alcove, knocking on the wall to find it was solid.

'We need Scooby-Doo,' sighed Marnie, then started to explain to Herv that he was a crime-solving cartoon dog, but Herv cut in and started singing the theme tune in Norwegian.

'*Se på Scooby-doo, så mye skrekk og gru* ... We have him in Norway. And we also don't like Scrappy-Doo.'

'I used to look like Velma when I was younger,' said Marnie. 'But without the glasses.'

'No, I can't see that. You are a Daphne.'

'I wish.' Daphne had always reminded Marnie of Gabrielle.

'So am I Fred or Shaggy?' asked Herv.

'A hybrid.'

Herv laughed, a deep merry boom of a sound that bounced back from the cellar walls, and she had a sudden vision of lying in bed with him, her head against his great chest, his arm draped possessively around her. A lazy Sunday morning where they'd be trading information about themselves, their histories, their memories. He would be talking about flowers and loving families, happy times in Norway and a perfect childhood and she'd be like a black cloud of doom with a backstory of rejection and resentment and her *Guinness Book of Records* entry for most mistakes in one lifetime. It couldn't ever have worked between them. He might have been able to plant flowers in his soil and let something good grow from it but her garden was full of triffids. He'd had a lucky escape.

As they were walking back upstairs, Marnie told Herv that Lilian had seen something in the ledgers that might indicate where Margaret Kytson's well was. He told her that there was a village meeting at seven that night and he thought that she should be present too.

Marnie went back to trying to read the ledgers through Lilian's eyes but nothing sprang out at her at all. Nothing even made her curious, and she wondered if there really was anything to see or whether she'd be better employed concentrating on matters that needed her more immediate attention, such as trying to find costings for rebuilding those four dilapidated cottages or combing over the accounts again to see if she could find any more of Titus's misappropriation of funds. The ledgers held still more secrets, she was sure.

HISTORY OF WYCHWELL BY LIONEL TEMPLE
Contributions by Lilian Dearman.

In 1849 Cecil Dearman, who inherited the manor after the death of his sibling Rodney, challenged his younger brother Tiberius to a dual. Both men were involved in a three-way relationship with 'Fat Bessie' Nevison of Pike Farm in Troughton. Miraculously both guns failed to go off so Cecil beat his brother to death with the end of his pistol and was executed for murder in the same year. Bessie married the last remaining brother Vestigen but she died in suspicious circumstances in 1851 – poisoned by sweets laced with arsenic. Vestigen was suspected of ridding himself of an unfaithful wife, but there was no evidence with which to charge him.

Chapter 34

The closer the clock hands swung around to seven, the more Marnie's nerves began to jangle. Could she really walk into Titus's house uninvited to face people who resented her presence in the village because she'd 1) put up their rents, 2) slashed their private funding, 3) snogged their heartthrob and 4) shoved cheesecake in their faces.

The first time she'd had to do a presentation in front of the industry demi-god that was Laurence Stewart-Smith, she'd almost walked out of her job rather than face him. He was well known for being impossible to impress and of being a closet misogynist. She'd thrown up the night before, had chronic diarrhoea in the morning. She was pretty sure, at least, that she wouldn't vomit or mess herself during her address because there was nothing left in her system to expel. It was always good to find a positive, she thought.

It was whilst she was putting her make-up on at the kitchen table that fateful morning that she heard something that would stay with her always. The radio was on and playing an anniversary programme which featured an interview with

Sammy Davis Junior. He was talking about the prejudices he had endured throughout his career.

'You always have two choices: your commitment versus your fear,' he said and that resonated so deeply with Marnie that she dropped her mascara. Commitment versus fear, which was it to be? She'd arrived at Café Caramba that morning with a whole new attitude. She presented her ideas to a room packed full of men expecting something weak and full of holes and instead she'd dazzled them into silence.

Now she was facing the same: which was more important, her fear or getting Wychwell back on its feet? Titus Sutton was big and bullish but he didn't have the power that Laurence once had over her: Titus couldn't sack her. Titus couldn't sully her name so she never worked again. Titus was simply a big bag of hot air – and a corrupt one at that.

So Marnie put on one of the power-suits she used to wear for work, applied 'don't-fuck-with-me' red lipstick and as she walked up to the Lemon Villa, recited Sammy Davis Junior's quote like a mantra. She had deliberately delayed her arrival until quarter past, to allow the meeting to be in full swing. She rang the doorbell, her jaw tight with tension. Hilary answered.

'I hear there's a village gathering tonight,' said Marnie, head held high.

'There certainly is,' said Hilary, smile pulling at the corners of her lips. 'Would you like to push past me to gain entry. It's just to your right, there.'

Marnie didn't have to push past her, of course. There were fourteen steps because she counted them in an effort to offset her spiking anxiety level. She didn't give herself time to think, but opened the door and walked straight into the room full of people. Marnie took them all in with a sweep of her eyes from Derek at one side of the table to Una at the other. Zoe's head was down, Titus was glaring at her, Cilla was wearing a small smile, Herv gave her a secret wink.

Titus was the first to speak. 'Hilary, what on earth are you doing, letting her in?'

'I didn't give your wife the option of not letting me in,' said Marnie. 'If this is a village meeting, about the village, and me I expect, then I reserve the right to be here.'

Titus's eyeballs began to bulge. 'This is my house, madam . . .'

'Well it's your home, but the house itself belongs to the village, which I'm presently in charge of,' she fired back. Something in her head gave her a high-five for that.

'I think it might be a good idea if Miss Salt stays,' said Dr Court. 'She can answer our questions then.'

There were grumbles of agreement. But not from Kay and Una, who were trying to kill her with their narrow-eyed stares.

Herv got to his feet. 'You can have my seat, I'll stand,' he said.

'Thank you,' said Marnie, taking him up on the offer and sitting down demurely. Underneath the table, though, her leg was vibrating with nerves as if an over-enthusiastic puppeteer was jerking on a string tied to her knee.

'So, questions?' she said, dovetailing her fingers together and sitting primly. 'Do ask me anything you aren't sure of.'

'Why does my rent agreement say that I have to pay a penalty of five pounds extra per month?' Kay Sweetman dived straight in.

'And mine does as well,' said Una.

'Do you really have to ask?'

'You can't do that,' Una protested.

'Well yes, actually I can and I have,' Marnie replied. 'And

if you don't like the arrangement then why not go and live in Skipperstone where you will be paying a hell of a lot more than you do in Wychwell. That's the deal – take it or leave it. Anyone else?'

Una's mouth gathered into a cat's-arse pucker of fury.

'You've obviously made a huge mistake in what you think you're going to charge me for living here,' snickered Titus.

'Not at all,' said Marnie, with a coolness belying her inner stress. 'I worked out the rents per square footage. You have rather a lot of square footage in this house, Mr Sutton. Quid pro quo. It's fair and – if you'll excuse the pun – square.'

Titus's red face moved further up the angry spectrum towards purple.

'How solid are the promises you made in the letters?' asked Cilla, and Marnie knew she was giving her the chance to appease people's worries. Bless her.

'The new deals have been made with the approval of the new owner. They are binding. You all have your homes for the duration of your lifetimes, subject to the rents being paid of course. If you work for the estate and then retire, the rent will constitute part of your pension.'

'Thank you,' said Cilla.

'I can't afford to pay rent,' said Una, her chin and bosom jiggling with indignation. 'I haven't got a job.'

'Well, you'll have to get one then, won't you,' said Marnie, starting to enjoy herself now.

'I can't work,' said Una. 'I have bad feet.'

'I do believe there are actual jobs you can do sitting down these days,' replied Marnie with faux sweetness. 'You pay, you stay, say no, you go. Next.'

David Parselow raised one hand whilst rubbing his chin thoughtfully with the other.

'The loyalty payments that the businesses have received in the past, do we have to pay them back?'

Marnie had to be careful how to answer this because she'd written to Titus that he had to.

'The two businesses in the area, i.e. the pub and the post office, were given a bonus payment in compensation for lack of custom, from what I understand. By increasing the amount of people who live in, and who know of, Wychwell, it is hoped your businesses will have a much-improved turn-over. There is absolutely no other reason for anyone else to have received a loyalty bonus.' She looked pointedly over at Titus, who was firing daggers at her with his rheumy eyes. 'But to answer your question directly, David, no. I think that would be unfair.'

He sagged with relief, as if he'd been a balloon and a pin had been stuck in his back.

'Who is the new owner?' asked Emelie. 'Do you really not know, Marnie?'

'I have no idea,' she replied.

Titus gave a short bark of laughter and everyone's head swung around to him.

'I have no idea,' Marnie reiterated. 'One of you is, I'm sure. One of you has a set of keys – the owner's keys – to the manor. One of you was up there last night.' She looked around hoping to spot some giveaway body language, but she saw nothing. 'Now, is there anything else?'

Silence answered her. 'Okay, well, if there is and you want to discuss it with me in private, you know where I am. I do need your intentions to stay and abide by the new agreements in writing by the end of the month. I will take any non-responses as a desire to terminate your residency in Wychwell and will then issue a thirty-day notice to quit your property. Thank you for your time.' She stood and pushed the seat back with her legs.

She was at the door when Roger asked, 'So where has all the money gone?'

'Maybe Titus can explain that one,' said Marnie.

A church-like hush fell upon the group after Marnie departed from their midst. Cyril Rootwood, an old quarry miner with a resultant bad chest, was the first to break it.

'So, where *has* all the money gone, Titus? What did she mean by "Titus can explain that one"?'

'I have absolutely no bloody idea,' he replied, with convincing confidence. 'Always a clever ploy to shift the focus onto someone else when you are trying to divert it from yourself.'

'Well, with the greatest of respect, Titus, she can't be held responsible for there being no money in the estate.' This from Mrs Court. 'You must know what's happened to it all. You looked after that side of the business.'

'Dear lady,' began Titus in the most patronising tone he could muster, 'Lilian had absolutely no fiscal sense. I could only advise, not dictate.'

'Did she invest any of her savings with you?' asked Griff.

'I don't like what you are inferring, Griff Oldroyd,' Titus replied, his expression hard.

Lionel, sensing a meltdown, asked for calm. 'I think that Marnie has answered all the questions we were going to raise. I didn't realise she hadn't been invited, Titus. What would have been the point in a meeting without her?'

'Lilian was half-senile when this ... this stranger breezed into her life and two minutes later Lilian is dead and the woman is running the estate. Is there any wonder that I do not trust her?'

'Lilian was sound enough of mind to recognise a good soul when she saw one, Titus,' said Emelie.

'Yes,' he spat back, 'and that's why she had a Nazi as a friend.'

'Whoa.' Herv was on his feet now. 'There is no need for that.'

'Shame on you, Titus Sutton,' said Lionel, also moved to stand.

Emelie picked up her handbag to leave.

'You horrible, stupid, ignorant man . . .'

'Our business is done, I think,' snarled Titus. 'Can't you see what that Salt woman is doing to us? Setting one against the other? Wychwell was a haven of peace before she came here.'

'It wasn't Marnie who started with the insults though, was it?' said Herv, towering over Titus, his blue eyes sparking fire, but the money-bloated man wasn't in the least cowed.

'Well don't blame me if you're all turned out of your houses before the year is out. Whatever it says on those let—'

Hilary, at his side interrupted him, 'But Titus, she said that wouldn't—'

'Oh do be quiet, Hilary,' he snapped. 'You don't know what you are talking about.'

'I think we should go,' said Lionel, before things got even uglier and he was sacked from his post for belting one of his parishioners. 'Thank you for the tea, Hilary. It was much appreciated.'

'A pleasure, Vicar.'

Silently the villagers filed out of Titus's house. Ruby pushed past the Rootwoods to catch up with Herv.

'We're going to the Wych Arms, Herv, would you like to come for a drink with us? I think we all need one after that.'

'Thank you, Ruby, but I'm going to make sure Emelie gets home and is all right,' he said, without breaking his stride.

Kay Sweetman saw her daughter's face crumple.

'You want to watch who you mix with, Herv Gunnarsen,' she said, loud enough for her voice to travel past Lionel and Dr Court and reach him. 'I have it from a very reliable source that your perfect Miss Salt isn't interested in men unless they're attached. She's one of those home-wrecker sorts. Her last man was married with three children and a pregnant wife and she ran off up here with her tail between her legs when the wife gave her what-for in front of everyone she worked with.'

Kay saw the slight hesitation in Herv's step before he carried on at an increased pace and she knew she had hit home with that bullet. She'd been saving it for the right moment. But she hadn't finished yet.

'She told Lilian all about it, that's why she offered her a house here. Because she did to some poor other woman what your wife did to you.'

'Mu-um, you shouldn't have said that,' Ruby said with an annoyed huff. 'It'll not make any difference.'

'Oh yes it will,' said Kay Sweetman triumphantly. 'You just wait and see.'

Chapter 35

The rest of the week passed without incident or drama. Marnie didn't see Herv to talk to, he was working away from the manor, mending windows, fixing tiles on Dr Court's roof, doing general maintenance around the village. She spotted him at the top of a ladder when she was strolling back to Little Raspberries on the Wednesday. He turned, saw her – or so she thought – she waved, but he turned back, so she presumed he couldn't have. She thought nothing more of it than that he needed to concentrate on not falling and breaking his neck.

Letters were either pushed through her own letterbox or were waiting for her at the manor from the villagers all accepting the new agreements. Una's arrived with a hole in the paper at the end of her signature as if she had stabbed it hatefully with her pen. Herv's hadn't come yet, but she knew it would. Nor had Titus's, not surprisingly. By Marnie's latest calculations – and she was sure there was more she had to still uncover – he owed the estate well over a million pounds. Mr Wemyss had since found out that Mr Helliwell at the farm had been paying his due after all – and had a rent book to prove it. The monies had been going directly into a mysterious company bank account, it seemed, and the farmer hadn't had sight nor sound of any loyalty payments.

Titus drove past her in his E-Type on the Thursday morning as she was walking up to the manor, and deliberately swerved to hit a puddle and drench her. She gave a throttled scream and shook her fist at the car hoping he would see her in his rear-view mirror. She was swearing a bouquet of profanities when Lionel caught her up.

'I saw that,' he said. 'What an odious man.'

'Sorry about the language, Lionel.'

'I would have said the same,' he replied, though Marnie doubted it. She twisted her shirt to squeeze out some water. Her whole right side was soaked.

'Marnie, I wanted to say I thought you were magnificent at the meeting the other night,' he said. 'It's been a long time coming. And I know that Lilian gave me a small stipend from the estate but—'

'But nothing,' Marnie broke in. 'That will continue. Lilian would rise up and lynch me if stopped that.'

'Marnie, that's exceptionally kind of you.'

'I might have to start coming to church to save my damned soul,' she said and Lionel laughed then and said, 'You are very welcome to call and see me if ever you need any spiritual guidance.'

'I don't think you'd know where to start.'

'If Lilian Dearman liked you, I'm pretty sure you haven't strayed too much from the path of righteousness.'

Marnie sighed, suddenly emotional. 'I've made so many cock-ups in my life, Lionel.'

'You wouldn't be human if you were perfect, Marnie,' he replied.

'Oh I'm about as far from perfect as you can possibly get.' She could feel rainwater dripping down her back from her hair. She must look like the woman from *The Ring*. 'I was just off up to the manor house. I'll have to go home and change now.'

'Let me walk with you,' said Lionel, and they fell into a step together, a companiable silence between them until Lionel spoke again.

'Have you noticed Lilian's collection of ceramics?'

'The broken pots and plates?'

Lionel smiled. 'Those are the ones. I'm presuming then that you haven't heard of the ancient art of Kintsugi?'

'Nope. I'm guessing it's Japanese though,' Marnie answered, given the exaggerated accent which Lionel had used to say the word.

'Indeed. It's the art of repairing pottery with gold in the understanding that the piece is more beautiful for having been broken.'

'Oh, really?' said Marnie, not really understanding why they'd moved from her soggy appearance and damned soul to an art lesson.

'Take a good look at them when you go up to the manor because they're very valuable, Marnie. More valuable now than they ever were in their original perfect state.'

She still wasn't sure where Lionel was going with this.

'Lilian was completely smashed by life and it was love that built her up and made her more beautiful and whole than she ever was before. Love is the gold that can mend a broken heart and make it stronger than ever.'

Ah, now she got it.

'Are you talking about George Purcell?' Marnie asked and saw Lionel shoot her a look as if he was shocked that she knew about that affair. 'Lilian told me all about how he'd broken her heart. I didn't realise there was someone after him who . . . mended her.'

'Yes, there was. Not only mended but recreated her into the Lilian you adored.' He moved the subject on. 'By the way, you have quite a few well-wishers in the village. Derek Price for one thinks you should be canonised.'

Marnie cringed visibly. 'Is he all right in his new abode?'

'Happy as the proverbial pig in muck,' Lionel chuckled. 'As I said to Una, no one forced him to go. He was given the option and he took it. Lilian did consider letting him have Little Raspberries after Jessie died, but something held her back. Then she asked me if I thought it was wise to let him have Autumn Leaves and I said I wasn't sure, so I presumed she'd changed her mind.'

'Autumn Leaves?' She had a sudden vision of Derek living in a huge pile of brown leaves. And still looking happier than when he resided with Una.

'The old name for the gravedigger's house, although no one ever calls it anything but the gravedigger's house. That's why Lilian didn't bother to rename it when she did all the others, at least the habitable ones. She hated Wychwell, and who could blame her, so I suggested that it might help endear the place to her. I think it worked, in part.'

'I saw the Pink Lady on Monday,' said Marnie.

'Did you now?'

'For the second time. I'm not convinced it's a ghost, Lionel.'

'I have never seen her, so I couldn't comment.' They were at Marnie's door. 'And now I have escorted you safely, I must take my leave because I have an appointment with Griff and a chessboard. I've been practising my opening gambits.'

'Right-o,' said Marnie.

'Hasta la Vista, as Mr Schwarzenegger might say. And thank you again.'

'Pleasure,' said Marnie.

Lionel made a courteous half-bow. 'Remember that word: Kintsugi.' Then he was off.

Marnie went inside to change. For such a relatively short conversation Lionel had given her a lot to think about there: broken valuables and mended people and something else that had piqued her interest. Something to do with the gravedigger's house. And, unless she was very much mistaken, Lionel didn't seem half as surprised as she would have expected to hear that the Pink Lady might not be a ghost at all.

The manor was silent that afternoon. Herv and Johnny were out buying building materials and Cilla and Zoe finished at lunchtime. Marnie unfolded a huge blueprint of the estate plans which she had found in the box containing the ledgers. She studied it for clues, but she couldn't find anything of interest, then she sat down with the History of Wychwell, a coffee and a plate of biscuits.

The Gravedigger's House, is a one-bedroomed property on the edge of the church gardens. The cottage is the smallest property on the estate and was built c1790. It was originally a single storey building, a second floor was built approximately one hundred years later.

The house was originally called Autumn Leaves, inspired by the banks of leaves that always drift against it from the churchyard trees in Autumn, yet the name was never used. The last inhabitant of the cottage died in 2012, ninety-year-old Diggory 'Ox' Hoyle who had to be forced into retirement at eighty-five years old. Diggory's father Seth was also . . .

There followed a long list of names and dates but nothing more about the house itself. Her moment of enlightenment, like Lilian's, had flittered away before she'd had the chance to get her net out and catch it.

In all honesty, filling her head with a whodunit was preferable to leaving it empty so that Justin Fox could take up residence in it. She had no idea why she had agreed to meet him. What if his wife turned up with a machete? She permitted herself to think about snogging him in the car. He'd been a good kisser, or so she'd thought then: urgent and passionate and lip-bruising. It had seemed exciting, naughty, thrilling having sex on the back seat, snatching illicit moments with him, outlawed by Laurence and cocking a snook at his controlling wife. Looking back it was tacky, tawdry and bloody uncomfortable and she felt sickened. Herv Gunnarsen's kiss had set a new standard, as brief as it was. And his big hands holding her face so carefully had done more to fire up her sexual hormones than Justin Fox and his hasty, blind-dart-player, way-off-the-bullseye fumbling had ever done. It hadn't mattered at the time because she knew that the more they got to know each other, the more they'd get into each other's rhythm. She'd taken care to read his satisfied *ums* and *ahs* but, thinking about it, he hadn't really changed his technique to suit what she wanted. Maybe he was too attuned to what he did with his wife. Wham, bam and thank you, ma'am.

Why the farts did she say yes she would see him?

Because I want that apology, her inner self said. *Because I want to have the last word. Because I want to show him that I don't care.*

She just hoped that when she saw him the following day, she really didn't care.

Chapter 36

Justin had said more than once that he liked her hair down, flowing in gentle waves of black, so she pinned it up. His favourite outfit was her navy-blue dress with the peplum which showed off her figure and her trim legs, so she wore a dark green trouser suit. Her make-up was mother's-funeral subtle, her shoes a block heel giving her a bit of height and also the chance to escape any wife wielding a sledgehammer.

She arrived at the Blue Boy ten minutes before the allotted hour and was aware that she felt trembly from the inside out, not because she was excited to see Justin, but because she was afraid. Afraid of herself. Afraid of feeling things for him that she didn't want to feel. She hoped she wasn't kidding herself by assuming she was strong enough not to let him back into her life again. She had managed to build herself up from the stack of broken pieces she'd been reduced to a couple of months ago, but it wasn't thanks to any Kintsugi gold; she was held together with Pritt Stick.

Well, you're here now, said the voice inside. *Pretend you're in the SAS, get in, then get out with minimal damage to self.*

She checked her face in the vanity mirror for lipstick on

teeth and mascara transference and then walked over to the pub. There was no sign of his car yet. Just a very swanky brand-new Audi and a couple of Toyota Aygos parked up. She recited her Sammy Davis Junior mantra and headed for the front door. She had to be more committed to finally ending this episode of her life on her terms than scared of him making sure it ended on his.

She spotted him immediately. He was sitting in the booth where they'd sat last time they were there together. That was by design, she suspected. Stupid though, if it was, because she'd been really pissed off with him that day. He heard the door bump shut behind her, turned, smiled and waved and she felt something inside her involuntarily respond to the sight of him, as if it were looking at a star that had long since burnt out but was still visible to the eye.

'Justin,' she said, as he rose. She kept her distance and didn't give him the chance to move in for a kiss or an embrace.

'Marnie, it's so good to see you.'

He was wearing jeans and a shirt – both Armani. The scent of Joop drifted towards her and attempted to poke fire into memories she'd thought were cold ashes.

He'd already got himself half a lager and her a diet cola. Well, she wasn't going to touch it. And she wasn't going to say it was good to see him either. The Pritt Stick was holding up well; she was impressed.

She sat down opposite him and noticed the dark circles under his eyes and wondered if he'd been kept awake last night from thinking about this meeting.

'So,' she opened quickly. 'I was surprised to get your texts.' She made the point of making the word plural, so he could be assured she'd ignored the first one with all the contempt it deserved. She, like Lionel on his way to see Griff to play chess, had been practising her opening gambits. In the bath last night. Move that pawn in front of the king forward and free up that mother of a bishop.

Justin steepled his fingers, elbows on the table. He'd stolen that from Laurence because that was his default pose when talking to someone on the opposite side of his desk. There was no flirty twinkle in his eyes, which was a shame because she would have liked to have had the pleasure of shutting it down.

'I thought we needed to clear the air, in order to move on,' he said, caution evident in his tone.

'From what I remember, you moved on very quickly.'

His eyes dropped from hers. 'I'm sorry.'

'I might have thought better of you had you had the decency to return my calls after you left me to the wolves.' Bring the white knights into play. Get them both neighing that they're going for that black king.

'I . . . didn't know how to handle it. I didn't think things would get that far.'

'You drove the pace, if you remember. And I let you because of your subconscious uncrippling.' She knew immediately she'd got the phrase wrong and saw the side of his lip tweak towards that gorgeous sexy grin that always made her insides warm. Now her internal thermometer didn't even waver from resting zero.

'Oh, I have missed you,' he said to her. Or at least she thought he did, because his voice was lower than a whisper. If that was an attempt to get her to lean towards him so he could kiss her, he could piss right off.

'Why am I here?' she asked, brooking no nonsense.

She saw his tentative smile wither. Surely he hadn't thought that a glass of pop and a 'sorry' would have her dragging him to the back seat of her Renault.

Justin took a deep fortifying breath. 'We thought a meeting would help us . . . recalibrate.'

She didn't like the sound of that 'we'.

'We?'

'Suranna and I.'

Was Marnie hearing this right? 'I beg your pardon.' She stood up.

'Please don't. She's just gone to the toilet. She says she'll leave me if she doesn't meet you and sort this out.'

'I absolutely couldn't give a flying fu—'

'Marnie.' A female voice behind her.

Marnie turned around to face the small woman who had tried to rip her head off at their last encounter. She was a damned sight thinner than the last time they'd met. And not as blotchy-faced. And she was holding her hand out in greeting.

Chapter 37

The day could not have gone more bizarrely if the landlord had ridden towards them on the back of a Tyrannosaurus Rex. It was like the trip Marnie once had at college after she'd licked her first and last acid tab and had seen worms wriggling out of Caitlin's eyes.

Marnie did not shake Suranna's hand. She left it hanging there and then turned to Justin.

'I have no idea what sort of sick game you think you're playing . . .'

'Marnie, please, just sit down and save my marriage,' he said, throttling back on the volume when a man passed him carrying two pints.

'Why should I?'

'Because he nearly wrecked it,' said Suranna with controlled calmness. 'And I need to get everything in the open before I can forgive him.'

'I had no idea that he was still very much married,' said Marnie, with emphasis on the '*I*'.

'I know,' said Suranna. 'He told me that.'

That surprised her.

'Please, give me half an hour of your time – max – and then you never need see either of us again,' said Suranna. There was a scratch in her voice as if she was upset but trying not to be. 'Please.'

Against her better judgement screaming at her to go, Marnie sat back down, but she was ready to spring if Suranna turned back into a nutter. Suranna slid in next to her unfaithful husband.

'You've had your baby,' said Marnie.

'I wasn't pregnant,' said Suranna. 'It was a cushion.'

The black queen, it appeared, *was* full of dirty tricks. She'd thought as much. 'A cushion?'

'I thought it might add to the drama,' Suranna replied coolly.

'If I'd known at the time it was a cushion, I'd have punched your face in,' replied Marnie.

'That's why I made sure I chose one that didn't look like a cushion.'

Marnie laughed. She wasn't amused, but her confused reactions short-circuited to the nearest response, which happened to be a hoot.

'I am pregnant now, really,' said Suranna, picking up the cola, which had been hers then. So Justin hadn't even got her a drink in. Marnie found herself quite annoyed at that. 'Two months,' Suranna added.

'Congratulations,' replied Marnie, dryly.

'We've only had full sexual intercourse once since . . . since I found him out and that's all it took.'

Whoa – too much info.

'But I will leave him, pregnant or not, if I don't get the answers to my questions,' said Suranna. 'And as you are probably aware, Justin lies. It's not the first time I've been here, so when I heard about you, I had a plan of action already in place.'

Marnie nodded. 'A cushion.' And an impressively effective cushion too. It had assured Suranna sympathy, and saved her from a broken conk and very probably arrest.

'Justin covered all your neighbour's costs plus extra to stop her going to the newspapers,' said Suranna, as if she were talking to a fellow parent about making reparation for some destructive antics of her wayward child.

'Well done, Justin,' said Marnie, allowing herself the sarcasm.

'What did he tell you about me?' asked Suranna.

Marnie glanced over at Justin and found him looking downwards, probably willing the pub floor to open up and take him prisoner.

'That you and he had decided to part, that you had taken a leaf out of Gwyneth Paltrow's book of conscious uncrip . . . uncoupling but were taking an age about it. And that if he didn't dance to your tune, you would stop him seeing his children.'

Suranna's mouth opened in an O of incredulity.

'He said that?'

'Yep.'

'Did you, Justin? Did you say all that?' Suranna's voice was a mouse-squeak.

'Yes,' he answered with an Eeyore sigh.

'And that you hadn't had sex for fourteen months.' Marnie's white queen was swaggering down that board and shaking her booty.

'Justin?'

'Yes, I did say that.' The black king was scratching his neck nervously now.

'Did he tell you that he loved you?' asked Suranna.

'Yes. Usually after he'd . . . you know what . . . I think it was more of a reaction to his er ... *offloading* than genuine emotion. He confused gratitude with love,' Marnie answered coldly, watching Justin squirm and adding for evil good measure, 'Didn't you, Justin?'

Justin coughed. A mottled pink pattern was spreading over his neck.

'Did he mention his children? Arrange for you to meet them?'

'No,' answered Marnie and she saw the relief in Suranna's expression. 'It was very obvious he loved his children. There was never any mention of me meeting them.'

'One point to Justin,' Justin said, not quite under his breath.

'It's a very small point, you bloody bell-end,' growled Suranna at him, before turning back to Marnie. 'Did he give you any indication of long-term plans?'

'He asked me what size ring I took. I did get a little excited at that. He hinted at holidays, we talked about what sort of house we'd like to live in. It was all bollocks though,' – Marnie swept her eyes over him, head bowed, saw how he'd nudged his hair over a small bald spot on his crown – 'he had no intention of doing any of it. But he was very good at creating an illusion.'

'Did he ever put strawberries on your pubic area and eat them?' asked Suranna, wobble in her lip.

'What?'

'Oh God,' Justin's head fell into his hands.

'You've led me to this, Justin, so shut up.'

For all Suranna's waspish tone, Marnie knew she must be in a terrible place to have to wash this sort of linen in public. It wasn't so much dirty but putrid. And very possibly stained indelibly.

'Well, did he?' Suranna asked again.

Something intimate that she thought he only did with her, obviously. There was hope for her then if Justin gave her some foreplay, which Marnie thought about saying but was glad afterwards that she'd overridden the impulse.

'No. There was no love-making, just rushed, urgent, horny, sex between two people – one with an insatiably large ego that constantly needed feeding, and the other grateful and stupid enough to believe the bullshit was true.' Crazily, she hadn't realised that until she'd said it. She'd thought it was passion, when in reality, he was simply emptying his balls expediently in the allotted timetable slot.

Marnie saw a single tear land on Suranna's skirt and stain the material dark. The black queen was folding and the white queen was starting to feel a little sorry for her.

'Thank you,' said Suranna, no trace of the aggressive harpy now, just a sad little woman trying to patch up her marriage. 'It can't have been easy to come here and face me.'

'I didn't know that I was,' replied Marnie. 'I came here expecting Justin to try and worm his way back into my life and wanted the satisfaction of telling him to go fuck himself.' Which he probably would if he could, she added to herself with a snort.

'You didn't tell her I was coming?' shrieked Suranna. She picked up the half of lager and poured it over his head and he merely sat there and dripped, saying just the one word.

'Sorry.'

It was time for Marnie to go. She stood up and left them to it. Suranna would make it work for the sake of their children, but she would always be waiting for the next Marnie to appear. She would be the one in their disparate relationship who loved more, the one surviving on a knife edge, the begging end and it would eventually exhaust her. *Break* her. This,

Marnie knew, would have been her destiny if she'd been led
to the altar by any of her exes. She would have spent her life
building a family then desperately trying to hold it together,
to keep intact what she craved most of all: security and love.
And she would have failed.

Marnie opened the pub door. The white queen had left
the board, and the building. This game was better conceded
than caught up in an eternal stalemate.

*

Marnie walked into Little Raspberries, kicked off her shoes
stripper-style and flopped onto the sofa. She had no job, no
man and yet she felt ridiculously happy, as if she were an
animal that had just spotted a trap in the undergrowth and
avoided it. She hadn't thought it possible that she'd feel sorry
for Suranna, but she did. She hadn't thought it possible that
she could look at Justin and feel nothing but contempt and
stirred in with that, a smidgen of pity. Where did all that love
go, she wondered. How could it fill you so much, inflate you
like a big balloon enough to make you float over the ground
and yet the next minute drain away through a hole that no
one knew was there.

But not always.

There were some lovely templates of what marriage should
be like, even in a village as small as Wychwell. Cilla and Griff
laughed a lot together, Dr Court and his wife walked everywhere arm in arm, David at the pub and his missus, Roger
and his wife, the Rootwoods. When it worked well, it really
worked well. Then she wondered, not for the first time, who
had mended Lilian's heart and why they had never married.

There had been a disparity in every one of her relationships, the scales had always been tipped against her, but it wasn't as if she'd surrendered easily. Aaron had chased her for weeks, in fact he'd been a borderline stalker and she hadn't batted her eyes once at Justin before he'd made a move on her. She'd always hoped that *this* time it might lead to a trip down the aisle, not a garden path. She wanted the little girl's perfect dream – a church, a white dress and a big cake, a honeymoon, a relationship stable enough for a family to nest in. She wasn't so stupid that she hadn't done all the self-analysis and realised that she was probably drawn to life's arseholes for the most warped of reasons. *You're not fit to be a mother, love. So best we fall at the first hurdle and not at the last, eh?*

That's why Herv Gunnarsen getting close terrified her, because her receptors didn't know what to do with him. He wasn't her usual type: he was decent, thoughtful, kind and as gorgeous on the outside as he was on the inside. And he fancied her and was she mad turning down the chance to have his lovely hands caressing her face again and his soft lips falling onto hers?

So, as Marnie drove from Leeds back to Wychwell, she made a brave decision: she was going to let Herv Gunnarsen in. She couldn't go through life denying what her heart craved. Maybe she'd been right to keep hope alive after all. He had nothing to fear from her, she would never let him down and betray him like his wife had done. Most of all, she wanted to undo the mis-knitted pattern of her life and start it again. She wanted to love and be loved in equal measure and be the kind of mother who always let her children know that she was on their side and would never blame them for what others had done. And that it was okay for them to have imperfections and make mistakes.

If Herv Gunnarsen tried to kiss her again, she wouldn't

push him away. It was time to show her mother's voice the door.

Marnie put the kettle on and whilst she waited she wondered what she should do with all the flat-pack Tea Lady cheese-cake boxes that were taking up too much space in the corner of her kitchen. She had really enjoyed making the orders for Mrs Abercrombie and she knew they had gone down well with her customers. Was it so important that they were outsourced and not baked on the premises? She toyed with the idea of ringing her and talking through an idea that had come to her between putting the water in the kettle and the steam coming out. Why not call herself 'the Little Tea Lady' who made cheesecakes for the (Big) Tea Lady in her country kitchen? She knew it was good and Mrs A just might buy it.

Then a stop sign flashed up red and brightly in her head.

Actually Mrs Abercrombie didn't deserve them. She was making a ridiculous profit on the cheesecakes and yet hadn't had the decency to ring Marnie to discuss it when a couple of customers started shouting their mouths off in her shop. And to take them at their word, too. She'd let her carry on baking a fridge-full of cheesecakes, all to go to waste, as far as Fiona Abercrombie knew. Yes, the old bat could sod off. Marnie's cheesecakes, complete with Mrs McMaid's secret ingredient, were way too good for her over-priced, over-hyped, up-themselves cafés. Marnie hadn't a clue where her fabulous cheesecakes did belong, but she'd figure it out. She was an ideas person and a bloody good one at that. And if she didn't realise her own value, what chance had anyone else of knowing what she was worth. She couldn't remember where she'd heard that before, but it was flipping true.

She settled down with her book, shutting out everything

but Penelope Black's words. She was six chapters from the end with number three – *Black Manors* – ready and waiting to be opened and the tension had really cranked up.

It was only when a character made an appearance in the last chapter that Marnie's senses really began to sit up and take notice. *Emma Tybalt, an old lady who lived in the woods, descended from witches. Eunice Prince, Titan Sonnett, Kate Sowerby?* Penelope Black knew Wychwell intimately or Marnie was a monkey's uncle.

Chapter 38

Marnie was on her way up to the manor the next morning when she saw the woman coming out of Herv's house, closely followed by the man himself, his hand gently on her back. The woman was very tall, very slim, very blonde, very glam – and clearly wearing the clothes she had been out in the previous night. She was very everything Marnie wasn't. Herv caught Marnie's eye briefly when he was holding his car door open for the blonde woman, but looked immediately away. The blonde reached up, pulled down his head and kissed him on the mouth before getting in and Marnie knew that they'd spent the night together. Tears pressed at the back of her eyes like acid and a heavy weight of disappointment landed with a thud in her stomach. Well, what did she expect? That he'd wait around for her to honour him with her assent? Become a monk? She'd had her chance and blown it. *C'est la bloody vie.*

Emelie was in her garden hanging out washing on her line. Or rather standing by the basket, holding her side. She waved to Marnie, who conjured up a smile from somewhere as she heard Herv's car turn left behind her.

'Good morning,' Marnie called, fighting the tremble in her lip. 'You all right?'

'Damned arthritis,' grumbled Emelie. 'It's a nuisance.'

'Here, let me.' Marnie opened the gate and walked over the grass. 'I'll peg them up for you. Go and have a sit down.'

'Have you got time for a tea?' asked Emelie.

'I have,' replied Marnie, though it was company she could do with rather than tea. She missed Lilian. She would have given anything to have sat down with her over a big pot of tea and let it tumble out that she'd been an idiot and allowed Herv Gunnarsen to slip through her pathetic fingers. She felt stupid-cow tears push out of her eyes and she flicked them away as if they were irritating insects crawling down her cheeks. She hung out the sheets and towels; then she took a deep breath and walked into Emelie's house where that pungent smell once again worried her nostrils.

'That damp can't be doing your arthritis any good, Emelie.'

'It's a very old house, Marnie. Damp happens.' Emelie brought in a tray of tea and Marnie took it quickly from her because she looked as if she barely had the strength to carry it. The cups were delicate china, light green with hand-painted edelweiss.

'Emelie, are you all right?' she asked, as the old lady dropped heavily onto a chair.

'I'm fine,' she replied, with a trill of laughter. 'It isn't that much fun getting old. If you aren't visited by one pain, you're visited by another. I don't want any fuss nor do I like to think about anything going wrong with me.' She leaned close to Marnie as if whispering a secret: 'I don't want to turn into Una Price.'

'You are about as far from Una Price as it is possible to be,' smiled Marnie.

'Maybe, but I do have a bone to pick with you, young lady.' Emelie pretended to frown. 'You gave so many people a cheesecake, I hear, but not me.'

'I'm so sorry, Emelie,' replied Marnie. 'I shall make you a special one, I promise. Name your flavour. Apple strudel?'

'I'm joking,' said Emelie. 'I heard what happened.'

'But I'd like to anyway. They were lovely as well. I ended up burning boxes of them. I was so angry.'

'I'm not surprised,' nodded Emelie. 'Una and Kay have both changed so much over the years. Kay didn't used to be so bad, but she's protective over Ruby and since she became friends with Una, she's absorbed her personality. Una has been spoilt, Derek should have stood up to her more. He helped to make her the way she is. They can't force Herv Gunnarsen to put his affections where they don't want to go. Besides, I think he has his eye on you.'

'No, he doesn't,' said Marnie bluntly. 'I've just seen him leaving his cottage with a stunning woman who seemingly didn't bring a change of clothes with her.'

'Oh,' Emelie looked confused by that.

'So you're wrong.'

'I'm very surprised. To Lilian and me it was always so obvious.'

'Was it?' Marnie wanted detail, but there was no point in asking.

'Lilian said she could see it in the way that he looked at you and how his ear cocked when your name was mentioned. Herv is a man who wears his heart on his sleeve.'

'I turned him down. I made it plain that I didn't think of him in that way,' said Marnie, dipping her head to sip the tea and give those rising tears in her eyes time to settle. 'It's for the best.'

'For whom?'

'For him.'

'Why would you say that when it isn't the truth?'

'Because he's lovely and uncomplicated and he deserves the same,' said Marnie.

Emelie muttered something in her native tongue that Marnie didn't understand but the inference was clear from her tone. She thought Marnie was daft. She was right.

'I wonder ...' Emelie began, then stopped. Then she cringed, then she shook her head 'Oh, nothing.'

'What?' asked Marnie, because it clearly wasn't nothing.

Emelie reached over and put her small hand over Marnie's, a gesture of comfort to offset something nasty to come. 'I really don't want to tell you this, Marnie, but I think I should. When we came out of the Lemon Villa after the meeting on Tuesday, Kay Sweetman shouted something to Herv which we all heard. Ruby asked him if he wanted to go for a drink and he said that he didn't. Kay ...' She paused as if she wanted to get her next words exactly right. '... Kay said that he should be careful who he mixed with' – she swallowed – '... that ... that you broke up a man's marriage, a man with children and a wife who was pregnant, and that's why you came here. To get out of the situation.'

'Oh shit.' Marnie felt as if a rug she had been standing on had suddenly been snatched from under her to reveal a massive hole. One above a sewerage pit.

'I said to her, "Kay Sweetman, that was a terrible thing to say" and she said, "Well, it's true" and I reminded her that people in glass houses should never throw stones. She shut up very quickly then and ran on with Ruby asking her what I meant. I shouldn't have said it but I was very angry for you.'

Marnie's head was in her hands. Everyone here now, as

well, thought she was the world's biggest slut. Herv thought she was the world's biggest slut. Could Kay have told him anything worse, given his history? And how did Kay know? Marnie had only ever told Lilian. She'd told her *everything*. Kay could only have got it from Lilian. So, how much else did Kay know about her?

Marnie began to cry. She didn't want to but a wave of black despair engulfed her. The shame of Herv knowing about Justin wounded her with a rabbit punch that took her breath away.

'Oh you poor girl.' The compassion in Emelie's voice made Marnie's sobbing worse before she got control of it.

'It's true, Emelie. But he lied that his marriage was over. I ran away because I couldn't stand that anyone thought I was the sort of person that would ... that could ... And now I'm going to have to run away again because everyone here thinks I'm a ...' She couldn't say the word because it was one that belonged to other women who didn't care what carnage they caused with their selfishness. It was like waking up and finding she'd been branded on the forehead with the word as she slept and couldn't get rid of it.

Emelie's arms slid around her and Marnie clung to her and for a moment it felt as if she was holding Lilian because she caught the scent of her dear familiar perfume, the briefest ghost of it, then it was gone. Then Emelie pulled Marnie to her arm's length and spoke to her in a firm voice.

'You will not leave here, Marnie Salt. Kay Sweetman's word is not very reliable and won't be as easily believed as she imagines. She doesn't think anyone knows that she had an affair with Titus Sutton, but they do. I think it is very likely that Ruby is Titus's daughter. Lilian certainly thought so. And I am sure Hilary suspects. Why she has stayed with such a brute, I have no idea. Whoever the new owner of Wychwell is values you, Lilian loved you like a daughter and I too think you are a beautiful person. Wychwell is a much richer place for you being in it so no more of this nonsense about leaving.' She let go of Marnie to open a drawer in the dresser behind her, brought out a pressed linen handkerchief and pushed it into Marnie's hand for her to dry her eyes.

'"If anyone can find Margaret Kytson and her baby's grave, Marnie can", that's what Lilian used to say to me. You wouldn't let her down now, would you?'

*

Kay was serving in the shop when Titus walked in and asked for his usual cigarettes.

'I want a word,' she said and came from behind the counter to shut the shop door, dropping the catch. 'The other night, Emelie Tibbs made some comment about people like me not throwing stones when living in glass houses.'

Titus looked bewildered. 'I have no idea what you mean, Kay.'

'She knows about us,' said Kay in a low voice.

'Don't be ridiculous. That was years ago.'

'She knows. And she made sure that I know she knows.'

Titus didn't look perturbed at all. 'Why on earth did that crop up?'

'Because ... because I'd told Herv Gunnarsen that *she*'– and she thumbed in the direction of Little Raspberries – 'had to leave her last job for having an affair with a married man.'

'I see.' Titus guessed easily why she had done that. Kay had always been a vicious cat. Partly the reason for the initial attraction was that wicked, sexy spark in her, but also why their affair was short-lived. Luckily for him, Kay had never wanted to share her daughter with her real father. Quite the opposite in fact, which suited him perfectly. He dismissed the whole thing in five words. 'Village gossip. Deny, deny, deny.'

'I don't want Ruby to know,' snapped Kay.

'I don't either,' he snapped back. 'There's nothing to know. None of them can prove anything so it never happened as far as I'm concerned. Senile old woman's tittle-tattle.'

'Good.' Kay felt sufficiently assured to let that matter drop and move on to another. 'Have you found out anything else about you-know-what?'

'No, but I think it's pretty clear why she came here. I can't see there's a lot we can do other than wait for her to start demanding DNA tests. I'm only surprised she's taking so long about it.'

David Parselow tried the shop door to find it locked. Kay waved at him to let him know she'd be just a tick. 'Does Lionel suspect his daughter's turned up to expose his holier-than-thou status for what it really is?' she asked quickly.

'I don't think he has a clue,' said Titus. 'Yet.'

*

The sun streamed through the dining room windows of the manor and onto the ledgers as if it was trying to direct Marnie to the answer to the mystery which had held Wychwell in its grip for almost five hundred years, but it only highlighted the page showing details of the derelict cottages and there were no clues there.

Hilary Sutton had the best idea, buggering off to a city where people were too busy to nose into your affairs. Maybe she should take a leaf out of her book.

Chapter 39

Marnie hardly left Little Raspberries for the next three weeks. She didn't need to go up to the manor, she didn't want to bump into Herv. More importantly she didn't want to bump into Herv and a woman. Especially not one so damned physically perfect. What could be more damaging to the ego than to see the man you wanted to whisk you off to bed taking a woman home that he'd whisked off to bed the night before. Some perfect being that he'd have perfect sex with: no wet patches, no cramp, nothing but the sort of fantastic mutually satisfying screamy stuff that appeared in Hollywood films. The Pritt Stick had failed to hold and she found herself in bits again.

She wanted to leave Wychwell; she was about as popular here as a force twelve gale in a confetti factory. The new owner had done her no favours at all by putting her in charge of rescuing it because she'd only be remembered for making them all pay higher rents and being outed as a marriage-wrecking bitch. She decided that she would stay in Wychwell until she had set it up for its future success and had exhausted all avenues to find Margaret's grave, then she would go. She'd start again somewhere else where no one knew her and she would never tell anyone her secrets again, because that was the only way she could assure they wouldn't bite her from behind.

Maybe it was something to do with her Irish traveller parentage. People were instinctively suspicious of her, saw her as trouble personified and her destiny was to keep moving on. Maybe that's why any attachments she made were transient, unstable, fleeting because that's what the stars had dictated for her. Maybe she couldn't fight fate and so shouldn't even try.

Other than going for some shopping, she didn't venture out. She worked from her laptop on the kitchen table, throwing herself fully into future plans for Wychwell and how best to use the remaining cash in the village account. *Speculate to accumulate* would be her advice: rebuild the derelict cottages, turn at least a couple of them into businesses. A teashop would be good, she'd decided. They could give the Tea Lady a run for her money. Winter House was perfectly placed for that. It was small, but it could be extended at the back. A conservatory, west-facing, so it would have all the sun in the afternoon. Or would Summermoor next door be better because it had a larger garden?

The new properties would all be rented out on short leases. It was important any new people fitted in with the old residents; Lilian would have asked for that. Okay, it was maybe taking the duty of care thing a bit far, but she considered it important. The village hall needed knocking down and rebuilding. It didn't even have a toilet and probably transgressed every building law in the country. It seemed as if it had been originally constructed by a blind school-leaver with his plans upside down.

She contacted a few builders and asked if they had the man-power and the time to complete the suggested renovations that she emailed over, then took the names of those who did and sent them to Mr Wemyss for the owner's approval to forge ahead getting quotes. Then she played around with some figures, projecting the income if all the houses were full and paid their rents. The Lemon Villa would make a great B&B or a hotel, but she suspected that Titus wouldn't be moving out any time soon. If ever.

She had immersed herself so much in her plans that she lost all track of time and dates, especially as she hadn't even switched on her TV to see what was going on outside Little Raspberries. She suspected it was the same old, same old though: stabbings, bombs, disasters; there would be no won-derful news to lift everyone's mood. She hadn't missed being part of the larger world in the weeks she'd been a virtual hermit but she realised that she did need to go up to the manor and take another look through those old ledgers to try and locate Margaret Kytson's well because it was nagging at her brain. Plus she remembered that she had promised Emelie a cheesecake and hadn't delivered on it. The next day was Saturday; no one would be working up at the manor then. She wouldn't have to make small talk with Cilla and Zoe or witness first-hand the abhorrence that Herv must have for her. She drove to the supermarket for cheesecake ingredients and was delighted to find the fourth *Country Manors* book was out on the shelves – *All Manor of Hell*, which was great timing as she'd just finished the third one. After she had made an apple strudel cheesecake that night, she put on her pyjamas and started reading it.

Manfred, thank goodness, had got his manor back but his long-lost sister had turned up and there was a very dodgy attraction between them which had to be resisted. The fact that the sister was called Lalique Hartman was further indication that the worlds of Wellsbury and Wychwell were too intertwined for comfort. Marnie couldn't put the book down. The sparks from the unrequited passion were flying off the page. Their illicit love struggle was fabulous. *Illicit. Where had she seen that word before recently?*

Then she remembered picking up a ball of discarded paper in Emelie's house with that word on it. *Illicit . . . forbidden . . . love.*

Surely not . . . *Don't be daft, Marnie. Emelie is not Penelope Black*, she told herself. Still, she would have to ask.

Marnie realised she was anxious as she set off across the green towards Emelie's house the next morning. It was the first time in three weeks she had walked the length of Wychwell and she felt as if eyes were following her every footstep. It was probably true as all Una Price did was sit in her window and spy. She would be the first person Marnie would ask to join if they ever set up a Neighbourhood Watch scheme.

As she approached the end of Herv's lane, she sent a silent prayer upwards that she wouldn't see that blonde woman coming out of his house again. Or see him either, not smiling at her, disappointment and revulsion dulling his blue eyes. She jogged up Kytson Hill and felt a sigh of relief escape her when she reached Emelie's cottage without incident. The door was ajar and Marnie could hear Emelie coughing from the end of the path. She knocked.

'Come in,' said Emelie hoarsely.

Even with the fresh air blowing into the house, that smell of damp was awful and much stronger than it had been the last time she'd visited. Emelie looked delighted to see her.

'Emelie, you sound terrible,' said Marnie, giving her a hug.

'Oh, I'm fine.' Emelie waved at her concern as if she were batting it back to her. 'Is that a cheesecake?'

'A belated one,' said Marnie. 'So I made it extra-large by way of compensation.'

'I'll put the kettle on,' said Emelie. 'We will both have a piece now. I insist.'

'I wasn't going to argue with you,' replied Marnie.

Emelie walked into the kitchen, her back bent. She looked fragile and her long printed skirt was hanging from her.

'Is your arthritis playing up?' Marnie asked her.

'Always,' chuckled Emelie and began coughing again.

'Emelie, that damp is doing you no good at all.' Marnie wished she hadn't left it as long to come over now. She made a mental note to put this at the top of Herv's list of to-do's. There was a patch of wall behind Emelie's TV that appeared as if it would crumble if touched. That couldn't be good near electrics. The damp had to be coming from underneath the house. Maybe there was a water leak. She should check it out. 'Emelie, can I look in your cellar?'

'There is no cellar here,' Emelie replied. 'Marnie, I can't pick up the tray. Would you?'

Marnie went into the kitchen and carried it through for her. Emelie's typewriter wasn't out today, she'd been reading rather than writing. The first *Country Manors* book was open and face down on the table.

Marnie, nodded towards it. 'Isn't it great?'

Emelie wrinkled up her nose. 'I've had it for a while. I bought it to see what all the fuss was about. I'm not sure that I do though. I'm just skipping through it, not reading it in any great detail.'

'You should,' said Marnie. 'It's as if it was written by

someone in Wychwell itself.' She watched for Emelie's reaction at her theory, but there was none to indicate her big secret had been discovered.

'I can't imagine who,' she sniffed. 'I think that Miss Black is very clever, and good luck to her, but there are much more erotic books on the market which don't use all that gratuitous language. *Lady Chatterley's Lover*, for instance. I remember reading it when I was young, and falling madly in love with the writing. It felt so illicit' – that word again, Marnie noted – 'and so passionate. The lady and the gardener.' Marnie wasn't sure if she winked then or if her eye merely twitched as they sat down at the table. 'Anyway, Marnie, tell me what you have been doing since I saw you last,' and the conversation was pulled away from the mystery of the *Country Manors* author's identity. Marnie respected that and didn't ask her outright if she was Penelope Black. Emelie would have told her had she wanted her to know.

'I've been busy working out the future of Wychwell,' Marnie replied, cutting Emelie a slice of her special Austrian cheesecake. 'It's a shame it will have to let other people in, but if it doesn't it will die.'

'Of course it has to expand,' stressed Emelie. 'Dear Lilian realised that too late.' And she began coughing again, a horrible rasping sound and Marnie hurried to fetch her a glass of water.

'Right, that does it,' she said sternly. 'You are to move out of here and we are going to get that damp sorted before you come back.' A thought came to her. 'Why not live in the big house for a while? You can play at being lady of the manor.'

Emelie both smiled and shook her head. 'No, I wouldn't want that at all. I'll leave here in a box and not before. Tell Herv to come over and see what he can do if you must.' She lifted up her fork and started on the cheesecake. 'Oh my, Marnie, this was so worth waiting for.'

'I'm sorry,' Marnie said. 'I shut myself away. I didn't want to see anyone.'

'I am sorry that I told you what Kay said,' Emelie sighed. 'I really didn't want to, but I had to. But still, I have felt quite bad about it.'

'You did the right thing,' Marnie assured her. 'I did need to know.' *I did need to know what booted me out of Herv Gunnarsen's heart.*

'You haven't seen Herv since, I take it?' Emelie asked, as if picking up on her thoughts.

Marnie shook her head, tried to look nonchalant and failed. 'Have you?'

'Last week,' said Emelie, after a marked pause.

'Was he alone?' Marnie didn't want to ask, but her mouth had turned into a masochistic bitch.

Again Emelie hesitated before replying and didn't answer the question directly, which told Marnie everything. 'He was driving.'

He was driving that woman home after a night of adventurous shagging. He was probably falling asleep at the wheel because they'd been doing it all night. Marnie felt stupidly tearful, and the forkful of cheesecake she'd just eaten felt like a rock in her stomach.

'I'll leave him a note to come and see you as soon as possible,' said Marnie.

'Why don't you talk to him, tell him your side of the story?'

'I think that boat has sailed,' replied Marnie. 'Kay did a proper hatchet job there. Of all the things she could have told him about me, that was a direct hit in his Achilles' heel.' She was going to cry again and could barely hold it back. She needed to go up to the manor, do what she had to and then get home again, back to the sanctuary that the four walls of Little Raspberries afforded her, where it was all too easy to imagine there was no world outside it.

Marnie pushed her cheesecake around on her plate but she hadn't eaten any more by the time that Emelie had finished hers.

'It's no reflection on my baking,' Marnie tried to joke, but she could see that Emelie understood.

'Don't throw it away,' said Emelie, 'I'll polish it off later. It's nice to see the sun out, I was beginning to think it wouldn't make an appearance again until next year with all the rain we've had recently.'

Marnie didn't know what the weather had been like for the last three weeks, give or take the days when she had journeyed over to the supermarket, and then she hadn't taken much notice of it. She'd felt as if she were living under her own personal cloud dispensing a never-ending supply of drizzle.

The front door to the manor was unlocked and Cilla was in the hallway dusting.

'Oh hello, stranger,' she said with a delighted smile, when Marnie walked in, and then explained that the family had had a few days away in Whitby for a relative's wedding, so they were making up their hours. 'Herv's around too, he couldn't get a lot done in the garden with it being so wet this past fortnight,' she added and Marnie thought, *great*.

'Well, I'll leave you to it,' said Marnie.

'I'll send Zoe in with a coffee for you,' said Cilla.

'Oh it's fine, I don't want to disturb her.'

'You won't be.' Cilla checked to make sure her daughter was out of earshot before continuing. 'I'm trying to keep her extra busy if I'm honest, she's been ever so down recently. We don't know what's the matter with her.'

Marnie remembered being that age. As well as all the hormones raging, her wings had been flapping like crazy. She wanted to fly the nest so much and live in a flat with Caitlin. Then Caitlin had decided she wanted to go off to university and Marnie met and moved in with Warren who was probably the worst of her exes because he became violent when he was drunk and he was drunk a lot. Then she left him to live in a house near Sheffield with six other people who kept themselves to themselves and weren't the most hygienic people on the planet either, but she was happy there. She was perpetually skint and juggling finances between credit cards, but she somehow managed.

Marnie walked into the lovely dining room, shutting the door behind her. That first bedsit she stayed in would have fitted into here about eight times over. The people above her were noisy, the people below noisier still but she was standing on her own two feet and felt free, powerful, euphoric with independence. Lilian had once told her that she felt the same when her father died. He must have been an ogre, she remembered thinking.

Marnie could see that Herv was tidying up the plants around the lake. She sat on a chair which didn't allow her sight of him because then it was slightly easier to keep him out of her mind. She started at the first ledger again, reading it with the express purpose of only looking for clues to where Margaret lay. She was ten pages in when there was a timid knock on the door and Zoe entered with a cup of coffee and some biscuits on a plate. Her hand was shaking, Marnie noticed, and she appeared to have the weight of the world on her shoulders.

'Thank you, Zoe, that's very sweet of you. I told your mum

I didn't want to put you to any troub—' was as far as Marnie got before Zoe burst into tears, making Marnie rise from the table to shut the door and put her arms around the girl.

'Zoe, whatever is the matter?' she said. Zoe was breaking her heart. Marnie pushed her down onto a chair.

'It's my fault,' said Zoe, face hiding in her hands. 'I am so sorry, Marnie. It was too late when . . . I shouldn't have . . . Oh, Marnie, I can't stop thinking about it . . .'

'Zoe, what is it, because nothing is worth getting in this state for. What shouldn't you have—'

'Please don't tell my mum,' Zoe implored her.

Shit, she's pregnant, thought Marnie.

Zoe groaned loudly before continuing, bent over as if she had been hit by a wave of central pain. 'Marnie, it was me that told Kay Sweetman about that man you were . . . I'm sorry.' She dissolved again. 'She told me to spy on you. She said that you were up to no good and after Lilian's money and I should report back on anything I heard of interest.'

The realisation dawned. *Oh God*, thought Marnie. So that's where it had come from.

'It's fine, Zoe, go on,' Marnie reassured her.

'Lilian spoke about you so much that, in the beginning, I did think Kay might be right and I told her what I'd over-heard you and Lilian talking about one day. I'm so sorry. As soon as I'd told her I knew it was wrong. And the more I got to know you, the more I liked you and we all knew that you and Lilian were fond of each other and not pretending and then when Kay told Herv about what I'd said, I could have died because she only wanted to stop anything happening between you and Herv because of Ruby and you've been so lovely to me and then you said that about supporting me in university and—'

The girl was in bits. It would have been cruel to let Zoe know the damage she'd caused, especially when her sole motive had been to watch out for Lilian, so Marnie swallowed it and held up her hand to stem Zoe's tormented flow. 'Okay, slow down, slow down. It's fine, Zoe, really. You don't need to worry. I know you were fond of Lilian and thinking that you were protecting her. The fault is with Kay, she should never have tried to manipulate you like that.' She dragged her handbag towards her to pull out a packet of tissues. 'And the offer for help with your university costs still stands.'

'No, I can't now. Not after what—'

Marnie interrupted her yet again. 'Yes it does. We all make mistakes,' she let loose a little laugh. *Oh boy, don't we just.* 'Is this why you've been so down? Your mum said you've been worried and that's made her worried.'

Zoe nodded her head as she blew her nose.

'Well stop it, now. We're good, you and I, Zoe. Thank you for telling me. Now put it to bed, please. No harm done.' *No harm done? Oh, Zoe, if you only knew.*

'Three times I've got as far as your house to tell you and I chickened out on the doorstep,' Zoe went on.

'You silly girl,' said Marnie. 'If your mum asks why your eyes are so red, tell her that we've had a girl to girl chat about . . . about leaving home or something, otherwise goodness knows what she'll think.'

'I will,' said Zoe. She stood up to go and then suddenly threw her arms around Marnie.

'You are so lovely,' she said, sniffing hard.

'I know,' joked Marnie. 'Now cheer up.'

'I will,' said Zoe. Marnie escorted her to the door and opened it.

'You won't tell anyone?' Zoe asked again.

'No, and I don't want to hear another word about it,' said Marnie, sternly, which Zoe interpreted as kindness in context, although out of context it would have sounded harsh. As it did to Herv who had walked out of the kitchen to see Zoe standing there with bowed head, bloodshot eyes and red, salt-raw cheeks.

That's all I need, thought Marnie. *As if I couldn't sink any lower in his estimations, now he thinks I'm bullying teenagers.* She retreated into the dining room and, much to her surprise, he followed her.

'I wanted to ask you about the lake,' he said, his tone clipped and unfriendly. 'Are you keeping it or filling it in?'

'I'll ask the new owner,' Marnie said, in the same manner. 'It's not my call.' She picked up her pen and scribbled the word 'lake' on her pad.

'Why have you upset Zoe?'

'I haven't, actually.'

'She was crying.'

'As I said, I haven't.' *Oh bollocks, could his timing have been any worse?* And she couldn't exactly explain what it was all about so she moved swiftly on. 'Whilst you're here, would you mind taking a look at Emelie's cottage, the damp is terrible in it and she won't move out so we'll have to work around her. The wall behind her TV is especially concern—'

'Is it true?' There was demand in his voice.

'Yes. Rising damp, I'm sure of it.'

He took in an angry breath and said something unintelligible under his breath, something Norwegian and most likely a string of expletives. 'I don't mean Emelie's wall. Is *it* true?' He knew that she knew what he meant. She knew that he knew that she knew what he meant: what Kay Sweetman had said. And actually, now she was thinking about it, he'd believed it and judged her without question, just as Fiona Abercrombie had done about the cheesecakes. Maybe he wasn't so bloody perfect after all if he could take the gospel according to Kay Sweetman as the definitive version. Marnie's temper went from 0–60 in a nanosecond.

'Yes, all of it,' she spat. 'I'm a home-wrecking bitch because Kay Sweetman said I was so it must be true, mustn't it? Happy? Right, now that's sorted, I'm busy, Herv, so please sod off and leave me alone.' He turned from her immediately and shut the door in such a way that it was less an incidental action than a statement of what he thought about her.

Marnie flinched as it banged hard against the frame and it felt as if it had banged against her heart as well and bruised it a little more than it was already. But she was cross too. What business of his was it anyway? He had no right asking questions like that when he was bonking blondie. Marnie wondered if he'd held her face as tenderly as he'd held Marnie's in his cottage on Cheesecakegate day. No one had ever lit up every nerve in her body, just by brushing his fingers against her cheek. But Herv Gunnarsen was a hypocrite. What had he once said to her, something about letting the past settle and not raking it up, growing flowers from it instead – it was all rubbish, mere words that sounded nice but meant nothing. And she'd heard enough of those to last her a lifetime.

Chapter 40

Herv stomped straight from the dining room, out of the house and down Kytson Hill to Emelie's cottage hoping the strength of his emotion would dissipate by the time he arrived there to look at the old lady's damp wall problem, but there was too much of it for that to happen. He had spent the past three weeks – since Kay Sweetman had opened her mouth – in a state of such tension that he wasn't sure what he was capable of. To say he hadn't been himself was a gross understatement. He had never felt as disappointed in a person in his life as he had done in Marnie Salt. He'd thought he'd known what sort of person she was, outwardly bolshie because inside she was fragile. Lilian had warned him that she hadn't had the happiest of lives – without indulging in detail – and if he had any intentions towards her, then he should be prepared to be a little patient. He knew instinctively that she was battle-scarred and she would need some time to accept that he was a good guy without an agenda, and when he had kissed her, he knew he had been right to play the long game because she melted against his lips as surely as he had melted against hers.

Then he'd heard Kay Sweetman's words and they'd been the equivalent of an arrow in his heart, never mind his Achilles' heel. Marnie and Tine cut from the same cloth – it wasn't something he could handle. The fall-out from what Tine had done had spread far beyond him. She'd smashed a wrecking ball against so many lives. His best friend had fallen hard for Tine. His pregnant wife had been crushed by his leaving her. Then Tine had stamped all over him too, deciding she'd 'made a mistake' as casually as if she'd ordered the wrong size dress from a catalogue. He'd taken an overdose, survived it, but his wife, who'd been prepared to take him back, couldn't forgive him then for attempting to leave their three small sons in that way. It was a mess beyond mess and Herv knew he could never love another woman who could invade a marriage. He couldn't trust a woman capable of that sort of destruction.

He'd been half-mad with fury, determined to spit Marnie out of his life and he stemmed the bleed from his heart with another woman's soft touch. He'd met Suzy in a pub in Skipperstone, when he'd attended a fortieth birthday party there for one of the teachers he used to work with. She was skinny and tall, blonde and the physical opposite to Marnie Salt and he was ashamed to admit that that had been most of the attraction. He hadn't made her any promises, but he'd known she'd wanted more than he could give, despite her 'assurances' that she didn't. She was attractive and smiley and hung on his every word but he'd felt no quickening of his pulse whatsoever when he had kissed her.

His pappa had said that he had fallen in love with his mamma at first sight. They'd both been first-year students at Bergen university and she had leaned over him in the cafeteria to reach a serviette and accidentally brushed his hand. That's all it had taken for the sparks to fly up his arm into his brain and fry it. She still made his head tingle thirty years later, Pappa said. Herv had wanted that feeling too, but he'd never been that lucky. Not until he raised his head on the day of the May fair to charge a visitor an entrance fee, whilst he was wearing an old hessian sack and false brown teeth and found a black-haired woman with the prettiest, greenest eyes he'd ever seen and he knew exactly what his pappa had experienced.

'Come in,' called Emelie, hearing Herv's knock and he entered to find her waking up from a nap in her rocking chair.

'I'm sorry to disturb you, Emelie,' he said.

'I'm happy to be disturbed by you, Herv,' she said with a smile. 'Did Marnie send you?'

He answered her with a grunt and Emelie knew that her name had caused that sound of displeasure.

'I can smell the damp straightaway,' he said. 'How long has it been like this? It's not good. You should have told someone before.'

'It's only been this bad for a little while. Have you got time for a tea?'

'I always have time for a tea, Emelie, you know that.'

Emelie hobbled over to the kitchen and Herv thought that he hadn't seen her bent over so badly in all the time he'd known her. She was noticeably in discomfort. And he wasn't surprised at her cough as she waited for the kettle to boil. The black spores on the window frames would have aggravated any chest weakness.

'Plenty of milk, half a teaspoon of sugar and stir it well please,' Herv called to her as he went to inspect that wall behind her television set. He could stick his finger straight through the plasterwork. The whole lot needed to come off.

'Here you go, Herv,' said Emelie, bringing out a mug in one hand and a large slice of cheesecake on a plate in the other. She saw how he glowered at it.

'Thank you, but I'm not hungry.'

'I made it especially too,' said Emelie, with a disappointed sigh.

'No you didn't, stop fibbing,' Herv shook his head disapprovingly at her. 'Where's the damp coming from? Can I look in your cellar?'

'I don't have one,' said Emelie. 'The cheesecake is delicious. Apple strudel. Marnie made it for me.'

'I don't like apples.'

'Oh, Herv Gunnarsen, you are not a good liar.'

'I don't want to talk about her.' He lifted the mug which looked tiny in his hand, easily crushable. 'There must be a water leak somewhere.'

'I think Marnie likes you very much, Herv,' said Emelie.

'I don't think she does,' he said, his tone flat. 'Have you noticed any damp patches upstairs?'

But Emelie was determined to pin him to the subject. 'I also think that what Kay Sweetman said to you about her was evil.'

'I really don't care.' Herv returned his attention to the crumbling wall in an attempt to assess the extent of how far the damp had risen.

'Yes you do,' chuckled Emelie, dropping back into her rocking chair. 'You can't fool an old fool. You know, everyone thought that Lilian was a little cuckoo, but I swear she could see into people's souls. She told me that she knew from the first minute of meeting you, what a good man you were.

And how you'd fit into Wychwell as if you were meant to be here.'

'I thought a lot about her too,' said Herv.

'And she loved Marnie very much. Like a daughter.'

'I really think you should move out of this house whilst the work is being done, Emelie. I'll get my tools and some materials and come back tomorrow to start it.'

'Herv, it's Sunday tomorrow, it can wait.'

'It can't. I am free so I will do it. I'll leave a note for ... to tell ... her it's a definite priority.'

He couldn't even say her name, thought Emelie. He wouldn't have been so hurt if his feelings didn't run so deep.

'Thank you. I'm sure Marnie will agree to whatever you suggest. Lilian couldn't have left Wychwell in a kinder pair of hands, could she?' she said.

She saw him rub his forehead with his fingertips as if he was a genie rubbing a lamp to make an answer to that appear. And one that would avoid any reference to Marnie Salt's name. But Emelie persisted gently.

'You know, Herv, you might think I'm a silly old spinster who doesn't know anything about life, but you'd be wrong. Love is a rare privilege not a common right. Don't turn it away if you're lucky enough to find it.'

Herv smiled at that. 'My mother used to say the same thing.'

'Both of us can't be wrong,' Emelie smiled back.

Herv picked a crumb from the cheesecake plate and placed it on his tongue. The flavour spread in his mouth and with it a picture of Marnie flooded his brain. It was the same with everything about her, a touch, a smile, just being in her orbit had that great an effect on him. For good and bad.

'My mother and my father fell in love at first sight,' said Herv. 'They said it was the sort of thing that they'd only believed existed in books and films and imagination, but still they felt the full thunderbolt.'

'I know that feeling too, Herv,' said Emelie.

'I didn't think I ever would.'

'But you did. And with someone who couldn't have disappointed you more.'

Herv looked into Emelie's wise, blue eyes. It was as if she could see inside his head, see the thoughts madly tumbling around in it.

'People aren't perfect, Herv. Saints have pasts and sinners have futures, as they say. But are you really going to take Kay Sweetman at her word?'

'I asked *her* and she admitted it.'

Emelie came back at him more sternly now, 'Oh, Herv, did she really?'

'Yes she did. Only five minutes ago,' and he shrugged his shoulders. 'Why would she do that if it wasn't true?'

'So you came bursting into my cottage because you'd had a row with Marnie, hadn't you? Maybe she's as hurt and angry as you, Herv. Maybe she's disappointed in you also for believing too easily the word of a malicious woman with an agenda.'

Herv fell silent, processing her words. She was right. His knee-jerk reaction to Kay's revelation had led astray his common sense.

'Now, about my wall. If you insist on coming tomorrow, what time shall I expect you? I'm always up and dressed by half-past seven,' asked Emelie, moving away from the M-word. She didn't want Herv bracketing her with the village busybodies. She'd done what she set out to: make him think for himself, not just regurgitate the words that fell from Kay Sweetman's vicious tongue.

History of Wychwell by Lionel Temple
Contributions by Lilian Dearman.

Little Raspberries is the only cottage on Raspberry Lane. It is so-called because of the abundance of fruit which grows in its long sun-catching garden.

Little Raspberries was built as a charity cottage and has always been granted to someone in most need of its tranquil setting. There is a small bridge over Blackett Stream across to the wood where it is believed Margaret Kytson's cottage stood, though there is no firm source for this rumour, only hearsay.

Records show that past occupants of Little Raspberries have included Anne Mumford, John-James Settle, Jack Pettigrew (uncle of Lionel Temple Senior) and the last occupant Jessie Plumpton, who has lived there, at the date of this book, for seven years and is an expert pie-maker, taking full advantage of the rich raspberry harvest that occurs between June and October.

Chapter 41

Marnie marched home to Little Raspberries, shut the door and locked it against the village, against the world, against Herv Gunnarsen most of all. She clicked on the kettle and checked her emails to see if anything had arrived from Mr Wemyss whilst it was coming to the boil. It had, and also, she couldn't believe her eyes to see she had also received one from Caitlin.

She opened the message from Mr Wemyss first; Caitlin could wait. His mystery client would like to engage Dennis Whitby as the builder to carry out the renovations of the houses, and could Marnie arrange for him to visit and prepare quotes. He, apparently, had done work for Miss Dearman in the past and she had been very pleased with his services.

Marnie made herself a coffee before opening the email from Caitlin. The subject line said: Please read. She couldn't imagine what it could say because it would be neither a wedding invite, nor an apology. Maybe she'd heard about Marnie's mother and wanted to say something on the lines of, 'sorry to hear about your mum, had to say that, but it doesn't mean we are friends. I still think you're a shit.'

Should she delete it without reading and not give Caitlin a chance to stick the boot in again? The temptation to look was too great though. She clicked on it and found a considerable amount of typing.

Dear Marnie

I have no idea how to start this, I've rewritten this email a load of times and nothing seems right so I'm just going to jump in and say that I owe you the biggest SORRY in the world.

You will not be surprised, I'm sure, to hear that Grigori and I have split up. I found out he had been sleeping with Tawny his PA. He was so arrogant when I confronted him and he said something, though I can't quite remember what in all the drama, that made me realise he really had come on to you on the staircase at Lucy's wedding, blaming it on drink of course. After all the years we were mates, I cannot believe that I took his word above yours. I feel ashamed.

Let's go out for a drink and talk. I really miss you and could do with a friend right now.

Lots of love

Caitlin xxx

PS. Sorry to hear about your mother.

Marnie read it and initially a candle flame of joy ignited inside her that her friend wanted to be back in her life, then she re-read it and the light was snuffed out immediately. So, if Grigori hadn't been so stupid as to drop himself in it, she would still be enemy-zoned – correct? And that line 'I could do with a friend right now' might as well have been written in a highlighter so yellow, it could have been seen from Mars. And though Caitlin knew that Marnie and her mother didn't get on, a post scriptum mention for her death – really? Where was the 'how are you?' for a start. But then Caitlin always was less about *you* and more about *me me me*. These were crumbs from the apology table, and Marnie didn't do crumbs any more. She wasn't someone on a piece of elastic that could be dropped and picked up again when it suited. Nope, she wasn't that Marnie now and the awareness that she wasn't shocked her in a warm way. Could she be actually growing up at last? Thanks to a batty old lady who had seen her warts and all and still valued her as something precious . . . ?

Marnie didn't answer straightaway. She took her book into the garden down by the stream. The raspberries had ripened early, she noticed; they were fat on the brambles and would need harvesting soon. They would have made wonderful toppings for Mrs Abercrombie's cheesecakes: raspberry and champagne, raspberry and white chocolate, raspberry and even more raspberries . . . but that was a closed avenue. Maybe someone in the village made jam or pies, like Jessie Plumpton had, and could use them. Or maybe Lionel or David would take them for their wine-making; it would be a shame to waste them so she'd ask around. She wondered who the next occupant of Little Raspberries would be when she left. It had been the most wonderful bolt-hole. In winter, when snow fell, the garden would look like Narnia. She could imagine sitting in this spot with a fire crackling in an iron basket and drinking a mug of warm spiced cider. She imagined kissing Herv Gunnarsen with cinnamon lips and gave her head a shake to rid it of the image.

She forced herself to focus on the *Country Manors* book, willing it to pull her into the story again so she could forget all about her future and Caitlin and really annoying Herv

Gunnarsen and Christmas snogging, and it worked for a while until Manfred's nephew Jurgen Goss arrived at the manor all the way from Austria – a whopping great hunk of a bloke with a lion's mane of blond hair, blue eyes and a penchant for gardening and fornicating with some very inventive uses for his garden twine. Marnie closed the book; she'd read enough today.

She replied to Caitlin just before she turned in for the night.

> Dear Caitlin
>   I am so sorry to hear that you've been through all that. You don't need me to tell you that you are so much better off without G. Onwards and upwards - good luck.
>   My best wishes
>   Marnie x

That said all she needed to really.

Lying in bed, she started to think about her own plans for Wychwell. That lovely tearoom she had envisaged. It would have been the ideal place to sell her cheesecakes in, if she'd stuck around. Screw Mrs Abercrombie and her rubbery crap. As for the question of which one would be better – Winter House or Summermoor ... well, why not both? It would make perfect sense to knock them together into one big tearoom.

As Marnie started to lift off the shores of consciousness and drift into sleep imagining how the combined buildings would look, her eyes flashed open. She sat bolt upright, switched on the bedside lamp and starting frantically hunting for a pen and paper. There was something she had to write down before she did a Lilian and forgot it.

She had a hunch where Margaret Kytson's well might be. Lilian hadn't found a clue in the ledgers – which is why she couldn't locate it again when she looked. It's what Lilian *hadn't* seen in them that had given her the answer.

Marnie got up and made herself a hot chocolate in an effort to reboot her bedroom routine because her mind was spinning. Going out for a walk around the block was not an option. Knowing her luck she'd see the Pink Lady floating across the manor gallery, and there were only so many mysteries her brain could deal with in one evening.

Chapter 42

Marnie was awoken at half past seven hearing the squeak of her letter box. It was Sunday so it couldn't be the postman. There was a note waiting for her on the doormat when she padded downstairs to investigate. A handwritten one, no envelope.

> I wanted to warn you, Titus has been asking a lot of questions about you, I have no idea why though I have tried to find out. I do know that today I overheard him on the phone and he mentioned that you had been a foundling and (quote) 'the dates tie in'. It has something to do with Lilian going off to Ireland in January 1984 and returning in late June. There has always been a story circulating that Lilian was pregnant and was sent away for six months to avoid a scandal. But this has never been substantiated. Wish I could be more help, but I thought you should know.
> H

Marnie's hands, holding the letter, were overtaken by the worst pins and needles. This couldn't be. Surely this was rubbish. It was a wild assumption. Bonkers. But Titus seemed to be taking it seriously. Was that why he asked for her birth date that day outside the shop? Was that why Kay Sweetman had once alluded to Herv sucking up to her *but it had nothing to do with fancying you*?

Emelie would know. Marnie had intended to go up to visit her that morning to see how she was. She thought she might perk her up telling her the theory she'd come up with about the location of the well and now she would ask her about this too, this mad rumour that she was Lilian's child. Emelie was an early riser but still, it didn't seem polite to call on her before nine. As soon as the clock on the wall started to chime that hour, though, Marnie was on her way, half-walking, half-running across the green to Little Apples.

As she passed the end of Herv's lane, she fixed her eyes forward so that she wouldn't see the blonde walking out of his house, his hand familiar on her back, or the two of them snogging on the doorstep, though the temptation to turn her head and torment herself was right there. She hurried up the path to Emelie's cottage and knocked on the door, but there was no answer, which was odd. Marnie knocked again and tried the handle. Emelie's tiny boots were in their usual place on the mat so she hadn't wandered over to the shop. Marnie pushed the door fully open and the smell of damp assailed her nostrils. Thank goodness she'd agreed to let Herv sort it for her.

'Emelie?'

Marnie stepped into the kitchen, but there were no signs of breakfast and the kettle was cold. She called up the narrow staircase.

'Emelie?' She hoped she hadn't woken her up.

'Marnie, is that you?' Emelie's voice was weak.

Marnie bolted up the stairs to find her on the bedroom floor.

'I think I might need a doctor, Marnie,' said Emelie. Marnie rang for an ambulance.

Emelie's breathing was coming in fluidy rasps; she was in pain and Marnie daren't lift her in case she had broken something, so she sat on the carpet and cradled the old lady until the ambulance arrived within a quarter of an hour, though it felt like much longer.

'We're up here,' Marnie called when she heard the knock on the front door. The paramedics – a man and a woman – moved in swiftly, took over with calm proficiency, asked questions, looked at the tablets on her bedside table.

'Don't you worry, sweetheart, we'll get you to hospital and comfortable,' said the male paramedic to Emelie.

'I'm dying,' said Emelie as they lifted her onto a carry chair.

'You're going to be okay, don't you talk like that,' insisted Marnie, holding her hand, feeling Emelie grip it back hard. 'And, what's more, you're moving into the manor and out of this cottage for a while, I won't take no for an answer.'

'No, Marnie, I really am dying.'

Marnie let go of Emelie's hand and followed behind as the paramedics descended the twisty staircase with expert ease.

'Emelie?' Herv was standing in the doorway, a bag of tools in his hand. 'What's happened?'

The female paramedic slipped an oxygen mask over Emelie's nose. 'You breathe in nice and steady,' she said, her attention fully focused on the old lady.

'I found her upstairs,' said Marnie. 'I don't know what's wrong.'

'We're going to need space in the ambulance,' the male paramedic said to Marnie and she nodded, understanding.

'I'll get my car.'

'I'll drive you,' said Herv.

Marnie followed Herv down the hill as the paramedics transferred Emelie into the back of the ambulance then set off at
a fair pace, but without the emergency bells and whistles.
Marnie was grateful for that because it would have scared
Emelie, she thought as Herv zapped open his car doors and
they got in.

He caught the ambulance up at the traffic lights on the
Skipperstone road, but then it went through the red light and
they had to wait. Until then, neither of them had spoken. It
was Herv who first broke the silence.

'What's wrong with her?'

'I've no idea. I found her on the floor at the side of her bed.
I don't know how long she'd been there, but she couldn't
breathe very well and she had a bad pain in her side.' Her
throat felt clogged with emotion and she had to cough it away
before continuing. 'The ambulance didn't take very long to
arrive at least.'

'It's good you were there.'

'Well, if I hadn't been, at least you would have found her.'

'I was late. I should have started work at half-past eight.
But I had another coffee . . .' Herv slammed his hand down
on the steering wheel.

'You're weren't to know, Herv.'

They had caught up the ambulance, but it was travelling
very fast now. Then another set of lights held them up.

'She said she was dying,' said Marnie as they saw the first
directional sign for the hospital. 'I told her not to talk like
that and she said that she really was.'

'She can't be,' said Herv, flatly. He recalled the Emelie of yesterday, forcing him to face facts, making him think, mind bright as a button. He took the corner into the crowded car park a little too fast, squealing his tyres.

'There's a space,' shouted Marnie, spotting someone just reversing out of one. Another driver had seen it too but Herv was quicker. This was no time for gallantry.

'Are you a relative?' asked the receptionist, when they enquired about Emelie.

'Yes,' lied Marnie.

They were directed to the emergency department where, eventually, a doctor took them into a cubicle and told them that Emelie had died and on her hospital notes was her explicit instruction that there should be no attempts at resuscitation.

It hadn't been the damp that had caused her breathlessness, she had a pulmonary disease that she'd know about for a year, apparently, but refused treatment for it because she didn't want to spend the time she had left in hospitals. And if she died, that was to be it, she'd made it plain that she must be allowed to go without medical intervention. Marnie and Herv went in to see her. Emelie looked peaceful and asleep, the lines smoothed from her face. Marnie gave her a kiss on her cheek, stroked her hair, said goodbye to her. Herv's kiss was gentle on her forehead, a thank you, grateful kiss. Then together they walked back to the car, in silent shock. They'd expected to find Emelie poorly and possibly looking at a couple of weeks on a ward. Separately, they'd both resolved to have Little Apples damp-proofed and replastered by the time she came home. Neither of them had expected that she wouldn't be home again.

'I'll go and tell Lionel,' said Marnie, as they left Skipperstone. She felt stunned.

'I can do it, if you like,' said Herv.

'Emelie will need a nice dress and . . .' she was going to say her handbag. How ridiculous.

Herv knew what she would need and what to do. He had been through this ritual before.

He pulled up outside his house and turned to Marnie; she looked devastated. He wanted to reach across and take her hand. His fingers twitched with intention and then Marnie opened the car door and the moment was gone.

'I should go and lock up her house,' she said.

'I'll come with you.'

The cottage appeared the same as always from the outside, apples now weighing down the tree in the front garden, most too small and green to be picked and Marnie thought that Emelie wouldn't be around to see them grow heavy and ripen in the late summer sunshine. They both walked inside her cheery, homely lounge to find Emelie's old typewriter on the deep windowsill, the *Country Manors* book on the coffee table, her crocheted blanket draped over the back of her rocking chair by the fireside, all normal and as usual, except for the clock on the wall whose tock sounded louder somehow, set against a silence in which it was apparent something important was missing.

Whilst Herv went upstairs to check that the windows were closed, Marnie bolted the back door then took the front door key from the hook on the wall. She dropped it and it landed in one of Emelie's short boots. The sight of them made her face crease with sadness that she wouldn't see the dear little woman again. Then she heard the top step creak as Herv came down and she forced herself to recover.

'All right?' he said. Marnie nodded. Outside, she gave Herv the key to take to the vicarage.

'Do you want me to walk you home?' he said.

'No, I'll cut across the green,' she replied. 'You go and let Lionel know.'

She wanted him to clear the two-step distance between them and wrap her in his arms but he didn't. She set off home, her straight back giving no clue of the grief that held her tight in its grip.

Chapter 43

First thing the following morning, Marnie asked Mr Wemyss to pass on a message to the mystery owner of Wychwell that she would not now be meeting the builders until after Emelie's funeral. Mr Wemyss was sad to hear the news of her death. Emelie had lodged her will with him, he said, and so he would be in touch with Lionel Temple to ensure that her final wishes were taken care of.

In the afternoon, she went over to the vicarage to ask if she could do anything for Emelie, knowing that she had no living relatives. Her brother had died years ago and had been childless; the Taubert line had come to an end. She found Lionel talking to Derek in the churchyard, standing by Lilian's grave. The closer to the men Marnie got, the more blurred her vision became. She burst into tears when she reached them and Lionel put his arms around her.

'I'm sorry,' she said, 'I came over here to offer help, not take it.'

'We have all been a little rocked by Emelie's passing,' said Lionel. 'Two extraordinary women gone in a ridiculously short time. She will, of course, be laid to rest here, next to her friend Lilian.'

'That's a lovely idea,' said Marnie.

Derek sniffed, pulled a handkerchief the size of a quilt cover out of his pocket and blew his nose. He was clearly very upset too and gave his eyes a discreet wipe.

'We thought we should have the funeral on Saturday – the sixth of August. That was the day that Emelie came to live in Wychwell in 1941.'

The sixth of August. Of all days.

'That's nice,' said Marnie, immediately cross with herself for saying something so lame. But Lionel agreed with her.

'It is nice, Marnie. A balance. We take comfort in balance and serendipity when there is none other to be found.'

'Is there anything you need? For Emelie?' she asked.

'I don't think so,' said Lionel. 'Herv has taken Pammy to the funeral home with an outfit. Mr Wemyss has communicated Emelie's wishes for the service. It's all in hand, but thank you.'

'We should have a tea back at the manor, Lilian would have wanted that for her,' said Marnie.

'That would be very kind,' said Lionel.

Marnie nodded. 'Well, if you think of anything, you know where I am.'

'Thank you.'

Marnie started walking away, then she turned. 'Lionel, do you ...'

'Do I ...?'

'It doesn't matter.'

It was not the time nor the place to ask about Lilian's trip to Ireland or Margaret Kytson's whereabouts. Later. She'd do it later, after they had laid Emelie to rest.

She went up to the manor then. No one was there, she could tell that as soon as she stepped inside. The house felt different when it was occupied, as if it were more alive. Ridiculous notion, she knew. She made herself a coffee and took it through into the dining room where the ledgers were waiting on the table. She found the one labelled *1980–1990* on the spine and flicked through the pages until she came to the 1983 entries and started there. Working forward she searched for something, anything, that might give her more clues about what was happening in the estate, the year she was born. She and Herv had stuck Post-It notes everywhere to remind them of how they had deciphered the ridiculous looping handwriting, or on the parts where entries had been written in pencil which had blurred or faded and they'd attempted to fill in the blanks.

There, in January of 1984, Marnie found an entry for *The Sisters of the Immaculate Conception Hospital, Connolly, Ireland.* They had seen it, but it hadn't flagged up as anything more than a legitimate donation from the estate, albeit a large one. A charitable donation of ten thousand pounds, to be exact.

Chapter 44

It was Herv who dug Emelie's grave in the end because Derek had put his back out tidying up the churchyard. It was now the day before the funeral and Herv hadn't seen Marnie since they had come back from the hospital. But she hadn't left his mind.

He felt the pull on his muscles as he lifted the earth loaded on his spade. Emelie had been right, he should never have taken Kay Sweetman at her word, a woman who would have stretched the truth until it fitted the best shape to harm Marnie. And he shouldn't have barked at Marnie asking her if it was true: could he have insulted her any more? If the roles had been reversed, wouldn't he have been hurt that she hadn't raised the matter with him directly before finding her guilty and condemning her? Wouldn't he have attacked her aggression with more of his own?

He'd acted like a brute, an idiot, storming in demanding answers for things that weren't any of his business to ask, going against his own principles and practices. He'd always judged as he found first-hand, prided himself on his loyalty – and yet he'd treated Marnie as if she were Tine wounding him all over again.

And then she had seen him with Suzy walking out of his

cottage the morning after the night before. *Oh boy*, he really occupied the moral high ground. His eyes had flashed at Marnie's for the briefest moment and yet they had still registered the hurt in her eyes.

He plunged the spade into the ground. It wasn't an easy dig, full of stones in this part of the churchyard. But it would be a perfect growing place for Emelie's beloved Edelweiss.

After the funeral, he would apologise properly to Marnie and ask her if they could sit down and talk. He would open up his heart and say what he felt, and how much he wanted her to let him love her. And she could take it all as slow as she liked.

Emelie's funeral was simple and beautiful. Her coffin was covered in a chaotic but lovely display of edelweiss that Una had arranged. That caused a Mexican wave of raised eyebrows in church because no one had actually realised that Una could lift up her hands.

In Lionel's eulogy he recounted how Emelie and her family had escaped the Nazi regime in Austria after the Anschluss, how they had fought prejudice and won the hearts of people in the village (Titus cleared his throat at this point as if in subconscious disagreement) and how her father had saved countless lives with his work for the British intelligence service. He told how she had found a great friend in Lilian, how they would no doubt be gossiping and taking tea now, because they both found so much happiness with each other; affection, acceptance, joy.

Lionel reminded everyone to venture up to the manor for refreshment. Then Mr Wemyss hijacked his speech and asked if all could please attend now because the owner of Wychwell had decided that his identity should no longer remain a secret and would be revealed today.

Chapter 45

Up at the manor, over a fabulous buffet which the Oldroyds had prepared, there were many twitterings of displeasure that the mystery owner of Wychwell should disrespect Emelie's day to claim the focus. He wasn't doing himself any favours, that was for sure.

Herv wandered over to Marnie in the dining room. She was pale as Emelie's funeral flowers, he thought. Drained and tired and her green eyes had no shine in them today.

'Hi,' he said. He had words crowding in his mouth to offer her but all he could manage was that.

'Hello,' she said, struggling to resurface from her thoughts, awful thoughts which had never really left her but she had been able to hold them at bay – mostly. But not on this day. Not the sixth of August.

'Tomorrow,' Herv said, after a ridiculously long impasse. 'Can I ... can we ...'

She looked far away, as if she had receded to a small dot inside herself. He wasn't even sure she could hear him. 'Marnie?'

'Sorry ... yes. What did you say?'

'Can we talk?'

She nodded but asked, 'What ... what about?'

'I owe you a huge apology,' he said. 'I should have ... I know this isn't the right time but it couldn't wait. I'm really sorry. I wanted you to know that.'

Titus blustered past them and out of the door. 'I'll be damned if I'm waiting half an hour for everyone to finish their bloody sausage rolls. Wemyss, it's time for this nonsense to end. Come on, let's get this over with.'

The Parselows followed him into the drawing room, then the Courts, then everyone else. For once, Titus had spoken for them all.

Johnny and Derek had been quickly moving chairs from other rooms in order for everyone to sit down. Titus claimed a seat right in front of Mr Wemyss who had taken up his position at the desk, the scene almost a direct lift from the last time they had all been here after Lilian's funeral. It was Titus, powered by his impatience, who called for order. Johnny tapped Marnie on the arm, indicating that he had put a chair behind her. She thanked him. She found herself next to Hilary, whose husband had not thought to secure her a place at his side.

'So, to business,' said Mr Wemyss, taking so long to remove his glasses from their case and loop them around his ears that Marnie suspected he was doing it to annoy Titus.

'The new owner of Wychwell decided that today would be the day—'

'Oh cut to the bloody chase, man,' bellowed Titus.

Mr Wemyss glared murderously at him.

'Very well, I shall indeed cut to the chase, Mr Sutton. The entire estate, ownership and management of Wychwell, manor, lands, residential and commercial properties et cetera belongs to Miss Marnie Salt. That fast enough for you?'

Marnie heard her name but her brain didn't register anything else because it was all too much to take in. Not even when the babble arose, not even when all eyes were turned to her and the air was so full of déjà vu she could barely pull it into her lungs.

'I knew it. It was her all along, the duplicitous bitch,' Titus shouted.

Marnie's head grew suddenly light to the point of dizzy, as if she had fallen from a great height at breath-taking speed with ten-kilo weights tied to both legs.

'Let me explain,' said Mr Wemyss, his booming voice crushing the cacophony. 'Lilian Dearman left Wychwell to Emelie Tibbs, Emelie bequeathed it upon her death to Miss Salt.'

'Emelie Tibbs?' spat Titus with disbelief. 'Why would Lilian have left it to her? If that doesn't prove the stupid old cow was not of sound mind, nothing can. Hence the will must be null and void.'

'Because Emelie was her friend, Mr Sutton,' said Mr Wemyss, adding with heavy sarcasm, 'an unknown quantity to you, no doubt.'

'So Lilian the loon left my forefather's estate to a bloody foreigner? A Naz—'

'Don't you dare.' Lionel was on his feet, his arm extended. 'Don't you dare call Emelie that word or disrespect Lilian's name again.'

'Well you would defend her, wouldn't you?' laughed Titus. A cruel, derisive sound, totally devoid of humour. 'You were in love with Lilian Dearman all your bloody life. Strange how Wychwell has ended up with *her* now, isn't it?'

As Titus nodded towards Marnie, Lionel lunged at him, his intention clear. Had Herv not thrown himself in the way, Lionel's fist would have been covered in Titus's nose.

Mr Wemyss, calling for calm from the front of the room, had no chance. He might as well have been Canute ordering back the sea.

'Bloody lunatic,' said Titus, straightening his waistcoat. 'I'll be contacting the bishop about your behaviour. Now – and in the past. And you know what I mean by that, Lionel Temple.'

'You vile man,' Lionel roared at him and even Herv had difficulty holding onto him.

'Come on, Hilary,' Titus strode past them all towards the door and beckoned his wife with a series of finger clicks. But Hilary did not budge an inch, she remained seated with her handbag resting on her knee.

'Hilary,' he demanded.

'No, I'm not going anywhere.'

Titus stopped in his tracks and glared at her.

'I beg your pardon?'

Hilary stared him straight in the eye and said, 'You heard me. I'm not going anywhere.'

Humiliation thrown in with nonsense was too much for Titus who made a grab for his wife's wrist. He was pulling her from the chair until Marnie karate chopped him mid-arm and he was forced to let go with a yelp. She noticed that Herv had moved to her side, ready to wade in, if required.

'Hilary. Now.' Titus was grinding the words through his teeth.

She was resolute. 'I'm not going anywhere.'

'Then you won't be coming back at all,' he snarled and threw open the door so hard that it banged into the wall panelling.

'You're right. I won't. I'm leaving you.'

The room fell silent. A sea of jaws dropped open.

'Whaaat?'

Hilary, in a cool, quiet voice, with no shake in it whatsoever, repeated every syllable slowly so it sank in.

'I. Am. Lea. Ving. You.'

Realising she was serious, Titus immediately switched from a bullying track to a face-saving one. He looked his wife up and down imperiously and sneered.

'Not before time, you ridiculous creature.' He took a step out of the door but Hilary's next words arrested him.

'At least I'm not a thief.' Then she stood and addressed herself to everyone. 'I had no idea of the extent of my husband's corruption. I had no idea he had taken your monies and invested them in idiot schemes, I had no idea he had been stealing from the estate, draining Lilian's finances, creaming from the very people in whose midst we live until I started my own investigations recently. I cannot bear to think you must all have thought me as guilty as he is and I will make sure, I promise you, that you will get every penny back that he has embezzled from you.'

Titus's face grew so red, it was a wonder it didn't burst into flames. He opened his mouth to protest, decided there were no words so turned on his heel and was gone from them.

Hilary didn't so much sit back down as collapse on the chair as hubbub erupted on a grand scale. Mr Wemyss let it continue for a while, hoping it would burn itself out, but it didn't so he brought his fist down hard on the desk and said, 'Now that particular scenario has ended, I'd like you all to bugger off so I can speak to Miss Salt in private.'

Chapter 46

The room emptied silently like an assembly hall full of admonished children. Marnie couldn't look at them as they filed out. Her focus fell on the cabinet full of Lilian's artefacts once broken and mended with gold. *Imperfectly perfect.* Or was it *perfectly imperfect*? Lionel was last out of the door. He closed it gently behind him and gave her a smile of support.

'Come closer, dear,' said Mr Wemyss, beckoning her forward from the back of the room to the chair which Titus had occupied, still warm from his great fat body. 'I expect this has come as quite a shock to you.'

'Bit of an understatement,' she answered.

'Congratulations, Miss Salt. You are now the Lady of the Manor of Wychwell. You can't sell it, of course, but the revenue it raises will all be yours and your heirs'. I understand you are already quite au fait with its potential.'

Marnie's mouth opened to ask questions, but it was as if they were all rolled up into a hard ball that refused to budge from her throat.

'Why . . . why me?' was all she eventually managed.

Mr Wemyss pulled out an envelope pressed between the

pages of his notebook. It bore Marnie's name on the front, in old lady spider scrawl.

'This should explain. Or, at least lead to the explanation.'

'Can I open it now?'

'Be my guest.'

Marnie hesitated. This, she suspected, was a life-changing moment. This was when she found out if she was a Dearman herself. If it was more than coincidence that she shared the dark, green-eyed looks of the woman who had her portrait on the staircase and that her birth date matched that of Lilian's pregnancy. Her heart felt as if it was beating in her mouth when she slit the top of the envelope open with her finger. She lifted out the heavy hammered sheet of paper, unfolded it and read.

My dear Marnie,

If you are reading this, then I am with you no more. But I die knowing that Wychwell is in the safest of hands, of that I have no doubt now. Lilian was right to trust you.

I have written the full story in my journal, but let dearest Lionel tell you, in his own words, about us.

I wish you a long, healthy and happy life and one full of love. God bless you.

Your great friend Emelie Tibbs x

Lionel. Why Lionel. *About us*? Who is *us*? She was no more enlightened and felt the crush of disappointment deep in her chest.

'Emelie was a very wealthy woman, Marnie,' said Mr Wemyss. 'Her family might have arrived from Austria with nothing but the clothes on their backs, but her father was a shrewd investor and taught his daughter how to play the markets well.'

Mr Wemyss handed a sheet of paper to Marnie.

'The bulk of the money is bequeathed to the Wychwell estate to help with the rebuilding and upkeep. The sums earned from Emelie's literary works are to be for your personal consumption. I will prepare a breakdown for you in due course.'

Emelie's literary works. So, she was Penelope Black, Marnie had been right all along.

She read the figures on the paper and the numbers started to swim around. They could rebuild London with that amount, never mind a piddly little village in the middle of the Dales.

'Why ... I don't ... why did Emelie live in a tiny damp cottage then if she ... she had this?'

'I think you should let Lionel Temple explain everything to you,' said Mr Wemyss, reaching down for his briefcase. 'I shall be in touch re the transfers of money and various other paperworks of which there are many.' He stood and held out his hand and Marnie lifted hers to meet it.

'Lilian and Emelie spoke very highly of you, Miss Salt. Enjoy your good fortune. It is a unique one and I hope a tide-turner.'

Marnie sat on the chair in front of the beautiful desk and she thought, *I own that desk now.* She owned the carpet it was sitting on, the room it featured in, the manor in which it was housed. And the lake, the lands, the farm, even Titus Salt's house. Everything. She owned the beautiful Japanese Kintsugi pieces mended with gold. All of it. She would need to absorb this in bite-sized pieces. She knew how lottery winners must feel now. She'd nearly had an aneurysm the day she won a hundred pounds on a scratch card so she had no chance of taking all this in in one gulp.

She heard a soft knock on the door and then it cracked open. Lionel.

'Can I come in?' he asked. Marnie nodded. He put his hand on her shoulder and she raised her eyes to his.

Emelie's voice whispered from the page: ... *but let dearest Lionel tell you, in his own words* ...

'Are you my father, Lionel?' Marnie asked.

'My lovely girl,' he smiled, sitting beside her, taking her trembling hands in his. 'I only wish I were.'

Chapter 47

'Lilian thought that you managing the estate would allow you to get used to the idea of one day owning it,' said Lionel. 'Looking at you now, I'm not so sure that's true. I don't think I've ever seen anyone as white with shock.'

'I don't think I could ever get used to the idea,' said Marnie, beyond stupefied. 'This ... this doesn't happen in real life.'

'But it does and it has,' said Lionel. 'I'd like you to take a walk with me.'

'Where are we going?' asked Marnie.

'To Emelie's House. To Little Apples,' said Lionel.

Marnie followed Lionel out of the room, out of the manor, along the drive that joined Kytson Hill to where Emelie's stone cottage stood. They walked down the path, past the apple tree. Lionel reached up and pulled off one of the larger fruits, polishing it on his sleeve before pushing it into his pocket and exchanging it for a key.

'Come on, Marnie, let's go inside.'

Lionel unlocked the door and they stepped into the cottage. The fusty smell rushed at them.

Marnie grimaced. 'I wanted Emelie to move out of here.'

'She wouldn't have,' said Lionel. 'Do you have a phone with you? Is it one with a torch on it?'

Marnie foraged in her handbag and brought out her iPhone.

Lionel went into the kitchen and then into the pantry. Inside it, there was a door that opened onto a flight of stone steps leading down. Lionel flicked on the light switch.

'Emelie said she didn't have a cellar,' said Marnie, with a gasp of surprise.

'She lied,' said Lionel. 'Dear me.' The further down they ventured, the more the walls were saturated. 'I've never seen it this bad before. The water falls down from the hill and it collects at the back of the cottage,' he explained.

'I know. Emelie took me strawberry picking. It was a quagmire.'

When she reached the bottom of the steps, Marnie found they were at the beginning of a tunnel with a low arched ceiling.

'You'll need that torch now,' said Lionel. Marnie switched it on.

'Wow.' *This is like something Manfred Masters might have constructed*, was Marnie's first thought.

'We don't know why the tunnel was built in the first place, but presumably it was intended to lead into the woods. Very handy for the Shanke family to help their priest escape, but of course it was built years before Henry the Eighth turned Protestant. Maybe the builder had second sight of what was to come.'

'What's at the other end of it?'

'You'll see soon enough.'

The tunnel curved to the left and they came to another door with an iron hoop for a handle. Lionel twisted it then pushed and it opened into the manor's cellar where Marnie and Herv had gone exploring. The door had a wine rack on the other side and when Lionel shut it again, it was undetectable.

'Imagine being here in the dead of night,' said Lionel as they walked up the steps, through the boot room, the scullery, then into the kitchen. 'You can't risk being seen because you're here in secret. Don't switch your torch off yet, Marnie.'

'Ok-ay,' said Marnie, still puzzled. She followed him into the body of the manor, up the main staircase and along the windowed gallery where Lionel sat down on one of the seats and took the apple out of his pocket. He turned it around so that she could see that it had started to redden on one side.

'Do you know what type of apples grow on Emelie's tree, Marnie?'

'I have no idea,' she replied.

'It does better in warmer climates, but it survives here in Wychwell for some reason. It's a Pink Lady.'

A Pink Lady, Marnie repeated to herself. Then Lionel watched the expression on her face change as the realisation dawned.

'A . . . the Pink Lady. The ghost?'

'Lilian's little joke,' chuckled Lionel. 'When Emelie used to come here at night, she walked with a lantern, or her torch, rather than switch on a light and alert the whole village to her presence.

'*Emelie* was the Pink Lady?'

'The chemical compounds in the glass here make any light behind it appear pink. Someone saw a strange glow, presumed it was a ghost. Lilian knew it wasn't, of course, but she nevertheless encouraged the misconception.'

Marnie laughed. 'The little monkey,' she said. 'But why would—'

'She was so full of fun,' said Lionel, cutting her off, the sun fading from his smile. 'At least she was after Jago died. Turn off your torchlight, Marnie. There's more to tell.'

Marnie did as he asked and they made their way back down the gallery. They passed the portrait of the Irish lady on the stairs and Marnie shivered as if they shared a secret, or maybe something implanted in their genes. Lionel led her into the library.

'Lionel, was Lilian my—'

'All in good time, Marnie. Lilian wanted you to inherit the manor before she'd even met you. You spoke to each other on the internet. You opened your hearts to each other, I know this. Emelie and I were . . . and you'll forgive me . . . concerned for her welfare. Lilian could get very confused. She had slight brain damage from unregulated electro-convulsive treatment.'

'Lilian did?' Marnie shook her head in bewilderment. 'When did she have that? I didn't know.'

'I'm coming to it. Emelie and I both recommended caution, until we could get to know you properly,' Lionel went on. 'It was an amazing coincidence, after all, that your birth date matched that of Lilian's . . . confinement.' He chose the word carefully. It was an old-fashioned term for pregnancy, Marnie knew.

'You have to tell me, Lionel, am I Lilian's child?' asked Marnie, her voice small, stolen by emotion, by expectancy.

'My dear girl, you aren't,' said Lionel, gently. 'There never was a child.'

Marnie's heart gave a delayed beat. She hadn't realised how much she had wanted Lionel to say that she was until the moment when he said that she wasn't. She felt punctured. Her face dropped into hands trembling with shock and she felt Lionel's arms around her, pulling her into his chest.

'I'm all too aware of rumours that I fathered Lilian's baby and she was sent away to Ireland to have it, but it's all untrue. But I let those convenient rumours persist. It kept people from sniffing around for more.' He gave a little laugh. 'It's no secret that I have been in love with Lilian Dearman for most of our lives. I would have married her in an instant, but it was not to be. Then it became an easier truth for Lilian to accept, that she'd had a child out of wedlock and it had been taken from her.'

Marnie drew back from Lionel. 'Why an easier truth? It was the nineteen eighties, not the eighteen eighties. If she'd had a baby and not been married, what difference would it make in this day and age?'

Lionel walked over to the books on the shelves and lifted one out. He found the page he wanted then set the book down on the library desk. It featured a photo of a large, puffy-faced country gent with bulging eyes and lots of facial hair. He looked like an obese wolf and had more than a passing resemblance to Titus.

'Jago Dearman,' explained Lionel. 'The most hideous man in our solar system. A bully, a brute, an abuser of women. When you have power and money and status and connections, Marnie, you can override any rule you choose. Lilian and Rachel were indelibly scarred by this . . . animal. He had his wife sectioned, then locked away in a secure hospital after he discovered the affair with her doctor. The girls were allowed to visit her only once and it terrified them. He threatened to do the same to them if they ever tested his boundaries. Rachel of course tried to escape and tragically suffered for it, Lilian complied but . . . she was very unloved. And love was what she craved more than anything. So, when she found it, she threw caution to the wind.'

'George Purcell?'

Lionel picked up the book and flicked to another page. Marnie could see, as he held it, that it was entitled *The History of the Dales Families*.

He put it back down in front of Marnie again. A formal family portrait. A beautiful blonde woman with a bouffant hairstyle in a sleeveless evening dress. In her arms a baby and two sombre-looking boys sitting beside her on a chaise. Behind her a ridiculously handsome man with short hair and wide shoulders in a white shirt and evening jacket. Generous lips, dark brown eyes.

'George Purcell,' said Lionel.

'Handsome man,' nodded Marnie.

'And her husband Edwin.'

Marnie's eyebrows sank under the weight of puzzlement. 'Sorry? Is that not . . .'

'Georgina Purcell, George to her friends,' said Lionel.

'Lilian had an affair with a woman?'

'Yes,' said Lionel. 'A passionate and not very careful affair. George Purcell would never have left her husband, whom she loved; Lilian was a mere dalliance and the affair ended but Lilian . . . dear Lilian . . . was deeply in love and couldn't let her go. Edwin came to see Jago who was of course livid that he had "an aberration for a daughter". He arranged for Lilian to be taken – forcibly – to a hospital in Ireland, where they attempted to *cure* her.'

Marnie noticed how Lionel's jaw twitched, how his fist clenched at his side.

'What they did to her in that place was unspeakable. All in the name of religion.' He shook his head in disgust. 'My father was in charge of St Jude's then, he was horrified at what Jago had done. He was instrumental in getting Lilian home again. Oh my, Marnie, you should have seen her. She was completely and utterly in pieces. Broken beyond help, we thought.' Lionel stood up quickly, turned from her and she knew that he was hiding a tide of great emotion. She gave him time to recover, shifting her attention to the items on the library desk: a silver roller blotter, an art deco perpetual calendar, a vase; once broken but mended with melted gold.

Then Marnie understood. The edelweiss in her gardens, flooding at the feet of her favourite lilies.

'Emelie and Lilian were lovers weren't they?'

Lionel nodded slowly. 'Lilian was terrified of her feelings. Even after her father died and she was in charge of her own life, she still believed she would be taken away, back to Ireland, back to that *hospital*. And Emelie fought her feelings for as long as possible because she was older than Lilian and saw how fragile she was. No one had to know. Lilian wouldn't have risked their secret being made public. She would have killed herself before exposure because of what those ... bastards put her through. I guessed, but then I knew her better than she knew herself. That love made Lilian whole again, better than whole.'

'And Lilian supplanted her memories with a false one that she'd had a child in Ireland and it would one day come and find her and everything would be all right?' suggested Marnie.

'That's about it in a nutshell,' Lionel replied. 'It was an easier truth – *a better truth* – for her to believe.'

'And so that's why she wanted Wychwell to come to me. Because she thought I was her baby grown up and come home.'

'Yes.'

Marnie looked horrified. 'But that means I'd be inheriting Wychwell under false pretences. I couldn't—'

'But Lilian didn't leave it to you, dear,' Lionel cut in. 'She left it to Emelie and Emelie left it to you. Emelie knew of

course that you weren't Lilian's daughter. But you could have
been, she loved you as if you were. You were similar in so
many ways and you both have those beautiful green eyes; we
almost came to believe it ourselves that you were hers. Emelie
was in no doubt that you were the best person to take care of
Wychwell. But I didn't know she was ill. That was one secret
she kept from us all.'

The clock on the wall sounded so loud in the ensuing
silence. A deep, comforting *tock* marking time.

'There's a lot to take in,' said Lionel. 'I'm so sorry I couldn't
give you the news you really wanted. I think you would have
liked to have had Lilian as your mother.'

Marnie, unable to speak, gave a small sad smile.

'And I know, Marnie, that she believed that she was your
mother and that made her very happy.'

Marnie walked home to Little Raspberries across the green,
aware of eyes on her through windows making her conscious
of every step. As she turned the corner, she saw Hilary sitting
on her low wall, still in her funereal garb and her mood rose.

'I appear to be homeless,' Hilary said with a smile. 'Do
you think the new lady of the manor might let me have a
cup of tea?'

At the side of her doorstep was a posy of flowers and a bag
of home grown onions, plus a bottle of David's cherry wine,
so the label read.

'I can stretch to something stronger if you like,' said
Marnie, picking up the presents and opening the door.
Company would be good today.

'What a lovely house,' said Hilary, walking in and looking
around. 'Though, I suppose you'll be living in the manor soon.'

'I haven't even thought about it,' replied Marnie. 'I'm

waiting to open my eyes and find out it's all been a dream.'
So long as she didn't wake up at her desk in Café Caramba
with Suranna King about to land her a punch, she thought.
All that debacle felt like a million lifetimes away.

Marnie took two glasses out of her cupboard and uncorked
the wine.

'Cheers,' said Hilary, raising her glass to chink against Marnie's
as they sat at the kitchen table. 'Here's to new beginnings.'

'And here's to your . . . freedom?' Marnie asked tentatively.

'Oh yes,' Hilary said with emphasis. 'Julian is driving up
for me as we speak. I shan't be taking anything with me.
I've moved everything I have of any value out of the house
already.' Hilary didn't look the same dowdy woman as she'd
appeared the first time Marnie had seen her. Her eyes were
shining, her complexion dewy, even her grey hair was bounc-
ier. 'I'll make sure that Titus leaves Wychwell, too. I have an
offer he can't refuse.'

'I'll miss you,' said Marnie. 'I mean, I hardly know you,
but I've known other people for longer and yet less, if you
know what I mean.'

Hilary smiled again, the smile of a truly content woman.
'I do.'

They sipped the wine and it was sweet and punchy and
tasted of summer.

'Marnie, I have an apology to make to you,' said Hilary. 'I
really didn't know that Titus had been stealing from the estate
funds until I started snooping around when I was trying to
get my own finances in order to leave him. How much has
he taken?'

'I haven't got a final figure, but, it's a lot. At least a million.'

'Oh hell.' Hilary let out a long breath and raised her eyes
to the ceiling. 'I've been a fool too, trusting him. I really

believed we were living from wise investments, but I hold true to the promise I made and I will make sure it is all paid back to the estate. And whatever he has taken from the people in the village, I'll get it returned to them too. I have a plan.'

Poor Hilary, thought Marnie. *She must feel terrible.*

'Mr Wemyss is on the case,' she said, hoping that might relieve her of the obligation to fulfil such a ridiculously ambitious pledge.

Hilary picked up the copy of the fourth *Country Manors* book, which was sitting on the table next to a duo of salt and pepper pots.

'Titus has forbidden me from reading these, says they're pornographic tripe. Which is rich considering what I've recently found he views on the internet. But then again, he is the emperor of double standards.'

'I can give you book two and three if you haven't got them yet,' Marnie offered, 'but you're not having that number four until I've finished it. I have to find out how it all ends.'

'It doesn't end at book four, surely?' said Hilary, flicking to the last page. 'She'd be an idiot if she killed the cash cow.'

'You'll laugh,' said Marnie, 'but I bet there won't be another one. I think Emelie Tibbs was Penelope Black.'

Hilary looked at Marnie, realised she was serious and then burst into laughter. 'That isn't true.'

'I'm sure it is,' said Marnie. 'Someone in Wychwell wrote that series. I'd put my life on it.'

'I know they did. Me,' said Hilary. 'I'm Penelope Black.'

For the umpteenth time that day, Marnie was stunned into silence. Hilary topped Marnie's glass up and handed it to her.

'These are the sorts of days that enrich my writing,' she said. 'The days when fact out-fictions fiction.'

When Marnie eventually found her voice it was to say just one word: 'You?'

'Yes, me,' said Hilary with a deep curve of a grin. 'And I owe so much to Titus really. If he hadn't kept telling me that I had no imagination whatsoever, I wouldn't have tried to prove him wrong. I picked up a notepad one day and I started a story about a hideous dick' – Hilary's beautiful voice made a hideous dick sound something to aspire to – 'with a giant chip on his shoulder. Married to a woman with passions surging under a very ordinary exterior. Then I added a masterful anti-hero who realises her true worth.'

'Lara, and Manfred?'

'My middle name is Clara,' grinned Hilary. 'My maiden name is Stamp.'

'Oh my lord, *Penelope . . . Penny Black.*'

'I never expected to be published. I certainly didn't expect the tsunami of interest and the clamouring for more.'

'And who is Manfred based on?' Marnie couldn't wait to find out.

'He's a collage of all my favourites: Julian of course, Michael Bublé, a little bit of Orson Welles and a lot of Liam Neeson.'

Marnie laughed, then stopped suddenly as the full implication of Hilary's alter-ego hit her like a slap from a heavyweight boxer.

'You're super rich.'

'I am,' Hilary agreed. 'And that means that Titus will be gunning for me financially soon. Julian Fosse is my publisher as well as my lover and he's managed to delay some payments on my books so I look officially much poorer than I am, but I will still need to give Titus quite a sum to get out of my marriage. I shall repay everything, plus interest, that he has stolen directly back to Wychwell as part of the divorce settlement, so please forward me the final figures. A little insight: if he doesn't agree to it, between us we will combine forces to sue him for embezzlement and also to drag the family name through the mud, which is of stupid importance to him. He wouldn't want it tarnished, which is more than ironic. You hold a cocked shotgun to his head with that threat, trust me.'

Hilary's phone rang and she excused herself whilst she answered it.

From the smile on her face, Marnie didn't need to ask who was on the other end of it.

'My chauffeur has arrived in the car park,' she said, replacing the phone in her bag. 'Thank you for your friendship, Marnie. I always had my sister to talk to and I've missed her so much. The day you pulled up beside me in the rain was one of those awful low times when I really needed her. I was so grateful for your company. You're a good soul, I sensed that from the beginning.' Hilary picked up her handbag. Even that small action showed off her innate elegance.

'I'll miss you,' said Marnie. 'I hope you're so happy.'

'And I shall miss you too, Marnie. Come down to London and see me. I'll send you books. We will stay in touch.'

'That'd be lovely.'

At the door Hilary embraced Marnie. Tightly.

'Break the curse, Marnie. Be the first person to live out a long and happy life in the manor. Are you Lilian's daughter?'

'No,' sighed Marnie. 'Sadly.'

'I'm glad, though,' said Hilary. 'Too much bad blood. I think a family curse might be the theme of my next *Country Manors*.'

And with that, Hilary walked out of Marnie's cottage to the car park where an Aston Martin was waiting to zoom her away to her own new life.

*

The cottage felt like a hug after Hilary had gone. Something small and snug and tight around her that would keep her safe with its firm walls, low ceilings and uneven floors. Today there had been too much information, too many words, too many secrets blown open. But one stayed closed in her heart, folded like a bud that could never blossom for even Little Raspberries couldn't protect her from the long, cold shadow of the past. Nor could Emelie's fortune buy her a passage back in time to change the biggest mistake she ever made.

Chapter 48

It was three days before she saw Herv Gunnarsen again. Or anyone. She shut herself away in the cottage, not even bothering to get dressed, because she didn't know what else to do. The manor was hers to live in, but the notion was unreal. She felt stupidly fragile and lost. As if she were standing at a signpost not knowing which way to go because the lettering had faded too much to guide her.

It was Fiona Abercrombie who put her back on the road to reason.

Marnie's mobile rang and she pressed accept rather than decline by mistake. And then was too polite to hang up.

'Marnieee.' Fiona Abercrombie's voice was at the top of the pleasant scale.

'Mrs Abercrombie,' Marnie replied, with flat politeness.

'I'd like to offer you my congratulations. I hear you're the new owner of Wychwell.'

Mrs Abercrombie's voice had sugar overload. Marnie wasn't taken in.

'Thank you.'

'I expect you're wondering why I'm ringing.'

Marnie could make a stab at a guess if pushed.

'I think I acted rather hastily,' Mrs Abercrombie went on. 'I was understandably cross when we last spoke but we can't find a cheesecake maker in your league. How about we strike a new deal?'

Marnie could imagine her sitting at her desk, fixed grin on her face, pen hovering over her diary to make a date for negotiations. Well, she could work for it.

'What sort of deal?'

'Oh, one to your advantage, of course.'

'Really?' Interest crept into Marnie's voice and Mrs Abercrombie leapt on it.

'I can guarantee double the quantity I was taking from you before. And shall we say a pound more per cheesecake? I can stretch to one pound fifty if you are going to insist on driving me to a hard bargain.' Tinkly laugh.

'Hmm, let me think about that for a moment,' replied Marnie. She fell silent for a three-second count. 'No.'

More glockenspiely-type laughter from Mrs Abercrombie then, as though she thought Marnie must be joking.

'I really mean no,' said Marnie. 'I know my cheesecakes are good enough to be marketed as mine, not masquerading as yours so no, I'm not dealing with you. Not after you cut me off like you did. I think Wychwell is the perfect place for a teashop and one that can sell my cheesecakes exclusively.'

Mrs Abercrombie tried to argue but Marnie disconnected the call mid-plea: 'Oh, let's not be too hasty, Marnie, I—' No – for once, someone needed her more than she needed them. Actually, it had happened quite a bit in recent times. Caitlin, Justin and now Fiona fatarse. All it needed was for Gabrielle to turn up at her doorstep imploring that she needed a sister's advice.

Mrs Abercrombie's call made her think. Marnie had only said it to put the wind up the woman but there was no reason why she shouldn't sell her own home-made fare in the teashop she had planned for the village. It could turn out to be the cheesecake capital of the North, the world, the universe. If Fiona Abercrombie and her sub-standard offerings could make it in the marketplace, why the hell shouldn't she have a go?

And the matter of teashops brought her neatly round to the mystery of Margaret Kytson's well. With an injection of much-needed energy, Marnie got showered and dressed and set off with a spring in her step towards the vicarage.

Lionel greeted her warmly and Marnie was a little sad that it had transpired that this wonderful man wasn't her father after all.

'Come in, come in,' he said, ushering her into his lovely bright kitchen. 'Can I get you a cup of something?' There was a newspaper spread over the table.

'Not disturbing you, am I?' Marnie asked.

'Absolutely not. I would rather have your company than read about doom and gloom any day. Milk? Sugar?'

'No, I'm fine, thank you.'

'When are you moving into the manor then?'

'I have no idea,' said Marnie, puffing out her cheeks. 'It all seems too ... dreamlike.'

'You'll get used to it very quickly, I'm sure. Lilian used to say that the house liked you,' and Lionel smiled fondly. 'She said that it wanted to be loved. And if it were, then it would give it all back.'

Lilian was bonkers though, she could have said, but she knew exactly what Lionel meant. She'd always felt welcomed there. Possibly by the ghost of the Pink Lady, who she now knew didn't exist.

'Didn't Emelie want to live there at all?'

'Not without Lilian. She told me that she went back a couple of times, in the night, hoping to feel Lilian's presence there . . . but sadly, no.'

Marnie had known it was a real live person she'd seen that one time when she had run up to the manor hoping to catch the ghost before it walked through a wall. It was Emelie, retracing her familiar steps.

'Lionel, I've come to ask you about Margaret Kytson and the well.'

The vicar sat down next to her and Marnie couldn't work out if the resulting creak came from him or the chair.

'Well, you can ask, my dear, but I have no new information.'

'You may have, but not know it,' said Marnie and Lionel's head moved forward by interested degrees.

'Oh? Do go on.'

'Emelie said words to the effect that Lilian had been looking through the manor ledgers and had found something which made her think she was on to where the well might be, but she didn't write it down and so she forgot it.'

'As we all do,' said Lionel. 'Most annoying.'

'Well, Lilian tried to refresh her memory by going back over them again but she couldn't find it . . .' she left an enticing pause '. . . I think that might have been because she found something that wasn't there.'

Lionel waited for her to continue and when she didn't, his brows dipped quizzically. 'I'm not sure I'm with you.'

'Lionel, where is Spring Cottage, Spring House, Spring whatever?'

Lionel tapped his lip in thought. 'I . . . I don't know that there ever was one. I've never come across mention of it. Why?'

'There are two derelict houses named after Winter and

Summer, and Derek's house – Autumn Leaves, but no Spring one. I find that a bit odd.'

The vicar processed this and nodded slowly.

'Yes, I see what you mean. But there isn't.'

'There must be. Lilian told Emelie that whatever she had found was more or less hiding in plain sight.'

Lionel considered this for a moment.

'Wait a minute,' he said and walked out of the room, reappearing soon after with a blue cardboard folder. He pulled the contents out onto the table.

'This is all the stuff that wasn't of any use but I didn't throw it away, just in case. You never know. Here's the child's picture we found in one of the cottages.'

It was a drawing, of no interest so she put it back into the folder. Along with everything else because Lionel was right, it was rubbish.

'We have a complete list of all the cottages – past and present names – but there is definitely no Spring amongst them,' Lionel reiterated.

'There has to be,' replied Marnie. She had looked at the layout of the village so many times it had become tattooed on her brain. She went back to the blue folder and took out the drawing again.

'Do you have a present map of the village here, Lionel?'

'No, I don't. I only have this collection of research rejects.'

'Can I borrow it?'

'Of course,' said Lionel and gave a chuckle. 'It's yours now anyway.'

Marnie, a woman on a mission, said a quick goodbye and headed over to Little Raspberries to pick up the key for the manor house.

She was near to finding Margaret now, she absolutely knew it.

Chapter 49

Marnie opened the heavy door and walked into the manor.

'Hello,' she said in the quiet. 'Nice to see you again. I'll be living here soon, if you want me.'

There was no reply, simply a feeling that she would be welcome when she did. She was getting as batty as the Dearmans. She clapped her hands together.

'Okay, house, you and me are going to find Margaret Kytson. And I won't take no for an answer, all right? Good.'

She strode into the library where the ledgers had been stored to make way for Emelie's funeral tea, and she carried them back through to the dining table. She pulled out all the maps and plans of the village that she had found and unfolded them. *Oh, where to start?*

She turned her head upwards and implored, 'Come on, Margaret, give me a hand here.' And her heart nearly bounced out of her chest when someone rapped loudly on the window behind her.

It was Herv. Beautiful, lion-maned Herv with his large blue eyes that seemed to hold the sunshine in them. He pointed to the left and mimed unlocking the door. She was aware of how quickly she moved to do it.

'Hello, how are you?' he said.

'I'm good, how are you?' she replied. He seemed bigger, wider, his accent sounded stronger, his lips looked even more kissable and the sensation of them upon hers drifted across her mind.

She saw him smile, cross his arms, shake his head. 'It's so strange that you're here. As Lady of the Manor.'

'Yep, well . . . it's odd for me too,' said Marnie, jiggling her head nervously.

'Are you . . . are you moving in? Do you need any help?'

'No, I'm not moving in, but I could do with your help. If you aren't too busy?' She asked hopefully.

'You're the boss.'

Whatever Emelie might have said about Lady Chatterley and the gardener, somehow being Herv's boss was a further wedge between them. Marnie picked that up in his only half-jokey tone.

She told him her theory and waited for his reaction and his eyes narrowed as his brain spun behind them.

'It would make good sense, but there is no Spring House or Spring Hill or Little Springs . . .'

Hill. Little . . .

'Herv look at this.' She opened up the file and pulled out the drawing found under the floorboards in Winter House.

'I have seen this before,' he said. 'It's just a child's picture.'

'Or is it?' Marnie positioned the three formal maps they had of Wychwell so they were in date order. She put the drawing in first position. 'Let's call this Map A, those B, C, D, okay,' then she tapped the top right-hand corner of A with a heavy finger.

'Here, look how it compares to the other ones. Can you see what I'm seeing?'

Herv's eyes journeyed across the four maps. All he could see was that on the proper ones Emelie's cottage was in the right place and on the drawing, it was much further into the woods.

'Obviously not,' he answered her, flummoxed.

'Look at the manor and the church and the vicarage and the Wych Arms. The oldest still-standing buildings.'

Herv did as she asked. 'They are the same on the maps and the drawing.'

'Yep. These are the only buildings in the village which are in the same position on all four. Exactly the same position. And in the right place. So what if A isn't a child's drawing, what if it's a very accurate map and the earliest one we have of the area.'

Herv looked again, studied the proper maps, compared them all to the drawing. She was right.

'This isn't supposed to represent Emelie's house then?' He tapped the top corner of map A. 'This was another house built before Little Apples, is that what you mean?'

'Yes, I think it was.' She excitedly flipped over to a clean page in her A4 notepad and started scribbling. 'Here's a timeline. I'm guessing but I feel I'm onto something. One: Margaret Kytson's house gets burned down and the well is closed up in the mid-sixteenth century. Next, trees grow, time passes. People remember the witch but it's a long time ago. They have a vague recollection of where she lived and the well she was drowned in but by now she's probably become more of a myth than a real person. Maybe something to scare naughty kids with. Then maybe later ... yes ... I know, so that kids *aren't* scared, they make up a story that the witch lived at the other end of the village, and in time that's what leads people to believe that her house was near Little Raspberries.' The excitement was adding pace to her speech; she was so close to solving this, she could almost smell the hubble and bubble in Margaret's cauldron. 'Anyway, the Lord of the Manor decides that he wants a cottage built near to him. Maybe for a worker or his mother or his bit on the side. It's close, but still tucked away. So he has the trees cleared and up the building goes.'

Herv tapped on the drawing, at the misplaced house they'd presumed was Emelie's on map A. 'This one?'

'Yep. For the sake of argument, let's call it Spring Cottage. Named after the fabled natural spring that is in the area some-where nearby, though no one can remember quite where it is. Next, more cottages are built in the village and whoever names them presumes that 'Spring Cottage' is named after the season, so it makes sense to call three buildings after the other seasons.'

Herv clicked his fingers. 'I have it,' he said. 'I know. Yes, but the water from the spring has been pushed underground and over the years it makes the land unstable.'

'Precisely. Here on B – the second oldest map – this is not Spring Cottage because it has collapsed or been pulled down. The house has been rebuilt nearer to the village sometime after map A was drawn.' She tapped the top right of maps B, C and D where the small square sat on the lip of the wood. '*This* is Emelie's Cottage. And it's been put there because it links to the manor house via a tunnel. It's no longer needed to smuggle priests out into the woods, but it is rather handy if the Lord wanted to secretly visit a mistress that he's ensconced there.'

'There's a tunnel?' Herv asked.

'I'll show you where it is later,' replied Marnie, resolute on keeping her thoughts on track. 'Emelie presumed the water was running down the hillside and collecting there, and it does, but that's not what caused all the damp she's been getting. The water was coming up from underneath. It's the spring. It hasn't been able to drain into the well so over the years it's got closer and closer to the village and then it found Emelie's cellar.'

'She said she didn't have a cellar.'

Marnie gave a little laugh. Emelie hadn't wanted anyone snooping down the stairs, that's why she had lied.

'We've all been thrown off the scent because of that story that Margaret was at the other end of Wychwell. For hundreds of years, we've been looking in the wrong place,' said Marnie, all too aware she'd said *we*. As if she was as much part of the village as the green, Blackett Stream and the wood.

Marnie pressed her fingertip into map A again, right on the house that was no longer there and felt a tremor of excitement ripple through her like an electric eel. 'Margaret Kytson is somewhere here, I know it. Have you got a spare shovel, Herv?'

Herv rang Johnny Oldroyd for an extra pair of hands and some tools. Johnny turned up with those and Lionel, the Mumfords, the Rootwoods, Derek, David and Pammy Parselow with theirs. Marnie was ankle-deep in mud when they arrived. Another pair of her trainers were absolutely ruined, but she didn't care.

'Where are you, Margaret?' she said to the claggy ground. 'We know you're here somewhere.'

Zoe and Cilla turned up carrying two wide planks of wood so that Griff could ride over some of the mud in his wheelchair.

'Watch out,' David grinned, 'foreman's here.'

'Just shut up and get your back into it, you,' Griff returned.

'We can't dig up the whole wood,' said Roger, surveying the expanse with dismay.

'We won't have to, Roger. She's here,' said Marnie, hoping she was right otherwise the estate was going to have to cough up for some chiropractor sessions.

'Look for trees that are narrower in the trunk. They'll be younger,' Griff suggested.

'This is a thin one,' Zoe called. 'In fact, there's a few over here.'

'It's as good a place to start as any,' said Herv, striding towards her in his monster-sized wellies.

Dr and Mrs Court arrived with a bag full of small bottles of pop. Then Ruby and Kay arrived with a spade and a fork and joined in. No one expected Una Price to turn up, but she did. Last, of course, and she hadn't brought any tools with her, and she stood watching with Griff, arms folded, but she was there. Only Titus was significant by his absence.

The more they dug down, the more water-clogged the mud became and collapsed immediately back onto itself. Some made more impact on the ground than others, none more than Herv. He dug like a machine, and in second place was the string-thin Johnny who had a deceptive amount of strength, and plenty of youth on his side.

'You be careful with your back, Derek Price,' Una yelled at him.

Derek looked pleasurably shocked by her concern. 'I will, Una. I will.'

'Don't overdo it, Dr Court,' Marnie warned him, as he stretched an ache out of his shoulders.

'I won't, but I don't want to miss the find,' he beamed.

Ruby squealed as she hit something solid, but disappointingly it turned out to be only a large rock.

'I've got to have a sit down for a bit,' said Una, waddling over to the fallen tree that Emelie had rested on, when she and Marnie went picking strawberries. She was steps away from it when she disappeared into the ground with a screech that owls everywhere would have envied. It was as if a trapdoor had opened beneath her.

Those who could rushed over. Lionel was nearest.

'Una, are you all right?' The hole was at least four foot deep.

'My bloody ankle,' she winced.

'Take our hands, Una, we'll pull you up,' said Herv. He and Lionel carefully hoisted her out.

'Chuffing sinkhole,' she said, putting her bare foot down on the mud. 'And I've lost my shoe.'

'It's a well,' shrieked Johnny, staring into the hole that Una had so recently vacated. 'It's a round well.'

'Oh my lord,' said Lionel. 'Here, dig here.'

Una hopped to the tree trunk and sat down to rub her ankle. With renewed vigour, the diggers plunged their spades and forks into the ground around the newly found hole, loosening the stones where they could. Herv reached down, tearing up huge rocks that had been placed there to press down the soil. There was a feeling of great excitement thrumming through the air now, like an engine of anticipation building up steam because this had to be *the* well – Margaret's well. Herv scooped out more rocks, Lionel and Johnny threw down their spades and followed his lead.

'There's something else here,' said Herv. 'It feels like metal, not rock.' It was lodged under more stones and he was having difficulty getting a purchase on it. Then his fingers managed to grip it and he gave one almighty heave. He handed it to

Lionel who took it from him reverently and turned it around in his hands, wiping the mud off it with his jumper sleeve.

'What is it, Vicar? Treasure?' Johnny's eyes were wide with fascination.

'A chalice,' replied Lionel.

'There's more,' said Herv, tugging hard and then handing over a tarnished metal cross.

'Oh my,' gasped Lionel. 'Church artefacts. If they've been down there as long as Margaret, these must be things stolen from churches and monasteries when they were destroyed in Henry the Eighth's rule. We'll have to declare it to the authorities of course.'

'Will we buggery,' said Griff. 'It's on our land so it's ours.'

'Absolutely,' said Kay.

'I think you'll find it's on Marnie's land,' said Derek, and all eyes turned to her. She felt herself colouring under the splatters of mud which had taken over most of her face.

'I'll have to check,' she said. Not the answer some of them wanted, but she would do things properly, they knew.

'They're here.'

Attention shifted to Herv who had found something else in the well. Something far more valuable to the village. A human skull.

*

They had to leave the digging there, once there was evidence of a body. Ancient or not, Marnie knew they'd have to phone the police, because she'd found it out from the internet in case it ever happened. If they decided these were 'bones of antiquity' then it would be a matter for the county archaeologist.

'If that turns out to be a sheep, I'll bleeding murder

someone,' said David, looking down into the hole at the partly unearthed skull.

'If that turns out to be a sheep, it'll have had the funniest shape head on an animal you'll have ever seen,' replied Roger.

It wasn't a sheep, it was definitely human: it was poor Margaret, they were sure of it.

'Can we all say a little prayer,' said Lionel.

Everyone bowed their heads.

'Dear Lord, thank you for leading us to find Margaret and her child. May she be buried amongst us soon, properly, where she belongs, and at peace. Amen.'

'It was me that found her, not God,' Una argued, under her breath but still loud enough for everyone to hear.

'Ah, but who led you over there,' said Roger, with a twinkle in his eye.

Una huffed. 'I'm changing religions if my God wants to shove me down a well.'

Lionel offered her his arm. 'Dear lady, you are the hero of the hour.'

Una beamed as a ripple of applause offset the ache in her ankle.

'I think celebrations might be in order,' said David. 'Anyone fancy a pint? Your wellies are most welcome. Oh, the joy of easily moppable rustic stone floors.'

No one needed to answer in words. Their smiles said it all. If ever they deserved a pint, it was now.

The whole of the village of Wychwell – bar Titus – trooped down to the Wych Arms. Una hobbled theatrically, but no one minded her being a drama queen on this occasion. If she hadn't been Una, lazy and very heavy, the ground might not have caved in. Marnie wondered how many times tiny

Emelie had crossed over the exact spot where the well lay underneath her feet.

David brought out the carrot wine, Lionel went across to the vicarage to fetch his beetroot, determined not to be outdone. Never had the pub been as full, never had the roof threatened to blow off with the amount of camaraderie stuffed inside its walls. Those who had been slightly worried about how to speak to Marnie now she owned the village, found that a little wine helped ease down any barriers. Una even wished her every success and Marnie thanked her for finding what had foxed so many for so long. Marnie looked over at one point and saw her talking to her estranged husband, although by that time she was plastered and Derek was eager to be off.

The only two people who didn't speak were Marnie and Herv. But his eyes flicked to her often, and hers to him. At one point he smiled at her and she smiled back, but neither crossed over to the other. She secretly studied him talking to Kay and a very tipsy Ruby and thought how gorgeous he was. *Strong, lovely, kind* . . . he was absolutely perfect. And she was about as opposite to that as could be. Kay went off to the toilet, strategically Marnie suspected, leaving her daughter with that hunk of Viking and Marnie thought that maybe they'd make a good match after all. Ruby was pretty and bubbly and would probably be really nice away from her mother and she'd love him, oh boy she'd smother him with affection . . . and she was blonde so she was on to a winner with him because he obviously liked those. And, more importantly, she didn't have a lot of past hanging around her neck like a scabby albatross.

When she saw him crook his arm and Ruby take it, she wondered if he'd eventually realised how uncomplicated and easy a relationship he'd have with her, after the brush with evil that she'd given him. She wished them well and tried not to watch them walk out of the door, though her eyes were so clouded that even if she had turned her head, she wouldn't have seen them anyway.

Herv showed Ruby to the door and bent to receive her kiss on the cheek. He was okay with that, because he knew that Ruby's affections had found a new home with a teacher at her school. Change was present in the air; he also knew there had been a seismic shift in Wychwell as soon as they had found Margaret. Marnie had lifted the curse and with it, slipped properly into the role of Lady of the Manor; Wychwell was all hers now and she would make her mark on it. One curse gone, another one started. The curse of good fortune had put her out of his league.

Chapter 50

It took over two and a half months for the results to come back from the laboratory for the skeletons they found down the well. Experts ascertained that one set of bones came from a woman, aged between thirty and fifty and were approximately four hundred and seventy years old. The date fitted. Strangely though the second set of bones was not a baby but a cat.

The well also yielded other treasures which had to have been buried at the same date: religious artefacts, stolen from churches. It couldn't have been far from the truth to assume that Edward Dearman himself had stored these secretly in Margaret's grave for safe-keeping to be retrieved later, but after his premature death, they were lost.

Marnie sold them to the British Museum and the funds would pay for a new swanky village hall, and repairs to the church roof, the vicarage and the gravedigger's cottage.

The diverted waters from the spring had caused the ground to become extra fertile, trees had grown quickly and covered the area over with foliage, disguising the site of Edward Dearman's dreadful deed. Finally, after hundreds of years, the spring had found its way to the surface again and helped them unearth Margaret.

Marnie, for a reason she couldn't fathom, deferred moving into the manor until Margaret was laid to rest. In truth, leaving Little Raspberries would be a wrench and Marnie knew why it was always given to someone who could appreciate the sanctuary it afforded. She felt inordinately sad packing up to leave it, but she didn't need it any more and Little Raspberries should be made ready for the next person upon whom it could work its healing magic.

October 31 – the day of Margaret's funeral – was the first day off that Marnie had had since the big dig. She had thrown herself into the affairs of Wychwell with vigour, in fact she didn't recognise herself without a hard hat on. If she didn't have a meeting with an architect, she had one with a builder or a bank or a prospective tenant. The tearoom was almost finished now and a manager had been appointed. Marnie nearly fainted when Una asked her if she could apply for the job. She'd probably eat more of the cheesecakes than she could sell, but sometimes you had to put your faith in people, thought Marnie, and offered it to her on the spot. Lilian had put faith in Marnie, it was time to pay it forward.

Ruby had fallen head over heels in love with a teacher at her school and her mother, no longer on maternal Rottweiler duty, had become a much softer creature.

And Titus was gone. Hilary offered him the deal of a lifetime – a house in Sandbanks, Dorset where Titus could show off a prestigious postcode. She cut him a generous full and final settlement in the divorce on the condition he played nicely, knowing that Titus would have eaten his own backside for cash. She couldn't avoid giving him a chunk of her fortune, but her divorce – as she disclosed to Marnie in one of their many email exchanges – really was money well spent. Plus she was earning so much from *Country Manors* that any hole in her finances would soon be closed over. Number five was done – *Country Manors – The Witch is Back*.

Marnie saw Herv only briefly – here and there, a quick *hello, how's it going* between appointments, nothing more than that. It was always Marnie who set the pace. *Lovely to see you, take care.* Always her feet that started walking away first. It was better that they were cordial, she reasoned. Their moment had come – and gone. He was a lovely man who should have someone straightforward and simple, not someone who had more history than the Romans and more psychological baggage than a Louis Vuitton stockroom.

Lilian had seen to it that a plot was reserved in the churchyard for Margaret, for when she was found: a sunny spot under the giant wych elm. Margaret's skeleton, and her cat, were put in the coffin together. The village turned out to say goodbye to her. Una had discovered a real talent for flower-arranging and had made a wonderful autumnal wreath from simple coloured leaves and twigs and fruits, and she took great pleasure from the compliments she was given. She and Derek sat together in the church. Though they were better apart, somehow they had rediscovered the friendship that had brought them together many years ago.

Marnie lingered behind in the churchyard to inspect the new stone which had been erected at the head of Lilian and Emelie's graves. It had just three words on it, apart from the names and dates: 'Oh Perfect Love'.

Emelie, Marnie had been astounded to know, had been a celebrated Sapphic poet in Europe, writing in Italian and German. Marnie had had some of her work translated into English so she could read it and it was beautiful. She knew that many pieces had been inspired by her darling tortured Lilian with whom, Marnie hoped with all her heart, she lay at peace now.

Marnie and Lionel, when she'd had any time, had been working on an updated history of Wychwell. Emelie had written a chapter about herself and Lilian. It would cause a few eyebrows to be raised in surprise, Marnie knew, but it wouldn't make any difference to the affection in which people had held them both.

'Well, ladies, I hope I'm doing okay,' said Marnie to the ground. Lilies and edelweiss had been planted there and it was too soon to know if the plants would take, but then again Herv had done it, so she bet they would. 'I miss you both so much. I'm moving into the manor tomorrow but I don't think anyone is going to be sneaking down a secret passage to see me. Say hello to Margaret for me. Oh, and I'm getting a dog. Greyhound rescue. She's grey and was called Irish Lady – how could I resist? I'll look like Rose's portrait on the staircase.' She blew a kiss. 'God bless you, my darlings.'

She was picking the dog up the following week. Poor thing was the worst racer in history, lost every one despite coming from a champion mother and father. As soon as Marnie heard that, she decided that they were a match, because she knew what it was to be the family disappointment. She could imagine herself as a portrait on the staircase one day, black hair, green-eyed with a sleek hound at her feet, but she'd have no ring on her finger. She'd be the lonely lady of the manor, married to the village and all the people in it, the temporal version of a nun married to the church.

She joined the others for a drink in the Wych Arms after they had laid Margaret to rest. Lionel had upped his game to apricot brandy and David Parselow had to carry Pammy home. Herv stayed for a couple of drinks and then slipped away. Marnie wondered if he had a date. The thought of him with someone else still tore a hole in her heart.

She couldn't sleep that night and she blamed it on the brandy. She didn't know what Lionel had added to it to make her head spark with activity so much, but she suspected those apricots had been grown next to an amphetamine factory. She dressed and did a few laps of the green, as she so often did, and then flopped onto Jessie Plumpton's bench in the middle of it and stared up at the manor – her new home – and thought how amazing it was. The moon was high above it, a huge pink-tinged round of light as if it was doing its best to impersonate an apple, she thought. A Pink Lady. She laughed and deduced she must still be half-pissed, having stupid notions like that. She should get back to bed, she had a big day ahead of her.

She had only taken a few steps, when she heard a voice behind her. A voice that sent shivers tripping down her nerve endings.

'You too?'

She turned, tried to sound cool and not as if her heart had started flapping around inside her like a landed trout. 'Oh hello, Herv.'

'Sit with me for a moment. Help me find my sleep,' he said, then immediately corrected himself. 'Not that I think you're boring.'

Marnie smiled. She sat beside him, a person-width away.

'So, here we are again,' he said, after a ridiculously long silence.

'We are indeed.' Well this wasn't awkward at all.

'We've barely spoken for weeks ... months.'

'It's been a busy time, what with all the building work and stuff.' The lamest excuse on the planet.

They sat looking in the direction of the manor for a few moments before he sighed heavily.

'Do you know what I think?' he said.

'No.' And that was true, she had absolutely no idea.

'I think you've been avoiding me.'

'Don't be silly. I haven't . . . at all . . .' she said; the world's most unconvincing reply.

'Know what else I think?'

'No.'

'I think I've been avoiding you.'

'Have you? Why?' She didn't even ask if he was joking because she knew he wasn't.

'You're the lady of the manor and I'm the gardener.'

'I'm still the same person.'

She wasn't though and they were both more than aware of that. She was queen of a small private kingdom and his pride couldn't take that people might think he wanted to be with her for that reason. At least, until he had come to his senses tonight thanks to Lionel's apricot brandy. It might have made his walk wobbly but it also caused him think more clearly than he had done for a long time. '*Til helvete med alle Kay Sweetmans i denne verden.*' *To hell with all the Kay Sweetmans of this world.* He wasn't going to let them stop him from saying what he should have on the night of the big dig, when he had thrown the towel in instead.

'Know what else I think?'

She chuckled. 'No.'

He twisted to face her. 'I think I love you,' he said. 'No, that's wrong, I know I do. Because I can't get you out of here' and he hit his skull with the heel of his hand, '. . . you won't leave it. And I told my head, "Look, you plant bulbs and dredge leaves out of the lake, Herv Gunnarsen. People will think you're after her money." But I watch you and I don't see any happiness in your eyes and I think, *Herv, you can make her happy. You can love her, you can mend her.*'

She was aware of his eyes, his lovely blue eyes trained on her, waiting for her to respond. She didn't because she knew he couldn't mend her. She was beyond repair.

He reached for her hand and took it between both his own and felt it trembling like an injured bird. 'I think I've loved you from the first moment I saw you. I know you can't say the same because of the brown sticky-out teeth and I don't really look good in hessian.'

She laughed and she felt her eyes sting and she blinked hard because she didn't want to cry.

'I see you and my mood lifts, you walk away from me and it sinks.'

She pulled her hand from his because it felt too good.

'Tell me what is it that stands between us, Marnie, please.'

'There's nothing.'

'You're a terrible liar,' he said. 'There can be nothing so bad that—'

'There is,' she insisted.

'Marnie, tell me. This is killing me.'

Don't. A kind voice inside her urged. *He is yours. Let him love you.* And she felt that voice despair when the words moved up her throat and into her mouth and were then released into the air.

'We went to the best school in the area, my sister and I. All girls. Not a fee-paying one but really good,' began Marnie. 'There was an English teacher there, Mr Trent, married with a young son, all the girls fancied him. Me included. I was thirteen and we were reading *Wuthering Heights* and he was my own personal Heathcliff in my imagination. He offered to give me extra lessons after school because I was "bright", he said. I didn't think I was, really. There was one girl in my class destined for Oxbridge but she didn't get extra lessons. Still, it was something to tell my mum that I'd been selected. I thought I'd impress her with that.' She stalled, gauging Herv's reaction, waiting for his mind to gallop ahead and for that look of revulsion to appear on his face, but found only that he was listening carefully.

'You can probably guess what happened. Plain girl full of new sexual hormones, handsome teacher giving her attention she's never had, knowing all the right things to say, looking into her eyes as he reads poetry. I thought I was being loved, not groomed. *It* only happened twice. I didn't like it. I knew it was wrong . . . it hurt, I felt sick. He said that was natural the first time and it would be better after, but it wasn't. Textbook stuff, I was special, he said. He'd never felt that way about anyone before. I didn't want to go to any more lessons after that. I told Mum that he'd stopped them, she wasn't surprised. She put my weight gain down to comfort eating because I'd been dropped. I put my weight gain down to comfort eating because I felt ashamed. I didn't know I was pregnant until I went into labour. Three months after my fourteenth birthday.'

Herv's eyes were on the ground now, his hands knitted tightly together.

'I didn't know what was happening to me. I thought I was dying. It was the school holidays and I was arguing with Mum about something when the pains came from nowhere. She thought I was putting it on until my waters broke.'

Her voice gave up and she had to cough to clear away the frog that seemed to have taken residence there.

'I gave birth to a beautiful tiny little girl. She had to go straight into special care because she was so early. Mum said I couldn't keep her. She said that even if I didn't sign her over to be adopted, she'd be taken away anyway. She told me all sorts of lies and I was fourteen and confused and believed them all and she wouldn't let anyone give me any alternative. Mum said what sort of life would she have with a schoolgirl mother and a father who was already married? I'd ruin hers as well as everyone else's. So I let her go and then I found out that I could have kept her, I could have gone into a home and let social services help us but it was too late by then. One of the nurses took a polaroid of her and Mum found it and tore it up because she said I had to forget her, but I never did, how beautiful she was, how perfect. And on the sixth of August, the day of Emelie's funeral, she would have had her eighteenth birthday. She would be a woman, a grown-up.'

Marnie sensed Herv getting up from the seat and she thought he would start walking away but then she felt his arms around her, pulling her to her feet, holding her tightly.

He was talking into her hair, words in his native language, words she didn't understand but she knew that they were tender, loving.

'I'd ruin a man's marriage, his career, his family if I told, Mum said, but there had been rumours in the school and the police came to see me and . . . Oh God, I felt so guilty after I said his name. He was sacked, prosecuted. His wife left him. We moved away, to another town and another school and she never forgave me for the mess. Then I found out he'd done it before. In a private school. He'd had to leave but they'd hushed it up to avoid the scandal and sent him on his way with a good reference. The girl wrote to me but I didn't find the letter until after Mum died. She'd kept it from me.'

'It wasn't your fault,' said Herv, holding her tighter. 'Kjære jenta mi.' *Oh my darling.*

Her legs were shaking, she sat back down before she fell.

'I try not to think of her, but I do. What if she was adopted by a woman like Judith and has been unhappy all her life?'

'More likely a couple who have loved her as if she were the most precious child in the world. Like my parents loved me,' he smiled. 'Marnie, you were especially unlucky.'

'What if she's turned out like me, Herv?'

He didn't leave a beat before he answered. 'Then I think that it's not such a bad thing. Obviously without all the hang-ups.' And Marnie couldn't help the blurt of laughter that escaped her.

Herv sat down beside her, put his arm around her and pulled her close. The moon had sunk into a quilt of clouds; *Time for bed,* the sky said. *Time to sleep for a final time in your old life and waken in a new one.*

'You are the perfect man,' said Marnie. 'You really are.' He was way out of her league, not the other way around.

'Whaat?' said Herv, throwing his head back and giving a hoot of incredulity at that. 'Anyway, Lilian once said to me that perfection was an imperfection in itself.'

'What does that mean?'

'I have no idea, she was . . . *gæren.*' And he rotated his finger near his temple to indicate that Lilian was slightly bonkers, but he was smiling and it made Marnie smile too. *Imperfection personified,* that's what Lilian's father had labelled her. And he was right, because she was the most perfectly imperfect woman Marnie had ever met. The mother she had grown in her heart.

'My God, Marnie, look at that,' said Herv. 'What the . . . ?'

A light in the gallery window of the manor claimed their

attention. A pink dot hovering. But it couldn't be? Because Emelie was the Pink Lady, wasn't she?

They sat mesmerised, watching the light bounce in gentle arcs from left to right.

'You'll be living with a ghost after all,' chuckled Herv as it halted for a long moment and then melted into the darkness.

'I don't mind,' said Marnie. 'I can learn to share.'

'Can you?' asked Herv. 'Can you learn to share yourself with me then?'

Marnie turned to him, saw the tenuous smile on his mouth, pinned there by hope. His hand rose to brush against her cheek, such a gentle touch yet she felt the reverberations shoot all the way down to her fingers and toes and beyond as if they were too big and powerful to stay within the confines of her skin. His head bent towards hers, tentatively, expecting her to edge away at any moment, but she didn't. As he placed his lips softly on hers, she felt a warmth bloom in her heart as if his love was slipping between the many breaks and cracks in it, gluing it back together, mending it like liquid gold.

Kintsugi.

Her lips pressing back against his answered the question perfectly.

THE UPDATED HISTORY OF WYCHWELL

Author's Note

At the other end of Yorkshire, Denby Dale has its crowd-drawing giant pie. Wychwell now has its crowd-drawing giant cheesecake. Brainchild of the present Lady of the Manor, Miss Marnie Salt, the Wychwell cheesecake even overtook the popularity of the May Queen, who this year is Mrs Una Price.

It would be no exaggeration to say that this May Day fair was attended by more people than in the previous ten years put together. Entry was prohibited to anyone not in medieval dress, which could be rented at the entrance for a very small fee. Visitors included two Richard the Lionhearts, a Geoffrey Chaucer (Vicar Lionel Temple) a Lady Godiva, in a flesh-coloured bodystocking, complete with real horse, and a coven of witches and their cats. Even Miss Salt's greyhound, Lady, joined in the festivities with a Maid Marian headdress.

Alas last year's May Queen Miss Ruby Sweetman, now Mrs Ruby Beswick, was absent as she is on honeymoon in Italy.

The well, despite its grisly history, has been reconstructed to its, we hope, original form. A small log cabin has been erected nearby (The Witchery) as a museum telling the (much-edited) story of the village and its history.

The village headcount has increased to more than double what it was the previous year. New residents have settled in well and footfall to the Wych Arms and Plum Corner stores and post office is much improved. The Maid of Cheesecake tearoom is extremely popular. The cheesecakes are made by our own Miss Salt (with a little help from Cilla, Griff and hopefully – when she is home from Edinburgh University – Zoe Oldroyd). The cheesecakes (quote from the press) 'have that extra little secret ingredient that makes them special, yet Miss Salt refuses to disclose exactly what it is'. But then, what is Wychwell without a secret or two in reserve?

The coffers of the estate are richer by one and a half million pounds, thanks to the ex-Mrs Sutton, now Mrs Hilary Fosse, who has never publicly disclosed (by mutual agreement) where she found her inspiration for the fabulously successful Country Manors novels. Seven to date and one Hollywood film in the can.

The old Dearman coat of arms may stand but the motto has been changed.

In Imperfectione Perfectio Est

A wonderful innovation for there truly is perfection in imperfection.

Miss Emelie Tibbs left us, in manuscript form, the full story of her rather beautiful relationship with the previous Lady of the Manor, Miss Lilian Dearman. That and some of her wonderful, poignant poetical works make up the next chapter, though it will by no means be the last.

I, Lionel Temple, will be delighted to add to it after the wedding of Miss Salt and Mr Herv Gunnarsen next month (December) and then in March when Master Gunnarsen is due to be born.

I foresee quite a few more chapters in this History of Wychwell book. Maybe – looking forward (we hope) – some even fit for public consumption.

Revd Lionel Temple. 30 November 2017.

Acknowledgements

As always, I have a few people to thank because getting a book to you is a team effort. I'm just a cog in a big engine.

To my fantastic agent Lizzy Kremer at David Higham Associates and the team there – especially Alice, Olivia, Margaux, Guilia, Maddalena, Harriet and Brian (who hands the cash over). And my smashing publishing team at Simon & Schuster – Ian, Suzanne, SJ, Jo, Emma, Dawn, Dom, Joe, Jess, Rich et al. And the fantastic Sally Partington, my copy-editor. Working with you, Sal, is my favourite part of the whole process.

Thank you Raimonda and Chris at the New York Cheesecake Company in Barnsley for giving me the idea to include cheesecakes in my next book while sampling their delicious wares. You really are masters at what you do.

And my new friends up in Ayr – The Handmade Cheesecake Company www.handmadecheesecakes.co.uk. Yes, folks, you can have them posted to you!

Thank you to my friends both in the profession and out of it who keep me (mostly) sane. Especially Maggie Birkin who sent me a copy of an article about the sale of the North

Yorkshire village of West Heslerton and said it might make good subject matter.

Thank you to the very lovely Yvonne Staley who adopts rescue greyhounds and introduced me to Leon, Holly, Fran, Dancer, Storm and Jenny. Greyhounds are fabulous dogs, lazy and affectionate and there are so many of them needing a good home. Yvonne would like to recommend Northumberland Greyhound Rescue http://northumberlandgreyhoundrescue. org.uk, but there are many of these beautiful creatures stuck in other centres ... so do go and rescue one.

Thank you to Rita Elvea Berntsen for all the Norwegian bits. And for rescuing me from almost having Herv sing the Scooby Doo theme in Danish. Rita – you are magnificent.

And if you are wondering who I had in mind when writing my hero ... you should check out Lasse Matberg on the Internet. Then you'll realise why the chapters with Norwegian Herv in were quite joyous to write.

Thank you to my readers who send me their lovely missives and keep me in the job.

And thank you to my family. Without them, I would never have found the path hidden in the undergrowth, that led me to this bloody brilliant career.

If you loved reading

The Perfectly Imperfect Woman

Turn the page for an extract of

The Yorkshire Pudding Club

Out now in paperback and eBook

Prologue

The previous September
They took a day off and went with her because in the three
million years they'd all been friends, it was the first time
Helen had ever asked them a favour. That was how Elizabeth
came to end up carrying a picnic basket in a grassy middle
of nowhere, watching one of her two best friends wriggling
out of her drawers and about to sit on the giant appendage
of a club-bearing man carved into an alien county hillside.

'Hels, are you actually right in your head?' she asked.

Janey said nothing but her equal disbelief showed in the
dropped-open jaw as Helen stuffed the discarded pants in her
handbag and then sat down squarely and triumphantly on Mr
Big's phallic enhancement.

'Now if I had told you what I wanted to do, would you
have come?' she said. 'I don't think so! You would have tried
to talk me out of it, wouldn't you?'

'Too bloody right I would,' said Elizabeth, whilst thinking,
She's lost it.

'And this is the something you needed to do that is really,
really, really important then?' Janey asked, her eyebrows
raised as far as they could stretch. 'Dragging us halfway across
the bloody country to see a chalk drawing?'

'Aw, come on, we're here now. Just sit down and have a

sandwich,' said Helen, straight-backed and sitting there as if she was waiting for something extraordinary to happen.

'Where are we, like?' Janey looked at the surrounding countryside, dominated by the thick white outline of the naked man with the enviable asset. 'And more to the point – why?'

'Oh, I'm having a sarnie, I'm flaming famished!' Elizabeth decided. She was almost brain dead with tiredness, even though she had spent most of the long, long journey snoring on the back seat. She threw herself onto the grass next to her knickerless friend and dragged the picnic basket purposefully over. Janey huffed in a 'can't beat 'em, join 'em' sort of way and grudgingly followed suit, muttering something about them all being bonkers.

'He's an ancient fertility symbol,' Helen explained.

'I'd never have guessed!' said Elizabeth, ripping so hungrily into a giant sausage roll that the chalk man almost winced.

Helen went on, 'Well, I was watching this programme a couple of weeks ago about how all these women who hadn't been able to conceive came here as a last resort and sat on his ... well, here, for a while, and seventy-eight per cent of them – that's seventyeight per cent of them – became pregnant.'

A dramatic silence ensued in which Helen waited for the others to be impressed.

'Well, I have to say it and I hope you'll excuse the pun,' Elizabeth spat through a flurry of pastry flakes, 'but that is positively the biggest load of bollocks you have ever come out with.'

Janey laughed derisively at the same time.'Oh Hels, come on!'

'I know what it sounds like, that's why I didn't tell you

where we were coming,' Helen said, her voice fighting off a wobble, 'but if I don't get pregnant soon, I'll die. I want a baby so, so much. Believe me, you two have it a lot easier not wanting children, but I don't care who laughs at me any more, I just Want. A. Baby.' Then she turned her head suddenly skyward, blinking hard, a little ashamed at her outburst but more than that, hurt that they of all people were mocking her.

Janey and Elizabeth exchanged the slightest of glances but each knew what the other was thinking. She'd always been so light about the fact that she hadn't caught on. How many times had she led their joking about it? Neither of them had had the slightest idea that her pain ran so deeply.

Elizabeth plunged her hand into the picnic basket again, in a brave effort to break the heavy silence that had descended upon them like a thick, depressing cloud.

'So, let's have a good look at this lot. What have you made us then, Hels? What feast have you concocted this time?'

'There's egg and cress, beef and horseradish, goats' cheese and tomato …' Helen began to reel off, dabbing at her eye, trying to make it look as if she had something in it '… sausage rolls, spicy scotch eggs, chicken filo parcels, lemon Swiss roll, banoffee tarts, Victoria sponge, crisps, Twiglets, there's a red hummus and onion dip, strawberries dipped in dark chocolate and there's some Diet Coke and wine.'

'That all?' said Elizabeth and Helen blurted out a laugh and the mood was lifted once again.

Aw bless, thought Elizabeth, as she spotted all the little flags on the sandwiches; everything was homemade. Who the chuff could be bothered making real puff pastry these days but Hels? If she did have kids, their sandwich boxes would be the envy of the school.

That little thought bubble gave her another taste of her friend's desperation and how very severe it must be to trick them into travelling so many miles to do something as ridiculous as this. How had she missed this before?

'Pass me an egg and cress, would you, please,' Helen said, all tears abated.

'When are the fish and Disciples arriving?' Elizabeth asked, rummaging deep before handing over the clingfilmed triangle bearing an egg and cress sticker.

'I know you're a pig ... I didn't want you moaning that I'd dragged you all this way and I hadn't fed you,' Helen said, managing a little smile.

'I'll have a beef, please, and pass the plonk seeing as I'm not driving,' Janey said with a deep sigh. 'Tell me you haven't forgotten an opener.'

'It screws,' Helen said.

'That's appropriate!' Elizabeth snorted and got her usual disapproving look from Janey.

The latter then gasped suddenly and said, 'Oy, I hope we'll be all right, sat here on this bloke's genitals. I can't afford to get pregnant.' She looked worriedly down at the segment of chalk line disappearing up her skirt. 'My Head of Department is about to peg it – I'm in line for his job.'

'Oh nice!' Elizabeth said, batting back some disapproval for a change.

'Cough, cough, cough – I'm sick of listening to him,' Janey went on. 'That's a lifetime of fags for you,' and she nodded a warning in Elizabeth's direction. 'I think they'll get rid of him in an early-retirement swoop – he's been with them for about four hundred years so he'll get a good pay-off. Mind you, he'll probably spend it all on Bensons, knowing him. It's only a matter of time before the vacancy comes up; he's always flaming off ill and I'm running the place as it is so I don't want any surprise sprogs knackering up my career hopes, thanks very much.'

Helen tilted her head. 'Well, all I can say is that not all of those women on the TV programme took their pants off when they sat on him.'

'Oh great!' said Janey, shifting her bottom off the white line. Not that she believed in stuff like that, but it didn't hurt to make sure.

Elizabeth poured herself a glass of the wine and reclined to let the gorgeous September sun shine down onto her face. She was too comfortable to move from her position on the ancient willy. Mumbo jumbo crap, she thought inwardly, but she was here now and might as well enjoy it, as it really was a cracking day for a picnic.

Chapter 1

The following February

Her arms and legs spasmed outwards, she let loose a very loud scream and then Elizabeth awoke to find herself not on a nose-diving plane but on the seven thirty-six to Leeds and the focus of half a crammed carriageful of 'glad that wasn't me' faces. However, not even their cold-water stares, the probability that she had been snoring and two mega-strength coffees slopping around her digestive system could keep

Elizabeth's eyes from shuttering down again – she was exhausted. She was last off the train and, in fact, had the fat, sweaty bloke sitting next to her not caught her with the hard edge of his briefcase as he heaved his carcass out of the seat, she might well have slept through to Barnsley again on the return trip. She had better buck up for later; she was hardly going to be the life and soul of Helen's birthday party face down and asleep in her minestrone.

As usual, the train station was full of suits zipping in straight lines to their destinations clutching a laptop case in one hand and a grabbed breakfast bag in the other. As usual, there were a few early shoppers making a leisurely way up to the main city stores and managing to get in the way of the rushing executives, who did not take too kindly to having lumpy human obstacles on their own personal work paths. And as usual, there was a large contingent of big-bellied workmen staring at women's breasts from the scaffolding as their more industrious colleagues worked on extending the station, yet again. The train used to dump Elizabeth right in front of the ticket barriers, but these days it deposited them all so far away on one of the new platforms that she almost needed to catch another train from there to the exit. That morning, it felt a particularly long way.

At least the ten-minute walk in the crisp February air served to startle her brainwaves into some activity, and by the time she had reached the great, smutty-bricked offices with the giant blue Handi-Save sign above the entrance she felt considerably more human and less like a dormouse again. It was an old, weary-looking building in the middle of a sea of younger, more dynamic structures, with its exterior reflecting the majority of the people on the inside – dull, tired and uninspiring. She pushed open the giant stiff revolving door that had given everyone who had worked there for any length of time a deformed bicep. It was easy to spot a longtimer at Handi-Save for they all had one arm bigger than the other, like a male Fiddler crab. Yep, she felt decidedly better for the walk.

'Flaming Norah, you look rough,' said Derek the security man. He, being ambidextrous, had two massive arms. 'Good night, was it?'

'I was in bed for nine,' Elizabeth held up her best shushing finger as his mouth sprang open, 'and before you say it, yes, I was alone. I don't know what's up with me at the moment. I think I've been bitten by a tsetse-tsetse fly.'

'Tsetse-tsetse? Going round in pairs now, are they?' grinned Derek. 'Maybe you're coming down with something. Mind you, in a place like this someone's only got to say "cold" and everyone gets it through the air conditioning.'

'I feel all right in myself, just tired,' she said, hunting in her bag for one of her menthols. She proffered the packet to him. 'Want one?'

'Do I chuff!' he said, warding them away like a vampire who had just been offered a garlic bulb. 'If I want mints I'll suck a Polo, if I want a fag I'll have an Embassy, thanks for asking.'

'Please yourself then! Right, now, I better do something with my face then if I look that bad.'

'I've a carrier bag behind Reception. I could poke two eyeholes in it for you.'

'Thanks a lot, Ras.'

He nudged her playfully. 'Ah, you still look bonny!'

She turned away, mock-insulted. 'Nope, sorry, the damage has been done, you can get stuffed,' and though she could hear him laughing behind her, the smile slid off her face as if it had been greased with three pounds of melted butter. Not that she had taken offence, for it took a lot to wind Elizabeth up – at least it had done until recently, when this infernal tiredness threatened to turn even her cool disposition to something as brittle as the toffee she used to get as a kid that snapped off into artery-severing shards.

Derek, or Rasputin as everyone called him, would have been mortified even to suspect that he had upset her because they went back such a long way. He had only been at Handi-Save a week himself when she had turned up at the Reception desk aged sixteen, all wide grey eyes, smashing blouse buttoned up to the neck and her dark gypsy curls tamed into a ponytail. She had been half-fearful, half-excited by her important-sounding destination – 'the typing pool' – to where Ras volunteered to escort her. She'd had a picture in her mind of lots of typists working around a pool full of warm, blue water and was critically disappointed when it turned out to be just an airless office full of women with perms and frumpy frocks banging away on word processors. Ras was string-thin back then, with a number one haircut and a moustache like Ron from the pop group 'Sparks'. He ended up getting them both hopelessly lost which caused a standing joke that was still running.

Twenty-two years later, they were both still there, crossing paths in Reception each morning, though Elizabeth had long since left the pool and was now the Managing Director's secretary. Ras, on the other hand, had concentrated his energies over the years into evolving physically into a heavyweight wrestler who would fail a Roy Wood's Wizzard audition for being too hairy. He'd had four kids, three wives, two motorcycle crashes and a steel plate in his head. The only things that seemed to have stayed constant about him were those friendly facial features and the warmth in his morning greetings. He alone these days put a smile on Elizabeth's lips at work, or as she preferred to call it, 'the Hammer House of Handi-Save'.

The worrying part in all this was that if Ras thought she looked rough, then Julia definitely would – and the only reason Elizabeth had pushed herself out of bed that morning was because Julia and Laurence had made it perfectly clear that being absent on a Monday was tantamount to admitting to a hangover. So ironically, there she was dutifully turning up but looking as if she had been on a weekend ciderfest. A picture of the pair of them flitted across her mind, which made her growl inwardly. She was wound into the ground before she had even set eyes on the Gruesome Twosome and it was so not like her to feel this way. Hardly anything ever got to Elizabeth and even if it did, she never showed it.

She grabbed a coffee from the machine and slid into the tiny and horribly smoky room that the militantly anti-tobacco Laurence had 'allowed' the smokers to have and, as he said 'pollute as their own'. The rebellious air in there usually calmed her down before she had even lit up, but that morning it felt thick and unpleasant, and welded itself like glue to the back of her throat. She sat on a table in the canteen instead, gulping back the lukewarm gritty coffee whilst pitter-patting with her fingertips at the fluidy swellings under her eyeballs. She didn't dare risk another look in the mirror in case it threw back a worse reflection than the passable one she imagined was there before making her way to the lift.

She pressed the button (only four times that morning) before it started to shudder and rattle upwards at a pace that a snail with a weight problem could beat – even the machinery didn't want to work here! She hadn't always felt like that, for there had been a time when she used to belt up the staircase in the mornings, glad to get to her desk. Obviously that was before the days of that well-known double act Laurence Stewart-Smith, a name impossible to say without hissing, and his wonderful side-kick, Julia Powell – Powell as in the contraction of 'power crazed troll'.

Laurence Stewart-Smith: also known as 'Eyebrow Man' on account of the long furry caterpillar which ran the width of his forehead before scuttling into his hairline to hide the 666. Laurence Stewart-Smith: in the opinion of the City, The Man – business genius, whizz-kid, darling of industry, multi-millionaire manof-the-people, demi-god of the hoi polloi – but in the opinion of anyone who really knew the man behind the title: total plonker.

Julia did not lift her head as Elizabeth walked past her desk, which had long since failed to surprise her. Julia could not communicate with females on a lesser grade unless it was by email, even when sitting two metres away as Elizabeth did. There were bagfuls of evidence to substantiate the theory that Julia was threatened by other women, who were creatures to be ignored, or destroyed. Men, however, were a different kettle of fish. Then she would start flirting and sticking out her chest and batting her eyelashes in the general direction of the flirtee – the number of bats being directly proportionate to the quality of his suit.

Sometimes, to be controversial, Elizabeth would open a mail and shout across the reply to Julia as it really seemed to annoy her, but this past week or so she was just too tired to play the dissident. Was this the onset of old age, she wondered. Was she about to start dribbling and nodding off after a morning Rich Tea biscuit and exchanging her cappuccinos for a nice cup of cocoa? She was only eighteen months off being forty, after all.

FIND OUT MORE ABOUT

milly
johnson

Milly Johnson is the queen of feel-good fiction
and bestselling author of fourteen novels.

To find out more about her and her writing,
visit her website at
www.millyjohnson.co.uk

or follow Milly on

twitter @millyjohnson
Instagram @themillyjohnson
facebook @MillyJohnsonAuthor

All of Milly's books are available in print and eBook,
and are available to download in eAudio

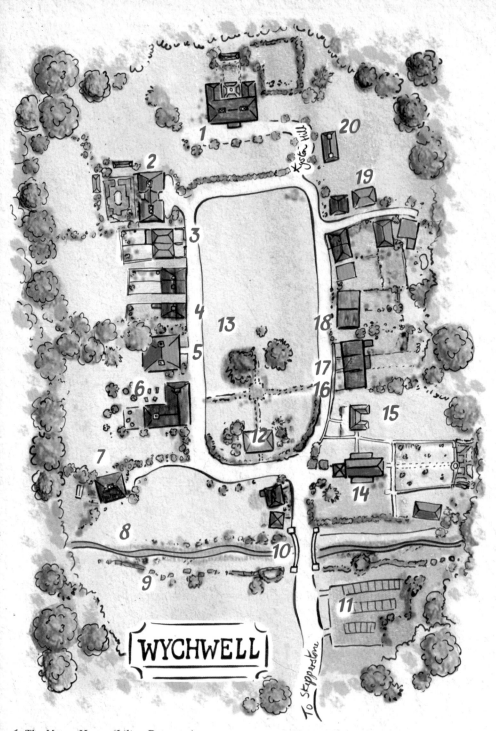

WYCHWELL

1. The Manor House (Lilian Dearman)
2. The Lemon Villa (Titus & Hilary Sutton)
3. The Nectarines (Cilla, Griff, Johnny & Zoe Oldroyd)
4. Quince Cottage (Kay & Ruby Sweetman)
5. Plum Corner Post Office (Roger & Sarah Mumford)
6. The Wych Arms (David & Pammy Parselow)
7. Little Raspberries (Marnie Salt)
8. Blackett Stream
9. The Old Village Defensive Walls
10. Blackett Bridge
11. The Car Park
12. The Village Hall
13. The Village Green
14. St Jude the Apostle Church
15. The Vicarage (Lionel Temple)
16. Tangerine House (Una & Derek Price)
17. Orange House (Cyril & Alice Rootwood)
18. Peach Trees (Dr & Mrs Court)
19. The Bilberries (Herv Gunnarsen)
20. Little Apples (Emelie Tibbs)